DRAGON TAMER

SPECIAL EDITION BOXSET

J.A. CULICAN

J.A. ARMITAGE

Paperback ISBN: 979-8-839020-07-8

Hardback ISBN: 978-1-949621-20-4

Dragon Realm Press
Cape May Court House, NJ 08210

CONTENTS

SLAYER

WARRIOR

PROTECTOR

SAVIOR

TRIAD MOUNTAINS
DRAGON VILLAGE
TO THE SLAYER VILLAGE
CLIFFSIDE HOUSES
FIREPIT
TRAINING GROUND
TOWNHALL
VILLAGE SQUARE
E

SLAYER VILLAGE
TRIAD MOUNTAINS
TO THE DRAGON VILLAGE
TOWN SQUARE
JULIANNA'S HOUSE
TRAINING GROUND

SLAYER

DRAGON TAMER BOOK 1

SLAYER

1

I held the sword up in the air as the sun glinted off of it, blinding me for the briefest of seconds. That was something I'd have to watch out for in the future. It was also heavier than I expected it to be after unofficially training for so long with the old, battered swords. Normal swords. Boring swords. But this was no ordinary weapon. Apart from being the traditional sword of my family and my eighteenth birthday present to boot, I knew it to be hollowed out down the thickest part of the main shaft.

"You aren't going to kill a dragon holding it up in the air like that, Julianna," Jasper said with a smirk. "Do you expect them to just fly down from the sky and impale themselves on it?"

I lowered my sword and stuck my tongue out at my brother. At nineteen, he was exactly one year and one day older than me, a fact he liked to lord over me at all given opportunities. He was also taller, more popular, and downright annoying.

"Jasper, leave your sister alone. This time last year I seem to remember you nearly slicing off your big toe. We all have to start somewhere." My father's voice boomed toward us.

Jasper's smirk transformed into a scowl and I snickered. I knew why he had a bee in his bonnet but it was hardly my fault. He had also received a sword for his eighteenth birthday which was practically identical to mine. Both had our family crest and a dragon forged onto the handle, the eyes inlaid with our birthstones. If he'd been born a day later or I'd been born a day earlier, they would be exactly the same. As it was, his had eyes of jet, a common element found naturally in the Triad Mountains, while my dragon's eyes glittered with fire diamonds, an infinitely rare and therefore more expensive jewel. Both swords cost more than the average family in Dronios paid in a month's rent, but thanks to the two fire diamonds, mine could also feed and clothe them for the same month if I ever had any inclination to sell it, which, of course, I never would.

"Now!" My father clapped me on the shoulder nearly causing me to drop the sword. "Your brother is going to show you some moves so you can get used to the weight and feel of it and when I think you're ready, the two of you will spar. I don't expect you to win but I do expect you to pay attention to what Jasper tells you and to at least block him. Do you understand?"

"Yes, Papa!" I turned to him and, lifting myself up on my tiptoes, kissed him on the cheek.

"Come here, baby sister. I'll show you how a real warrior holds a sword." Jasper's tight voice met my ears.

The dust swirled around my feet as I crossed the

training ground to him. I idly wondered if my father would declare me the winner if I stuck the sword right in his only son's gut. Okay, probably not, but it was a nice thought.

"You're holding your sword like a girl," he said, taking it out of my hands.

"If I hold my sword like Morganna, then I'll be quite happy," I replied. The legendary swordswoman brought men to their knees both figuratively and literally. Holding my sword like a girl indeed!

He took hold of my hand and placed the sword back into it, this time in a slightly different position. Damn it, it did feel better.

"Now, when I give you the say so, lift your sword and copy the pose I show you."

I waited until he picked up his own sword and got himself into a position I knew to be a blocking stance. One foot was slightly behind the other to steady him, should he need it. He angled his left arm behind him while his right held his sword out in front of him so that it crossed his chest. I followed his lead and put myself in position, but as I did, it didn't feel quite right. I wasn't steady enough. My feet weren't far enough apart and if I was in a real sword fight, I'd left too many parts of myself exposed. I widened my stance slightly.

"Pay attention Jules," Jasper snapped. "This is important."

I looked over my shoulder to see that my father was still exactly where I left him, watching us with his hand held up to block the glare of the sun. It was important for me to do exactly what Jasper said. I didn't want to let my father down. Closing the distance between my feet, I tried to position myself exactly how my brother stood.

"That's better. You're learning already!"

He took me through more blocking stances before he moved on to other forms of defense. After an hour and a half of protecting myself—mainly from barbed comments from my brother, but occasionally from pretend jabs of his sword—I began to tire.

"I'm done with defense. You're teaching me to protect myself against another swordsman, but we'll be chasing dragons. I need to learn how to attack." I was being childish but he was treating me like a child and I was annoyed.

"The concept is the same. You'll still have to defend yourself against dragons."

I couldn't see how any of the moves he'd just taught me would help me if a dragon decided to flame me.

"Go get yourself a drink of water if you're fading," he said, his mouth twisting back into its spiteful smirk. "We'll start on attacking moves in five minutes." His eyebrows narrowed and he turned away, effectively dismissing me.

I didn't want to admit it to him, but I did need a break. The sword was much heavier than the ones I was used to practicing with. I'd actually started my training a year ago on the same day Jasper did, watching him and my father from my bedroom window, wishing I was old enough to join them. The next day, as I was grabbing seedlings from the shed, I found an old practice sword and took it for myself. The feel of the sword as my hand grabbed the hilt that first time was seared into my brain, the strength and power that it represented burned into my being. Every day, I watched Jasper's training sessions and then practiced the same moves in my bedroom. Today I'd finally be sparring with a real person and not just the shadows.

I grabbed the jug that had been left on an old wooden table and poured myself a goblet of water and one each for Jasper and Papa. The water was warm after being out in the burning sun, but it refreshed me all the same.

"You're doing well, little one." My father took his goblet and drank before pulling a face. "This would be better if it was ice cold ale."

"Yes, but then you'd be too drunk to watch me kick Jasper's a— butt, and please don't call me little one. I'm eighteen today, a woman now!"

Papa just laughed at me but Jasper had heard what I said and turned from where he'd been practicing his footwork. He took the third goblet and drained it easily. "I think you'll be lucky to block me at all, let alone kick anything," he said. "I'll have yours on the ground before you know what's hit you."

"Now, now, you two," Papa started before draining his drink. "Save your squabble for the fight."

I put my goblet down and stalked back to the center of the dusty training ground to wait for Jasper. I did love him. He was my only brother after all, but he was a complete and utter pain in the neck.

I stalked around the training circle kicking up more dirt as I took in my surroundings. Our home sat on the outskirts of Dronios, the small village my family had belonged to since the beginning of time. The Triad Mountains hovered in the background with the promise of power only a dragon could bring me. The only known place dragons lived.

Two hours later and he'd shown me every move he knew, both attack and defense, and watched as I'd practiced each one ten times. The sun was considerably lower in the sky when Papa came over to us. I was glad that the heat of the day had gone with the lowering sun, but now that it was directly behind Jasper, I had a hard time seeing him, and he, of course, refused to move.

"I think you've worked hard enough today," Papa said as he wrapped an arm around my sweaty shoulders. "I'm going to let you spar, but Julianna, you should use the moves you've learned today to block. If you think you can get an attack in, by all means, go for it but I don't expect you to get a hit in."

"Yeah, like that's going to happen," said Jasper as he pulled on his training armor. "I don't know why I'm even putting this on." He smirked at me as I lifted up the armor set aside for me.

"Don't wear it. I just hope you got enough birthday money yesterday for your healer's bill," I retorted.

"Children!" My father rolled his eyes at us and a pit of unease grew in my stomach. I wanted him to be proud of me, not think I was a pathetic little girl.

"Sorry, Papa." I lowered my head.

Jasper picked up his sword and walked to the circle drawn in chalk on the ground.

"Papa?"

"Yes, my girl?"

"How can this be a fair fight?" I picked up my sword, now much more comfortable with its weight.

"This is your first day. I expect it will take you

months, if not years, to be as good as your brother. He is becoming quite well known for his swordsmanship. He will not hurt you."

"That's not exactly what I meant." It irked me that my father was expecting so little of me. "Jasper's sword has been imbued with the soul of his first dragon kill. Mine is still empty."

"What do you suggest? I can ask your brother to swap swords if you like but even though his sword gives him strength from the dragon, which will pass to you if you have it, I'm still certain he'll beat you."

"I don't want his sword. That won't be fair either. I want to use yours." It was unbelievably cheeky of me to ask. I wouldn't normally have dared, but I was beginning to get angry with both my father and Jasper for treating me like I was a hopeless case.

He looked down to where the sword was sheathed by his side. It had been forged in the Triad Mountains over thirty years ago by the goblins that mined there. The legendary blade was made from the rarest metal of all and had won the soul of over three hundred dragons. I'd never once seen it leave my father's side. He stared at me as he rolled the idea over in his head.

My hopes began to rise. Would he really let me borrow it?

"No, Julianna. I cannot let you use my sword."

That was that then. I was going into a fight at a disadvantage before I even started. I could have cried.

"But," my father continued, "I do understand your point of view. You are right. You must do this fairly. Jasper!" he called out to my brother who ran back over to us.

"Don't tell me she's chickened out." He grinned.

"Hand me your sword. You'll both use old training swords of mine. They aren't quite as heavy as these swords, but they are identical to each other which will make the fight fair."

Jasper's face fell and now I was the one grinning.

"I'll get them, Papa. Where do you keep them?" I asked innocently. I could hardly tell either of them that I'd had one of them in my possession for a year.

"They're in a shed behind the house."

I ran around the house to the back where I retrieved one of the swords. Thankfully we had a back door, so neither of them would see me running up to my bedroom to retrieve the other from under my bed where it had laid hidden for the past twelve months. I brought both swords back outside and handed them to my father.

He took something small out of his pocket and dabbed it on the tip of one of the swords.

"What's that, Papa?" I queried.

"This ink will show up as a blue mark every time Jasper hits your armor. The less blue you have on you at the end of the duel, the more successful you've been at defending yourself."

"Just make sure you put it on my sword too," I replied. I might not have been fighting to attack but my father had told me I could try.

Jasper still had a sour expression on his face when he took up the starting position. I faced him and bowed. The niceties should always be followed in any duel, even one where everyone thinks you are going to lose. Jasper bowed too.

"On my whistle," I heard my father say, but I didn't break eye contact with Jasper.

"One, two, three." The shrill call of the whistle blared as my father backed away. Immediately, Jasper lunged at me. I blocked him but only just in time. He wasn't playing. He was really trying to hurt me! Papa obviously thought the same because he blew the whistle a second time to signal the end of the duel. The quickest duel ever, after which Jasper would get a telling off for going too hard on me and I'd get a pat on the back for blocking him.

No, this wasn't how this was going to go down. I ignored the whistle and thrust my sword forward. It was designed to put him off guard and it worked. He wasn't ready for me. He looked over at Papa with a raised eyebrow. I flicked my eyes over to see my father's expression. He shrugged his shoulders as if to say, "Carry on." Fine! Carry on I would!

Jasper pulled his features back into a sneer and lunged again. This time I was ready for him. I didn't need to block; I was too quick for that. By the time his sword should have hit the armor covering my stomach, I was five inches to the right. I hopped around to his back and planted my first blue dot right in the middle of his shoulder blades. He whipped his sword around but I saw it coming and ducked, rolling around to his front. Before he had the chance to defend himself, I plunged the sword forward again, this time staining a spot on his chest. Papa's laugh echoed around me, fueling my movements. He was enjoying this, as was I.

"Beginner's luck, Jules," spat Jasper as he lunged

forward trying a fancy move he'd not bothered to show me.

So, that's how you want to play it, huh? I blocked his sword, which he anticipated, and pulled back only to lunge again straight away. I had some fancy footwork of my own and after blocking him a second time, I was able to attack again. I drew dot after dot all over his armor and it was only when my father blew the whistle again that I was able to truly see just how much damage I'd done to Jasper.

He was covered in hundreds of tiny, blue kisses. When I looked down, my armor was still the plain gray it had always been.

"Julianna," Papa said, striding over to us. "That was amazing! How did you do that?"

"She got lucky, that's all." Jasper scowled and threw his armor onto the ground along with the old sword.

"Lucky? You have more blue on you than the Parvanian Ocean." I couldn't help but gloat.

Jasper's scowl got meaner and he stormed off into the house, leaving Papa and me to clean up.

"Should I take his sword back to him?" I asked as I grabbed his jet sword off the ground.

"No, give him some space. You embarrassed him out there. I'm so proud of you. I just didn't think...I mean I didn't expect..."

"It's fine Papa. I surprised myself too if I'm honest."

"I feel bad for underestimating you. It's not something you will have to worry about again. I'm taking you out tomorrow."

"Out?" I asked, picking up the armor that Jasper had thrown down.

"Into the mountains. You're going to fill up that sword of yours. It needs the soul of a dragon and you're going to be the one to put it there."

I looked at my father incredulously. It had taken Jasper nine months from getting his sword to having his first kill.

"I'm not ready, Papa!"

"Twenty minutes ago, I'd have agreed with that statement. You've shown me how wrong I can be and I'm sorry."

"You're sure?"

He put his arm around my shoulder and handed me my fire diamond sword. The final rays of the sun glinted for the last time that day.

"My love, I've never been surer of anything in my life."

2

Dawn sent rays of sunshine filtering through the ragged curtains in my bedroom. I jumped out of bed with an air of trepidation. Fear mingled with excitement as I pondered the day ahead. Today was my first hunt, the most important day for any dragon slayer. It was the most important job anyone in our village could have. The job all younglings yearned for. The one I was destined to have since the day of my birth, thanks to my slayer parents.

I checked my reflection in the mirror. Long wavy hair cascading around my shoulders was completely inappropriate for any slayer. I was going on a hunt, not to a party. I tied it on top of my head in a messy bun and turned my attention to the clothes that I'd left out the night before. They were actually pretty basic—khaki colored leggings with a similar colored tunic and a thick, brown leather belt that my mother had bought me for my birthday. The shield of our family was engraved on the buckle, complete with the requisite silver dragon. It had the same fire diamond eyes as my sword so I knew to keep it away from Jasper.

The floor shook as Jasper stomped around his room next door, no doubt still being the sore loser he was yesterday. Thunderous footsteps on the stairs followed by a slamming door told me he had left the house. I peeked out and sure enough, Jasper was stalking across the training ground towards the road that would take him to the village less than a quarter mile up the road. He was already covered in armor with his sword sheathed neatly at his hip, and I'd not even had breakfast yet. As if on cue, there was a knock at my door and my mother's small voice came through.

"Julianna. Honey, I've brought you some breakfast. I thought you might need it today."

I opened the door and kissed my mother on the cheek before taking the plate of bacon and eggs from her and setting it on my vanity desk.

At just under four feet, she was the smallest person in the village and the most unlikely dragon slayer my family had produced. I couldn't imagine her out of her flowery dresses and the white apron she always wore.

"I'm not sure I can eat anything, Mom, I'm too nervous!"

"I was watching you out there yesterday. You put your brother to shame, not that I'd ever tell him that. I have faith you'll be an excellent dragon slayer just like the generations of Slayers before you."

"How did you do it, Mom?" With her small size and gentle personality, I doubted she'd be able to pick up my sword, let alone wield it at a dragon.

"Oh, I was hopeless," she said with a grin. "The

sword was almost as big as I was and I was a complete bag of nerves. I honestly thought I was going to cause an avalanche with all the quivering I was doing walking up that mountain with your grandfather. And then we saw it. It was the biggest, ugliest mountain dragon you ever saw in your life and it was angry. Your grandfather charged at it, sword blazing, but tripped over a stone and knocked himself out." She giggled as she replayed the memory.

"So, it was just you and the dragon?" I'd never heard this story before. My father told us stories all the time about his escapades but my mother was usually quiet on the subject.

She nodded her head. "I almost turned and ran down the mountain but I couldn't leave my father."

My eyes widened at the thought. "So, what did you do?"

"I pulled out a slingshot I'd borrowed from your uncle. He was eight years old at the time and had given it to me for good luck. I found a stone and shot it right at the dragon's eye." She chuckled quietly. "I got a clear shot and half-blinded the thing. He must have been disorientated because he began to rampage, spewing flames everywhere. I managed to pull my father into a crevice and the stupid dragon ended up setting himself on fire.

"When the flames died down a bit and it looked like my father was stirring, I picked up my sword and plunged it into the dragon. My father opened his eyes and thought I'd fought with the dragon. I wasn't about to dispel the notion. I told him that night that I couldn't bring myself to do it again. He was just so proud of his dragon-slaying daughter that he let me be." She took my hand and stroked it. "I've never told another soul that story so I'm hoping you'll see fit to keep it to yourself. Your grandfather will never forgive me if he knew the truth."

I couldn't help it. I laughed loudly then flung my arms around my mother.

"Just so you know there is more than one way to skin a cat, or kill a dragon in this case. Now eat up, they'll be waiting for you in the village."

I wolfed down the breakfast and my nerves dissipated. If my mother could do it, then I surely could. So what if she cheated a little? The end result was the same. Maybe I'd take some of her luck onto the mountain with me today.

The armor was much trickier than the clothes had been. Every piece weighed me down, heavy with flame repellent magic. There were buckles to fasten and ties to knot and as each piece was put on, my ability to actually move became more and more impaired. I had no idea how I was going to manage to walk down the stairs, let alone climb a mountain. When my father came to see if I was ready and then kindly told me I'd put it all on backward, I was relieved to find that it was much easier to wear correctly. He handed me the weapons that would fasten to my belt—an 8-inch dagger and a waterlogged grenade. Finally, he passed me my sword so I could fit it into its sheath. In a few hours' time, after it was weighed down with the soul of a dragon, it would be the heaviest piece of equipment I possessed.

My mother kissed my cheek and I felt her slip something into my pocket. I had a pretty good idea what. She winked and I left the house, ready for my adventure to begin. The walk to the village was a slow one. My father showed endless patience as I kept stopping to adjust something. Getting used to this armor was going to be tricky.

Dust on the road swirled around my feet, dry from months of sunshine. It would have been so much easier if I'd been born in Spring or Autumn when the air was cooler, but no, I was born at the peak of the year, when the sun was at its hottest. I reminded myself that it was a day much like today, not too long ago, when Jasper had done his first kill and I'd already proved I could do better than him. I only hoped I didn't let my father down. I understood my mother's reluctance to tell her story. I needed to prove myself at all costs.

Music met my ears as signs of a celebration began at the very outer reaches of the village. Red and gold bunting was strung from post to post. Excitement flooded through me at the thought of what lay ahead. I knew that when I got further into the town center, there would be banners hung from windows and lamp posts with my name on them. All the villagers would come out to greet me, to wish me well for my big day. It was a small village so it wasn't often someone turned eighteen. Before Jasper, it had been three years since they had been able to put on a party like this. And what parties they were.

The newer slayers who had already acquired their dragon soul would go up into the mountains with the birthday boy or girl, but they were only there for back up. It was up to the person whose birthday it was to make the first kill. Of course, the village never knew when the festivities would begin since it depended on when during their eighteenth year they were ready for their first kill. Those left behind would spend the day baking and preparing for the celebration that was to come. A huge space on the village green was always left for the body of the dragon, and around the edges would be tables full of delicious food. Musicians would perform on the small stage and everyone would dance late into the night.

A sudden thought hit me and memories of celebrations drifted away.

"What happens if we don't find a dragon?" I actually wanted to ask what would happen if I didn't kill one but I didn't want to appear weak.

"You can always find a dragon, as long as you know where to look," he replied heartily.

"But what if—"

"Julianna, I've lived in this village for forty-eight years. I've been to so many of these celebrations, I've lost count I'd be lying if I said there haven't been one or two injuries along the way, but I've never—not once—seen a new slayer come back down from those mountains without a dragon. Hell, your mother managed it with her kid brother's slingshot!"

"She told me that this morning. She said you didn't know."

"Honey, everyone knows. I personally think it's the best dragon killing story I've ever heard, God bless her."

I smiled. There had never been a single new hunt without a dragon. It made me feel better until a niggling thought bored its way into my brain. What if I was the first?

"Don't you worry about a thing," Papa said as he placed his hand on my shoulder. "After today, you will know everything there is to know about being a slayer. Today, you will learn our secrets." He winked and strolled to the center of the square.

———

IT SEEMED everyone had come out to greet me. I could barely move for the shouts of "Good luck!" and claps on the back. Smiles were aplenty as I shook hands and nodded graciously to the excited crowd. I breathed deeply and tried to hold back my nerves as words of congratulations were thrown at me. As the crowd thinned, I made out Jasper sitting on an old marker stone sharpening his already sharp sword. He still had the same grouchy look on his face that he'd had when I beat him yesterday.

I scanned the other villagers, looking for the slayers who would be accompanying me up the mountain. There were so many people milling around it was difficult to see them all, but the tell-tale armor that slayers wore was visible here and there between all the other people.

"It's time, slayers!" someone shouted, and as if by magic, the crowd parted and the slayers congregated on the small patch of scorched grass that surrounded Jasper's stone.

I walked forward to join them, knowing all eyes would be on me. There was no need for introductions. I'd grown up with them, but it didn't stop each and every one of them coming up to me and shaking my hand. Well, all except for Jasper who just looked at me moodily.

I gazed up at the Triad Mountains. They looked spectacular in the bright morning sunshine. The middle of the three had snow on its peak, even in the summer sun. I'd never been allowed to climb higher than the village border before, marked by a fence that had been dug into the hard earth before I was born. I'd spent so much time looking up to these mountains, dreaming of the day I'd finally be able to conquer them, and now that day was here at last. I gulped at the thought of what lie ahead but a couple of deep breaths calmed my nerves. I was ready.

I put my best foot forward and took the lead to the sounds of cheering behind me. The wonderful energy provided by the remaining villagers buoyed me.

The fence beckoned to me in the distance and so I marched purposely forward toward my destiny.

"You might have beaten me, little sister," Jasper hissed into my ear. "But fighting me doesn't compare to fighting a dragon. You're not ready; you will fail."

I ignored him. He might be known as the strongest newbie slayer in the village, but as I looked up to the sun-bathed mountains, I knew that I'd prove him wrong yet.

3

The hike up the mountain was more taxing than I thought it would be. I was fit but I hadn't been given time to get used to the weight of all the armor. To take my mind off the struggle, I admired the view around me. At the other side of the village border was a thick band of giant evergreen fir trees that appeared to give the mountain a skirt. It was cooler under the shade of them which I was thankful for, but it wouldn't last. I unhooked a canteen of water from my belt and took a deep swig.

"Not so fast, Julianna!" said Marcus, one of the boys from the village. "We have a long way to go yet and dehydration will kill you faster than an angry dragon if you aren't careful."

I slipped the lid back on and put the canteen away. I knew to listen to the more experienced members of the group. At twenty-three, Marcus was one of the younger ones but he'd been on enough of these expeditions to know what he was talking about. Brown pine needles carpeted the ground beneath us, making it soft and springy. Sounds of wildlife filled the air, birds in the trees and hidden animals scurrying in the undergrowth.

I turned to Marcus. "Why is the village border below the tree line? It's beautiful in here. Surely dragons don't come into the woods."

"They don't, but once we get out of the trees the terrain changes dramatically and that's when you know you need to keep your wits about you. It's rare that they come so low down the mountain but it's not unheard of. You'll see one or two scorched trees at the upper border. That's the work of dragons!"

Light filtered through the dense copse of trees much more freely now as we neared the upper edge of the woods. In a couple of minutes, I might be coming face to face with a dragon for the first time. Fear whipped through me and adrenaline pumped through my body. Scorched trees? I knew how to wield a sword but what good did that do against flames?

"What if the dragon breathes fire in my direction?" I asked him, feeling woefully under-educated.

"You duck!" he replied. "Quickly!"

Great! I could barely stand up straight in the armor, I wasn't sure I'd be able to duck, and I was positive that even if I managed it, I wouldn't be able to do it quickly.

I didn't have time to panic as the trees gave way to a rocky gray terrain. Occasional weeds and the odd hardy flower grew between the cracks in the stones but that was the only sign of life. I tried to ignore the black marks on some of the rocks. Burn marks.

The air turned from the sweet-smelling fragrance of pine to a faint acrid smell.

"What's that smell?" I asked, turning my nose up.

"You'd better get used to it. It's the smell of sulfur. It gets stronger the higher up you go. It's the smell of dragons." I turned to see Marcus grinning. He was enjoying this a lot more than I was.

If I ignored the smell and immediate barren terrain, it was actually pretty beautiful up here. Once we'd cleared the treeline, I could see far into the distance. Looking back, I picked out our house with smoke coming out of the chimney, no doubt thanks to my mother's baking. The village was tiny from this high but I could still make out the colors of all of the banners and decorations for the party tonight.

I couldn't look behind me for too long, because like Marcus had told me, I needed to keep my wits about me. The last thing I needed was to be flame-grilled when I was too busy admiring the view.

The skies above me were clear except for the odd wispy cloud that scudded across the sky. It was perfect slaying weather. Occasionally, from the village, I had seen dragons flying around the peaks but they were often so far away, they looked like birds, but there were none flying about today. I'd only ever seen dragons from such a distance that they were no more than dots in the sky, or the dead ones brought back to the village. I'd grown up surrounded by lore of dragons and I knew everything about them except anything practical.

Three hours later and the terrain had become even more difficult to climb. Rocky outcrops and caves were everywhere so, although Marcus had told me to keep my wits about me, I didn't really know where to look. It seemed like a dragon could be hiding waiting to pounce from anywhere, and there was evidence of them dotted all around us in the form of the discarded bones and carcasses of small mammals. The heat and the smell of sulfur intensified, and it was all I could do not to pass out. The trek was so much more grueling than I had expected and I'd already guzzled my way through half my water rations.

My father who had been walking ahead stopped suddenly and raised his arm as a signal for us to follow suit.

"There is a well-known dragon roost just round those rocks there," whispered Marcus. "It's where I got my first kill. Good luck!"

For the first time, the fear that had been plaguing me throughout the entire trek turned into full-on terror. My time was nearly here. Just another fifty or so more steps and I'd be face to face with my first dragon. My father beckoned me forward. I'd be expected to go in there first.

I put one foot in front of the other and began to walk forward.

"Good luck, little sister," hissed my brother as I passed him. "Don't let the dragon burn you on the butt!" He laughed lightly but I held my head up and ignored him. I might be quivering on the inside but I wasn't going to give him the satisfaction of knowing that.

"Julianna," my father said, clapping me on the shoulder with his huge hands and nearly shaking some of my armor off in the process. "Whatever happens up there, I just want you to know I'm proud of you. I'll be behind you the whole time and you've got the others as back up. If we see you struggling, we'll step in but I want you to do everything to get that dragon without our help. Only that way will you capture his soul. You don't want to fight him almost to the death and then have someone else come in to finish the job. You have to be the one. Do you understand me?"

"Yes, father."

"The carcasses here are fresh and the scorch marks on the rocks are old. That means there hasn't been any other slayer up here for a while. They only breathe fire if they feel threatened. Now go on in there and do your best!"

I managed a half-hearted smile and set off up the rocks alone. Harsh breathing came from behind me although there was no sound of footsteps. Either they were being incredibly quiet or they were giving me a head start. I didn't turn to see which.

Pulling myself up the last ten feet or so, I peeked my head around the corner, wondering what exactly I'd come face to face with. It could be anything from a small immature Triad dragon to a fully grown Royal Scarlet Flame, the biggest and deadliest breed of dragon in our kingdom.

At first, I thought the crevasse was empty. An old roost built from reeds and stones was perched under a rocky outcrop which had been blackened by years of dragonfire, but there was none in sight. I breathed a sigh of relief until I realized it meant more climbing until we found one. I was just about to turn and let the hunting party know when I spotted something in the middle of the roost. I moved forward cautiously to get a closer look. At first, I thought it might be a huge pearl from the giant oysters that lived off the coast of our land, but when I peered over the edge of the roost I saw it for what it was. A dragon's egg. Its opalescent shell glimmered in the noonday sun.

I was confused for a second. Why would there be a dragon's egg without a mother dragon? But then a huge screech from above me told me there wasn't. I looked up to see the whole sky above me had turned scarlet.

4

I stood rooted to the spot. Now was my time to shine but I had absolutely no clue what to do. My training went right out the window. The dark red dragon circled above, dropping lower and lower in the sky but it was nowhere near close enough to impale with my sword. How did the others do this? More importantly, why didn't I know how to do this? I'd been waiting my whole life for this and now I couldn't even move, let alone slay a dragon. I felt like a kid on the first day of school.

My mother's story came back to me and I remembered the thing she'd slipped into my pocket. I already knew what it was but I still felt relief when I pulled out the slingshot. I scoured the ground quickly for a loose stone of the correct size, grabbing the first one I found and fitting it into the pouch.

The dragon had seen me, I was sure of it, but it hadn't attacked yet. I pulled back hard on the leather string of the slingshot, ready to fire, when a hand grabbed hold of my belt from behind and pulled me backward so fast I ended up stumbling and then falling, sending both me and the person behind me flying back down the rocks.

"What are you doing?" I hissed angrily, turning to find Jasper rubbing his head after banging it in the fall.

"Are you a complete moron?" he asked, pulling himself up and dusting himself off.

I gave him a look of disgust before doing the same myself. "What are you talking about?"

"What do you think is going to happen if you use that children's toy?" he spat. "Do you seriously think a small stone will fall a dragon? Because if you do, you are out of your mind."

Anger coursed through me. "Okay, hotshot. What else was I supposed to do? Wait for it to land and bring out a white flag? If you hadn't noticed, it was up in the air!"

It was then I noted that we were alone. "Where is everyone else?"

"They've gone around the other way." He pointed to a rough trail at the side of the rocky outcrop. "You can climb up onto the higher rocks up there which will put us about even with the dragon. Father told me to come get you. I guess he knew you'd make a mess of it."

That really stung. I needed to make my father proud.

"Right then," I said, setting off briskly up the path he'd pointed out. "Are you coming or not?"

The dragon was now completely out of sight but I could hear it. With each step I took, the noise of the flapping wings grew louder. The path was steep and shaded by the cliff to my right that turned into the cleft that the dragon was flying over. I could see Jasper's point. If I kept climbing up, I would be much closer to where the dragon was, making it a much easier target. I pulled myself up the last bit and found myself on the very top of the rocky outcrop that formed the cliff. The others all stood there, swords raised ready to fight. To my surprise, the dragon was still circling around, seemingly oblivious to the men poised to kill it.

My father saw me and beckoned me over. "We waited for you. You have to be the one to kill it. I must warn you, a Royal Scarlet Flame is not the easiest kill. Usually, they attack without warning and shoot fire without being provoked. This one is acting very strangely. You might be in luck, it could be sick. I've never known one not to attack before."

"Maybe it hasn't seen us yet?" I guessed.

"It's seen us all right. It's even flown past a couple of times close enough for us to kill it but you have to be the one to do that. If it's sick, you're going to have an easy job. Just go to the edge of the cliff and wait for it to circle back around. When it gets near, you'll need to stab it. Go for the brain or the heart. If you get it anywhere else, you've effectively given yourself a death sentence."

I'd felt better for a minute but it's funny how phrases such as "death sentence" can instill fear into someone.

The others moved back when I approached, giving me room to run if I needed to. Walking slowly towards the edge of the cliff, I kept my eyes on the dragon, making sure I had room to move if he breathed fire. To my immediate front and about five meters to my right were sheer cliffs. I peeked behind me to see that the slayers had formed a line, keeping their distance while ready to spring into action. I inched closer to the edge, my gaze returning to the dragon. He was still lazily flying around, sometimes ducking into the crevasse below. I wondered if its behavior had something to do with the egg. Perhaps it didn't want to fight us on the cliff for fear that someone else would harm its precious egg? Were dragons really that clever?

My feet came to the very edge of the cliff. One misstep and it wouldn't be the dragon I had to worry about. I hazarded a peek downward and immediately felt dizzy. The valley below was nothing more than a green blur. I'd been gearing up my whole life to be a slayer, but no one had thought to give me lessons on heights. I could see the egg about thirty meters below me. A fall from this height would undoubtedly kill me. Instinctively I took a step backward and a few deep breaths to clear my head. The dragon flew right past me. A rush of air pulled some of my fiery hair from its bun, obscuring my view for a couple of seconds. Pushing my hair back out of my face, my eyes followed as it once again circled around.

"For goodness' sake, kill it!" Jasper shouted from behind me. "Even a toddler could have gotten it that time."

He was right. I'd missed my chance. I'd not even unsheathed my sword, but the dragon circled around again. There would be another chance and this time I'd not fail to take it. My heart rate increased as I put one foot in front of the other to steady myself and drew my sword. This was it. It was now or never. The dark ruby-colored dragon turned back around, flying towards me in the same trajectory as before. For whatever reason, it was planning another swoop past rather than an attack. Maybe I was lucky and it really was sick. It certainly wasn't acting as I'd expected it to. As it flew in my direction, I looked into its eyes and poised myself to fight.

I thrust my sword forward but at the very last second, I hesitated, missing the dragon's chest by millimeters. For the briefest of moments, time stood still. It was just me and the dragon. The dragon I was there to kill and yet there was a voice deep within me screaming not to harm her. She was just protecting her egg, just as any other mother would.

"What are you doing?" Jasper screamed behind me. I turned to see a grim expression on my father's face and my brother hopping up and down in ill-hidden anger.

I turned back to the retreating dragon. What had I done? Or should I say why hadn't I done it? Jasper had been right again. Anyone could have killed that dragon, but I'd hesitated. It just didn't feel right killing it when it wasn't able to defend itself. If it was sick, it had no way to fight against me. That should have made me feel happy but it didn't. This should have been easy but it wasn't. My thoughts returned to the egg and I found myself feeling sorry for the dragon.

"Stop it!" I hissed to myself under my breath. "It's a dragon. You're a slayer."

I blew out a harsh breath and focused my mind, mentally psyching myself up to really kill it this time. Sunlight bounced off the dragon's red scales as it began its trip back my way. I pulled myself as tall as I could and readied my sword again. As the dragon came closer I primed myself for the kill. This time I wouldn't hesitate. I pulled back my sword ready to strike when I felt someone running up to me.

"If you can't kill it, I can!" It was Jasper shouting behind me.

Everything happened in a split second that seemed to go on for a thousand years. As the dragon flew past, Jasper's sword glinted in the corner of my eye. I didn't know what inspired me to do it—whether some misguided empathy for the mother dragon or the fact I didn't want him to take my kill, I'll never know—but I ran to the side, blocking him. We crashed into each other and the blow knocked me right over the edge and into the valley below. As I felt myself falling to my death, my father's voice called my name, dying in strength the further I fell.

"Julianna!"

I landed much earlier and on much softer ground than I expected and it took me a couple of seconds to comprehend I was still alive. In my disoriented state, it was a couple more before I realized I'd landed on the dragon's back. It was no accident. It must have seen what happened and flown to catch me. It went against everything I knew about dragons. They were monstrous killing machines. I flipped over so I was the right way up and grabbed hold of the dragon's spines that ran the length of her back. It would be so easy to kill it now but that would send both of us tumbling to our deaths.

We soared into the air and then back towards the men we left behind. Fear etched on their faces as a huge blast of flame erupted from the dragon's mouth, scattering them as we flew past. It took a swoop into the gorge and then out into the open air, leaving my family and the troop behind.

Well, as far as messing up a dragon slaying goes, I think I could definitely claim to be the best. Not only had I failed to kill it, I was now riding on its back to goodness knows where with no way to get down without plummeting to my death. I decided the only thing I could do was hold on for dear life and pray that it landed soon.

The scenery was stunning although I was too scared to really appreciate it as I forced my eyes to stay open and not squeeze closed in fright. Red light bathed the flatlands to the right as we soared over the gray rise of the mountains in front of us. It was heading up to the highest peak of the Triad Mountains. None of my people had ever ventured this far before. There were enough dragons to kill on the lower mountains that we didn't bother coming this high.

We were now flying lower in the sky as if coming into land. The snowy peak of the mountain was still some ways ahead of us but we were miles above where we had left the others behind. The dragon pulled back slightly to slow down as we landed gracefully on a ledge near a cave entrance. At the last possible second, I jumped down and waved my sword around in a very unpracticed manner, all thoughts of my training completely forgotten.

The dragon was about fifteen feet in front of me. I glanced around. The ledge was only about fifty feet long with sheer cliffs dropping away to the right and the same rising above me to the left. If I did nothing, it would kill me. If I killed it, I'd be trapped on the ledge and die anyway.

What a stupid position to find myself in.

I was just weighing my limited options when the dragon made the most sickening sound. Its bones crunched and its skin seemed to fall inwards. Well, Father was right, it really was sick. It looked like it was dying on the spot with no help from me. I wanted to watch to make sure I was ready if it attacked, but it quickly became apparent it was in no position to do so. I closed my eyes, unable to look at it as it let out the most agonizing scream of pain. The grinding of bones turned into a sickening squelching sound that made me feel sick to my stomach and deathly afraid. When it was finally silent, I opened one eye to take a peek.

What I saw before me was not the dead dragon but a man lying face down on the ground.

5

Where had he come from? And where was the dragon?

I scoured the skies, both confused and worried. Whatever had just happened had happened so quickly, my brain hadn't had a chance to process it. The dragon was nowhere to be seen. The man stirred slightly, bringing my attention back to him and making my heart thump so loudly, I was sure he'd hear it.

"Hello," I called out hesitantly.

He lifted his head and ran his eyes from the tips of my toes all the way to my now disheveled hair. He looked tired, exhausted even, but it was his eyes that threw me, piercing green and staring right at me. It was unnerving.

I unhooked my armor with blundering fingers and pulled my tunic over my head, leaving me in just my vest and leggings. It wasn't ideal but it was better than the alternative. I took a few tentative steps towards the strange man, holding my tunic in front of me.

"Did the dragon bring you up here too?" I asked nervously. Those eyes!

He took my tunic but his eyes narrowed as an expression of intense confusion crossed his face. A wrinkle appeared on his forehead as he studied me. I had an overwhelming feeling that I'd done something wrong. It didn't help that he still hadn't covered himself.

"The tunic is for you," I said, gesturing at the garment. "It's cold up here." He still appeared confused as he pulled my tunic over his head. It was entirely too small for him, the green material stretching over every muscle on his torso. At least it covered him although it would do little against the cold. I shivered slightly, feeling it myself.

"You didn't see me?" he asked. His voice was deep and warm like molasses.

"Not at first. The dragon must have been blocking you. I don't know how we're going to get out of this."

He smiled then, dimples appearing on his cheek. His stunning green eyes, framed by the longest black eyelashes I'd ever seen, crinkled at the edges. If he wasn't so utterly beautiful, I'd have felt affronted by his lack of fear and obvious humor at our situation.

"Come with me," he said.

He walked past me, affording me a generous look at his tunic-covered behind and disappeared into the cave directly behind us.

I stood still, rooted to the spot. Did he really want me to follow him? What exactly did he expect to find in the cave? I suspected there to be nothing more than the bones of animals and quite possibly those of the occasional human. This dragon obviously liked to play with its food before eating it.

He stuck his head out of the mouth of the cave.

"Are you coming or not? I can assure you there is no other way out of here."

I threw my armor back on haphazardly, picked up my sword and followed him. What other choice did I have?

The cave was a lot deeper than I had expected and surprisingly devoid of bones. A pile of clothes lay by the mouth of the cave and it was these that the man went to. Without any embarrassment, he pulled my tunic off, throwing it to me before pulling on the pants and top that had been left there. What the hell was going on? There was no way it was a coincidence that those clothes were there.

"Who are you? What's happening?" I probably should have felt more scared than I did. Maybe I was in shock?

He came toward me with something in his hands. It was only when he wrapped it around me that I realized it was a coat. Thick fur-lined the inside, warming me instantly and almost pulling me down with its weight.

"The coat if for you. It's cold up here." He smiled at me again and pulled the coat tighter around me, my heart flipping at his closeness. If I stood on the very tip of my toes, I'd be eye to eye with him, but as it was I had to look up to meet his gaze. A thick mop of messy black hair that was way overdue for a haircut sat atop his head, giving him a raw, feral look. His clothes, although perfectly suited to the altitude, were messily sewn together and had almost certainly never seen a sewing pattern. Unlike my own; our seamstresses were very dedicated to their skill.

For the briefest of seconds, I wondered if I'd inadvertently been dropped into his home and he actually lived in the cave before brushing the ridiculous idea aside. He was thoughtful in a way no cave dweller would be and he had manners.

Although a little voice inside reminded me that he'd shown no discomfort in being completely naked around a stranger.

"Follow me," he said, beckoning me towards the back of the cave which was completely black.

"What if the dragon is back there?" I asked, wondering if I hadn't just jumped from the frying pan into the fat.

"The dragon will not harm you." He laughed and headed towards the dark. I waited until it had swallowed him whole before making a decision. On one hand, I could walk into what was almost certainly a dragon's lair with a complete stranger who I'd already seen naked; or on the other, I could go sit on the ledge outside and wait to die of frostbite or starvation. What a choice.

"Wait!" I called out. "I can't see you."

He stepped back into the light. "I'm sorry. I forgot that your eyesight won't be as good as mine."

"My eyesight is perfectly normal, thank you!" I replied haughtily, making him laugh at me once again. What was it with this man?

"Forgive me. I only meant that you might not be able to see as well in the dark as I can. Let me help you." He held out his hand in such a way it was obvious he wanted me to take it. Part of me wanted to tell him to stick it but another part didn't want to be left alone on a freezing cold ledge hundreds of feet above the ground. I was completely ignoring the much larger part of me that wanted to touch him so badly, to feel the warmth of his skin.

Just thinking about it caused my cheeks to redden. The heat rising into my face made my mind up for me. Maybe going into the dark cave where he couldn't see just how much he'd affected me wasn't the worst idea after all.

I took his hand and let him lead me into the darkness. He was much warmer than he had any right to be after being naked in these freezing temperatures. His hands were softer than I had imagined they would be and that source of heat was both comforting and thrilling at the same time. The whole thing was confusing—the insane condition I had found myself in and the feelings the situation was generating inside me. I was probably in shock. Perhaps riding a dragon could do that to a person.

"Something tells me you know something I don't," I said, feeling my way along a narrow tunnel. The ground was rocky beneath my feet and the going was slow. How he was managing with no shoes on was beyond me.

"Very astute," he replied, infuriating me further. I stumbled on a rock, tightening my grip on his hand to stop myself from falling. The walls of the tunnel were damp back here. My hand dragged against the side of the cave and the water accumulating there.

"You know where you're going, don't you? Those clothes weren't there coincidentally."

"That's right."

I could actually feel him smiling. I couldn't see him at all but I knew the corners of his mouth were turned upwards. He was having fun at my expense.

"Are you going to enlighten me?" I queried.

"What do you want to know?"

"Who are you?" I figured we'd start with the basics. I'd get on to the whole question of why he was naked on a ledge later.

"My name is Ash."

"I'm Julianna," I said, then paused. "Is that all? Are you going to tell me where you come from?"

"My people live up here on the mountain."

I laughed, thinking he was telling a joke, but his silence told me he wasn't.

"You're serious? No one lives on these mountains. The terrain is too difficult to climb. There's no possible way to get back to the village from here without falling to your death."

"Who said anything about going to your village?"

"But how do you get food without going down the mountain? It's too cold to grow anything up here."

"You'll see," he replied. "Look, there's light ahead."

And he was right. The cave wasn't a cave at all but a tunnel through the mountain. As it grew lighter, the less I needed his help. I could see well enough to navigate the rough ground beneath me but I was reluctant to let go of his hand. He didn't seem in any hurry to let go of mine either.

We emerged on another ledge with no way down. Below, a lush, verdant valley spread out into the distance, surrounded by snowy peaks. A tiny town hundreds of feet below us looked like a toy village from this height. The view took my breath away. It was like nowhere I'd ever seen before and not in a million years would I have guessed that the aged Triad Mountains would hide such a utopia.

"It's...it's...stunning!"

"It's home," he replied simply, shrugging his shoulders.

As I gazed in wonder at the spectacular view below me, it dawned on me that two tiny dots on the horizon I'd taken as birds were in fact dragons.

"Don't you have a lot of problems with dragons up here?" I wondered aloud, glad that they were so far away.

"Much more than you could imagine," he smiled again.

"There's no path down the mountain," I pointed out. The cliffs were as sheer on this side as they were on the other. "How are we supposed to get down there?"

"You really haven't figured it out yet?" he asked, amusement filling his voice. He pulled his shirt over his shoulders, exposing his muscled chest, before moving to his belt.

"Hey, hey," I shouted, taking a step back in alarm. The ground crumbled beneath my feet and I could feel myself begin to fall.

A pair of strong hands caught hold of the coat's collar and pulled me away from the edge.

"You need to be careful."

"I need to be careful?" I shouted, my heart hammering at my near death fall into the valley. "What do you think you're doing?"

"Oh God, I'm sorry." He pulled away from me and sat at the mouth of the tunnel on a smooth boulder, his head in his hands. "I sometimes forget. We're so isolated up here that I didn't realize how rude I was being."

"Darn right you were being rude. What is it with you and having no clothes on?"

"I promise, I wasn't trying to scare or offend you," he said looking at me, contrition filling his features.

I didn't know what to think. He was acting so strangely and yet I could see that he was genuinely upset at scaring me.

"I have to take my clothes off to get us down the mountain."

"I really don't see the connection between the two."

For the life of me, I had no idea what he was trying to tell me. Not unless he had a plan to build a makeshift parachute out of his pants.

"I can't change with my clothes on. They'd rip to shreds."

"Change? Change into what?"

"Those dragons over there? They're my family, Julianna. I'm the dragon that brought you here."

6

———

"You're what?" I looked at him uncertainly.

"We are an ancient colony of dragons. We're shifters."

"The dragons are humans?" I asked incredulously.

"Not quite, no. We have a human form, that is true, but we do not identify as such. Nor do we really identify as full dragons. We are somewhere in between and happy to be that way. We keep to ourselves and only ever come down the mountain when absolutely necessary."

"But I'm a dragon slayer," I muttered, feeling a mixture of confusion and intrigue, not to mention a healthy dose of guilt about my own ancestry.

"Are you?" He looked at me with such warmth that my guilt began to melt away. "Julianna, I've lived up on these mountains my whole life and I've been brought up on stories of our enemies, the men and women of your village who call themselves dragon slayers, but not once have I known anyone to do what you did today."

"What did I do?"

"You hesitated. You could have killed me but you didn't. You actually risked your own life because deep down you really didn't want to harm me, did you?" The warmth in his eyes made me feel unsure of myself.

"I thought you were a mother dragon. I saw the egg and thought it was cruel to take a mother away from her baby."

He laughed which only added to my confusion. "The egg is a decoy—polished rock in a fake nest. It's been there as long as I can remember. As you can see below us, we live in houses, much the same as you do."

"But why?"

"I guess it was put there in a misguided attempt to ward the slayers off." He shrugged. "We hoped that your people would leave us alone if you thought we had babies to look after. Of course, the opposite happened. They saw that we were breeding and stepped up the amount of people coming here."

"I didn't know," I said, feeling ashamed.

"I know you didn't, but you're the first of your kind to think before mindlessly killing us. I'm going to give you two choices, Julianna. There is no way off this mountain without wings. I will happily transform back and take you home, or at least to a place that will be safe for you to get home."

"I want the second choice!" I butted in.

His mouth curled up at the edges as he regarded me. "I've only given you one choice so far."

"You were going to invite me to your village." As soon as I said it, I hoped I was right. Now that I knew it existed, I knew I wasn't ready to go home and forget its existence.

He chuckled. "You're a mind reader, no? I was indeed going to offer to let you come to my homeland but I must warn you, if that is what you choose, it will not be without risks. My people are fiercely proud and much like your people, we have a deep-rooted fear and dislike of outsiders."

"So why were you going to invite me?"

"Because fear is brought about by misunderstanding. War could so easily be avoided if the two parties communicated."

"Is this war?" I asked.

"Isn't it?"

I looked over the pretty little village hundreds of feet below us. I wondered for a second what my father would make of it.

"I'm going to have to strip again. You might want to cover your eyes."

Despite my fear of heights, I walked to the edge and sat, dangling my feet over. The village looked tiny from here, not scary at all as long as I didn't think of the fact that it was full of dragons, or dragon people. Dragon people who had spent centuries being hunted by my people.

I tried to ignore the sickening sounds coming from behind me. Shifting sounded really painful. I'd heard of shifters before but they were creatures in distant lands and were spoken about in almost mythical terms. It was difficult to imagine a whole colony of them so close to where I lived. My shoulder suddenly got very warm as a blast of fire flew over me. I turned to see a dragon waiting for me to climb aboard his back.

Climbing up was trickier than I had imagined. He was just so big. He lifted his leg for me to use as a step and I grabbed the base of his wing to pull myself aboard. It felt much weirder sitting on top of him now that I knew what he really was. The discarded pile of clothes only served to make me more uncomfortable.

Flinging my arms around his neck as we took off, I held on tightly for fear of falling. The wind blew around me sending my hair flying out behind me. It was so strong that I could barely keep my eyes open, but I did, just so I could enjoy the magnificent sight. Adrenaline pumped through my system as Ash circled high above the village, giving me a bird's eye view.

"Woohoo!" I shouted as he did a steep dive before pulling back up straight moments later. The thrill of flying was like nothing I had ever felt before, not even close. Blood rushed through my veins and my heart pounding in a mixture of fear and utter excitement. I had never felt as free as I did now, soaring high in the air.

All too soon, my thrill ride ended and we came to a gentle landing on the very edge of the village. Another neatly folded pile of clothes greeted us, ready for his return. I jumped down and ran towards a fence at the edge of a neatly tilled field while he changed into his human form and dressed. I was eager for him to finish so I could tell him how wonderful the flight down had been, how exhilarating. I peeped around to find him buttoning the top two buttons on his shirt.

"Oh my goodness. That was amazing!" I jumped up and down making him laugh. "I flew, Ash. I really flew."

I knew I sounded dorky but I didn't care. I felt high as a kite. I might have touched down but I was still flying.

"Yes, you did. Did you enjoy the dip I did for you?"

"Next time can we do a loop-the-loop?" I held my hands together almost pleadingly.

"I know I could but you'd probably plummet to your death. Maybe we should put that idea on a back burner for now. Come on, I'll introduce you to Spear, our leader."

"Okay," I said, full of excitement.

"Before I take you into the village, I have to warn you. Spear does not like slayers, with much reason. His mother was killed by one. He makes sure our village is defended from your kind and he will not take well to me bringing you here."

My excitement swiftly turned to fear.

"He will not hurt you; he is a proud man and he is angry with your people, but he is not a bad man."

"Are you sure?" He must be pretty livid if we slayed his mother, not that I could really blame him. I would be too.

"You'll be safe with me, come on." He took my hand again, just as he had done in the caves. The warmth of his skin reassured me as we walked past fenced fields. The houses were built in a similar way to ours although they were much closer together. Each house had a flat roof, unlike the ones in my own village which were sloping.

I wondered why for a second before I saw a dragon

land on the top of one of them. They were landing spots. Despite the fact I knew the dragons were really people, I still shied away from the one on the roof. Years of having it instilled in me that dragons were killers was enough to make me wary and afraid. Even Ash's warm hand was not enough to stop the fear running through me.

The houses became denser as we got closer to the center of the village, and more and more commercial buildings appeared. I was surprised to see shops although I didn't know why. Unlike the shops in my world, everything they sold seemed to come from this small valley—grains and vegetables from the fields, a butcher's shop selling beef and pork, a basic clothes shop selling handwoven attire. All the buildings were made out of wood.

"That's our town hall," Ash said, pointing out a circular building ahead of us. It was thatched with straw which I couldn't help but think was a fire hazard with all the dragons around. Ash gripped my hand more firmly as we entered through a set of double doors.

I found myself in a curved corridor, more than likely circling the entire building. Posters of events and news from around the village were pinned up on the walls haphazardly. Instead of turning left or right, we walked through another set of doors ahead of us, bringing us out into a huge circular courtyard with strange holes evenly distributed around the edge. One side was raised slightly like a stage although there were no chairs. Ash guided me forward and slightly to the right where there was a set of stairs leading down into the ground. At the bottom was a heavy wooden door which Ash pulled back easily, despite the fact it looked extraordinarily heavy.

The room we walked into was the strangest room I'd ever seen. Unlike the building above, this was made entirely of stone although it had some handwoven rugs on the floor to give it the appearance of being homely. The use of the holes above suddenly became apparent —they were windows to let light into this strange room. It looked very much like a courtroom that we would have back home with a raised podium at one side and rows of wooden benches at the other. Behind the podium was a door which was where Ash led me. This time, instead of just entering, he knocked and waited.

I shivered slightly, partly because of the cold, mainly out of nerves.

"Maybe I should go home," I whispered. "This is a mistake."

"Come in," a deep voice boomed.

"You'll be fine," he replied warmly and opened the door.

"Ash, what are you doing?" asked a great big man sitting behind a long desk. He looked to be in his early forties although his black hair was graying slightly at the sides. His voice was even and calm and his face showed no emotion but his eyes flashed with anger. Anger at me.

"Hear me out, Spear. She doesn't want to kill us."

"Of course, she wants to kill us," he replied as if I wasn't standing before him. "She is one of them." He spat the last word out as if he was talking about vermin.

"She had the chance to kill me and she didn't. Even with all her men behind her, she chose to spare me."

"Ash!" Spear stood up and slammed his fist on the table. The resulting boom echoed around the room, making me jump in fright. "I don't care what she did or didn't do. She is a slayer. For centuries, her people have been killing ours. That's all they know how to do. She's no different. She will need to be killed now that she knows where we live.

"I didn't want to kill him. I don't want to kill anybody," I replied nervously, trying to ignore his last statement.

"Nobody needs to be killed. That's exactly why I brought her here. To see who we are. To give her a chance."

"Are you suggesting we just let her go free? Within days there will be swarms of slayers up here and we will all be dead."

"You know as well as I do that there is no way they can get up this high on the mountain. We're perfectly safe up here."

"I've heard rumors of flying machines built in distant lands. If they know we're here, it's only a matter of time before the slayers figure out a way to get up here. I'm sorry, Ash, but she has to be disposed of. We cannot trust her to keep our colony a secret."

"I will!" I shouted before I'd even thought about what I was saying. As a slayer, could I really promise anything of the sort?

"She has said she will keep out secret and I believe her. You can't make decisions as big as this without the rest of the village elders anyway. There has to be a majority vote."

Spear's eyebrows scrunched as defeat reflected in his

eyes. I took a deep breath as I realized that there was a chance of surviving this after all.

"It will take a week to gather everyone," Ash continued. "There are still a couple of scouting parties out over the eastern rim. Let her stay here and get to know everyone before just deciding she must die. Let her prove she means no harm."

"I don't like it but protocol must be maintained. If she proves that she can be trusted and the Elders believe her then I am powerless; however, if, like me, they pass the death sentence, then she will have to die. I'm putting you in charge of her, Ash, and if I hear about her putting just a toe out of line, it will not only be her head on the chopping block. Do you understand?"

"Completely. You have my word, I'll look after her."

"As well you might. She is as unsafe here as we are in her world. With any luck, I won't have to bring this to the elders in a week. I'll be surprised if she lives that long."

He went back to his writing as Ash and I left the room. My nerves, already frayed from everything else that had happened that day, were now on a knife edge.

"He's all bark and no bite," said Ash in an attempt to reassure me. It didn't work.

"No bite? He just sentenced me to death!"

"The elders won't allow it. Once they meet you and get to know you, they'll know that you're telling the truth. I know that you won't tell your family about us; we just have to prove it to them."

I gulped. I'd only said what I'd said because I was faced with certain death otherwise. If I never spoke of this place, it would be a massive betrayal to my family. Was I really able to do that? I wasn't even sure myself.

"Where are we going?" I asked Ash as we left the circular building and headed down a street I'd not previously seen.

"I'm taking you home."

Ash's hand squeezed mine and I suddenly realized that he'd not let go of my hand the whole time.

7

We headed back toward the cliffs we had flown down from, but this time proceeded much further along.

"Do you live in a house on the outskirts of town?" I asked as the houses once again thinned out to be replaced by more of the farmed land.

"Kind of," he replied mysteriously. We passed a field full of cows munching lazily on grass.

There was only one house I could see now—a pretty little cottage with a thatched roof and smoke drifting out of the chimney. It was here I thought we were headed but we walked past it.

"There are no houses left," I exclaimed as we left the cottage behind.

"Look ahead of you."

I looked towards the cliffs and that's when I noticed a series of caves in the sheer rock. There were lots of them, maybe fifty or sixty, but unlike normal caves, they were uniform in the rock and each had a doorway or window intricately carved with effigies of dragons. There was no way these were natural. Someone had spent years lovingly carving homes out of the hillside. Ten of the holes were at ground level and had wooden doors on them. The rest were windows, some with balconies. They stretched quite a way up the cliff, showing the immense size of each dwelling.

We arrived at a periwinkle blue door that Ash pushed open. A huge, gangly dog came running up to him, its long ears flopping behind it. It jumped up and began to lick Ash as if he had been away for months.

"Hey, Firecracker," Ash said, giving the dog a friendly ruffle of its hair.

It surprised me that a dragon would have a pet dog. A lot of things were surprising me today. The dog finally put its two front paws back on the ground and came to give me a sniff.

"He's very cute." I grinned, patting him on the head.

"She. She's a girl. Come on, I'd like you to meet my mom."

I hesitated. I felt comfortable around Ash but Spear had scared me. What if Ash's mom felt the same way about me that Spear had?

The entrance hall was the strangest place I'd ever seen. The walls were roughly hewn out of the rock but the floor was polished wood. Framed pictures of unknown people lined the walls and coats hung on a row of hooks. A mirror hung next to where I stood, a shelf below it. A couple of unlit candles sat on an old table, waiting to be lit.

I hazarded a glance in the mirror. My hair had settled into a frizzy mess and I was covered in dirt.

When I pulled Ash's coat from my shoulders, I realized I looked like a warrior with my armor still on over my clothes.

Straight ahead was another door and to the right of that, stairs leading up to the next level.

"My mom will be in the living area, come on."

He seemed eager to take me to his mom, but I couldn't possibly meet her looking the way I did.

"Do you have a bathroom I can use first?"

"Sure. That door over there is a guest toilet."

I opened the door expecting to find a hole in the ground but was quite surprised to find a true bathroom with a little sink and another mirror. Water poured out of a little channel and streamed into the rock basin where it gurgled down a hole in the middle. The water was freezing but it refreshed me as I splashed it over my face. I did my best to tame my hair with the few pins that had survived the journey and then pulled off all my armor. I wanted to meet Ash's mom as an equal, not as a slayer. My tunic was filthy but it would have to do.

Looking in the mirror, I tried to imagine what Ash's mom would think of me. Did I look like a slayer? I didn't think so, not now that I had taken my armor off, but I hardly looked like a lady either. I was just about to tell Ash to forget the whole thing when he knocked on the door.

"Are you okay? You've been in there a long time."

"I'll be right out."

Steeling myself, I opened the door and followed Ash to a landing with two doors. The stairs continued up to another level but it was the first door that Ash opened. Just like the hallway, this room had been cut out of the mountain. The walls were nothing more than jagged edges of rock but there was carpet on the floor and family paintings hanging alongside landscapes. Whoever had painted them was quite an artist. The room was also a lot lighter than I imagined it would be thanks to a large window at one end. At the other end of the room was a table with four chairs. An elegant lady with her hair in a long braid down her back sat at one of these.

"Hi, Mom. I've got someone I'd like you to meet."

She looked up with a beautiful smile on her face but when she saw me her face dropped.

"Ash, who is this?" she asked although I could tell from her expression and the tone of her voice she already knew what I was, if not who.

"This is Julianna. She's—"

"No!" said his mother, cutting him off mid-sentence.

"No, what?" asked Ash but he knew what she meant. We both did.

"Maybe you should just take me home," I said quietly. It was obvious I wasn't wanted here.

"No!" replied Ash. "Mom, I want her to stay with us. This is what we've been talking about for years. You've said it yourself a million times how you wished things didn't have to be as they are. Well, now is our chance to make that happen."

"I didn't mean invite one into our home. I'm sorry, Julianna, is it? I have nothing against you personally although what Ash was thinking by bringing you here is beyond me. But you will have hardship here." She turned back to Ash. "If Spear catches her with you, we'll all be in trouble. Take her home quickly before he finds out what you've done."

"He already knows. I took her to meet him first."

"Spear knows? I'm surprised she's still here to tell the tale."

"He wants to put her to death but he's giving her a week to prove her loyalty to us."

"Ash, she has no loyalty to us and why should she? I'm surprised at you after what happened to your father."

"That was nothing to do with Julianna and you know that. She had the chance to kill me today and she chose not to. All slayers are not what we have painted them to be. What if we have been wrong all these years?"

"Hundreds of our people slain over the centuries tell a different story, Ash."

"If Julianna hesitated, why wouldn't there be others who would also spare us? I'm only asking for her to be here a week. Spear told me I have to look after her. After that, if she has not persuaded enough of our villagers that she's loyal to us, then I'll take her to Spear myself."

"If that is what Spear has said then we cannot go against it, but it will be for one week only, Ash. She can have the top bedroom. I'll bring her some clean bedding later."

"Thank you, Mom," said Ash, crossing the room to kiss her cheek.

"Thank you, Mrs.—" I paused, not knowing what to call her.

"Edeline." Her eyes met Ash's for a brief second

before turning to me. "If you're to live among my family, you may as well know my first name."

"Thank you, Edeline."

"I have no fight with you child, but you must know that being here among us will not be easy. People here hold grudges. Ash, show her to the top bedroom." She sighed as she turned from us and disappeared down the hall.

"Yes, Mom."

I followed Ash through the overly wide doorway and up the stairs which wound back on themselves. We passed at least three floors before the stairway opened into a large room. The walls were smoother up here and blackened by fire but there were none of the home furnishings of downstairs. The whole room was empty save for a mound of straw.

"I'm sorry, it's not very homely. We don't normally use this room as a bedroom. I guess you can say we don't have many overnight guests." Ash shrugged his shoulders. "We use it to fly in. Our landing pad is through those glass doors."

Opening the doors he motioned to, I stepped out onto the large terrace. The view over the village was stunning, even in the fading light, with verdant fields laid out below me and the houses of the village in the distance now lit up with twinkling lights.

"I could sleep up here and you can have my room if you prefer."

"I love it!"

"You do?" asked Ash as I followed him back into the room.

The hay looked dry and clean and was as good a

place for me to sleep as any. It reminded me of our barn back home. I had fallen asleep there many nights, just gazing at the stars through the holes in the roof. If I ignored the faint burning smell, I could be comfortable here.

"I'll find a bed for you to sleep on and bring it up."

I bit my tongue, embarrassed that I had assumed they slept on hay, and thankful that I hadn't said as much.

"That's very kind of you. Thanks."

"It's beginning to get late. I'll get it now."

When he had gone, I stepped back out onto the terrace. The light was fading quickly. A whole day had passed since I'd jumped on Ash's back. I wondered where my father and Jasper were now. Would they still be out looking for me or would they have gone back to the village to tell my mother that I was gone?

Either of those options was enough to bring tears to my eyes. Ash had promised I'd be loyal to the dragons but was that something I could really do?

A few moments later, a clattering in the room behind me told me that Ash had arrived back with the bed. He'd brought it up in four pieces which he dropped on the floor.

"It just slots together. Do you think you can manage while I bring up the mattress?"

"I'll try."

In reality, having something physical to do took my thoughts away from the situation. I'd just slotted the last two bits together when Ash came back with the mattress and a huge fabric bag, out of which he produced blankets and a pillow. Following that, he pulled a loaf of bread and some butter.

My stomach gurgled at the sight. I'd not had a bite to eat since my mother made me breakfast that morning.

"It's not much, sorry. It's all we had." He chuckled quietly. "We hunt most of our food."

"It looks delicious." I eyed the bread still sitting in his hand.

We both sat on the newly made bed and Ash ripped chunks from the bread and dipped them in the warmed butter. I couldn't help but smile at the thought of my mother's face if she ever saw anyone eating like that. She was the type of person that cut the crusts off her sandwiches.

Ash handed me the first chunk, gooey with butter. I bit down on it and let the liquid butter ooze down my throat.

I don't know if it was because I hadn't eaten all day or because it felt naughty to be eating in such a savage manner, but it tasted utterly delicious. We devoured the whole loaf between us and drank a bottle of milk that Ash had also brought out of the bag.

I felt completely at ease but something that Edeline had said was gnawing at me.

"Ash?"

"Hmmm?" he responded around a mouth full of bread.

"What did your mother mean earlier? What happened to your father?"

He chewed thoughtfully before swallowing the bread and turning his eyes to me. I could see the pain in them but there was no malice.

"My father was killed by a slayer last year."

The way he looked at me was enough to break my heart. It took everything I had not to reach out to him, but how could I? One of my kind killed his father. Who was I to offer sympathy?

"I should leave you now. It's getting late," said Ash, standing and putting the empty bottle back in the now depleted bag. "Will you be okay?"

I nodded my head numbly, not knowing what to say to him. He was acting as though nothing had happened, as if everything was okay.

"Ash," I called out as he was leaving the room.

He turned to me and nodded slightly. It was his way of telling me that he didn't blame me. He closed the door, leaving me alone with my thoughts.

I laid my head back on the surprisingly comfortable mattress and pulled the blanket over me. The only light in the room came from the glow of the town through the window. Strange sounds filtered from the outside, although it was so much quieter than I was used to. I heard shuffling from someone moving about downstairs and hushed voices although they were far too faint to tell who they belonged to.

My mind flew to my father and Jasper searching for me, the thought of them making me homesick even though I'd only been away for a day. No one had ever gone up to the mountains and not returned before. Some had been unsuccessful in slaying a dragon, but we had never had one of the villagers go missing. I wondered if they thought I was dead. Even if they still hoped I was alive, they would never be able to reach me —not this high up.

I closed my eyes and thought of Ash. How could he be so nice to me when one of my kind had murdered his father? I had felt no blame from him but my guilt was palpable. More than anything, I wanted to make it up to him, but how? I closed my eyes and shivered even though the room was warm. Thoughts turned into dreams which turned into nightmares of dragons and fire, and by the time I woke up, I still felt conflicted about my feelings towards Ash and the situation I had found myself in.

8

The smell of something cooking wafted up the stairs and woke me from my bad dreams. It was definitely some kind of meat and smelled delicious. My stomach gave a gurgle to concur. I followed the smell downstairs, expecting to find Ash or Edeline cooking. I searched the whole house, calling out their names but no one answered. I saw no sign of the sister that Ash mentioned, nor Firecracker.

As I searched from room to room, it became apparent that they did not own a kitchen and yet the smell of food was stronger down here. It was only when I got to the bottom floor and the entrance hall that I heard the sound of people outside. I opened the door hesitantly to find a large group of people sitting around a huge fire pit. Flames licked a grill that had been laid on top and filled with great slabs of meat.

"Here she is!" Ash stood up from the circle of people and walked towards me. Two dozen eyes swiveled my way, making me feel more nervous today than I had yesterday. I also spotted Edeline in the group and a young girl sitting beside her that must have been Ash's sister.

Firecracker bounded over, passing Ash and licking my fingers. I gave him a pat on the head for his troubles.

"Come. There are some people I would like you to meet." Ash held out his hand for me to take but I was reluctant to do so. I could see the expressions on some faces and they weren't happy.

"They know about you. I've already told them. You'll be fine," Ash said in an effort to comfort me. I held out my hand to his reluctantly but when our fingers touched, I suddenly felt safe. It was as if nothing could hurt me when Ash was at my side.

I walked with him to the group of people. There was a pretty even split between women and men, of young and old and of those smiling at me and those grimacing at my presence. Not that I could blame them.

"Everybody, this is Julianna."

I gave a shy smile and waved. An elderly man to my right patted the rock beside him to indicate that I could sit there. I let go of Ash's hand and took the offered seat so as not to cause offense. The young girl came over to me carrying a plate with a huge steak on it and handed it to me, grinning. She looked to be about twelve years old with burnished red hair in short braids at either side. Her coloring was different from the dark-haired Ash, but her cheeky face was the spitting image of her elder brother's.

"What's it like over there? I've never been over the mountain. I'm too young but I can't wait until I'm big enough to fly there. Do you have rivers? Ash told me that the roads are made of gold."

She was a whirlwind but I immediately liked her.

"We have rivers," I laughed. "But we have roads much like yours. Very few of us have any gold. Only the richest people of our village own any and they make it into jewelry."

"Wow!" Her eyes rounded like saucers. "I'd love some gold jewelry. I only have this." She showed me a polished rock threaded through a bit of string that hung around her neck.

"Maybe one day I could give you one of my brooches. I have a couple of gold ones."

She jumped up and hugged me, nearly causing me to drop my plate. "I'm so glad you brought her here, Ash," she squealed before letting me go.

"Yes, that's right, give her some gold," sneered a voice from the other side of the fire pit. "That's really going to make up for you murdering her father."

I looked through the flames to a very good-looking man with blonde hair. Even sitting down, he was obviously tall. His shoulders were wide, topping off muscular arms and I could see the outline of his muscles under his tunic. His nose was scrunched as his eyes tracked me.

I had just opened my mouth to reply when I felt my arm being pulled up by Ash. I rose to my feet in surprise, knocking the steak to the ground. Firecracker ran over to my feet and picked it up between her teeth.

"Stop it, Aluss. I warned you not to talk to her in such a way."

He stood up, his huge size almost blocking the light

from the sun. He was at least a head taller than Ash and three times wider. I'd never seen someone so huge and so strong. "Yeah, you warned me, but what exactly are you going to do to stop me?"

FEAR GRIPPED me as Ash skirted around the campfire, pulling me closer to the brute.

"I'm not fighting you. We need to stop this ridiculous war once and for all. Killing ourselves is only going to make the slayers' jobs easier, don't you think? Now get out of our way. I'm going to show Julianna around the village. I was hoping we would show her how welcoming we can be but thanks to you, you've only cemented her assumption that we're all savages."

"He's got every right to voice his opinion. We're all thinking the same thing." The speaker was a woman about my age who would have been attractive was it not for the way hatred twisted her features.

"What is wrong with you all? Julianna hasn't done anything to you, Lisa, or you, Aluss. You weren't out there yesterday. I was. I saw what she's like. She chose to risk her life to save mine. They're not all bad people on the other side of the mountain."

"You are such a fool, Ash," replied Lisa. "She didn't kill you then so she could find out where we live and bring her family back to slaughter us all. You're such a sucker for a pretty face."

"You're wrong!" Ash's hand tightened around mine. "Come on, Julianna."

I had no choice but to follow him and leave the others behind. He took me along the same track we'd walked down the previous day, moving at such a pace he was almost dragging me.

"Wait up!" I said, barely able to keep up with him.

"Sorry!" He turned and kicked a rock behind us. "I'm just so angry. They knew you were going to join us and they treated you like that anyway."

"How can you expect them to treat me any differently? I'm more surprised at the way you treat me."

"What do you mean?" His eyes softened as he looked towards me. There was a hint of something in them, not fear exactly, but worry.

"My people killed your father and countless others and yet you treat me with such warmth. I don't understand it."

I saw him glance behind me to see if there was anyone in earshot.

"I want you to understand that I don't blame you for the death of my father."

"The others do."

"Aluss looks mean but really he's just stupid. He's all brawn and no brain. He likes to flex his muscles and throw his weight around but you've nothing to fear from him."

"What about Lisa?" From nowhere a surge of jealousy rose up within me. It was as though just saying her name gave her some connection to Ash. I couldn't even begin to fathom why I cared, but I knew that I did. I almost didn't want to hear what he was about to say.

"Lisa was my girlfriend."

"Was?" I knew it was none of my business but I couldn't keep myself from asking.

"We dated a while last year. She cheated on me with Aluss."

"Oh," I said, not knowing how to respond. I couldn't deny that a feeling of relief rushed through me, as undeniable and as strange as the jealousy I had felt moments before.

We walked in silence around the perimeter of the little village. Once on the other side, the terrain was more rugged than the farmland. Soft rolling hills covered by the greenest grass and hundreds of pretty pink and red flowers made a valley for the clearest stream I'd ever seen to wind through.

We crossed the stream, stepping on flat stones that had been placed there for that very reason. As we strolled up the low hill, a couple of dragons took off by the cliffs, a large gold one followed by a smaller green one. They flew closer to us, getting larger as they soared above our heads.

"That's Aluss and Lisa," said Ash

"Where are they going?" I squinted into the sun as they disappeared over the cliffs at the opposite side.

"To hunt," he replied, sitting on the soft grass. I followed his lead and sat beside him, trying not to flatten any of the flowers as I did.

I gazed out over the village, seeing the farmland in the distance.

"You have cows and pigs. Why do you need to hunt?"

"We do farm, but it's not enough for us. You've seen the size of us when we are dragons. It takes an inordinate amount of energy for us to change forms. We have huge appetites. Most of the food we eat is hunted. Aluss and Lisa will bring home a few goats between them, or maybe if we're lucky, a couple of the wild buffalo that live on the plains on the other side. After lunch, another group will go out hunting and we'll eat whatever they bring back for our dinner."

"There are a lot of you and you so easily outnumber the people in my village. Why don't you...?"

"Why don't we kill your people?" He finished the question so that I didn't have to. The shame I felt was so overwhelming that I couldn't look at him. Instead, I gazed at the broken stem of a flower on the ground near my feet—anything to stop me having to raise my eyes to his.

"My people do not kill. We hunt for food but we do not hunt out of malice. You and I are the same really. Yes, I have the power to turn into a dragon but that doesn't make me a savage beast."

"I don't think you're a savage beast," I said, flashing my eyes towards him to find almost a smile on his face.

"But yesterday you did."

"Yesterday I didn't know you."

"And therein lies the solution." He picked a flower and handed it to me, taking me by surprise.

"Thank you," I replied, taking the flower from him. It was one of the red ones, with a long stem and six perfectly shaped petals. I didn't have to bring it to my nose to smell it; the whole field was filled with the fragrance of these flowers. Nothing remotely like them grew on our side of the cliffs. "These flowers are so beautiful. They're perfect in every way."

Ash just smiled which made me blush. It occurred to me that this was the first time in my life that a boy had given me flowers. I turned my head away to hide the color in my cheeks and went back to the conversation we'd been having before he'd handed the flower to me.

"What do you mean by solution?"

"It's easy to kill someone when you don't know them. Even easier when you believe them to be dangerous, and yet hand a man a sword to kill an equal, someone they know, and the job is a much harder one. You wouldn't kill me now because you've taken the time to get to know me."

"I didn't want to kill you yesterday when I didn't know you at all."

"Ah, but you are like that flower in your hand."

I could feel the blush deepen in my cheeks at his words. I'd called the flower beautiful. Was he saying the same about me?

He lay back on the carpet of grass, his hands behind his head. I followed his lead and lay back next to him, gazing up into the pale blue sky and enjoying the heat of the sun on my face. A small dragon with a yellow belly flew overhead.

"What do you see?" asked Ash as the dragon soared across the sky above us.

"I see a dragon."

"Yesterday it was a dragon. What are you seeing now?"

I looked at the dragon once more, tilting my head to follow its path. Above its belly, its skin was a dark red. Something about it caught in my consciousness. I'd seen that color already today.

"I think it's your sister."

"Lucy. Yes, it is. She likes you. When I told her last night that a villager from the other side of the cliffs was staying with us, she was so excited I had to order her not to go barging into your room. She's been begging to be allowed to fly over the cliffs since she first learned to talk, but she's too young. It's dangerous for her over there."

I thought back to the whirlwind of red hair and the exuberant little girl I'd met only a couple of hours before. She was so sweet and full of life. Would the slayers really have killed her? With a heavy heart, I knew that we would. We'd had smaller dragons brought to our village before. Why hadn't it occurred to anyone that these smaller dragons were nothing more than children?

"This needs to be stopped! Your sister should be free to fly wherever she wants without fear. We have to do something about this."

"That's why I brought you here. So you could see who we really are. Do you think you'll be able to convince your people that we are no threat?"

I looked back up into the sky as I pondered Ash's question. Lucy had disappeared from view. My father was a proud man and he was set in his ways. I'd been brought up a slayer, as had he and all the other villagers. However much I'd like to tell Ash yes, I wasn't sure if I could change centuries of hate, but as the small dragon flew back into view, I knew then that I'd do everything I could to try.

9

———

The sky darkened as a dragon blocked out the sun overhead.

"That's our cue, come on."

I sat up to see Aluss and Lisa pass overhead. Both had something in their mouths.

"Cue for what?" I rubbed my eyes and yawned. We'd spent the whole day lazing on the grassy hillside amongst the flowers, enjoying the sun and chatting effortlessly. It had been the most blissful way to while away the day and I didn't want it to end. Not just yet.

"Dinner. You must be hungry. You didn't even get breakfast this morning."

"Do we really have to go back now?" My time with Ash had been perfect and I wasn't sure if I was ready for it to end. I felt so comfortable around him. He listened when I talked about life on the other side of the cliffs without passing judgment, and he told me about his father and what a great man he'd been. Despite the fact that I was starving, going back to the other dragons meant I had to share his company and I wasn't ready for that. I liked having him all to myself. It felt as though going back amongst the other dragons would change everything although I couldn't quite put my finger on why.

Unfortunately, my stomach didn't have quite the same thoughts and betrayed me by gurgling loudly.

Ash jumped to his feet, holding his hand out to me. I'd held his hand before but after spending the day with him, it suddenly felt different. Before, he'd been either guiding me somewhere or offering support. This time it felt like something more. I took his hand and let him pull me to my feet, telling myself that he was only helping me up. It would have worked if he'd have let go once I was upright but he didn't. How was it possible for all my nerve endings to congregate in just one place? I had never been so aware of the palm of my hand before. His was warm and his touch made me feel safe but nervous. It was only as we walked back through the village that I realized he'd not given me the tour we'd set out to do in the first place.

In the distance, roaring flames lighted the cliff fronts in a warm orange glow. It caused me to pause.

"That's Aluss cooking the food," Ash said, gripping my hand tighter at my hesitation and pulling me forward.

The same group of dragons I'd seen this morning was sitting around the campfire. Even from a distance, I could sense an easy familiarity between them. It made me feel like even more of an outsider. Nerves took over as I recalled the way some of them had spoken to me this morning. I slowed my pace as we got close.

"I can't do this. I'm not really hungry."

Ash stopped and turned to me. "They're good people, really. Old prejudices die hard but that's why you need to stay strong."

"Their hatred towards me is understandable."

"They've been less than welcoming but they don't hate you. They just need to get used to you. I won't let them hurt you. I'll be there with you the whole time, right by your side."

My nerves dissipated slightly but I was still scared when we joined the circle. The chatting stopped and everything became silent as they all turned their eyes toward me.

Lisa threw me a look of pure loathing as I took a seat on one of the rocks, doing nothing to allay my fears. I gripped Ash's hand harder as he sat next to me.

Edeline walked toward me carrying a plate heaped with food. Whatever it was smelled delicious. Flame-cooked meat had never looked more appealing. There was also bread and salad on the plate she handed to me.

She addressed me while everyone watched. "I trust you had a good day?"

"We did. Thank you," I replied nervously. I felt like I was center stage with all eyes upon me, or like prey waiting to be devoured in the midst of hungry carnivores. Either way, it was disconcerting to have everyone looking at me, waiting for me to say or do something.

"I have an apology to make. We all do," began Edeline, loud enough for the whole group to hear. "Ash is very important to us and it has long been a dream of his to unite the dragon folk with the slayers so we could all come to understand one another and live in some kind of harmony. I must confess to thinking it a harmless daydream on his part and dismissed it as such. Yesterday, his dream became a plan when he brought you to us, and I for one felt uneasy about what it actually meant. We've all lived under the threat of your people for so long that they have become almost mythical. We've all suffered losses as a direct result of what your villagers have done and it has made us both angry and scared. However, we as a group have come to realize that if we treat you the way that we ourselves have been treated, then nothing can possibly change.

"Ash made it very clear that you had the chance to kill him and you made the decision not to. I know of your custom of having the first kill on your eighteenth birthday and I understand how important it is to your people. It is a rite of passage. It must have taken great strength of character and compassion to choose to let Ash live, therefore we must offer the same compassion to you. We've all had a talk and we would officially like to welcome you to our land. You are a guest of Ash's and that makes you a guest of all of us."

I peeked around to see Ash beaming next to me. Edeline's speech had left me more than a little overwhelmed. I carefully placed the plate to my side and stood to give her a hug. Somewhere, someone in the circle began to clap and then one by one, everyone else joined in, first by clapping, then by stamping their feet in a cacophony of noise sounding like the center of a thunderstorm. When I let Edeline go and the noise had subsided, Aluss came up to me.

"I'm sorry about the way I treated you," he huffed. "I was wrong."

I gave him a shy smile and then, without thinking, gave him a quick peck on the cheek to which he grinned stupidly back at me. It was only when I sat back in my place that I noticed Lisa staring at me with such hatred that goosebumps sprouted on my arms and a shiver ran down my spine.

"See, I told you everything would be fine," whispered Ash, making me turn my eyes away from Lisa. I wasn't so sure. Okay, on the surface I had been accepted, but I still had Spear to worry about and the way Lisa looked at me told me that not everyone was so easy to forgive or to give others a chance.

The sound of music suddenly cut through the air and I looked up to find that some of the dragon people had started to play a lively jig by the side of the fire. Their instruments were completely alien to me—sets of wooden pipes, drums, and stringed instruments I had never seen before—but the music they played was joyous and fun and I couldn't help but tap my foot as I ate my dinner. Now that the awkwardness was over, the dinner had almost turned into a party. The elder dragons were drinking something that looked suspiciously like mead and the younger ones danced around to the music.

"Is this a special occasion?" I whispered to Ash who had already finished his food and was now clapping along to the beat.

"Just dinner. It's like this every night. Don't you have meals like this?" he asked, his eyes focused on the band.

The only times we ate like this was when we slayed a dragon but I could hardly tell him that. As I looked around at the group of people, it struck me how at ease they were together. Laughing, joking, eating and dancing as one family. The sense of easy cohesion and community between them made it very easy for me to have a sense of belonging. It felt wonderful but I knew that I didn't belong. These people were my sworn enemy, ingrained in me since birth, and thoughts of belonging to them were dangerous. And yet, when Lucy came to me and held out her hand for me to dance with her, I couldn't help but laugh and follow her onto the makeshift dance area that was really no more than a circle of well-worn dirt.

She giggled as I spun her around and around, under my arm and then both of us together. She loved every minute of it and if I was honest with myself, so did I.

"Can I have this dance?"

I stopped spinning Lucy to see Ash waiting patiently by my side. Lucy grinned and backed off to go sit with her mother. Dancing with Lucy had been effortless and a whole lot of fun. Why was it that the thought of dancing with Ash made my stomach turn to mush and my knees turn to jelly? He took my hand and spun me around in much the same way I had with Lucy except this time it was slower.

At some point, the music had changed from a festive jig to a slow dance. With his free hand, Ash grabbed my waist and pulled me close, leaving me no choice but to drape my free arm over his shoulder. The closeness between us was electrifying and terrifying at the same. I'd danced at slayer parties many times but never like this. I could barely breathe with excitement. The close-ness of his body against mine scared me but made me feel both warm and safe, like being in the center of a hurricane of new emotions.

"Tomorrow is my day to hunt. I want you to come with me."

I was glad that my head was resting on his shoulder so he couldn't see the expression on my face. I rearranged my features so I didn't look so shocked, then pulled back to look him in the eye.

"I can't fly!"

He just grinned lazily back at me. "No, but I can." He gave me a wink and pulled me back to him. I wasn't sure if the thumping in my chest was from nerves about tomorrow or the thrill of the now.

10

I barely slept a wink that night. Every time I closed my eyes I could feel myself soaring through the sky. As I finally drifted off to sleep, I woke with a jolt, free-falling through the sky only to find myself safe and warm in the bed.

The morning dawned in much the same way as the previous one, with all the dragons eating breakfast together around the huge campfire and the wonderful smell of food cooking. I gave Edeline a warm grin as I sat in the circle with the dragons. Lucy immediately came over to me and gave me a hug, and even the others smiled at me and said hello. As I looked around at the group of thirty or so people, it struck me once again just how close they all were. Every meal was like a party—festive, friendly and full of fun although the band was no longer there. I looked around for Ash and found him at the other side of the fire talking to two young men. He turned and saw me so I waved, thinking he'd wave back. Instead, he brought the two men over to meet me.

"Julianna, this is Stone and Ally. They're my hunting partners and the ones we'll be with today."

I looked up at the pair of them. Both were at least a head taller than Ash and you could tell right away that they were brothers, more than likely twins as they were so similar with chiseled jawlines and easy-going smiles. Curiously, one had hair so dark it was almost black and caramel-colored skin with eyes like chocolate. His brother was pale, with white-blond hair and eyes the color of the sky. It was as if they were negatives of each other

"Hello," I said shyly, holding out my hand to shake theirs. They both took my hand and kissed it in turn, causing me to blush and Ash to roll his eyes.

"They both think they are God's gift to women but don't be fooled by their charms. They're really a couple of idiots." Ash grinned as he said this and I could tell that he was ribbing them.

"At least we aren't ugly, right, Ally?" retorted Stone, playfully punching Ash on the arm.

"Yeah," replied Ally, joining in the humor. "I don't know what you see in him personally. I've seen prettier gorillas."

They sat on either side of me, dark-haired Stone to my right and Ally to my left. I was blushing so hard at both their words and their presence that I could probably have rivaled their dragon fire with the heat in my cheeks.

Thoughts of flying through the air with these three, hunting for gazelle or some other food, had my nerves in tatters.

"I don't know how good I'll be at hunting with you

guys," I said, bringing the conversation round to the day ahead, hoping the topic would stop my cheeks from burning.

"Don't worry," said Ash, standing in front of me with a plate of meat and bread that Lucy had just passed him. "We're not going to send you out to hunt before we train you. That's why I've roped in the moron twins here in to help.

"Oy!" said Ally, throwing a chunk of bread at Ash, which he ducked expertly. The bread fell into the fire to become toast.

"Nice try!" said Ash, doing a comical jig on the spot. "Let's hope you throw better than that in training!" Just then, another chunk of bread soared through the air, hitting him in the center of his forehead.

"Bullseye!" Stone and Ally high-fived, causing me to giggle. Today was going to be much more fun than I had anticipated and the fears I'd harbored were beginning to melt away.

Once breakfast was over, I was taken to another stone circle I'd not seen before. This one was much larger than the one with the campfire and had a white wooden wall at one side about fifteen feet long and six feet high. The circle looked a little like the training ground by my house although blackened stones and ash showed that they also practiced here in their dragon forms.

"We're going to start with hand-to-hand combat," said Ash, showing me a flat rock to sit on. "I'll let Ally and Stone go first just so you can see how we train."

"Yeah, and the fact that you are way too much of a

chicken to go up against either of us," said Stone with a grin.

"Just fight, will you?" replied Ash, rolling his eyes once again.

Watching the two fight was almost like being at a dance. The way they moved together was almost magical; it was obvious that they had been fighting like this since they were young. It was almost brutal in nature and yet, despite the magnificently wild and fierce way that they moved, neither really wanted to hurt the other.

"Show offs," muttered Ash beside me as Stone brought Ally toppling to the ground, straddling him to stop him from getting back up. As Stone's hands flew into the air to mark himself a winner, I couldn't help but clap, much to Ash's annoyance.

"I win. Do I get to fight the fair lady now?" asked Stone, pulling himself off of his brother and dusting himself down.

"I'll fight with Julianna. You guys can watch," said Ash irritably. I couldn't help but smile. I'd never had anyone be jealous over me before, but I could sense it in Ash now and it made me feel warm inside. Any fears of fighting were long gone as we took our positions in the center of the circle while Stone and Ally sat where we had on the edge. Instead, butterflies filled my stomach for a completely different reason. I'd watched how Stone and Ally had fought, the beautiful yet savage way in which their bodies had moved together, and now here I was about to do the same with Ash.

"Don't worry. I'm not going to hurt you."

He must have seen the trepidation in my face that

had nothing to do with getting hurt. One of the brothers whistled to start the fight. I had been practicing for so long with a sword in my hand that I had no idea what to do without it. With no clue how to bring him down, I charged at him with none of the finesse I'd seen in Stone and Ally's fighting. He ducked to the side, catching me on my arm as he did. With a maneuver so quick I barely saw it, he had me on my back in the charred dirt.

"Round one to Ash," I heard someone say as Ash grabbed my hand and pulled me back up.

"Don't just run at me. I'm bigger than you. Use that to your advantage," whispered Ash as we faced each other again. That was all right for him to say but my heart was beating so loudly in my chest at the thought of being so close to him that I could barely concentrate. I also couldn't see how being smaller would put me at any kind of advantage in combat.

"Before you run at me, find my weakness."

I looked into his eyes, barely a foot away from me, and a strange intensity glowed back at me. Electricity flowed between us and I could hear him breathing as heavily as I was even though our first round had lasted mere moments. Then, without thinking I bridged the gap between us and kissed him. It was the quickest of pecks on the lips but it did the trick. I seized the moment of surprise, hooked my leg around his, and pushed his chest. He fell backward, landing flat on the ground to the brothers' hollering and clapping.

I couldn't help but grin at the look of shock on his face as he stared up at me from the dusty ground.

"You said to find your weakness," I said coyly,

holding my hand out to him to help him up as he had done with me.

The smile that cracked his face was so wide that it finally sent the shivers down my spine and goosebumps up my arm which had been threatening for the last two minutes.

It was only when Stone and Ally wolf-whistled that I realized exactly what I had done and my cheeks began to burn.

"I think it's about time we showed you how we train as dragons," said Ash, still grinning. I couldn't help but match his grin even though I felt like a loon for doing so.

"Come on guys." He motioned with his hand and Stone and Ally stood. They all walked over to the wooden wall I'd seen before and disappeared behind it. I could see the foreheads of Stone and Ally and just the top of Ash's hair over the top. I was just about to follow to see what they were doing when someone flung a pair of trousers over the top, quickly followed by a sweater.

It dawned on me that this was the place they undressed to change into dragons, so I instead returned to the flat rock that Stone and Ally had just vacated.

Seconds later there was a huge roar and a blast of flame as one dragon took off into the sky. Judging by the black leathery skin, it could only be Stone. He was outstanding, long and graceful in the sky with a shimmer of green on his scales when the sun hit them at just the right angle.

A pure white dragon followed and then finally the scarlet dragon I recognized as Ash. They flew in perfect formation, swooping and twirling in the sky, putting on an aerial show just for me, before flying back down to the circle and landing with effortless grace. I couldn't believe I'd spent the whole night worrying about flying. Just watching them in the sky made me long to be up there with them. The sense of freedom they must feel would be breath-taking.

This time, they didn't fight in twos, but in a kind of free for all, each man—or dragon—for himself. Ash reared up, extending his claws and savagely laying into Stone who was snarling back at him, giving as much as he got. If I didn't know that they were friends and this was only training, I'd have been terrified at the beautiful savagery of it. Ally rose a couple of feet from the ground and rained fire down around them, causing Stone and Ash to break apart and fly after him.

This time, there was no stunning formation flying; they were fighting. Fire filled the sky, bathing it in flashes of warm red and orange. Even though they were quite a way above me, I could still feel the heat of their breath as they blew fire at each other. One of the brothers caught Ash square on in a burst of flame. Fear coursed through me as I stood up, peering into the fiery sky. I had to use my hand to shield my eyes but I saw him fly through the fire as if it wasn't there. I couldn't keep my eyes from him and how elegantly he flew, shooting between the two brothers as they both directed another blast of fire at him, accidentally getting each other instead. My heart was in my mouth the whole time that they were in the air, fearing for their safety, and I was glad when they all landed unscathed.

As they disappeared around the other side of the wall to dress, I realized that they were just like me, like us on the other side of the mountain. They ate together, lived together and trained together in perfect harmony. This new world was so similar to my old one and yet the two were like oil and water and could never mix. The time when I would have to choose between the two was drawing closer and with each passing moment, it was getting more and more difficult to know which decision I was going to make. If Ash had his way, I wouldn't have to decide at all. Both sides would live in harmony, but it wasn't just up to Ash.

As he appeared, fully clothed and completely burn-free from the side of the wall, I ran to him, determination coursing through me.

"We need to make this work!" I said, causing a look of confusion to appear on Ash's face.

"Make what work?"

"This!" I said breathlessly, indicating first myself, then him. "Us. All of us. I want to help the dragons!"

"You're already doing just that by being here and letting them see you mean no harm."

"We have to tell my family the truth but I don't know how. I don't want to hurt them."

"I know you don't. Neither do I. Come on, let's go home."

I held his hand. Something had changed within me. Maybe it was the kiss or maybe it was watching him and his friends train, but when he said we were going home, I knew that that was what this place was beginning to feel like.

11

Someone yelling woke me early from my slumber. I'd slept like a log compared to the previous night, and the fear-filled nightmares I'd experienced the night before had been replaced by much happier dreams. My heart was filled with wonder and even the commotion outside my window and the noisy awakening could not dampen my spirits.

I dragged myself out of bed as the noise got louder. The night before, I'd asked Edeline if I could borrow some clothes and she'd graciously lent me some of hers. I pulled on a green summer dress which was only slightly too large for me and opened the balcony doors to see what was happening. Looking down to the campfire, I could see many of the dragons I'd already met, some in human form and some in dragon form, plus a few I didn't recognize. They were definitely arguing but from this height, I couldn't hear what they were saying.

I picked Ash out in the crowd. He was talking to one of the dragon men I'd seen around but not spoken to.

When I saw the look on Ash's face, I knew something bad was happening. The man he was with waved his arms animatedly and looked angry. Ash was trying unsuccessfully to placate him, but there was a sadness I'd not seen before on his face. Even at this distance, I could tell that he was upset.

I ran down the stairs calling for Edeline and Lucy, but the only one who answered was Firecracker who bounded up to me with a woof and a wagging tail.

I patted her on the head absentmindedly.

"Not now, girl. Do you know where your mistress is?"

Firecracker responded with another bark.

I patted her once again and left the house to find out what was going on, making sure she was safely shut inside. There were so many people that it was impossible to see what had happened, but I could see the man prodding Ash in the chest angrily by the side of the cliff. No one had noticed me; they were all consumed by whatever it was that had happened, so I took the opportunity to sidle along the edge of the cliff to better hear.

When I was almost upon them, the angry man turned and saw me.

"You!" he roared. His voice was so loud it was enough to make everyone else silent. "This is your fault!" He turned his attention away from Ash and walked toward me, his face set in an angry grimace.

I couldn't help but hold my breath as he approached with angry strides. I had no idea what I had done but whatever it was, I'd made this man extremely angry. I'd spent the whole evening in my bedroom alone so I couldn't for the life of me think what it might be.

"You shouldn't have come here," he shouted. His face was incandescent with rage, and he was pointing his finger at me. I took a step back, hitting the base of the cliff. With the rock wall behind me, I was trapped. The man was one of those that had hugged me just a day ago. What could I possibly have done to evoke such anger in him within the last twelve hours? He prodded me in the same way I'd just watched him do to Ash.

"Leave her alone, Bill. She had nothing to do with it and you know it." Ash came up behind him and grabbed his arm, swinging him away from me. Bill pulled his other arm back as if to strike Ash, but he was too quick. Ash ducked and then spun, kicking Bill down into the dusty ground in much the same way I had done to him yesterday.

"If you touch her again, you'll get worse than that," said Ash, his own anger evident.

Bill turned and spat at the ground. "Just get her away from me and out of my sight."

"What's happening?" I asked fearfully. Everyone was looking at us, some of them with the same anger Bill had displayed, others only looking upset. Lucy had tears in her eyes.

"I'll tell her," said Ash to the others. To me, he simply said, "Follow me."

He took me back to the training ground where I had kissed him just a day ago. It had been the most wonderful day and yet here we were the next morning, and I knew that Ash was going to tell me something I didn't want to hear.

"What is it?" I looked into his pained eyes and held my breath.

"Stone was killed last night."

My hand flew to my mouth in shock as I gasped at the news. I could barely take it in. He'd been so vibrant and full of life.

"What happened?"

"He decided to go out to the other side of the cliff. Julianna, he was killed by one of the men in your village. A slayer murdered him."

I could barely comprehend what he was telling me and yet he had no reason to lie. One of my friends had killed him. One of my family even. I didn't need to ask what had become of his body. It would be taken into the village like all the others. The ones that were killed on special days, the first kills, were always taken to the village green where their body would be displayed whilst the village partied around it. It had never occurred to me to find out what happened to the bodies after that. Nor had I ever asked what had happened to the bodies of the dragons killed on the non-special days. They were probably left to rot somewhere on the outskirts of the village. Stone was dead and I didn't even know where he would be buried. I had never felt so utterly dreadful in my whole life.

I felt eyes bore into me and as I turned, my eyes met Ally's as he stood by the campfire. The others had gone back to crying and arguing and hugging each other, all of them dealing with the news of Stone's death differently, but Ally just stood there. He didn't look angry, just sad and lost, like a man who had misplaced his shadow.

I'd only met him the day before but he looked diminished without his dark-skinned twin next to him.

There was nothing I could do to bring his brother

back to him and nothing I could say that would make this right, but as I looked at him, I tried to convey how sorry I was and how much my heart was breaking for him.

Edeline appeared then, wrapping her arms around him, and his eye contact with me broke.

I turned back to Ash and it was as if the dam inside me cracked. Tears fell onto the parched ground. Everything I had learned within the last few days had not prepared me for this moment. Even though I knew that my people had killed hundreds of dragons over the years, Stone's death finally made it real. Ash's arms circled around me as I cried. My body was wracked with quiet, anguished sobs. There was nothing I could do to make this better. My head filled with memories of easygoing Stone, how cute and how funny he had been. I couldn't believe it was only yesterday we had all sat around this very stone ring and I'd watched him train with Ally and Ash.

"I'm sorry," I murmured almost inaudibly. My face was buried in his chest. His arms tightened around me, making me feel safe. A feeling I had no right to have.

"Don't apologize. You've done nothing wrong."

"But Stone—"

"Stone shouldn't have even been on that side of the mountain. He knew the risks and chose to ignore them. We only go over there when we need to. Most of the time it's only to keep a look out, and even then we try to keep as far away from the slayers as possible. He was a grown man, and the decision that cost him his life was ultimately his."

"You didn't stay far away from me as possible," I said,

remembering just how close he'd flown to me the day I had first walked up the mountain.

"Yeah, but I thought you were cute. I just wanted a better look."

I gave a sad laugh, more for his benefit than mine. He was trying to cheer me up but it felt as though my heart had been replaced with a heavy stone.

"Listen," he said, pulling away from me so he could look into my eyes. I couldn't bear to look at him so instead, I gazed at the ground. He gently placed two fingers under my chin and lifted my face until I had no choice. My face was a mess of tears and snot but I was too upset to care. Ash had no malice in his eyes. Instead, they showed nothing but kindness. If anything, it made me feel worse.

"No one blames you for what happened to Stone."

"Bill does," I reminded him.

"Bill is just upset. He doesn't know what he's saying. He worked with Stone. They were pretty close. He doesn't really blame you."

"Well, he should!" I shouted, feeling wretched. The anger inside me was nothing to do with Ash and everything to do with how I felt about myself. Anger and guilt and grief swirled through me. "It was my people that killed him."

"You're right!" he countered, his voice matching my own. "Your people. Not you. You didn't stab him with your sword. It wasn't your fault."

What was I doing? Why was I shouting at the one person who was on my side? I fell into him once again, needing his warmth and protection, desperate to feel his arms around me. He stroked my hair, calming me.

"This has to stop!" I said. "No more blood can be shed over some ridiculous, ancient feud. We need to put an end to this."

"That's exactly what I've been saying all along," replied Ash. "Between us, we have the power to put an end to this."

He gently pulled back a stray strand of hair and kissed me lightly on the cheek. Yesterday the action would have delighted me, but today I took little pleasure in it. I felt like all the happiness had been sucked out of me, leaving me empty and afraid.

Then, some other emotion came over me. I don't know whether it was because of Ash holding me or something I had inside me all along, but I suddenly felt a strength I had never known I possessed.

With every bone in my body, I vowed to put an end to this. Soon enough I'd have to speak to the other dragons, but for right now, I had Ash.

I pulled away from his arms and instead held his hand. I turned slowly to the grief-stricken villagers. If they hated me for Stone's death, I wouldn't blame them, but sooner rather than later I'd have to answer to them. To the man who lost a workmate. To the brother that lost his twin and to the village that lost a son and friend. I'd have to answer to them all. I gripped Ash's hand tightly and took a step back to the campfire. I knew I had to be strong and with Ash beside me giving me courage, I had everything I needed in order to do what had to be done.

f I was nervous five minutes ago, it was nothing compared to how I felt when I saw Spear standing by the campfire. There were also many more people than I had previously met. They, like Spear, must have come from the houses in the village. With Ash by my side, I tried to hide my fear as I entered the circle of dragons. He'd managed to get them into some semblance of order and now the stone circle was filled with people all looking his way. I took the opportunity to sit toward the back in the hope that no one would see me.

The sound of sobbing still surrounded me but the chaos from ten minutes ago had subsided.

"Right!" said Spear. "I think everyone is here so I shall begin. As you all know, a courageous young man died last night…"

"He was murdered by a slayer, you mean," shouted someone although I couldn't tell who. I pushed myself farther back on the rock in an attempt to hide.

A couple of people jeered at his words.

"He was one of our very best," continued Spear, ignoring the man who had heckled him. "He will be sorely missed by all of us, but especially by Eleanor, Tom, and Ally."

An older couple stood next to Ally, presumably the twins' parents. The woman was crying into her husband's shoulder. My heart went out to them.

"Do you want to say a few words about Stone?" asked Spear to the couple. The old man set his mouth into a grim line as he shook his head and held onto his inconsolable wife. Ally pushed into the circle, taking Spear's place.

"I want to talk about my brother. He was my twin and my best friend." His voice cracked with the pain of speaking. "Everyone thinks that twins have this unique connection and it's true. It does exist. When Stone scraped his knee, I felt the pain in my own knee. When I fell out of a tree at the age of eleven and broke my arm, he went home complaining of a sore arm way before he knew I'd hurt myself. We knew what the other was thinking. He was half of me."

He broke down into loud sobs but didn't give up speaking. I could see that he needed us all to understand just how special Stone was, but I had a feeling everyone already knew.

"I can still feel him! How can that be if he's dead? How could I still feel him so strongly within me?"

A young woman I didn't know came up to him and threw her arms around his neck and gave him a tight squeeze.

"I'm sorry, Ally. I was out there with him. I saw them kill him. He's definitely dead."

"But I can feel him," he pleaded to the young girl before descending into uncontrollable crying. She led him away from the circle so that Spear could take his place again.

He began to talk about how connected they all were to this land and how they could never leave, but something about what Ally had said resonated within me. Of course, he could have been in denial about his brother's death and the weird twin connection thing could mean nothing, but what if he was right? What if Stone was out there somewhere? The woman had said that she had seen him die, but if his soul was trapped within the slayer's sword, then maybe that was why Ally was so sure he could still feel his existence. Because he wasn't dead at all. His soul was just not inhabiting his body.

Once the thought entered my mind, I couldn't shake it. Was Ally still alive out there somewhere? I thought of my own sword that I'd left in the bedroom in the cliff house and how it was supposed to be filled with the soul of a dragon by now. My father's sword was said to be filled with the souls of a hundred dragons. Before I'd come here, it had been nothing more than an abstract thought that didn't really mean anything. Sure, I knew the souls strengthened the swords, but I'd thought that dragons' souls were worth very little, that they didn't mean anything. The thought of a hundred or more of them trapped within my father's sword was enough to bring bile up my throat. It was worse than death, the thought of being trapped forever within a metal object.

I looked across to Ash who was listening intently to Spear speak. He was still talking about the connection they felt to the land and to each other, and how they could never leave, despite the danger on the other side of the cliffs. It became clear to me just why they felt so connected. The souls of their ancestors, their fathers and their brothers, were still here, albeit trapped at the other side of the cliff and they didn't even know it. The way Spear was talking about it being a spiritual connection was right. I had to tell someone! If it would bring Stone back, I'd stand in front of the whole crowd and speak myself.

I opened my mouth to tell Ash when I suddenly realized what telling them would mean. It wasn't as simple as getting the dragon souls back. They'd have to go to my village and take them back. By force.

Most of the villagers were trained dragon slayers. They'd fight to the death before even knowing who the dragons really were. Causalities would be high on both sides and then maybe it would be Jasper or my father that would get killed. Maybe it would be Ash.

"Come on," I heard Ash say, breaking me away from my thoughts. The people were beginning to disperse. It seemed the meeting was over. "We need to get you out of here."

I followed him silently as we ran behind the people into the cave house and shut the door. Firecracker came bounding over, her tail wagging enthusiastically.

"At least someone likes me," I said, giving her hair a friendly tousle.

"I like you," said Ash, coming toward me. He gazed at me with such concern in his eyes but something else too. It wasn't happiness. It was warmth and safety and friendship and something else I couldn't quite decipher. I couldn't look at him without the tears welling up. I couldn't help it. My eyes stung and I knew that if I held his gaze just one moment longer I was going to cry. He pulled me into a hug and the dam finally burst. I sobbed onto his shoulder, wetting his outfit. The hug could have lasted two minutes or two hours, I couldn't tell, but it was interrupted when Edeline and Lucy walked through the door.

"We'd be better stay indoors today," remarked Edeline. "I think a storm might be brewing. We'll eat away from the others in here."

I glanced out the window. There wasn't a cloud in the sky. The storm she was talking about had nothing to do with the weather.

The day passed slowly. I hung out with Ash up in my bedroom, and we sunbathed a little on the terrace. He tried to engage me in conversation but I was so distracted with thoughts of the slayers' swords that I wasn't much of a conversationalist. We ate dinner there until great black clouds blew in. Maybe Edeline was right after all. When the first big, fat, heavy drops of rain began to fall from the sky, we moved indoors.

"Are you okay?" he asked as he closed the door to the outside. "You've been quiet all day."

"I'm sorry. Today has been hard. I just need some space." His face fell as I said the words but it was true. I knew he was hurting too, and I had the feeling that he'd been glued to my side all day because he needed company, but my company wasn't worth much at the moment. He'd been wonderful to me but the truth was I felt guilty about getting him into this. He shouldn't be inside with me; he should be outside with his friends so they could all share their grief. "Goodnight then," he said, kissing my cheek sadly.

I watched him go, leaving me alone with only my own misery for company. It was early but I flopped onto the bed, listening to the hammering of the rain against the window. Usually, I loved the sound.

I tried sleeping but the thought of those dragons locked within the swords was haunting me. Guilt had me lying awake for so long that it was completely dark before I eventually got to sleep. I couldn't have been asleep long before a huge roll of thunder rattled the windows. I sat up in bed, fearful of the noise, before I realized what it was that had woken me.

Someone needed to find out if we could get the souls back from the swords. I jumped out of bed and put on the warmest clothes I could find. I also attached my armor and sword, not because I thought I would have to fight anyone, but because I wasn't sure if I'd make it back.

I crept quietly through the house, only disturbing Firecracker who was her usual exuberant self. Thankfully, she didn't bark as I let myself out into the night. The rain was pounding down, making it difficult to see, but I only had to follow the cliff to get to where I'd seen the stairs cut out of it earlier. I had no idea if they would lead me up over them, but I had to try. I couldn't bring myself to look at the circle where we had trained only a day or so ago. It only reminded me of Stone.

By the time I came upon the steps, my clothes were soaked and I was freezing cold. It was too late to turn back though. Someone had to save those dragons and that someone had to be me. I placed my foot on the first step and looked up. The steps seemed to go on forever. It was going to be a long and arduous journey but in my heart, I knew it was one I had to make. I whispered a goodbye to Ash and started the journey up the cliff face.

13

The rain lashed down as I fought my way up the mountainside. The going was tough as each step was slippery and the wind blew a gale in my face. I clung to the rocks, drenched to the bone and fearful for my life. The steps were narrow and, without a rail of any kind, it would be easy to take a misstep and fall to my death. I could barely see a thing with the rain stinging my eyes and the darkness of the clouds. There would be no moonlight or starlight to help me out tonight. Using my sense of touch, I climbed the dangerous path, feeling my way along the wet roughness of the rocky cliff face. My eyes were stinging so much that I couldn't tell if it was from the rain or tears. Nothing rivaled the pain in my chest though. Not my stinging eyes or my body that screamed with the blistering cold of the storm. My armor weighed heavy as I trudged upward, each step feeling like a mountain all on its own.

I tried to think of something, anything, to keep my

mind from the agony in my hands and feet as the cold bit down hard. I thought of Ash, asleep in his bed, and the pain became unbearably worse because now it was inside my heart as well. The thought that he would wake up the next day and I'd be gone filled me with such guilt, but what choice did I have? It was the only way to get Stone and the others back. I could almost see the moment when he would wake up and realize I'd gone home. He'd think I was betraying him, wouldn't he? And yet I felt that he knew me. When he looked into my eyes, it felt like he saw into my very soul. He had to know that I wouldn't leave if it wasn't important.

I couldn't get the image of him out of my mind all the way up the cliff face, and when I reached a platform with a cave, I'd have done anything to have him by my side. The cave mouth was a wide, gaping chasm and without any light flooding it from outside, I couldn't see more than a foot or two into it. I should have turned back but when I saw how far I'd come, the thought left me. It was the image of Stone and the reason I was doing this in the first place that spurred me on. I had made my way up the cliff face in almost complete blackness just by feeling the wall. If I could make it this far, I could keep going.

My hands waved in front of me as I felt my way into the inky blackness. Just a couple of feet in, I stumbled on something and tumbled to the ground, banging my knees and making my armor clatter as it hit the hard floor of the cave. I reached out, hoping to find something that would help pull me up into an upright position, but when I scrabbled around I felt something much better—a long stick with a cloth around the end.

If there was a torch here, there must be some way to light it.

I was proficient in making fires—it was all part of the slayer training—but I needed some flint to make a spark. I'd also not tried setting fire to cloth, always using dry twigs and paper, but I could smell the bitter odor of some kind of fire accelerant emanating from the cloth so I knew it would light pretty quickly. I felt around the floor near where I'd found the torch until my hand came upon a smooth flint stone. Luckily, the floor inside the cave was dry so I ripped the flint along the floor just near the head of the torch. Sparks flew, lighting up the cave for a fraction of a second before it was once again plunged into darkness. I tried it again, this time getting as close to the torch as possible.

A spark hit the torch, igniting the accelerant and bathing the cave in a warm orange glow. Relief flooded through me that I could finally see. This cave, like the other one, went back much further than just a few feet. Even with the light of the torch, I couldn't see the back. I walked forward, keeping my eyes on the ground for any more loose stones. If I were to fall and injure myself, I might end up stuck up here forever.

I followed the tunnel deep into the cave. My spirits were beginning to rise, knowing that it wouldn't take too long to get through the mountain as long as I kept in a straight line. This, however, was where my luck ran out. I came to a T-junction with my only options being left or right, neither of which were the direction I wanted to go. I waved the torch down each corridor, but both were equally uninteresting and neither looked like a way out. I took the path on the right just because it bent slightly to the left. After another ten minutes of walking, the path forked again. I scoured the floor and walls, looking for some kind of sign that someone might have left, but found nothing.

"What did you think you'd find? A glowing sign reading this way out?" I asked myself. The sound echoed hauntingly around the walls, doing nothing to calm my frayed nerves.

I'd heard about a trick to use when stuck in a maze, for this was a maze and if I ventured deeper, I'd surely lose my way. It was something about picking a direction, left or right, and sticking to it until I found my way out, but that didn't seem right. If I took another right turn, I'd end up heading back towards the cliff face and that was the complete opposite of where I needed to be. I took the left-hand tunnel, hoping for the best, even though I had lost my sense of direction.

I had never felt so alone in my life as I did in that tunnel, trapped between two different worlds. The darkness scared me more than I liked to admit. Even though the torch light covered everything within a few feet, I saw nothing at all beyond its reach. The lullaby my mother sang to me on the morning of my eighteenth birthday popped into my head. It kept my heart warm, thinking of it as I walked through the network of paths, my decisions based on intuition instead of reasoning. I must have been walking at least half an hour before deciding I was hopelessly and terrifyingly lost.

Suddenly, there was a huge whoosh and the torch went out, plunging me into darkness. Then the wind came again followed by an intense heat as flames licked the ceiling of the cave. I screamed, wondering what could cause such a strange phenomenon until a large dragon with a pair jeans in one claw came around the corner. I only caught a glimpse before the fire stopped, but it was enough. I'd recognize those red scales anywhere. It was Ash. He'd come to rescue me.

I held the torch aloft, waiting for him to breathe fire again. When he did, I held out the torch and watched it ignite before turning away from him to give him the chance to turn back.

"Why are you leaving?" he asked a few moments later. I turned to find him fastening the top button of his jeans. He wasn't angry. It was fear in his eyes. Putting the torch down carefully, I ran to him and threw my arms around his neck. He felt so warm and yet the hug was awkward thanks to all the armor. I couldn't help but begin to sob again as he held onto me, comforting me, making me feel dreadful because it should have been me comforting him.

"I'm sorry," I finally said as I pulled back. "I have to go home."

"Without telling me?" I could see the pain in his eyes matching my own.

"I couldn't tell you because I didn't want to hurt you or get your hopes up, but I think there might be a way to get Stone back. That's why I left."

"He's dead, Julianna. You heard it yourself. One of your people killed him."

I blanched at his words but I had to make him believe me.

"We don't kill just because of centuries of hatred. Each kill we make is said to take the soul of a dragon that imbues our swords with power. It's their soul that the sword takes, not their life. I've not once seen where the dragon's bodies are taken after death. What if they are all lying somewhere in an eternal slumber? Alive and yet empty at the same time?"

He regarded me for a second as I willed him to believe me.

"You don't kill the dragons?"

"I don't know, but what if I'm right? I have to try to find out. I was planning to go to my village and see if I could somehow get the souls out of the swords."

"I just don't understand why you didn't tell me all of this before. I'd have come with you. I want to protect you."

"I know." His words made me feel guilty and yet elated at the same time. He had protected me throughout all of this and yet hearing him say it filled my heart. "I didn't want to put you in danger. I'm scared that the other dragons will turn against you because of me."

He came closer and held me tightly once again. This time, I managed to keep the tears at bay.

"I'm a big boy, Julianna. I know how to handle myself. I don't want you to worry about me, but there is something you can do for me."

"What is it?" I asked, pulling back slightly so I could see him.

"I want you to tell me everything from now on. We're in this together and the only way we can do this is if we are honest with each other."

"I'll never lie to you again. I promise."

"Good." He took hold of my hand. "Now let's go to your village and find these swords."

He held my hand, expertly guiding me through the maze until we were at the other side. In the distance, the lights of my village seemed small and insignificant, especially from this great height.

Minutes later I was soaring through the rain on Ash's red-scaled back. I was finally going home.

<h1 style="text-align:center">14</h1>

Water stung my eyes as we flew through the angry clouds, blinding me for the whole journey. I trusted Ash to know what he was doing and only hoped that his dragon vision was better than my human eyesight as we flew down the mountains.

The rain came down in hundreds and thousands of big, fat drops that not only drenched me, but Ash's clothes that were squeezed in my hands. Only I would be crazy enough to pick the wettest night of the summer to sneak out.

We landed just outside of the village with a great thump. Lightning crackled across the sky, illuminating the small houses for the briefest of moments. The darkness of the night and the clouds kept us in the shadows and made me feel grateful for the storm, even though I was soaked through and freezing cold. I threw Ash his clothes and walked to the fence that marked the border between the village and the mountains. All the houses were dark. However, in the distance, I could make out the road that would take us to my house. I turned and gazed up at the mountain we had flown down from, holding my hand above my eyes to shield them from the pelting rain that still came down in torrents. The mountain range was shrouded in clouds to the tree line, almost like the towering peaks weren't there at all.

"What now?" asked Ash, making me jump. He'd changed and dressed already, the sound of the rain hitting the pathway beneath us covering the sound of him changing.

"I need to go home."

"Do you think that's a good idea?" he asked. Concern filled his voice and I understood why. He thought that I wanted to see my parents. In a way, he was right. I missed them terribly, maybe even Jasper too, but that wasn't the only reason.

"It's the only place I know where some of the swords are kept. My brother, Jasper, has one, and my father too. His is said to be one of the most powerful swords in the village."

"Does that mean he's taken the most dragon souls?"

I nodded, unable to speak. I'd spent my whole life looking up to my father, wanting to follow in his footsteps. I could barely believe that I was now planning to break into my own house and steal his sword. What would he think of me if we got caught? I wasn't even sure what I thought of him anymore. "I'm sorry."

He kissed the top of my forehead. "You have nothing to be sorry about."

I heard his words, but, not for the first time, I wasn't sure if they were true.

The road to our house was deserted and yet we kept to the trees, partly for the cover they offered from the rain, but mainly because if anyone were to turn their lights on, we could dash into their cover.

The rain had turned the usually dusty track into a muddy bog. Ash held my hand as we trekked through it, giving me the strength to do what I had to do and reminding me how important it was that we did this.

"Do you think you'll know?" I whispered, as we approached my house.

"Know what?"

"Will you know whose soul is in each sword when we get close to one? Will you be able to feel it?"

"I don't know. I don't feel anything other than freezing at the moment. Are we nearly there?"

"This is it. This is where I live."

The house looked almost deserted with the lack of light but I knew it was because it was late enough for them all to be asleep.

There was no way to hide as we snuck across the training ground in front. It was a wide-open space with the house on the opposite side. We could only hope that the darkness and the lateness of the hour would be enough to get us to the house without being seen.

The back door was locked but my mother always kept a spare key under a potted plant near the door in case of emergencies. I picked the pot up and scrabbled around in the muddy earth beneath it.

"It's not there!" I whispered.

"What isn't?" asked Ash, falling to his knees to help me look.

"The spare key. My mother always has one under

this pot and it's gone. Can you see it?"

"No. There's nothing there but mud."

"Why wouldn't it be here?" I asked, wiping my muddy hands on my tunic.

"You've been gone for a few days now. Maybe they think we'll come for them next."

"That's ridiculous," I replied.

"They lost a daughter. They're scared. People do strange things when they're scared. Is there another way in?"

The thought of my father being scared of anything was preposterous. He was the bravest man I had ever known. And yet...he never lost a daughter before.

"I think there might be a crowbar in the shed," I replied, trying not to feel overcome with emotion. We had a plan and we needed to stick to it.

I left Ash by the back door and ran to the shed. We never locked it as there were only a few tools that weren't worth a lot, but as Ash had said, things had changed. I closed my eyes and said a silent prayer before pulling on the door handle. It opened immediately; however, in the darkness, I couldn't see the crowbar. We kept all kinds of junk in here as well as tools—too-small bikes from our childhoods, bits of broken furniture that my father hadn't gotten around to fixing, and the miscellany that families accumulate over time. I could spend all day going through it all and not find the crowbar, especially in the dark.

I ran back to Ash and told him the problem.

"Use your sword," he suggested. "Slot it in the crack between the door and the frame and jimmy the door open."

I pulled my sword from its sheath and did as he instructed. After a few pushes the wooden door splintered with a crack and opened.

Thankfully, at the same moment, a roll of thunder crashed, hiding most of the noise.

"Are you okay?" whispered Ash.

"I just feel weird having to sneak into my own house," I replied. I looked around the kitchen, remembering the last time I'd been in here. The morning of my eighteenth birthday, we'd had a huge breakfast to get us ready for my first day of slayer training.

I thought about stealing a sword and it occurred to me that perhaps my father's wouldn't be the best one to go for after all. "I think we'll go for Jasper's sword."

"I thought your father's sword held the most dragon souls. Surely it makes sense to go for his so we can release more of my people."

"We need to check if my theory is correct first. We can do that with either of the swords, but Jasper's will be easier to get. He keeps it propped up against the wall in his room. My father's is in a locked cabinet in my parent's bedroom. We'll never be able to get it without waking either of my parents up."

He was eager to know if I was right about the whole thing, and excited to free his friends, family and ancestors, but if we got caught, my father would make sure that neither of us would have the opportunity to be near a sword again.

I held my forefinger to my lips to indicate we should be quiet. The noise of the rain was much less intense inside although I could still hear it tapping on the windows. Ash stayed behind me the whole way up the stairs until we reached the landing. How easy it would be to go through my own door and fall into a nice warm bed and forget the last week had ever happened. But it had happened and as long as I lived, I didn't think I'd ever forget it.

My father's snoring rattled the windows from the inside almost as much as the rain did. I pulled down the handle on the door to Jasper's room and pushed silently. The room was almost pitch black, making everything difficult to see, but I could hear his much quieter snoring coming from the general direction of his bed.

I tiptoed in and gazed around the room, trying to make out the shape of the sword in the shadows, but it was too dark. I couldn't see much at all.

"I've got it," a voice whispered quietly into my ear. Ash had found the sword straight away. How had he done it? Had he sensed his ancestors nearby or had it merely been that his eyesight was a lot better than mine in the dark?

He passed me the sword which I had to hold in my hand as my own sword was filling up my sheath.

"Let's go!" I turned to follow him out the door, but in my haste to leave, I knocked over something that made a loud crash on the floor by my feet.

Suddenly, light flooded the room, making me blink in surprise.

I should have run but the shock at finding my brother sitting up in bed, his eyes on the sword in my hands, was enough to have me rooted to the spot.

"Julianna?" he asked, the shock at finding me in his room evident on his face. "What are you doing?"

15

For a split second, he didn't notice Ash, but as his eyes widened, focusing on something behind my right shoulder, I knew he had been seen and that our chance to run had passed.

"What's this?" growled Jasper, jumping out of bed. I stepped back as he bounded towards me.

"Jasper, I can explain—" I began but he cut me off before giving me the chance to say anything else.

"Explain? Are you going to tell me why you're in my bedroom with whoever this is, trying to steal my sword?"

"This is Ash, he's..." How could I explain who Ash was? If I told Jasper he was a dragon, Jasper would go for him without listening to anything else I had to say. Jasper always had a tendency to react first, think later. We needed to get out of here.

I turned to tell Ash to run, but as I did, the sword was pulled from my hand. Jasper had taken the weapon back and now stood ready to fight, his sword arm raised.

"Jasper, don't!" I whispered. "This isn't what you think it is."

"So you aren't stealing my sword? Because that's what this looks like to me."

My hesitation was all he needed. The sword came swiping down at me and I only missed getting hit because Ash pulled me backwards quickly.

"I thought so," said Jasper, getting back into his stance and looking from Ash to me.

"I don't want to fight you, Jasper. You remember what happened last time we fought. I beat you."

"Yes, well this time is different," he growled. I guess he still hadn't forgiven me for beating his behind the last time we fought. He must be angry to strike before I even had a chance to draw my sword.

He was right though. This time was different. This time, we weren't training. This time, it was real. Someone was going to get hurt. I unsheathed my sword and copied his stance, hoping that when he saw how real the situation was, he'd back down, but he didn't. My decision to fight only angered him further. He thrust his sword forward, aiming for my stomach. I jumped back, just avoiding it by millimeters. Had he managed a hit there, it would have killed me. What was he doing?

"Jasper, stop!" It was my last-ditch attempt to not have to fight him. My back was now literally against the wall. If he tried anything else, I would have to defend myself and I wasn't experienced enough to fight him without hurting him.

He answered by swinging his sword again. I had no choice but to bring my own sword down against it to deflect it. He recovered quickly and tried again, but I was ready for him. I thrust my own sword forward, trying to nick his hand so he would drop the sword.

Out of the corner of my eye, I could see Ash, his wide eyes bouncing around the room, searching for a way out of the fight I was now embroiled in. But there was no way out. At least not with me in tow. If I ran now, Jasper would only follow and would be much quicker with his dry pajamas than I would be with my rain-soaked clothes and armor. Of course, the armor offered some protection against injury, but it wasn't the best, and he knew which bits of me were unprotected.

We both skirted the room, occasionally thrusting and deflecting. I was at the advantage with my armor, but only one of us was fighting to hurt and that wasn't me. I had no need to win except to finish the fight and get away, but if I only spent my time deflecting his sword, we'd be here all night. It wasn't helping that my wet clothes felt like ten-ton weights, severely impeding my reaction time and movements.

The only way to end this was to get the sword or to injure him. I didn't know how to do the first without having to resort to the latter.

Something in the air changed and it took me a few moments to realize what it was. The room was suddenly much quieter. Had the rain stopped pounding the windows? No, I could still hear it lashing down. It was then that I realized what it was. My father's snoring had stopped. Either he'd turned over in bed or the commotion had woken him up.

The door to my father's bedroom opened and I heard his footsteps on the landing.

Jasper must have heard it too. He hesitated for a

moment, and that's when I struck. I hit the handle of his sword hard enough to make him drop it. The sword clanged to the floor just as my father came into the room.

"Julianna?"

I stood there with my sword outstretched, pointing the blade at Jasper who had his hands raised as though I were about to hurt him. Ash was on my right, closest to my father. From my father's point of view, it must have looked pretty bad.

"Who are you? What did you do to my daughter?" he bellowed, lunging toward Ash who dodged to the side quickly.

"Daddy!" I screamed as he knocked over a bookcase, sending books scattering all over the floor. "Stop it!"

"What did he do to you?" he asked me, running after Ash again who cut between Jasper and me to escape him.

"Annie, fetch my sword!" my father shouted to my mother who must have still been in their bedroom.

I wanted to hold up my sword to my father to stop him chasing Ash. He was so much bigger than him and I knew if he caught him, Ash wouldn't survive to tell the tale. And yet, I couldn't do that to my own father. What if he got hurt? Besides, if I took my sword away from Jasper for a second, he'd be able to retrieve his own from where it lay on the floor.

My father passed me, nearly tripping over Jasper's sword. When he saw it, he bent down himself to pick it up.

"I've got you now!" shouted my father to Ash, who had run back to the open doorway. He lifted Jasper's sword and charged at the defenseless Ash. Without thinking, I jumped in front of the sword to stop. My intention had been to jump into it right where my armor was, but I missed slightly and the sword sliced a thin red line into the flesh of my forearm. It wasn't a deep cut—it wouldn't even need stitches—but the shock at what he had done was enough to stop my father from trying again.

A scream from just outside the bedroom door had us all silent. I looked to my left to see my mother holding my father's sword. She looked so tiny with it in her hands.

"It's okay; it's just a scratch," I said, trying to appease her although she could just as well have been screaming at the sight of Ash in the doorway. The whole thing was a great big mess, and I didn't know how to deal with it. For now, everyone stood still with shock, paralyzed by the fear of what would happen next. If my father got his own sword, Ash would not get away again. My father was the most skilled swordsperson in the whole village.

One of us had to move soon and I knew it should be me, but I couldn't budge.

"Julianna, you're home!" My mother ran forward to hug me, dropping my father's sword in the process. From then on, it was as if everything happened in slow motion. I moved toward my mother to embrace her while my father and Jasper both ran for the falling sword. Ash grabbed my arm and started to pull me to the door.

While all this was going on, something infinitely stranger was happening. Jasper's sword began to emit smoke from the tip. The hissing made us all turn our heads to look at it. Because of it, my father's sword hit the floor before either my father or Jasper could catch it, my mother and I didn't get to hug each other, and Ash completely forgot about our escape. The lurid purple smoke had us all mesmerized as it blossomed into a thick fog. There was a loud bang from the sword itself, followed by a bright orange flame that lit up the room in a flash before going out completely, but not before setting fire to Jasper's curtains.

Ash grabbed my hand and pulled me down the stairs and out into the wet night. I could barely keep up with him as my feet sunk into the thick mud. My clothes were now so heavy with rain that each footstep caused me pain and the armor rubbed against my bare arms, making them chafe.

Behind us, my father was hot on our heels with Jasper and my mother following behind. I screamed, not because of my family chasing me, but because of what I could see behind them. Flames licked the side of our house in the distance, illuminating the dark sky and turning it a deep orange.

"Ash, do something!" I yelled. Villagers opened their doors and windows to see what the commotion was all about, and yet Ash pulled me onwards.

"I can't do anything. I can only make fire. I can't put it out. The rain will do that if it keeps up like this."

He hopped over the fence and into the woods at the base of the mountains and I followed, knowing it was our only chance of escape. If he couldn't save my house, there was no reason for us to stick around. I turned and looked at my parents and brother one last time before disappearing into the trees. At least I knew they were all safe from harm. Before me, Ash's shape changed. He'd turned so quickly that his clothes ripped to shreds. I jumped onto his back and held onto his neck as he outstretched his wings, flying through a gap in the branches. It was only when we were half way up the mountain that I realized we had failed to steal either sword.

16

Before us, dark clouds covered the sky with a blanket of black, but behind us, fire painted the landscape every shade of orange.

"It's spreading!" I shouted pointlessly as the roar of the rain took my words away.

I could barely see my village anymore but the reach of the fire was unmistakable. The rain wasn't even touching it.

"Turn around!" I screamed out in a panic but Ash either didn't hear me or chose to ignore me.

We flew deeper into the clouds and the orange faded into black until there was nothing at all, and I once again had to close my eyes to block out the rain.

When we landed back on the ledge where I had first met Ash as a human, I immediately jumped from his back and ran to the edge. Freezing needles of rain lashed down, stinging my face, and yet I couldn't bring myself to enter the cave system which I knew would shelter me. Ash grabbed my arm and dragged me backwards until the darkness of the cave swallowed me.

"Why didn't you go back?" I shouted at him. "We shouldn't have left. All we succeeded in doing is burning my house and goodness knows how many others in my village to the ground. We didn't even bring a sword back except for mine and that's no use." I shook as I shouted, whether with fear, anger or cold, I didn't know, though it was probably a combination of all three.

"The rain will put it out. I already told you that. You need to get out of those clothes before you freeze to death. Your lips are practically blue with the cold."

"You didn't see how bad it was. It only looked like a small fire when we took off, but from a distance, it lit up the whole sky."

"Even a small fire would do that. You saw your family escape and your house was far enough away to not pose a danger to the other houses in the village. If it were a dry, hot day, maybe a stray ember might drift over and catch a straw roof, but look at the rain. The fire will be out in no time."

He moved towards me to hug me and for the first time since meeting him, I backed away from his embrace. It might have been irrational, but I was angry at him.

"Why didn't you turn around when I asked you? Even if you didn't think it was anything to worry about, you should have still listened to me."

"Julianna, if you want to go back, I'll take you back now. They're your family, and if you want to be there, we can go down the mountain. I didn't turn around because I didn't hear you."

"You mean it?"

"Of course! I don't know how you'll be able to help them but I wouldn't keep you away from them. Look, the rain is starting to let up. Get out of those clothes before you get pneumonia and I'll dry them with my dragon breath. There's a blanket behind that rock; wrap yourself in it and when the rain stops, I'll take you home."

I ran towards him and gave him the hug I'd dodged earlier. It was only then I noticed he was dressed.

"You have clothes on! They were ripped to shreds back in the village."

"I keep a few spares up here. At least, I used to. I'm going through them so quickly I'll have to bring more up. This is my last set."

I picked up the blanket with the intention of getting undressed behind it, but Ash disappeared into the tunnel to let me change in private. He was right; I was freezing and could barely keep my teeth from chattering.

I put my armor to one side and peeled the sodden clothes from my body, laying them out as straight as I could on some rocks. The blanket was dry but not warm enough to make my goosebumps disappear or keep my teeth from chattering.

A wall of flame shot up the tunnel, quickly followed by Ash. He curled his body in the small cave and blew breathed more fire. The cave turned a bright orange and heated immediately. I could see he was being careful not to burn me or my clothes. The heat flowing through the small cave and the intermittent light made the cave feel homely. I'd spent time with Ash as a dragon before, but in all of those times, I'd been flying on his back. To have him sitting near me like this felt weird. I could talk to him but he wouldn't be able to answer me.

"Thank you for agreeing to take me home," I said to him.

It was hard to tell but I thought he nodded his head slightly. I could barely see him at all when he wasn't breathing fire, and when he did, his whole body reflected the light of the flames as though he was on fire himself.

I pulled the blanket tighter, thinking of my parents. Ash was right about one thing. They and Jasper had gotten out of the house without injury. I loved my house, but at the end of the day, that's all it was—a building full of things. The things that made it a home had all escaped the fire.

"I wonder what started the fire?" I asked out loud, not expecting an answer. I thought back to the scene in the bedroom before the curtains caught fire. There hadn't been a naked flame nearby. "I don't suppose you can produce fire in your human form can you?"

Ash made a growling noise which could have meant anything but he accompanied it by shaking his head. He blew another blast of heat my way, warming me right to my toes.

It had looked like the flame had erupted from Jasper's sword but how could it? It was made of metal and no part of it was flammable. I picked up my own sword and examined it. It was different from Jasper's but not so much to make any difference to its capability to catch fire. I admired the intricate metal work. When Ash blew another blast, I held up my sword in the path of the flame. The heat slightly burnished the metal but set no part of it alight.

I knew nothing about the slayer's swords. Not only could I not see how it could produce or sustain fire, I also couldn't see how it would trap a soul. Why had I not been taught any of this? I'd spent my whole life being taught swordlore and yet I knew nothing at all.

My thoughts went back to Stone and all the other dragons who had lost their souls at the hands of the people in my village. Going home now would serve no purpose other than to alleviate my fears. What would my parents do if I went home anyway? Jasper had been so angry to see me with Ash that he'd attacked me without even thinking to ask why I was home. My father wasn't any better. He'd jumped to the conclusion that Ash had kidnapped me, and like Jasper, he had attacked without pausing to find out who he was. That was the problem with the people in my village. They mindlessly followed hundreds of years of traditions without pausing to question why they were doing what they were doing.

"I'm not going home." I'd made a promise to Ash and I was going to keep it. I moved to sit beside him, snuggling as close as I could to his curled body and resting my arm on his skin. For so many years I'd believed dragon hide to be tough and scaly and cold, but Ash's skin was warm and comfortable. He brought his long neck around so I was completely surrounded. I rested my head on his neck and closed my eyes, listening to the rhythm of the rain on the ledge outside the cave.

Later when I awoke, the sun was beaming down,

warming the cave. I stepped away from Ash, who was still sleeping in his dragon form, and grabbed my new dry clothes. Throwing them on, I stepped outside into the most radiant sunshine. Any evidence of the summer storm that had made me feel so cold the night before had gone, evaporated in the sunny morning. It was almost as if I'd dreamed the whole thing.

I peered down the mountain, trying to see my village, but of course, we were too far away. Now that the adrenaline had stopped pumping through me quite so freely and I'd had a decent amount of sleep, I knew I'd made the right decision to stay. Ash could try and convince the dragons to give the slayers a chance, but unless he had one on his side, his endeavors would be pointless. Despite what my parents and Jasper saw last night, or thought they saw, they knew me well enough to know how much I loved them, and the time would come when I'd be able to get the chance to put things right with them. Until then, there were plenty of families in the village that would take them in and make sure they were all right. Knowing the villagers as I did, they had probably already started rebuilding our house.

A warm pair of arms wrapped themselves around me. "You just say the word and I'll fly you back down there. I'll never stop you from going home."

"I know, and that's exactly the reason I need to stay." I brought my arms up to his and we just stood there like that for a long time, looking out at the incredible view down the mountain, the heat of the sun beating down on our faces.

We followed the same path through the mountain that we had taken the very first day I'd met Ash. This time, I had no problem holding his hand as we walked through the dark tunnel. Had that really been less than a week ago? It felt so strange that I'd gone eighteen years with everything being the same and nothing really changing, and then in just a few days, my whole life had turned upside down; now everything was different.

We came out onto the ledge at the opposite side of the mountain and it became apparent very quickly that something was happening. There were dragons everywhere. Previously, I'd only ever seen two or three in the sky at once, but now it seemed the whole sky was full of them. They looked amazing, so many different shapes and sizes, a kaleidoscope of colors circling around.

"Uh oh!"

"What?" I asked Ash. "What's happening?"

"They're looking for us. They've probably been on the other side of the mountain too. We need to get you home quickly."

He pulled his shirt off without even bothering to run back into the cave to change.

"Wait!" I yelled as he began to undo the buttons on his trousers. "I already told you. I don't want to go home. I want to stay here with you."

"I meant my home!" he said, flinging his trousers off and changing into a dragon before my eyes. I scooped his clothes up and jumped onto his back as dragons swooped towards us. Unlike the leisurely flight I'd first taken down this mountain, this one was fraught with panic. The other dragons weren't attacking us, but as soon as they had caught sight of us, they had formed a formation around us to escort us back down to the ground.

17

Wind whipped my face as we soared past the training grounds toward the center of the village. The thatched roof of the circular Town Hall greeted me. We flew over a village square that had been hidden before.

The square was surrounded by shops made in the same higgledy-piggledy construction as the rest of the buildings in the village. Many had flat roofs with stairs leading to the ground. Some of the dragons descended onto these makeshift landing pads, although most of them, like us, landed in the square itself. To one side of the square was a cafe with tables and chairs arranged outside. On any other day, in any other situation, I'd have liked to sit there and drink a hot mug of coffee while watching the world go by.

The ground was still damp from the previous night's rain and large puddles had formed, leaving less space for the dragons to land. When they did land, they immediately ran to the edge of the square where two fences had been erected. They were the same type of dressing rooms I'd seen at the training ground just the other day.

I hopped off in the middle of the square and Ash flew to one of the fences to join his fellow dragons.

I'd not had time to count just how many dragons had escorted us back, but there were a lot. Many more in their human forms had been in the village square, waiting for us to return. The way they watched me made me extremely nervous. The noise of the bones crunching as the dragons changed still made me feel queasy, but it was the fear of what would happen next that made my stomach churn the most. I was alone and exposed, but there was nothing I could do but wait. I crossed my fingers, hoping that Ash would be the first to change, but it was Spear that made his appearance first. I almost didn't recognize him as he wore a very formal robe and what could only be described as a judge's wig. It was likely meant to make him appear imposing but he just looked ridiculous, which somehow made me feel slightly more at ease. At least, I did until he barked at me to follow him to the Town Hall.

"I'd like to wait for Ash," I said, looking around at the fences to see if he was there. Some of the other dragons had changed and dressed and were now coming toward us, but there was no sign of him.

"He'll know where you are," replied Spear, catching hold of my arm and pulling me roughly toward the Town Hall.

The other dragons followed. Some I recognized but there were quite a few I'd never seen before.

I was taken through the circular building and into

the courtyard. Unlike before when it had been empty, the sandy courtyard was filled with chairs.

"Are we going down to the courtroom?" I asked as Spear dragged me toward the stairs that would lead us down there.

"Not this time. There are too many of us to fit today," he replied brusquely. We came to the small stage where Spear pushed me up the stairs, following close behind.

"Why are we here?" I asked innocently, but I knew. The dragons thought I had tried to escape. That's why so many of them had been flying up on the mountain— to try to find Ash and me.

"My people will not tolerate your behavior. I knew right from the start that having you here would lead to no good. Ash might be blinded by some ridiculous crush, but the rest of us aren't. Thanks to your little escapade last night, I think it's safe to say that you've shown your true colors. You're here, Julianna, to be sentenced to death."

The seats in the courtyard slowly filled up with villagers. They were all here to watch me die.

"I went to my village to find information that will help you!" I cried out.

"Of course you did. Good luck in convincing the court."

I looked out over the almost full courtyard, desperately hoping I'd see Ash in the crowd. It was then that I noticed something that I'd not seen when I'd been there previously—a set of gallows had been erected at the back. They had already made up their minds. I was going to die.

"Ash won't let you do this!" I screamed.

"Ash can't help you now. He's due to be convicted as well."

Ash ran in from the back. No one needed to pull him up onto the stage—he was making his way here all by himself. I felt an immense but misplaced sense of relief on seeing him run up an aisle between the rows of chairs. I wanted to shout out to him, to warn him, but something stopped me. I realized I knew him well enough to know that he wouldn't leave me. Not here and not like this.

"What are you doing? What's going on?" Ash demanded as he stomped to my side.

"I warned you, Ash. You've been brought here to stand before your peers for the crime of treachery. If found guilty, which I can assure you, you will be, you will be hanged."

"Shut it, Spear." Ash took my hand. I felt safer although my situation hadn't improved, just because Ash was by my side. Any safety I felt was just an illusion. There was at least one person guarding each exit, so escape was not an option.

"This is nonsense!" Ash shouted to the assembled crowd. "I admit, we did go to the slayers' village. Julianna took me to her home."

Gasps surrounded me as Ash spoke. I guess everyone thought we were going to deny it.

"She didn't take me there for her benefit, nor for the benefit of her people. She took me there because she thinks that Stone is still alive."

The gasp that I'd heard before was nothing compared to the interested babble that erupted among the crowd.

"It's a lie!" shouted a woman. "I was with him when he died. One of the slayers struck him with his sword. They carried his body down the mountain."

When she stood, I recognized her as the woman that had spoken to Ally the morning after Stone had died.

I couldn't stay quiet any longer. "My people took his body and his soul, but I don't think they took his life. The slayers' swords gain strength with each dragon soul they capture. There is an ancient magic that traps the soul within the sword. I don't understand it myself but I've seen it with my own eyes. My father's sword is one of the most powerful in the whole village. For the longest time, I thought taking a soul meant taking a life, but after hearing Ally speak yesterday about still being able to feel Stone, I believe that Stone might still be alive."

"I can feel him!" I looked to my left. Ally had been sitting in the third row back, but now stood. "I told you all. It makes sense. I knew he was alive."

The sound of the murmuring crowd swelled. They were beginning to question things thanks to Ally. If enough of them believed me, maybe Ash and I would live to see another day after all. The feeling of dread I'd been carrying in my stomach ever since we were escorted here began to dissipate. I didn't want to count my chickens before they hatched, but with Ally on our side, Spear would at least have to consider the fact I was telling the truth.

"If what you say is true, and your people's swords do harbor the souls of our kind, then surely Ally is sensing Stone's soul. Whether his body is dead or alive seems immaterial."

Ally slumped back into his seat as a man in the front

row spoke. He was right. How had I not thought of that? The gallows seemed to loom closer as I realized my best defense was completely useless. The best I could hope for was that they believed that I had left the dragon colony in good faith. Judging by the angry faces in the crowd, good faith was in short supply.

"I think we can all agree," began Spear, "that the slayer has acted in a manner that has caused our people grave danger and that Ash has abetted her. The penalty for both of them is death by hanging. I'd like a show of hands of those that believe they are both guilty."

I held my breath as I waited to see if I would live or die. One by one, hands rose. I didn't need to count them to see that a lot more than half the people in the room had deemed us guilty.

It was then that I noticed Edeline for the first time. She sat at the very edge of the courtyard holding on to a very scared looking Lucy. She looked even more terrified at the prospect of us being put to death than I felt. Of course she did. She was about to lose her only son. She'd already lost her husband to my people and now because of the slayers, her eldest child was going to die.

"Wait!"

All eyes turned to Ash. I didn't know what he could say that would get us out of this mess. Whatever it was, I hoped it was good.

"You're sentencing us to die for what? Neither of us has denied going to the village. Did we bring anyone else back here? No. Nor have we brought weapons to hurt anyone here. I've known all of you my whole life, and now you're raising your hands to have me hanged because I took a trip down to the village? It's crazy. If you were so worried that we were bringing the slayers up here, why aren't you out there guarding our town? You all know as well as I do that it's impossible to climb all the way up here. Think about it. What reason do I have for bringing the slayers up here?"

"You might not, but she does," someone shouted out from the back of the hall. Ash's hand tightened around mine.

"Julianna risked her own life last night. She climbed the mountain in last night's storm and attempted to get down to her village in the belief that she could steal a sword to test her theory. She didn't do it for herself. I was with her and I saw with my own eyes the devotion she has shown to the dragons. She even fought her own brother. Her house caught fire. She had to run away, knowing that her home was burning to the ground, and she did all of this for you. You should all be thanking her, not condemning her to death. I'm ashamed of all of you right now, and I'm ashamed to call myself a dragon."

Looks of unease and uncertainty passed through the crowd. Ash had stirred something in them with his speech, but would it be enough to save our lives?

A sharp clap to my left caught my attention. I glanced over to see Ally standing once again, bringing his hands together in applause.

Someone else stood and began to clap. It was Edeline, quickly followed by Lucy. Just as they had raised their hands to condemn us, the rest of the dragons were now standing and applauding us.

Not everyone stood and not everyone joined in, but it was enough to show Spear that they had changed their minds.

"Enough!" Spear strode to the front of the stage and waved his hands to quiet the crowd. Eventually, the clapping stopped. "It seems that your fellow villagers have listened to you. I am not convinced that Julianna knows the truth herself. Her theory has no merit whatsoever beyond Ally thinking his twin is still alive. Denial is a strong part of grief and I believe that Ally is mistaken; however, at this point, we have nothing to lose. I'm not going to send anyone who doesn't want to go to the slayer's village but if anyone wants to volunteer for this fool's errand, then I will not stop you either." He turned to me, anger drawing his brow together. "Once we have gathered the swords, what do you propose we do with them?"

"I don't know," I admitted. After Ash's wonderful speech, I felt pathetic.

"You don't know?" repeated Spear, making me look even more foolish.

"Let's get the swords first," said Ash. "Then we can worry about what to do with them. Who will come with me to the slayer village?"

A small number of people raised their hands. Not as many as those that wanted us dead ten minutes ago, but it was a start.

"Come on!" Ash carried on. "You felt brave enough to kill me by raising your hands five minutes ago. Why not raise your hands again, but this time to show me how brave you really are? These are our ancestors, the trapped souls of our brothers, sisters, mothers, and fathers. Surely that is worth a trip down the mountain!"

A few more hands raised. I started to count them when a flash of light at the back of the room took my attention from them. The gallows had gone up in flames. How was that possible? Had someone set fire to them to save us? The flames rose higher and then the inevitable happened: the thatched roof caught fire. Panic broke out with the people at the back of the courtyard rushing forward to escape the flames. People screamed as the fire quickly engulfed the thatching. Most ran for the exits, though some turned into dragons and flew into the air to escape. Still others turned to protect the ones still in their human forms. Someone grabbed my hand and pulled me through the crowd of terrified people towards the exit.

18

The heat of the fire became more and more intense as we tried to push our way through the crowd. The whole roof was burning away merrily while chaos reigned in the circle below.

"We aren't going to make it!" I cried to Ash as the fire took hold of the wall beside the exit nearest to us. Ash changed direction, pulling me away from the flames that now surrounded us and into the center of the courtyard. Nearby, someone shifted and flew up into the air.

I grabbed hold of Ash. "Change into a dragon. We can fly out."

"It's not that easy. It takes a lot of energy to shift from one form to another. It's been too long since I last ate or slept. I don't think I can do it."

I had wondered why the others hadn't all shifted into their dragon form and escaped. It would have been easy to fly up and out of harm's way, and yet there were still so many in their human forms wrestling for the doors that would take them outside. Except they wouldn't take them outside. Every door leading away from the courtyard would take them right into the burning building. Anyone trying to escape would have to run through a wall of fire to get through to the other side, and that's if they could even find their way out through the thick blanket of black smoke.

We stood there, just the two of us, right in the center of the chaos. There were still so many people trapped in the courtyard and yet I couldn't see how they would survive if they ran into the burning building. Smoke reached my lungs and I began to cough.

"Do you think we'll survive if we just wait for the building to burn around us?" I asked. Intense heat surrounded us but the walls of the burning building were far enough away to keep the flames from us unless the wind picked up.

"Normally, yes, but the chairs are made out of wood. The ones at the back have already caught fire." Ash guided me away from them, back to the stage.

"We need to make a run for the exits like everyone else then."

"We can't. The others will get through relatively unscathed. As dragons, we can withstand great temperatures, even in our human forms. We cannot withstand fire forever, but all those running for the exits will survive with little damage."

It was because of me that we were trapped. Ash could escape like everyone else, but my human body would burn in the fire. Even if the exits were clear and we could run right through, the chances of me getting through without being badly burned were slim. I couldn't even see the walls now, just a great wall of orange with thick plumes of black smoke billowing into the sky. Most had escaped, either up into the air or through the burning building, but I could still see some stragglers trying to get through the doors. It wouldn't be long until we were the only ones left.

"If you can run through fire—"

"Don't even think it." Ash wrapped his arms tightly around me as if just this small act would shield me from the flames. "I'm not leaving you."

"But you'll die with me."

"Then Spear will get his way."

"Don't say that!"

But he was right. For a second I wondered if Spear had wanted this to happen, had planned it out somehow, but then I remembered the look of shock on his face as the flames took hold, just before he'd changed into his dragon form and flown up into the sky. He could have pulled me up with him and saved me, but he chose not to. He chose to let me die in the flames, but he didn't start them. I tried to think back to what started them, but just as the fire had come from nowhere in my own house, the same had happened here.

"Why would a village of fire-breathing dragons make a town hall out of wood and straw?" I asked feebly. "You were just asking for trouble."

Ash didn't answer, and I didn't expect him to. I couldn't see anyone else now. The flames and their heat were close in every direction. It wouldn't be long before some part of me caught fire, probably my hair and then

I'd go up in flames just as the town hall had. Maybe then Ash would be able to escape. The thought gave me a little peace. At least there would be only one casualty in all of this. Ash still had a chance.

I closed my eyes and rested my head on Ash's chest, waiting for the inevitable. A huge gust of cold air made me snap my eyes open. Hot and cold air spun around us as if we were in the center of a small tornado. I couldn't see a thing except for my bright orange hair flapping across my face, mimicking the flames that had surrounded us only moments before. As quickly as it had started, the wind stopped.

I pulled my hair back away from my face to take in the scene before me. The town hall still stood but barely. What was left of the walls was charred black. Wisps of smoke curled into the sky. Most of the chairs were now nothing but ash, although a few closest to us were still intact, showing me just how close the flames had come to us.

The wind came again but this time in a powerful blast as a pair of massive wings flapped, causing my hair to fly out behind me. I shielded my eyes from the soot that blew toward me. The biggest dragon I'd ever seen landed in the center of the ruined courtyard, its wings spanning the entire space. It was green with a tinge of gold glinting in the sun on the tip of every scale.

It folded its wings as its feet touched the ground. I barely had time to comprehend what was happening and how the dragon had seemingly extinguished the flames when the tell-tale sound of bones creaking told me that it was shifting into its human form. I wanted to close my eyes but it was mesmerizing. I'd not seen a dragon shift before and now that I was watching it, I couldn't look away. He shrunk, every part of him seeming to curl up into itself. His snout shortened as his legs lengthened. The green color warmed until it was the pink of skin. All of this was accompanied by the horrible creaking and squelching sound I'd come to associate with shifting.

Finally, a man stood before us. He was tall and muscular and completely naked. I didn't know where to look.

"Dad!"

Dad? Ash dropped his arms from around me and ran to the man, flinging his arms around him. The man embraced him back.

This was Ash's father? The one who had been killed by a slayer?

He was supposed to be dead! Unless...

Unless my theory was right. I remembered the great green and gold dragon now, Jasper's first kill. I remembered its body being brought down to the village and the big party we had afterward. My mother had remarked on how the dragon's scales glowed in the sunshine.

It was a bizarre scene set out in front of me. The smoldering ruins of the town hall, Ash hugging his naked father. I looked around for something that would cover Ash's dad but almost everything around me was blackened and burned.

Ash's father looked very similar to his son. They had the same thick dark hair and strong jaw line. He was perhaps a couple of inches taller and his shoulders were broader, but it was unmistakable. He opened his eyes. When he noticed me, his expression changed almost immediately. I'd never seen a look of such hatred as the one that Ash's father directed at me now.

The world seemed to stand still.

"You," he said, "are a slayer."

"Dad, how are you here?" Ash's voice brought me back to reality. A dozen or so of the others had returned, still in their dragon forms. One of them had a blanket in its claws, which it dropped at Ash's father's feet. He picked it up from the floor, wrapping it around himself so he was fully covered. He pulled himself away from Ash, ignoring his son's last question, and strode toward me purposefully.

"You're the reason I'm here. You tried to kill me." His voice was menacing and the speed with which he came towards me made me step back in fear. I'd never seen anyone so angry in my whole life.

"Dad! Stop."

Ash ran forward as his father prodded me in my chest, pushing me back a foot. "Julianna came here to help us. Leave her alone."

Ash's father prodded me again, prompting Ash to pull him back. "No slayer ever helped one of our kind."

"She is helping us."

"Why are you defending her?" He finally took his eyes from me and turned to his son. "Do you have any idea what I've had to endure at the hands of her people? I've been trapped inside a sword for over a year. Do you have any idea what it's like to have your soul taken from your own body and imprisoned in a space as small as that?" He pointed at my sword. "It's cold and dark. I haven't been able to see or feel for over a year. I couldn't speak or hear or move, and yet I could think. I knew I still existed and yet I didn't know how to escape. For a whole year of torment, I was there and yet I was not. If hell exists, I have surely been living it."

"My theory is right." I had thought as much, but to finally hear it from Ash's father's mouth was something else. A small thrill ran through me to know that my friends and family were not murderers at all, but it quickly died when I thought of all those other dragons trapped in the swords, some for decades, even centuries. The thought of being trapped in the darkness for years on end with nothing but my own thoughts horrified me. Maybe death would have been kinder after all.

"What theory?" spat Ash's dad.

"Julianna is one of the slayers, Father, but she didn't know we were shifters. To her, we were nothing more than animals to be hunted."

His father interrupted him. "They know what they are doing. They have always known."

"I didn't. I swear. I knew nothing of your people. I

thought of us as hunters and nothing more. Now I see how wrong I was, and I'm sorry."

If I thought my apology would quell his anger, I was wrong. He seemed even more incensed by my words than he had been before.

"You are nothing more than a murderer. Maybe you didn't know that you were trapping our souls, but you cannot tell me that you didn't strike your sword into our bodies to kill us."

"Actually, she didn't kill anyone." Ash stepped in again. "She had the chance to kill me, but instead defended me against her people even before she knew we were shifters. While you can argue that her people did strike to kill us, are we really any better ourselves? We spend our lives training to hunt for meat."

"We hunt to eat, Ash. They hunt for fun, for the glory of the kill. That's what sets us apart from them."

I couldn't defend myself because he was right. We didn't eat the dragons or use their hide for shoes and belts. We killed them and then had a party to celebrate. Shame flooded through me. How had I not seen how sick and utterly pointless it all was? My village was surrounded by bountiful farmlands as far at the eye could see. We were in no danger of starving. If the dragons ever came down to the village to hurt us, perhaps it would have been justified, but yesterday with Ash was the first time I'd ever seen a living dragon in our village.

"You have every right to be angry with me. Ignorance doesn't seem like a very good defense, but it's the only one I have. I can promise you something though. Now that I know about you, I will never slay a dragon, and I'll make it my life's work to stop my people killing yours. I'm glad this has all happened because I would have spent my whole life mindlessly following a path that had been set out for me from birth. I will be blind no more. You have my word."

"Your words mean nothing—"

"Father!" interrupted Ash. He was still holding his father back. "I've been praying for a resolution to the conflict between our people and the slayers. I know that was something you wanted yourself before you went away."

"I was imprisoned."

"Yes, imprisoned, but the fact that you were imprisoned and escaped proves that we can save the others too."

"I want to save the other dragons, sir," I said. "I want to go into my village and let your people go free."

He seemed to calm down a bit while he weighed what I said. Ash finally let him go and he stayed away from me.

Sensing the shift in his mood, I felt safe to ask questions. "How exactly did you escape?" I asked, my voice hesitant but firm. "What was it that let you out of the sword?"

"The last thing I remember before I was trapped was a young man with a group of older men on the mountain. He stabbed me with his sword and at first, I felt pain, but then the pain subsided and there was a kind of whooshing sensation. It was as if I was being sucked out of my own body, and then it all went dark. It was dark ever since, until last night. There was no real sound, but the vibrations made me feel as if something was buzzing around me. Then I sensed movement, the clanging of my sword against another."

"That was me. You were trapped in my brother's sword when I fought him."

"You fought your own brother? Why did you do that?"

"I told you, father, she was fighting him for his sword. She believed that there was the soul of a dragon inside. She wanted to see if it was true."

"You fought for us?" The menacing look dropped from his face and was replaced with something else. If I was to guess, I'd say he was impressed.

"Yes, sir. I wanted to see if I was correct. Now that you are standing here, it seems that I am. Can you tell me what happened after the fight?" I now knew that it was Ash's father that had caused the fire in my house. His escape must have taken so much energy that he'd inadvertently set my house on fire as he left the sword.

"I don't know exactly. It went on for a few minutes and then something changed. It suddenly got very hot. I'd not felt anything for so long that just being able to feel the heat excited me. It meant something was changing. It got hotter until the whooshing sensation happened again. This time it went on for much longer. I felt like I was flying but I had no control. Everything was still dark until I opened my eyes. I was back in my own body. Darkness still surrounded me but this time there were specks of light. It took me a while to realize I was seeing stars and the moon. The ground was soaking wet from rainfall, but I didn't care. I could see and feel and move again. It took a couple of hours for me to readjust to using my body again. I had to relearn how to walk and fly, and by that time dawn had come.

"In many ways, being able to see again was a wonder, but it was also like waking up from one nightmare into another. The bodies of my fellow dragons lay next to mine. I tried waking one I recognized as my uncle's friend who had gone so many years ago. There was the faint beat of his heart, but he didn't stir. I couldn't wake any of them. There were so many dragons there that I knew, all sleeping in some kind of eternal sleep. I had the energy of a newborn, so it took me a long time to get out of there."

"Where were you being kept?" If there was a prison full of sleeping dragons, surely I'd have seen it.

"It was a great place with four large walls but no roof. There was a huge, locked door which I assumed was how we were brought in. I had to fly out over the walls. It was about a mile away from your village, in the forest that borders the Triad Mountains and the farmlands."

I knew where he meant. From the outside, it looked like a castle. I'd asked my father about it and he told me that a giant lived there. I knew he was making it up, but I just assumed it was an old building that was no longer in use. My father had never taken me into that part of the forest again, and as I grew up, I'd forgotten all about it. If only I had known it was full of soulless dragons.

"I spent the morning eating anything I could find. Squirrels, foxes, fruit from the trees. Once I had enough energy, I was able to fly and then I could catch some birds. I flew straight here. When I arrived, I saw that the village was empty of people. It took a few flights over to see everyone in the town hall. I had planned to land outside and change into a man, but I'd forgotten just how much energy that took. I'm afraid I accidentally set fire to the town hall."

"You caused this?"

I turned to see Spear standing behind me. I didn't know how long he'd been there, but he must have come in as a dragon. Unlike Ash's father, he was fully dressed.

"Spear! It's so good to see you." The two men embraced like old friends. "Please forgive me. I can assure you it was entirely accidental."

"No need to apologize, Fiere. It is just good to have you back. I cannot believe my own eyes. My dead best friend standing right in front of me."

"Believe it, Spear."

"I am the only one that owes anyone an apology. I've been wrong, and I can see that now." Spear turned to me. "Julianna and Ash, I hope you'll forgive me. I did not believe you and I did not trust you, and yet you have brought my oldest friend back to me. I thought he was dead. I thought they were all dead."

Someone held my hand. I didn't have to look to know it was Ash.

"I have just one question though," I said. "What made it possible for you to escape? Just fighting with the swords wouldn't have done it. I fought against Jasper and his sword before in training."

"What happened just before the fire started in your house?" asked Ash.

I thought back to the scene from the night before. My father had picked up Jasper's sword and then... and then he had cut my arm.

"It's the blood!" I exclaimed. "My father nicked my forearm, look." I showed them the small cut. "Just after my blood hit the sword, the house caught on fire. If what you said about the intense heat was correct, then it was at that point that your soul left the sword."

"So, it's a dragon's blood that entraps us, but the blood of a slayer that sets us free. There is some poetry in that, would you not agree?" Ash's father said.

I looked at Ash as he looked at me. It seemed that my blood was the key to saving the dragons.

20

An acrid, burning stench filled my nostrils. Almost without warning, waves of nausea washed over me. The world spun around me and I began to falter. Ash hurried me out of the ruined town hall and back into the village square where we had landed not an hour before. When the fresh air hit my lungs, I immediately felt better, although the underlying nausea was still there, waiting to consume me.

Part of me was elated at figuring out how to save the dragons, but knowing my own blood would have to spill to do it was too much. Just how many dragons were there? My people had been slayers for centuries and I'd lost count of how many dragons had been brought back to the village in just my short lifetime. How much blood would I have to give to save them all? Of course, if it was just a tiny drop and if it was just my blood, I might feel okay about it, but it wasn't just a small drop. When my father had nicked me with his sword, the cut had been superficial but quite a bit of my blood had hit the sword.

Multiply that by the hundreds, or even thousands, of dragon souls we had stolen and I wouldn't have any blood left in my body. The dragons would have to use the blood of my family, of my friends.

"Are you okay?" Ash gently placed his fingers under my chin and lifted it until I was looking at him. I couldn't lie to him.

"Not really."

"We'll figure all this out, don't worry."

"Don't worry?" Easy for him to say. He didn't have a hoard of dragons wanting to take all his blood. I shivered despite the warmth of the air.

"I'm not going to let anyone hurt you if that's what you're thinking. It can't only be your blood that works. There must be other's blood we can use instead."

I knew he meant well, but using other's blood was exactly what I was afraid of. Still, his arms around me were comforting, and just for a minute, I enjoyed his warmth and tried to forget about what I knew was coming.

It didn't last long. The dragons who had followed us had changed and dressed, including Fiere.

A couple of women brought chairs and tables from one of the cafes that lined the square. A neighboring restaurant did the same, bringing enough chairs for everyone to sit on. Ash took my hand and led me to one of the tables. Almost as soon as we sat, a waitress brought us both a cup of coffee and a slice of cake each. Spear sat to one side of me, making me feel nervous. The others had all changed into their human forms and joined the impromptu party or meeting.

Suddenly, a loud scream made me jump and spill

my coffee all over the table. Edeline ran towards us, tears in her eyes and arms outstretched. Lucy was just behind her, her small legs struggling to keep up with her mother. Edeline jumped into Fiere's arms, burying her head in his shoulder. Seconds later Lucy barged into them and was enveloped into the hug.

"You should go to them," I said to Ash. His back turned to me as he went back to his family. A pang of sadness hit me as I wondered what my own family was doing right now and if they were out looking for me.

"As many of you can see, our brother Fiere has returned to us," began Spear, standing to address the others. "I owe you all an apology. Julianna was telling the truth. Our ancestor's souls have been trapped by the slayer's swords but their living bodies remain, hidden in a secret place outside of the slayer village. Julianna's own blood is the key to releasing our people, and it is because of her that Fiere is back. The fire that destroyed the town hall was an accident and I know that Fiere wouldn't mind me telling you that it was he who started it. After so long trapped inside a sword, he's not quite used to being back in his body. I'm sure no one will hold that against him."

"I'm sorry everyone," said Fiere, finally extracting himself from his family. Ash came to sit next to me with his family on his other side. Lucy perched on her father's lap.

A cheer went up as I looked around me; a sea of smiling faces greeted me, glad to have one of their own back. I lifted the corners of my mouth to join in, but the thought of what my people and I would have to do to free all the dragons was a constant thought in my mind.

"What about Stone?" Ally shouted. "Did you see him? Is he still alive?"

"I'm afraid when I woke up I was very weak. I saw many dragons and tried to wake the ones nearest to me, but I can't remember who I saw. There were many, many of our people there. I'm sure Stone will be among them."

"I knew he was alive. I knew it!" Ally's fist pumped the air, his joy evident for all to see. "We need to go and get him."

"We need to go into the slayer village and rescue all of them," said Spear. "Most of you here have lost someone to the slayers so I think you'll agree with me; however, it's not just a case of flying into the village and waking our brethren. We have to get the swords first. Only then will we be able to save the dragons. We need to make a plan."

"How will we find all the swords?" asked a man I hadn't seen before.

"It's good that we have someone who knows the village very well." Spear's hand clapped heavily on my shoulder, pushing me down in my chair. If only he'd pushed a bit harder, I could have disappeared under the table completely. "Julianna has agreed to help us. She'll be able to tell us where the swords are and who owns them. She is a valuable resource indeed. With her help, we can make a map of the village and write up profiles on the owners of the swords."

Everyone began to clap again, this time for me. I picked up my cup and managed a weak smile. I'd said I'd help the dragons but I'd not mentioned anything about maps or profiles. I wanted to help the dragons and see the same look of joy on their faces that were currently being shown by Edeline and Lucy, but to do that, I'd be betraying my own kind.

"With Julianna's help, we'll know the slayer village intimately. We will know at what time everyone gets up and what time they go to bed, what time they eat and who goes to work where. I'm not going to send anyone down to the village until we're ready."

"But I want to go fetch my brother now," Ally said in protest. "He needs me."

"He does need you, but he needs you not to get caught. You will be of no use to him if you end up trapped too."

"So what?" replied Ally, standing. "I'd rather be trapped with him than sitting around here drinking coffee and eating cake."

"Fine, you go to him now, but which sword was it that took him? Because if you end up trapped in a different sword, you'll be even further from being reunited with him than you are now."

Ally sat down, defeated.

"Does anyone else want to start their own crusade, or are we going to do what we always do and work as a team?"

No one spoke.

"That's what I thought. Now here's what I propose. First of all, we need our strongest and most able men and women to go and fight."

I winced at the word fight.

A number of hands shot up into the air, Ally's among them.

"I also need volunteers to help rebuild the town hall.

Those of you offering to fight can start on that until we have our maps and plans. With Julianna helping us, they shouldn't take too long to write up, maybe a couple of days. Just how many swords do you think we'll need to look for?"

Ash nudged me when I didn't answer. Was Spear talking to me?

How many swords were we looking for? That was a tricky question. Almost everyone had a sword in Dronios. Receiving one was a rite of passage. I tried adding up just how many swords there were in the village. There must be at least a hundred. Granted, many of the villagers didn't use them and instead had them showcased in frames on their walls, but all of them at one point would have had to come up the mountain on their eighteenth birthday. Of course, there were also swords like my father's that had been used on many dragons, though I couldn't say exactly how many.

"I would say there are between eight and fifteen swords you'll need to find first. Not everyone in Dronios slays dragons, but there is a group of men who are up the mountain more than anyone else, the elders of our village. It's these men who will have most of your people trapped in their swords."

I felt like enough of a betrayer just telling them this snippet of information, so I could hardly tell them that they would need to target most of the people in town as well. My own father was one of the men in the group I'd mentioned. If he knew I was telling the dragons about him, he'd probably never speak to me again. At least not until he knew the truth about them, that they were shifters. My father was many things, but he wasn't a murderer. I knew he'd never take the life of another person. I hoped he'd find it in his heart to understand what I was trying to do and to forgive me because of it.

"It seems Julianna is now our biggest ally. I'll work with her closely over the coming days to define a plan that will allow us to free the dragons."

"Didn't you say that it was Julianna whose blood we would have to use to free them?" someone shouted.

I'm glad someone had noticed because Spear seemed to have skated over that small piece of information. Ash gripped my hand tightly under the table.

"Well, yes," said Spear, giving a little cough. "That's something to worry about further down the line. Today our priority is to make a plan and find the swords. As for the freeing of the dragon's souls, we can cross that bridge when we come to it."

"But we will need to use her blood, right? Why would she do that? She *is* a Slayer," the man pushed.

They were speaking over me as if I wasn't even there. A waitress refilled my coffee and handed me another slice of cake on a stone plate even though I'd not touched the first one.

"Well, as I've already said, she's agreed to help us. Isn't that right, Julianna?

All eyes turned to me. It was all well and good, Spear telling everyone I would help, but now that he was asking me to agree with him, I had to make a decision. On one hand, I wanted nothing more than to help these people, to return their lost loves to their community, but I knew that in doing so, my own people might be hurt. Having a plan was a good idea, but plans weren't infallible.

I thought of my father then, how he had been so proud of me on my last day of being seventeen. Was that really only a week ago? It felt like a lifetime. If I said yes to them, he would forgive me, right? All through Spear's speech, I'd been thinking of my family and how they had always taught me right from wrong, but doing the right thing now could hurt them all. They might never forgive me, and in that case, I might never see them again. It was breaking my heart, and yet how could I leave so many dragons trapped, knowing that I was the only one that could save them? I'd never be able to live with myself.

I took a deep breath, ready to utter the words that would change not just my life, but the lives of everyone, dragon and slayer alike

Ash's hand gripped mine hard. His emerald eyes glistened as he nodded at me. It was an almost imperceptible tilt of the head meant just for me, but I saw it and knew what it meant. He wasn't asking me to agree like Spear was. He was giving me his support to make up my own mind. He understood the position I was in as no one else did. Everyone was so keen to bring back their loved ones that any thoughts of my welfare and that of my family had not even been a consideration. Ash was different though. He looked at both sides of the issue and had an empathy I was yet to find in any other person or dragon. I knew Ash would support me in whatever decision I made, and for that I was grateful. That was also what led me to the decision I was about to make.

21

———

"Yes." There, I'd said it. "I'll help you. I'll help you find the swords but I have one condition."

Spear smiled. "And what condition is that my dear?"

"I want no harm to come to the people of my village. If we do this, we do it in peace."

"Are you proposing we fly down to Dronios and ask them nicely to give us their swords?"

A couple of the people in the crowd giggled.

"No, of course not," I replied feeling annoyed. "What I'm saying is that we do this at night without making a fuss."

Because that had gone so well last time. At least this time I had a couple of days to plan it. Hopefully, if I did a good job, we could retrieve the swords without making the same mistakes as last time.

"Of course. None of us wants anyone to get hurt but we must also be realistic. Even the best-laid plans can fail as you yourself discovered the other night."

"Now that I know that blood is the answer, I know not to bleed on any of the swords until they are safely away." The last thing I needed was to destroy any more of the village with fire.

"I'm sure that you didn't intend to bleed on the last sword, but you did."

"That's true, but it won't happen again." Of course, I couldn't know that for sure, but I was certainly planning to keep my blood in my own body for as long as possible.

"Let's hope so for all of our sakes."

Spear was really beginning to annoy me with his condescending attitude. I wanted to tell him to go shove it but I knew I couldn't. I'd already committed to helping them out.

"So," carried on Spear to the rest of the crowd, "those of you who have volunteered to go down into Dronios must do their level best not to do anything that might get anyone hurt. I know that retribution must be in all your minds as you fly down the mountain and that after centuries of them murdering our people, you'll want to have your revenge, but you must keep this instinct in check."

"That's not fair!" I shouted, standing up and knocking over my second cup of coffee. The waitress immediately ran over to mop up the spill. "My people are not murderers!"

"How do you explain all of our people that have been murdered by yours then?"

He had such a smug smirk on his face, I had half a mind to punch him in it. I didn't want to point out that not a single dragon had been murdered, just imprisoned within the swords. He already knew that; he was just baiting me.

"My people didn't know you were shifters. Had they known, we would have let you be. We thought the dragons were a threat to our safety. That is why we became slayers."

"Slayers. Yes, such an interesting term for a girl who doesn't think of herself as a murderer."

"Spear," Ash stood, matching my own indignation. "You've gone too far. You know as well as I do that Julianna isn't a murderer. Hasn't the fact that she's just agreed to help you been enough proof for you?"

"Maybe not," replied Spear, "but she's wrong about her people not knowing. Maybe she's just ignorant of it, but her people have always known."

I didn't like being called ignorant, but the alternative was worse—that my family and I had always known about the dragons being shifters and I was lying about it.

"I am not ignorant and I'm not lying. I know my family and I know my friends. They would never harm another soul." I was still shouting and I didn't care. I was the only one here that could defend my people.

"Interesting choice of words considering that's exactly what your people have been doing for centuries. I didn't mean to call you ignorant, but the fact of the matter is, the slayers have known about us being shifters for centuries. There's a book about it in the library here in town that I'm sure we can check out."

"Maybe it's a work of fiction?" I tried desperately, sitting back down in my seat. Another cup of coffee had magically appeared on the table in front of me. I had to be careful not to spill this one.

"It's called The History of Frokontas. Does that sound like a work of fiction to you?"

He directed the question at me but didn't wait for an answer. Not that I was planning on giving him one anyway.

"In the book, there is a whole chapter about the slayers. It is said that there was a meeting way back when between the elder from Dronios and the elder from Frokontas. They sat with each other and discussed their differences. It was made very clear to your elder at the time that we were shifters and that we were a peace-loving people, but your elder refused to cease slaying. He said it was all his people had ever known and they would keep fighting us until there wasn't a dragon left in the sky."

"That can't be!" I cried out. Surely the book was wrong. I looked to Ash for support, but he only whispered that he'd read the book too.

"Let's be clear on one thing, Julianna. Humans have always had a deep mistrust of shifters. From the battles of the wolves in the north to the war of the sea-shifters in the east, humans have never let us be. Where there is a community of shifters, there is a settlement of humans who believe it is their destiny to destroy them. Your village is no different."

He was right, but how could he possibly be? He'd used practically the same words my father had said to me—that it was our destiny to destroy them. How could my father have known? How could he have kept this from me, his own flesh and blood, his own daughter? I remembered the words he said to me the day before my birthday. *After today you will know everything there is to know about being a slayer. You will learn our secrets.*

At the time, I thought he was talking about learning to fight, but maybe he was going to tell me that the dragons were shifters. Maybe he knew all along. Jasper knew too. I remembered how haughty he had been about me not knowing everything.

They were going to tell me after my first kill. Once I'd already killed a dragon—or thought I had—it would have been too late to back out. I'd already be a murderer. The memory of all those parties came back to me. All the times we danced around the body of a dragon and celebrated the kill. They had known that it was a person. How could anyone do that, let alone a whole village? And they must have known. Everyone killed a dragon on their eighteenth birthday. There were few exceptions. Many didn't carry on in the pursuit of killing them, but almost everyone had blood on their hands. The thought made me sick.

I stood up quickly and ran into the café bathroom. Once there, I retched but nothing came up. Looking in the bathroom mirror while washing my hands, I wasn't surprised to see I'd been crying. My eyes were red-rimmed and salty tears had left tracks down my grimy face. I'd not even felt the tears falling. Perhaps I was in shock.

Someone knocked at the bathroom door.

"Julianna? Are you ok?" It was Ash.

"Not really." I splashed water on my face before stepping out of the bathroom. As soon as I'd closed the door behind me, he enveloped me into a soothing hug. I hated him seeing me like this again, all sad and misty-eyed. I'd been brought up as a warrior, not a cry baby.

"My whole life has been a lie. I swear I never knew."

"I know, Julianna. I've already told you I believe you. Whether your ancestors knew is another matter."

I pulled back and looked him in the eye. "You say ancestors as though they all died long ago. We're talking about my father, my mother, everyone! Is what Spear said the truth?"

"I've read the book he talked about. Everyone here has. We don't have school here like you do, but we're taught by our parents from a young age, and that book is the most frequently checked out book from the library."

"I can't believe it. I just can't."

"I don't know what's true and what isn't. That book was written a long time ago about a conversation that happened a long time before that. Stories change over time. What's to say this one didn't? For all we know, the two elders were drinking mead together and having a good time like old friends. It doesn't sound too dramatic now, does it?" Ash shrugged his shoulders. "The author had to add some excitement in there so he fabricated a fight."

I punched him playfully on the shoulder. "You're just teasing me."

"I wanted to see you smile, that's all."

"What now?" Outside, Spear appeared to have moved on to some other topic as he gestured wildly at the burned remains of the building.

"Now we carry on with our plan."

"To get the swords?"

"Yes, that is important. We need our people back,

but that is Spear's plan. Our plan is to make the dragons and the slayers see eye to eye."

I sighed. "I don't think that's going to happen in a hurry. Not if what Spear said is true."

"When my dad was taken from us, I was so angry. I wanted to go down the mountain and burn all your houses and hurt as many of you as I could."

"What stopped you?" I was fascinated to hear this. It didn't seem like Ash at all.

"Lucy. She asked me what that would solve and I realized she was right. It would solve nothing. Killing your people wouldn't bring my father back; it would just make the slayers angrier so they would come after more dragons. It was a self-perpetuating circle of hate, and I decided right there to break it. Of course, I could only think and act for myself, not for others, so the hate continued, but I've tried very hard to make the dragons see both sides of the story and not just what they want to see."

I looked at him and realized how brave he was. I wouldn't have been able to do the same if I were in his position.

I leaned forward, full of a need I'd not known before and brushed his lips with mine. This was nothing like the small peck I'd given him all those days before on the training ground with Stone and Ally. This was a kiss brought about by a fear of my past and a yearning to be with another person who understood what I was going through. I was aware that I was using the kiss to take away my pain, but perhaps it would take away some of his too. The intensity of the feelings rushing through me took me by surprise as our lips worked together. When he eventually pulled back, I knew that for both our sakes, the plan had to work.

"Come on. We should go back outside. They'll be wondering where we are."

"Can't we just stay in here forever?" I asked, only half-joking, but I knew we couldn't. Sooner or later, we'd have to go back to reality.

22

To give Spear his due, he didn't make any mention of my sudden disappearance. The talk had turned very animated in my absence and it seemed they were discussing how the new town hall should look.

"I'll tell you everything you need to know, but we have to do it now." I didn't want to give myself time to change my mind.

Everyone stopped talking and, not for the first time, all eyes were on me.

"Okay then," said Spear, looking directly at me. "I think we should discuss this somewhere a little less crowded. You can come to my house. Those of you that have agreed to go to the slayer village can come with us. Everyone else, thank you for your input, but I think we should adjourn this meeting here."

The sound of a hundred chairs being pulled back all at once filled the air. A group of people walked over to Spear. Ally was among them, as was the girl who had been with Stone at the time of his soul being taken. I didn't recognize the rest apart from Lucy, who had pulled away from Edeline and Fiere.

"I think you are a little too small to fight, Lucy," Ash said with a grin, ruffling her hair.

"Fight? Who said anything about fighting?" I asked, feeling nervous at what I was about to do.

"You know what I mean," he said to me. To Lucy, he said, "Go with Mom and Dad. I'll be home later."

"I can fight!" she said, pulling herself up to her full height which wasn't much. She placed her hands on her hips and looked at her older brother with indignation.

He kissed her lightly on the cheek. "I know you can, but we want to give the slayers a chance, don't we?"

I knew he was joking, but his words made my stomach churn.

"You've not seen Dad in a year. I have to go to this meeting because Julianna needs me, but Dad would be awfully upset if neither of his children was there for his homecoming."

She seemed to weigh it in her mind, then jogged back to her parents.

"Sorry about how I phrased it. I hope there won't be any fighting, but she's so young and doesn't really know what's going on. It was easier to word it like I did than explain."

"Surely that's precisely the reason we're in this mess in the first place?" I ventured.

"Okay, everyone," began Spear, not leaving Ash time to respond. "Let's go."

Frokontas was a small place so it didn't take long until we were at Ash's house on the opposite end of town. There were quite a few farms and pretty houses dotted around the landscape, but it didn't take a genius to guess which one belonged to Spear.

It was the largest house in the whole town and the only one that had more than two stories. Made out of white painted wood, it rose from the ground like a monolith. On the very top was a landing pad, but it was not there that we entered. Instead, we walked up a tree-flanked walkway to a huge door that must have been ten feet tall.

"It's so I can entertain people in their dragon form," he explained as he opened the door. "I don't like people coming in from the top and going through my house."

I followed him into a huge hallway with a polished floor and a wide, sweeping staircase.

A woman in a smart white uniform appeared. "Sir, can I get you anything?"

"Just bring some lemonade into the parlor, please. I think we've all had enough coffee to last a lifetime."

She curtsied and left through the door she had come from.

The parlor was a huge room with large windows that made it much brighter than the entrance hall had been.

Even though there were about twenty of us, we all found somewhere to sit comfortably on the sofas that were spread around the room.

"So," I began, feeling nervous. What I was about to do was a betrayal to my whole family. I cleared my throat and started again. "So, the swords. Everyone in Dronios gets one on their eighteenth birthday. They're all unique, although they all look similar to mine." I held my sword aloft for them to see.

"This one is light because it has never killed another being or taken a soul. Essentially, it's just a piece of hollow metal."

"You make your swords hollow?" someone asked. "Surely that would make them weaker."

"These are special swords. Yes, they are hollow. They need to be to hold souls but don't make the mistake of thinking that weakens them. They are imbibed with goblin magic."

"The goblins make them?" he asked, impressed now.

I knew why. Anything made by goblins was expensive. They mined the metal in the Triad Mountains and put their own magic into everything they made. Those that could afford it invariably ordered magic crowns, necklaces or other jewelry, but the slayers decided that was a waste of magic long ago and commissioned swords instead. Each one cost as much as a house in Dronios, but it was worth it. If a slayer lost their sword, they'd never be able to afford another one.

"Yes, so you can understand that this isn't going to be easy. Now I know that I said everyone in the village over the age of eighteen had a sword. That's true, but there are also others. When a person dies, their sword is deemed too special to give to someone else so they're put in the village stronghold."

"That's fine. We'll just go in there after we've found the other swords," said Ash.

"Not quite. I don't know where it is. I only know it exists because my mother told me that my grandfather's sword was put in there when he died ten years ago."

"This is going to be much harder than I imagined," said Spear. He'd not sat down yet but was instead pacing the room while I spoke. "We need a map. How are your drawing skills?"

He didn't wait for me to answer before unrolling a length of parchment on a table at the edge of the room and handing me a pot of ink and a quill.

I closed my eyes, trying to picture just how my village would look from above. On the far left of the paper, I drew a small square to symbolize my house. Of course, that had been burnt down, and I didn't know where my family was staying, but I felt that I should put it on the map anyway. If the dragons were flying in, they'd need to get the full picture. To the right, I drew the track that led to the heart of the village and a big circle to denote the center, with five houses around it. Then, to the far right, I drew another house. There were others of course, but as I drew the map, it occurred to me that only seven of them mattered. The seven I'd drawn in belonged to the founding families of the village and the only ones that were really considered slayers. In each building, I put a large cross, before filling in another few houses.

"What do the crosses mean?" Spear asked, looking over my shoulder.

"Dronios is a slayer village, but that doesn't mean that everyone in the village is a slayer. There are seven main families in the village. These are the ones that have swords, or at least the ones that have swords like mine. I've marked a cross in the houses where I know there will be the most valuable sword."

"Ok, seven families. Got it. Can you write the number of swords in each household next to it on the map? That way, we'll have a good idea what we're up against."

I nodded my head. Next to my house, I wrote the number four before crossing it out and writing three. I'd forgotten for a second that I had my own sword with me. Next to it, I drew a question mark.

"This is my house," I explained to Spear. "It burned down the other night and I don't know where my family is."

I was just about to write a five beside the next house when the maid bustled in with a large try of cups and a jug of lemonade.

"I'm afraid we 'e using the table, so you'll all have to pour your own lemonade and pass the jug around." Spear turned back to the chart.

I mentally added up everyone in the village and wrote the numbers in.

"Thirty-three," said Spear adding the numbers. "There are thirty-three people in your village with slayer swords?"

"Thirty-four," I replied, indicating mine. "Mine is the only empty one though. As I've only just turned eighteen, mine is the newest in the village. You've got to remember the ones that were owned by my ancestors though. I have no way of knowing just how many there are." I drew another box at the top of the paper and put a large question mark in it. Underneath I wrote "Stronghold."

"Wonderful, Julianna," Spear said, pulling the paper out from under my hands. "This will help immensely."

He held it up for the others to see as I sat beside Ash.

"There are thirty-three swords to find, plus some

more in a stronghold. Julianna doesn't know where this is but I'm sure we will be able to find it. I say we go in tonight and grab the swords under the cover of darkness. If you could all—"

"I thought you were going to wait a couple of days?" I asked, interrupting him. "Weren't you going to make a start on building the new town hall?"

"The town hall can wait. This is more important."

"No!" I shouted although I didn't know why. I'd agreed to this. It had to happen sooner or later. Did it really matter what day they went down?

And yet, the thought of my mother popped into my head. My dear, sweet mother who wouldn't hurt a fly. Sure, she was from a long line of slayers, but she had problems killing a chicken for dinner. She always had to get my father to do it for her. There was no way she would be able to knowingly kill another person, even if they were dragon shifters.

"Can't we just go to the village and ask them to give us the swords?" Even as I said it I knew it sounded lame.

Some of the people laughed and my cheeks reddened.

"I don't think that's an option, Julianna. Maybe you should go home with Ash now and let us plan for this evening."

"No, you need my help," I insisted. And I needed to be there to make sure that no one was going to get hurt.

"And you have helped. This map is invaluable to us."

"You can't just go blundering into my village. Someone will get hurt."

"She's right, Spear," said Ash "Thirty-three swords is a lot to find in one night, not to mention the ones in the stronghold. Why not just go and find some of them tonight and do the rest later?"

"Actually, that's not a bad idea. It will make it easier. We'll attack just these houses tonight," he said, pointing to two of the houses in the village.

"You can't attack anyone," I objected. "The men hold their swords close by because of the power they hold. You won't be able to do it without me."

"Attack was probably too strong a word. I want no casualties on either side, but I will get the swords. If they put up a fight, we will win. You should never underestimate the power of a dragon. Please take her home, Ash. Now."

"I'm not going," I stated, but Ash took hold of my arm.

"Come on. We may as well go home. I've not seen Dad in a year and I want to be home for the celebration."

I wanted to stay, but how could I ask him to stay with me when the father he previously thought was dead was at home waiting for him?

As I left the room, I heard them discussing their plans without me. The thought of them going to my village without me with information that I had given them made me feel sick.

"Why did you make me leave?" I asked once we were out of the house.

"Because I know Spear. If we didn't go, and you kept trying to undermine him, he'd have locked you up somewhere. It's better that we leave now while you're still free and come up with a plan of our own."

I already had a plan. I'd been thinking about it since

Spear had told everyone that they would be attacking my village tonight. I was going to go there before him. I was going to tell my family the truth. Once they knew that the dragons were shifters, they'd hand their swords over to me.

At least, I hoped they would.

23

T'd felt like an outsider many times since coming to Frokontas, but this was the first time I'd felt like that in Ash's home.

Edeline had prepared a huge dinner for Fiere to welcome him home, and even though I was invited to join them, I didn't want to interrupt the family reunion, so I took my plate and ate in my room.

My mind kept going over everything that had happened over the last few hours. I shouldn't have told Spear about my village, at least not until I knew for sure that I would be allowed to go too. It was too late now though. He'd made his plans and I wasn't a part of them. I cursed myself for letting it come to this, but what choice did I really have? I couldn't let my people keep killing the dragons knowing they were shifters. I wrestled with my conscience all evening, indecisive about what I should do. I could leave the dragons. Attempt one last time to reason with my family. Warn them what was coming and how to stop it. If they relinquished their swords, all would be over.

I'd made up my mind by the time I heard the family going to bed. I was going to sneak out. Okay, I'd tried once before and ended up lost in a maze deep within the mountains, dripping wet and freezing cold, but this time I'd go prepared. When the house was quiet, I tiptoed downstairs into the kitchen. There, I took a torch and some chalk I'd seen earlier on Lucy's desk to mark my way on the tunnel walls. I also took Edeline's heavy coat and threw it over my tunic. The only armor I carried was my sword, which I hoped I wouldn't have to use.

"I knew you'd try this again."

I jumped as I turned to find Ash staring at me from the other side of the kitchen.

"I have to go."

"You promised me that you'd always tell me. I don't want you getting lost in the mountains again. You know I'm coming with you, right?"

"That's why I didn't tell you. I knew you'd want to come and I didn't want to put you in the position of choosing between me and your family."

"Isn't that the choice you have to make?" Ash arched his eyebrow at me. "Julianna, we're a team. We're in this together. There are going to be difficult decisions that we will face, but if we don't confide in one another, we'll have to do it alone. Now go back upstairs."

"Go upstairs? I'm not going back to bed." I stomped my foot in agitation.

"And I'm not asking you to. We're going to fly and

the best place to take off from is the balcony outside of your room."

With a nod, I turned and once again tiptoed through the house. He was right of course. The balcony was the perfect place to fly from. Ash quickly shifted into his mighty red dragon and I jumped onto his back as he spread his wings and we took to the sky. It was so much nicer flying up the mountain as opposed to walking up the stone steps in a storm. The evening was calm and quiet, quite the opposite of how I felt. Normally I'd enjoy the feeling of weightlessness as we soared through the air, but my stomach churned as I thought about what I'd have to face in Drionos.

Last time we were both there, my family hadn't given me the chance to explain. They'd taken one look at Ash and attacked. Having him with me again might not be the best idea, but this time I would make them listen to us. I wondered just how badly our house had been burned, if they had somehow managed to control the flames or if it had burned down completely. Just thinking about it brought tears to my eyes.

We flew over the peak of the mountain, this time not bothering with any tunnels. It was a clear night with a bright moon. The mountains looked stunning bathed in pale moonlight, but I couldn't focus my attention on them too long. I wanted to see what had happened to my house. I strained my eyes into the distance, trying to see if it was still standing, but it was only when we came to land in the village that I finally saw the extent of the devastation. I threw Ash's clothes at him and waited for him to transform. We'd landed on the path at the edge of the village and my house, or what was left of it, was nothing but a silhouette in the distance. I could see enough to know that no one could possibly be living there anymore.

"It's gone," I said when Ash was back in his human form.

"It's too far away to know that. There is still a building there. Maybe it isn't as bad as you think."

I set off up the path at a brisk pace, hopeful that Ash could see something that I was missing and not just the burned shell that used to be my home. He did have much better eyesight than I did, especially in the dark.

As we got closer, it became obvious that I was right and that Ash was wrong. There wasn't a building there, just a blackened frame where there used to be one.

"I'm sorry," Ash whispered, pulling me into a hug. His wide arms comforted me. "It was the barn I saw back there, not the house. I confused the two."

I looked over to the barn. Thankfully it was far enough away from the house to not have sustained any damage.

Fear enveloped me and my breathing became ragged. I'd been trying so hard not to cry that I was over-come by a panic attack instead. I tried to regulate my breathing and get it down to a normal speed.

"Julianna," Ash spoke calmly and quietly. "We'll find them. You saw yourself that they escaped. Wherever they are, they're safe."

I nodded. He was right. I'd seen them all leave the burning building, but where were they now? I didn't know where to begin to look.

"Who's that?" a voice shouted, making me jump. "I

can hear you whispering, so don't try to pretend you're not there."

I looked over to see Jasper with a lantern. He'd obviously come from the barn. So that's where they were living. I felt a little relieved. The barn was safe and warm and would be cozy with all the hay.

"Jasper, it's me." I moved into the light, pulling Ash with me.

His eyes grew wide and his hand automatically went to his side where he usually kept his sword in a sheath, except he wasn't wearing it. By the way he was dressed, I guessed we had woken him up.

"I don't want to fight you," I said, taking a step toward him with my hands held in front of me.

He stepped back toward the barn door.

"Father!" he shouted, not taking his eyes from us. My father's bulky frame appeared at the door.

"What is it?"

"I told you it wasn't dogs. It's her...with him." He spat the last word out.

"Julianna?" My mother's hopeful voice sounded out and before either Jasper or my father could react, she ran over to me, her arms outstretched.

She was so tiny compared to me and yet I felt so safe in her arms. We both burst into tears as she hugged me tightly.

"Julianna, who is this and why have you brought him here again? Didn't he cause enough damage the last time?" My father sneered.

"Stay back, Elgin," my mother shouted. "This is our little girl, remember? Not one of your dragons. Don't even think about getting your sword out."

I'd never heard her stand up to my father before and I wasn't sure who was more surprised, me or my father.

"You'd better come in and you can bring your...friend."

"Thanks, Mom."

They'd done a good job with the barn. Someone had given them blankets which they'd laid on the hay for beds and seating. A couple of lanterns lit up the place, making it feel warm although I couldn't help thinking it was another fire waiting to happen.

I sat on a bale of hay with Ash beside me. My family sat opposite us. Jasper had a sullen look about him.

"Come back to do more damage, have you?" he asked, looking straight at Ash. "Or are you just here to kidnap someone else?"

"I wasn't kidnapped!" I replied.

"Of course you weren't. I can see that," said my mother before turning to Jasper. "And any more silly remarks like that and you can sleep outside."

Jasper pouted and folded his arms.

"Can you tell us what did happen to you? I've been worried sick."

My heart went out to my mother. I could see the worry lines etched onto her face and I hated that it was because of me that they were there.

"When Papa and Jasper last saw me on the hunting trip, I fell and Ash caught me. He wasn't kidnapping me. He was saving me."

"That's a lie. She was taken by a dragon. I saw it carry her off. This guy must have killed the dragon and then kidnapped her," said Jasper, not heeding my mother's warning.

"Ash didn't kill the dragon." I entwined my hands in his. I needed his strength now with what I was about to say. "Ash is the dragon."

I proceeded to tell them about Frokontas and the dragon shifter community there. My mother listened intently, although I could see the shock on her face. Even Jasper had been rendered mute with the revelation.

"I tried telling you all this before when I came down the mountain, but—"

Jasper sneered. "But you attacked me with your sword and set fire to the house instead."

"Jasper, I'm warning you!" My mother gave him a look of disgust.

"You attacked me if you remember, but that's another thing. The fire started when the dragon enslaved in the sword escaped. When you nicked my arm, Papa, my blood set off a magical reaction in the sword, allowing the soul of the dragon inside it to be free. It was not the fault of the dragon, but of the magic. This reaction was so fierce and full of energy that it sparked, setting the house on fire."

"That's preposterous," replied Jasper. "How do you even know that? It sounds made up."

"I know because I've spoken to that dragon. That dragon is Ash's father. His soul has been trapped in that sword since you slay it. When he was released, his soul went back to his body. There's a place somewhere in the forest where the soulless dragons lie. You didn't kill a dragon on your birthday. No one has killed a dragon. Instead, their souls are captured and taken into the swords to make them stronger."

"We've always known the dragons' souls end up in our swords, that doesn't mean they aren't dead." Jasper's eyes narrowed in a mixture of confusion and anger.

"They aren't dead. Ash's dad saw them. He says it's like they are asleep. What we're doing is barbaric and needs to be stopped. I've come today to ask you for your swords. We need to free the dragons because they're people, not animals for slaughter."

"Oh, my!" My mother put her head in her hands.

"What you're saying makes no sense. If we have their souls, why keep them alive?" Jasper shook his head, still not believing me.

"I don't know. Maybe they have to be alive somewhere to make the magic work."

"You aren't having my sword," Jasper said stubbornly. "If what you say is true, which I sorely doubt, then it's empty anyway."

"How can you doubt it? Surely you've felt the loss of power from it since the night the house burned down. You must have wondered why."

"I've not used it since then. I was waiting for you to bring this guy back so I could use it on him."

"Jasper, I've had enough. If you can't be civil, you can sleep outside with the cattle."

Jasper scowled, but he didn't dare disobey our mother. He picked up his sword and left, slamming the barn door behind him.

"Papa," I turned to my father, who hadn't said a word. "You are the greatest slayer in the village. I'm not going to ask if you know anything about the dragons being kept alive, because how could you not know, but I know you wouldn't have done this if you knew that the dragons were people. I need your sword. I need to set them free. Will you please give it to me?"

He stood and picked up his sword. "I love you my daughter, but I cannot give you my sword."

"Why ever not?" my mother asked. "She's told you why she needs it. I can't bear the thought of all those people trapped in there. We need to let them out."

"I captured those souls fair and square. They belong to me."

"But they're people!"

"I know they're people. I've always known they were people."

"You knew?" I asked my father, barely believing what he was telling me.

"Of course I knew. Just because they are people doesn't mean they aren't a nuisance. They're still drag-ons, too, and dragons kill people."

"No, they don't! When was the last time you remember a slayer being killed by a dragon from the Triad Mountains?"

"There have been times."

"Not many, and only then because we were tram-pling around up there waving our swords around. If they killed, it was only in self-defense."

"Enough!" shouted my father. "We have worked hard to keep this village safe from those dragons and this is how you repay me? By coming here and telling me to give up my sword? If you want my sword, you will have to fight me for it!" He growled and pierced Ash with his heated gaze.

24

I looked up at my father, barely able to comprehend what I was hearing. He was the one man I'd looked up to my whole life, my hero who'd always taught me right from wrong, and now he was telling me that he'd always known about the dragons. He was a murderer.

He stood so much taller than me, holding his sword by his side. He wasn't standing to fight, but I knew just by looking into his fierce brown eyes that if I drew my own sword, he would raise his. I couldn't beat him. He was the best slayer in the village. But even if I could, would I really have the courage to hold a sword up to my father? Probably not.

We stared at each other, unmoving, for what felt like a lifetime, neither of us backing down and neither of us starting the fight. Uncertainty coursed through me, rendering me unable to make a decision. I was saved by having to do just that by a loud noise and a flash like lightning from outside.

"Dragons!" Jasper came running in. "There are loads of them."

The light I saw must have been one of them shooting fire.

"What have you done? The dragons have never come into the village before. This is all your fault." My father glared at me as if I was a disgrace. If he'd ever looked at me in this manner before, I would have been devastated, but now I didn't care.

I looked him square in the eye. "This is not my fault. The fault rests solely on your shoulders and the other village elders for murdering innocent people. If they have decided to fight back now, then you only have yourselves to blame. Come on, Ash, we have some swords to get."

I ran outside with Ash beside me, leaving my parents behind. The scene we ran into was absolute chaos. Dragons flew overhead, lighting up the night with bursts of fire. The other villagers had heard the noise and were pouring out of their homes to fight. Some were dressed, but most were fighting in their nightwear. There were people everywhere. I saw Ally in his human form engaged in a sword fight with Wolfin, one of my father's best friends. Just behind them, Marcus chased one of the dragons. I could tell by the way it held its wing that it had hurt itself and could no longer fly.

Someone screamed and I saw the faces of two of the village children peering out of a window, watching as their father fought with someone I recognized from Spear's house. Spear himself was nowhere to be seen, but I knew he'd be nearby.

"Some of them have changed into human form," I shouted to Ash as he pulled me through the warring groups, trying to get me to safety.

"They would need to, to get into people's houses to retrieve the swords. I guess this is what they planned once we left."

None of this looked planned. People screamed in pain and bodies littered the ground. Thankfully, no one looked dead. The people I saw on the ground were still moving, but the peaceful raid I'd hoped for was not happening. There was blood everywhere.

Another burst of fire lit up the sky close to where one of the slayers lay prostrate on the ground. I noticed that the dragon missed by a good ten feet. For a second I wondered why, but then realized that he was only using fire for light. Not one of the slayers was burned. It was somewhat a relief, but not using fire in battle would put the dragons at a major disadvantage. It was one of the only weapons they possessed. A dragon in human form swooped in on the back of another dragon. As they passed the man on the ground, the human dragon leaned down and grabbed his sword before flying back into the sky.

I ran to the man. I recognized him as Ben, one of my childhood friends.

"Are you okay?" I asked, kneeling beside him. I couldn't see any blood but his face was contorted in pain.

"I stumbled," he said. "I think I twisted my ankle."

His ankle was already beginning to swell. I turned to Ash. "We need to move him. He's too exposed here."

Ben looked confused as Ash came forward. He obviously didn't realize that Ash was a dragon shifter, but we didn't get many visitors to Dronios. He didn't say anything though, as between us, we managed to get Ben out of harm's way. We dragged him into the first market on the strip.

"You should be OK here," I said, setting him down on a sack of flour. Behind me through the shop window, the sky lit up once again.

"Do you know what's going on?" Ben asked. "There are some humans out there with the dragons. If your friend wasn't with you, I'd have thought he was with them too."

At least it proved that there were more of the villagers that didn't know that the dragons were shifters.

Another scream came from outside.

"Julianna, we need to get out of here."

I turned back to Ben. "No time to explain, but I promise I'll come back when I can and tell everyone everything. Just do me a favor. When this is over, don't listen to my father or the other elders. They've been lying to us for years."

I didn't wait for him to question me further; instead, I took Ash's hand and we ventured back out into the night.

"What now?" I asked. The battle was still going strong, but I wasn't sure what I could do to help. Dragons were battling slayers everywhere I looked, some in their human form with swords and some in their dragon form.

"I think we need to get out of here," replied Ash. "Spear has this under control and us being here is not helping anyone. We're just in the way."

If this was in control, I'd hate to see confusion.

"We can't leave!" I dug my feet into the hard ground, pulling Ash to a stop.

"What do you suggest we do? Fight the dragons or fight the slayers? Because at the moment, I don't see any other option."

He had a point. Fighting on one side would mean hurting the other, and I didn't want anyone hurt. I'd never felt so utterly useless. Running away felt like a betrayal on both sides.

A war cry pierced the air. Out of the darkness, someone came running toward us, sword aloft. Whether it was a dragon coming for me or a slayer coming for Ash, it was too dark to tell. I hesitated. Ash, on the other hand, was ready. He pulled my sword from its sheath and deflected the opposing blade just as it came crashing down, missing me by only an inch. The assailant thrust again, this time going for Ash. I stepped back as the pair fought in the darkness. I could barely see them, although every couple of seconds a burst of light showed me how they were both faring. They were pretty evenly matched. The slayer, and that's what I knew him to be now, was a middle-aged guy from my village, and the best swordsman, but Ash had the advantage of being able to see much better in the dark.

Nerves congregated in my stomach as I watched the fight. I couldn't bear the thought of either of them getting hurt, but I didn't see any other outcome. I didn't know the slayer well, but I knew he was one of the men that regularly went up the mountain. There was no way he would ever back down. I was grateful for the darkness, for without it, Ash would surely be dead by now.

An idea came to me. I ran behind the slayer, praying that no dragon would choose this moment to let out its fiery breath. It would be a disaster if he saw me.

I couldn't see Ash, but I knew he'd be able to see me. I signaled from behind the slayer's back, pointing at his sword and making a motion that Ash should take it. Then I jumped onto the man's back. The shock of someone behind him was enough for him to loosen his grip and for Ash to grab the sword out of his hand. I tried to jump down to run away, but the slayer had already reached over his shoulder and grabbed me by the tunic. I attempted to struggle free, but it was no use. He was much stronger than me. I watched as his other arm came crashing down on me. I cried out as pain shot through my shoulder. I hit him on the head, but it was like a mouse hitting an elephant—I doubt if he even felt it.

A burst of fire illuminated Ash coming towards the man, ready to plunge a sword into him.

"Ash, no!" I shouted. I couldn't let Ash become a murderer for me. I clamped my teeth down hard on the slayer's ear. With a scream, he released me. Ash grabbed my arm and we both ran for our lives toward the path that would lead us out of the village. When the screams and fire were behind us, I let go of Ash's hand so he could change into a dragon.

It was quieter now. I wasn't sure if that was a good or bad sign, but at least the screaming had stopped. Despite all the fire, none of the buildings had burned. Spear had made a mess of this, but he'd kept to his word that they'd try not to hurt anyone. I'd only seen the dragons defending themselves. If they'd used fire for more than the purpose of light, they could have destroyed the village and everyone in it without having to land. It would have been easy to pick through the ashes of the burned down village later for the swords, but doing that would mean the deaths of many, if not all, of the villagers.

They hadn't done that. Of course, it didn't mean no one had been hurt. I'd seen enough to know that there were many injured. I only hoped no one was killed. The dawn was coming and I could see the village better now. Some people were still fighting, but it looked like most of the dragons had left. As I watched, one stretched out its wings and took off into the sky.

"Uh, Julianna," Ash called. I turned to find out why he hadn't changed yet to find his hands in the air and a sword to his throat.

"Jasper!" I cried, seeing who it was that held the sword. "What are you doing?"

"Is it true?"

"Yes. It's true. I've been living among the dragons for the last week. They don't want to hurt anyone."

"They've got a funny way of showing it." Jasper laughed, but it was joyless.

"Look around you. If they wanted to kill anyone, they would have done it. How easy would it be for them to breathe fire and decimate the whole village? They could have done it without even landing, and yet they chose not to. They only want their families back. All those men and women we caught and imprisoned."

Jasper scowled.

"We're the bad guys here," I continued. "We've hunted innocent people for centuries. The dragons have done nothing as we took their people, and yet it is only now that they know that the dragons are only imprisoned and not dead, and now they are doing something about it. Ask yourself why."

"Why should I believe you? You've been with them long enough for them to have brainwashed you. You could be planning to come back and murder us all in our beds for all I know."

"You and I have never gotten along very well, and for that I'm sorry. If you don't want to believe me, that's up to you, but I'm asking that you let us go. Papa admitted that he knew about the dragons being shifters right after you left the barn. Maybe you should go talk to him."

I could see he was struggling with what I was telling him, and I couldn't blame him. I could scarcely believe it myself.

"You're lying, you have to be lying." I could see the tears in his eyes and my heart went out to him. I'd just told him that his own father was a murderer. That *he* was a murderer.

"Papa isn't the only one. I think all the elders know. That's why I'm here—to stop a great injustice that our people have been perpetuating for centuries. Ash's own father was taken by us, and yet not once did he choose to come here and exact revenge. He wants peace as much as I do. You have the choice now. You can be one of them—a coward who lies and murders because of some century-old grievance—or you can do what's right and be on the side of peace."

I held my breath, waiting for him to make his decision, a decision that could mean Ash's death.

Slowly, he lowered his sword to the ground and I exhaled.

"You made the right decision."

His voice wobbled. "I hope for your sake that you're telling the truth because if I find out you are lying to me, I will hunt you both down and plunge this sword into both of your hearts."

"They are telling the truth, Jasper."

I looked around to find my mother standing beside us. She looked exhausted. Her clothes were dirty and ripped and her hair was wild, but she looked unhurt.

"I think you should have this." She handed her sword to me. I tucked it into my belt with mine and the one we had taken from the slayer.

"Thank you."

"It only has one soul in it and it might be no use. You remember the story I told you on your birthday? The dragon was already hurt when I plunged the sword into him. He might have already been dead by the time I did it."

"I appreciate you doing this for us," said Ash. "I want you to know that Julianna did not want any of this."

"I never knew. I wouldn't have let it happen if I had. I want you to know that."

"I know, Mama." I hugged her tightly, tears coursing down both our cheeks.

"Please promise me something," she said as I let her go. "Tell him or her that I'm truly sorry." She nodded at the sword and I knew she was talking about the dragon whose soul was trapped inside.

"I will." I gave her a final kiss on the cheek as Ash

turned back into his dragon form. I hopped onto his back and waved as we took off.

As the ground got further and further away, I scanned the village for any dragons. Most had left, but I could see the bodies of three left behind. There was nothing I could do for them now—we had to leave them. I held safe the knowledge that if they had been stabbed by the slayers, at least they wouldn't be dead, only appear that way. Their souls would become imprisoned within the swords, but I knew I was going to come back again and next time, we'd save them all.

25

The early morning sun cast a pink glow on the Triad mountains making them look spectacular as we flew over them.

A thousand emotions coursed through me as we crested the peak near Frokontas. Guilt about my people, fear of what we would find when we got back to Ash's village. Most of all, I was sad. Sad and utterly exhausted. I yawned as Ash flew lower over the other side of the mountain.

The plan had been to land in the village square, but as we flew over the fire pit by Ash's house, it became apparent that everyone had chosen to land there. Below us was a hive of activity. It looked like the whole town had come out to find out what had happened. Ash circled around a couple of times before landing.

Someone threw him some clothes, so I ran towards Edeline while Ash changed. She was busy bandaging the arm of one of the people who had gone to the village. All around me was chaos—people hurt and bleeding. Someone was shouting, another crying.

"Edeline, what happened?"

"I was going to ask you the same question. Is Ash with you?" Her face held an expression of worry.

"Yeah, he's safe. He's just getting changed. It was a disaster down there. Spear's group managed to wake the whole village. Do you know where he is?"

If anyone knew what had happened, Spear would be it.

Edeline nodded into the crowd. "Last I saw, he was having his foot seen to over there. Just to warn you, he's pretty mad."

He was pretty mad? I was fuming! I found him deep in conversation with another dragon. His right foot was bandaged and I could see he was putting most of his weight on his left.

I butted in, not caring how rude I looked.

"What happened? Wasn't this supposed to be a stealth attack? Do you need me to buy you a dictionary so you understand what stealth means? You couldn't have been noisier if you tried."

"Stop shouting. Come with me." He grabbed me by the arm and took me away from everyone else, to the base of the cliff.

"We did go in silently, but someone saw us. It only took that one person to raise the alarm. You should be happy I kept to my side of the bargain."

"What?" Was he kidding?

"None of your people were killed. Just before you rudely butted in, I was talking to Keth. He was the last one to leave the village, just after you. He confirmed that none of your people died. Those that were hurt were only superficially so. They will all live to see another day. Something that can't be said for us. Three of my team were killed." He held up three fingers. "Count 'em. Three! Three dead dragons and you can see the injured." He motioned to the people around the fire pit. It looked like most of those that went down to my village had been hurt in one way or another.

"Oh."

"Oh?" he growled. "Is that all you have to say?"

"Okay, I'm sorry. Thank you. Who...?"

"Ally, Gem and Fiona."

I didn't know Gem or Fiona, but the thought of Ally being hurt was bittersweet. Of course, I didn't want him hurt, but with some luck, the same slayer that pierced him was the one who had captured Stone. There was a possibility that they were reunited.

"They aren't really dead, though, are they?"

"Oh, well that's okay then," Spear responded with ill-disguised sarcasm.

"You know what I mean. We can get them back. We can get them all back. We just need to find where the bodies are being kept."

"We?" He raised his eyebrow.

"Yes, we! You were right all along. My father knew. He's always known. My whole life has been a lie. Some of the others know too, but not all. I think it's only the village elders. My mother and brother knew nothing about it."

Something else occurred to me then. That's what the eighteenth birthday tradition of killing dragons was all about. It was not just a rite of passage, but also a way to find out who was safe to tell the secret to. Those that killed the dragons willingly joined the hunting group. It was those slayers who would eventually be told about the dragons being shifters. The ones who were blood-thirsty and after years of killing, lacking empathy for the lives of dragons. They were the ones who would be brought into the inner circle. Jasper might not have known the truth yet, but there was no doubt in my mind that he would eventually have found out.

"That's all well and good, but your map was next to useless. After all that, we only managed to recover three swords."

"Four!" I drew my mother's sword from my belt and threw it to him. "This was my mother's. It only holds one dragon, but one dragon is better than none, right?"

"If you think this changes anything, you're wrong. You need to go back to Dronios where you belong."

"No!" I replied forcefully. "You're wrong. I don't belong there. Not anymore. I can do more good here than I can back home. Let me stay. There's so much I can do."

"What can you do?" he spat.

"Pass me my mother's sword back."

"Why?"

"What's happening here?" Ash put his arm around my shoulder.

"Your girlfriend was leaving. Ash, Take her home."

"I wasn't leaving. I was just going to tell Spear that I was going to let him use my blood to release the dragons."

Spear regarded me curiously. "You'd do that?"

"Of course I would. I'm not a slayer anymore." I took

a deep breath. "My father was a hero in my mind. Last night I found out he was a murderer. I'm not like him. Most of the villagers in Dronios aren't. Last night, they were defending themselves from an enemy. You have to know that. They need to know the truth and you need me for that. Setting the dragons free will mean nothing if the slayers carry on doing what they're doing. I only have so much blood to release them. Who are you going to use to free them once all my blood is spent?"

"There will be others," Spear stated confidently.

"Other slayers that give up their blood willingly?" I shook my head at the thought.

"Who said it has to be given willingly?" Spear countered.

"What are you saying, Spear?" Ash's arm tightened around me.

"That's not who you are," I said. "The dragons have always been peaceful. This needs to end for good. Peace needs to reign on both sides. We need to educate both sides. It's going to take a lot of work, but we can do it. Together."

"She has a point, Spear," interjected Ash. "This is what I've been saying all along. The people of Dronios are not going to listen to us, but they might listen to her. Without Julianna, we have nothing."

"If she does what she says she will."

The time for words was over. Now was the time for action. I lunged forward and took my mother's sword from Spear. Before he had the chance to stop me, I ran the blade down the palm of my hand. The cut was small, but it was enough. A burst of flame shot out of the end of the sword, sending us all flying backward.

The flames swirled into the air, taking on the appearance of a dragon completely made of flames. It spread its wings and flew into the sky. At the very top of the cliff, the flames rearranged themselves and turned into a howling tornado of bright orange fire. Then it disappeared over the top of the cliff.

I picked myself up from the floor where I'd fallen from the intensity of the blast and dusted myself off. One look at Spear's face was enough to tell me that he hadn't expected it to work. His mouth formed a perfect O and he was filthy with dirt from falling to the ground.

Silence rained down on us. I looked over to the others. They might not have seen how it happened, but there was no missing the escaped soul of the dragon. The gaze of the people lowered until a hundred eyes were on me.

"That's right!" I shouted loud enough for them all to hear. "You saw a dragon being freed. I used my own blood." I held aloft my hand to show them the cut I'd made with the sword.

"I've got an apology to make to you all. My father knew all along you were shifters. He's not the only one. There are others. I've never been so angry in my whole life, but this must stop. I'm going to stand with you if you'll let me, and fight this abomination. I'm going to save them all. We are going to save them all. I will not rest until every single dragon is freed."

A couple people began to clap. Then another, then another, until the air was filled with the sound of applause.

"It's not going to be easy," I said when the clapping died down. "What you just saw was the soul of one of your people. That soul is now heading back to the body it came from. That person is going to wake up scared and confused. They're going to be so weak that it will be difficult for them to escape. Fiere flew out from the prison, but I think we can assume that now the elders of Dronios know that we are freeing dragons, they will lock the bodies up more securely and make it impossible to just fly out. The good news is, there are a lot more of us than there are of them, and when the rest of the people in my village know the truth, there will be even more people on our side. Not everyone will believe us and of those that do, some may choose to fight with the elders. It's up to us to convince as many as possible to fight for what is fair and what is right. We need to go back to the village as soon as possible, before they have time to regroup and tell more lies. We need to find where the bodies of the other dragons are kept and free them."

"That could take days," shouted someone.

"Actually, that's going to be the easy part. We have three more swords with dragons trapped inside. You saw yourselves that the souls take the form of fire when outside the body. All we need to do it set one free and be ready to follow it. It will lead us back to the prison. You guys can fly so it should be easy. More than one dragon should go because, after last night, it will be heavily guarded. The biggest problem we face is getting the swords. Look at how many of you were injured and we only got four of them. We need to come up with a better plan."

I looked to where Spear was just pulling himself up from the ground.

"I'm going to be working closely with Spear. Today

we will come up with a better plan and this time, I'm going to be more involved." I emphasized the "this time." "Tonight, we go down to the village again and get the swords back. It's going to take more of you than before. I know many of you are not hunters or fighters, but the ten that went there last night wasn't enough. Everyone over eighteen and fit needs to go. We need to swamp them so there is no point in fighting. This has got to end tonight!"

I felt a hand on my shoulder. I turned, expecting to see Ash, but it was Spear. He had a look of grim determination on his face.

"I admit to being wary of Julianna since she first set foot in the village. Why would a slayer help us? But now I see the truth. It takes a great deal of strength and courage to sacrifice yourself for someone else, but it takes a whole lot more courage to stand up to your family. I need those of you who were out last night to rest. The rest of you, be prepared to save our ancestors. We're going in tonight! Who is with us?"

Some of the dragons cheered. Some, like Edeline, looked stunned. But they all raised their hands.

My hand instinctively found the hilt of my sword, like a moth to a flame. The sword that started it all. How quickly my life had changed. Just a few days ago I held this sword with the promise of slaying my first dragon, and today I held it as a promise to save the dragons.

The goblin-made gold held strong as my fingers wrapped around the intricate detail of the handle. With a clean whoosh, I unsheathed my sword and held it out front of me. The rising sun glinted off the blade as the cheers of the dragons met my ears once again.

Tonight, I would make right all the wrong my ancestors caused. Tonight, I would stand with the dragons and bring their families home.

Grab book 2 in the Dragon Tamer series TODAY:
https://books2read.com/dragontamerbook2

WARRIOR

DRAGON TAMER BOOK 2

WARRIOR

1

The early morning sun bathed the fields in a warm glow, painting the scenery in warm hues of pink and orange. In any other situation, I would have been happy to sit out in the fields, aimlessly watching the day go by. But today was no ordinary day and the beautiful view of summer fields in front of me was only part of the vista, for in front of them were hundreds of dragons. Dragon shifters to be precise. Each milling around, absorbed in their own task. Some were healing the battle wounded, some were sharpening swords and one was silently wrapping up my arm in a bandage where I'd purposely cut it just ten minutes previously. That one was Ash, the dragon shifter who'd been by my side right from the start of all of this mess we were currently in. I'd had to cut my arm so my blood could free a dragon from a sword. My blood, it seemed, was the key to their freedom. I looked down to the ground beside me. Three more swords lay waiting, the souls of dragons trapped inside. Next to them was the empty one. Just looking at it, you could tell it was now free of a dragon soul. It was black and tarnished and looked sad next to its gleaming brothers.

"No," said Ash firmly. It was the first word he'd said in the last twenty minutes.

"No what?" I asked.

"I saw what you were looking at. They can wait. You are exhausted. You need your blood more than they do at the moment."

He was right. I was exhausted. I couldn't remember the last time I'd had a good night's sleep. It certainly wasn't last night as I'd been down in Dronias, the Slayer village and my former home, fighting to get these swords. I yawned as if proving his point.

"I was just looking at them," I said, trying to suppress another yawn.

"Hmmm," he replied, obviously not believing me. "You need to sleep. I'm taking you home for some rest."

"No!" I said, standing up. The end of the bandage he'd not quite fastened hung loose and the whole thing began to unravel. "Spear is planning another attack on my village and he needs me there!"

Yesterday, he didn't want me to have anything to do with going into Dronias, but after last night, he conceded that I was on the dragon's side. Without me helping to plan, it could all go terribly wrong, just as it had done already.

"Will you sit still?" He pulled me back into a sitting position so that he could once again tighten my bandage. "I've spoken to Spear. He agrees that everyone who was out fighting last night should take the morning to sleep. There is no point in us all going down there again when we are too tired to fight. We are to meet him after lunch at his house."

"Oh." I could feel my heavy eyes begin to close. Spending the morning in bed might have seemed wasteful but the thought of it was very welcome.

I was so sleepy I didn't notice Ash had finished wrapping my arm, nor did I notice him carrying me to his house and laying me on my bed. He must have, though, because four hours later I woke up there with his arm wrapped around me. I turned my head to look at him. He was beautiful in sleep. Okay, he was beautiful awake, but somehow, in sleep, he looked serene, calm, as if all the worry and stress he'd been carrying around for the past few weeks was gone. He was breathing heavily. Not quite snoring, but there was a light grumble in the back of his throat. Outside the window, I could hear the sounds of people, still busy doing whatever it was they had to do, and I could smell meat of some kind roasting on the big, open fire they had. My mouth watered, but looking at Ash overcame any sense of hunger. I ignored the rumble in my belly and just looked at him. I wanted to kiss him so badly, but I didn't want to wake him. I settled for kissing his lips delicately, but despite my light touch, his eyes opened. His face cracked into a huge grin.

"Morning." He whispered through his grin.

"Morning? I think we are past that. I can smell lunch."

"What is it?" He gave a tentative sniff. "Mmm. Barbecue."

"Shall we go get some?"

"I'd rather stay here with you." He put his other arm

around me and pulled me closer. My head nuzzled his shoulder.

"Me too, but we have to eat. You have to keep your strength up if you want to shift into a dragon, and I need to eat red meat if I'm going to be using my blood to free the other dragon souls."

"You're right. You get up first," Ash said playfully.

His body heat was calming, and I felt warm and safe up against him, my head on his chest. I didn't want to move.

"No, you first!" There was no way I was going to be able to get up with him still keeping the bed warm.

"I would, but there is a gorgeous, red-haired woman currently laying on me. I'm afraid I'm pinned down and can't move."

"I'm hardly laying all over you. Just my head!" I grinned.

"And your arm."

"Okay, and my arm," I conceded.

It took another ten minutes for us to untangle ourselves and get up the motivation to leave the bed. It helped that Ash's little sister, Lucy, knocked on my door to tell me that lunch was ready.

The meat had already been served and placed on plates by the time we got down to the fire pit. Most of the others were already tucking into their food with relish. As well as the meat, which, judging by the charred carcass still smoldering on the fire, was beef, we also had fresh bread and a heap of fresh vegetables.

For the first time since being in Frokontas, I felt accepted. Some had accepted me from the start, but it took me drawing my own blood this morning for some of them to truly believe in me. The atmosphere was strange. It was one of both happiness and sadness. Happiness that we had found some swords, and sadness that there were so many yet to recover and many of the dragon souls were still trapped.

"I don't see Spear," I whispered to Ash.

"He'll be eating up at his home."

In the twenty minutes it took me to eat the meal, I had at least ten people come up and talk to me and every one of them was positive. Mostly they wanted to thank me for helping them. Even the ones who had previously shunned me were offering me more food. If it wasn't for the impending fight tonight, I could almost feel happy.

"What's it like being a great warrior?" asked Lucy after coming to sit beside me.

"I'm not a great warrior. Spear is a great warrior. Why don't you ask him when you see him?"

She wrinkled up her nose. "Spear is a boy. I don't want to be like him when I grow up. I want to be like you."

I couldn't help but smile at her.

"If I was such a great warrior, your brother would have his soul trapped in my sword now and I wouldn't be sitting here with you having this conversation. I'm actually a pretty terrible warrior. I just have a cool sword. You know, there is a great female warrior. Her name is Morganna. She is a Slayer like me."

"She kills dragons?" Lucy looked at me wide-eyed.

"No. She kills men. There is not one man that has gone up against her and survived. For a long time, I wanted to be like her. Her skill with a sword is legendary."

"But now you don't?"

"No. Now I have no desire to kill anyone or anything. Up until I came here, I thought I was a dragon Slayer, but being here has taught me that you can't just go around killing people or creatures without knowing who or what they really are. You've got to remember, I didn't know you were people, too. I thought you were just dragons."

"Just dragons?" teased Ash, eavesdropping into the conversation.

"You know what I mean," I said with a shrug.

"But I want a sword and to be like Morganna!" replied Lucy.

"I think you'll make a great hunter one day as long as you only kill for food and not out of anger or tradition."

"You think so?" Lucy clapped her hands together in excitement before running off to speak to her father.

"You've made her day," said Ash, finishing the last of his food.

"I just don't want her growing up thinking it's okay to kill like I did."

"She won't. She's just a little kid with a new hero. Come on. I think it's about time we headed to Spear's. He'll be waiting for us."

Spear's house was a twenty-minute walk along a dirt path with fields of crops at each side. We skirted around the main part of the village until we saw his house in the distance. It was huge and white and looked stunning in contrast to the golden fields surrounding it.

"Ah, you're here. Wonderful. The others just arrived." Spear answered the door himself. Last time it had been his maid that had answered. "Would you like tea? Coffee?"

"Coffee would be lovely, thanks," I replied and Ash agreed.

Spear clicked his fingers and the maid I'd seen last time I was at the house appeared. "We are all here now. Can you bring the coffee and tea into the parlor, please? Enough for ten people each."

She nodded her head and left through the same door she'd come through.

We followed Spear from the large entrance hall into the parlor where the others were seated. I'd been in this room before. The last time, I'd been asked to leave. It wasn't going to happen again.

I found a spare seat and Ash sat beside me. There were about twenty people in the room including Ash and me. Most of them had been with us in Dronias last night, but there were a few newbies too.

"Last night was a disaster, as I'm sure you'll all agree. I take full responsibility. Tonight will be different. Most of us here know what the village looks like now. We know where the houses are and hopefully, this map we looked at yesterday will make more sense to you."

He pulled out the crude map I'd drawn for him the day before.

"Out of thirty-three swords, we managed to retrieve four. It wasn't a good start, but at least we can cross those off the map. Julianna, you know better than the rest of us. Can you do it please?"

As I'd already marked the houses with swords using

crosses, I took a red pen and scribbled over the ones I knew we had retrieved. I'd not seen exactly who all the swords were taken from, but I recognized them easily enough, so being able to place them wasn't too difficult.

"This is my house." I began, pointing to the map. "You'd have seen it as a burnt-out mess. There are no swords there, but there are two in the barn behind. One belongs to my brother, Jasper. It is empty now and therefore worthless to us. It was the sword that held Fiere.

"There is another sword there, but my father will not release it easily and let me warn you all, he is an excellent Slayer. The best in the village. His sword holds a lot of souls, which makes it extremely strong. The Goblin magic imbued in it gets stronger with every soul, and he has taken many. Of all the swords in the village, I suspect this will be the most difficult to get. He will be on guard, too. The whole village will. They know that we were there last night and they know we are after swords. I'm going to say what I said before. I don't want anyone getting killed or hurt, but I think it's inevitable that we will have to be ready to fight. We also have to free the dragons from the three swords we have, and one person has to be in charge of following that soul until we find where the soulless dragons are being held."

"You should be that person," interrupted Spear.

"Why?"

"Because of all of us here, you have more at stake. We can fight for the swords, but I wouldn't want you to be in a position where you have to fight your own family or a friend."

I thought about it for a second and agreed. I couldn't

imagine having to have a sword fight with anyone I knew and loved.

"Okay, Ash will fly me down to the village just after I free the dragons from the swords. We'll set off about ten minutes after the rest of you so that we can follow the souls without distraction. Hopefully, the Slayers will be too busy with you to notice us, too."

The maid interrupted me by bringing in a large tray. On it were twenty cups, a jug of coffee, a large pot of tea, milk, sugar and a plate of cookies.

Once everyone had a cup, Spear got back to the map and making a plan for the raid into Dronias. For four hours we planned. I drew on the map, and we discussed who would do what. I wasn't naive enough to think that one of my people wouldn't get injured, but I said a silent prayer as Ash and I watched the others transform into dragons at twilight in preparation to fly to Dronias. Our part of the plan was simple. We would take the three swords up the cliff and through the tunnels there until we reached the platform. There, I would cut my skin with all three swords which would free the dragons. I'd then have to jump on Ash's back quickly and follow the fiery trails the souls made.

It all seemed simple enough, but as I watched the other dragons take off, I knew it wasn't going to be easy at all. It was probably going to be the hardest night of my life.

2

The sun was just setting on the horizon. It would be almost completely dark by the time we got to Dronias. It was hard to imagine that we were setting off from the same place just twenty-four hours ago. And in those hours, I'd learned that my whole life was a lie.

"You are going to have to let the dragons free once I'm changed, so please don't injure yourself too much because I won't be able to help you."

"I'll just make a small cut. I'll be fine." I'd packed some bandages into a backpack for this very reason.

"Actually, I've been thinking. We only need to follow one dragon. We can leave the rest of the swords here and free the dragons from them another time."

"Why would we wait?" I asked.

"Because," he said drawing me into a hug, "I don't like the idea of you hurting yourself any more than you need to. You can recuperate between letting each dragon free."

"Okay." I pulled out two of the three swords and took them back into the cave that would lead to a tunnel through the mountain. Dragging a large rock to one side, I hid them both behind it and pushed it back into place. It was doubtful that anyone would try to steal them, but I wanted to make sure.

The remaining sword I held aloft and waited for Ash to change into his dragon form. When he had, I pulled the blade of the sword over my skin, making sure it drew as little blood as possible and then threw the smoking sword to one side of the ledge. Ash ran to the opposite side and I jumped onto his back as he climbed into the air. The sword sent plumes of smoke up into the air before erupting in a great ball of fire. Ash was ready as the fire rose higher in the sky like a whirlwind of flames. Just like the other times, it took the shape of a dragon, which spread its magnificent fiery wings and took off toward Dronias.

I could tell Ash was flying as fast as his wings would carry him, but the fire dragon was much faster. It didn't have the problems of wind drag or air resistance that we did. I could feel his heart pumping away beneath me with the increased effort and I had to cling to him for dear life for fear of falling off.

Even with our increased speed, the journey still seemed to take forever. Perhaps it was because I was worrying so much about what this evening would bring. Any hopes that we would be able to retrieve the swords without anyone noticing had long gone out the window after last night's debacle, and even though everyone had promised that there would be as little bloodshed as possible, I knew that it was ridiculous in the extreme to think that no one would get hurt. I felt so angry at my village elders, none more so than my father who I had trusted implicitly my whole life, but that didn't mean I wanted him hurt. I just wanted the years of senseless killing ended.

As Dronias came into view, I strained my eyes to see what was happening. It was just about light enough to make out the little houses. A blast of flame in the distance told me that a battle had already started. It was enough to raise my nerves even higher and make me feel sick, wondering who that flame was directed to and if the dragon that made it would see another day. It didn't matter who got hurt; caught on both sides, I would be devastated if anyone was injured. To take my mind off it, I looked upward to see if I could still see the fire dragon. It was easy to spot in the dark, its bright wings blazing a trail for us. I watched as it began to fly lower in the sky and skirt the treetops in a secluded part of the forest at the other side of the village. That made sense. If the sleeping dragons were being kept anywhere, the forest seemed like a logical place to do it. Out of the way, large enough to build a prison for hundreds if not thousands of sleeping dragons, and surrounded by trees to keep it private. It tallied with what I remembered from when I was a child, too. My father had taken me out into the woods but then hastily brought me back to the village. I didn't remember much about it, I was only four or five at the time, but I guess I must have seen someone carrying one of the dragon's bodies to it. It would certainly explain why he'd turned around so fast and had forbidden me to go to that part of the forest ever since.

The fire dragon disappeared down into the trees and I thought we lost him, but as he flew through the branches, he set them alight so the very tops of the trees lit our way. We were still a good distance away, but seeing where we needed to go was easy. I looked down as we passed over the village and what I saw made my heart stop. The villagers had been ready for us. They were prepared in a way they hadn't been the night before. I could see many of them out, tiny specks, many feet below us, fighting other slightly bigger, but still tiny, specks. Bursts of fire lit up the village like a terrifying firework display beneath us and I could see that at least one house was on fire.

"Come on," I breathed quietly. There was no point shouting to make Ash go faster. I knew he was already flying at full speed, but I needed to be down there as quickly as possible.

Going to the dragons might have seemed pointless as they would all be asleep and nothing we could do, besides freeing their souls from the swords, would wake them, but we had let two dragons' souls free now and we needed to be there to help them. When Ash's dad, Fiere, came back to the village after we had rescued his soul, he told us how difficult it was to get used to being in his own body again and how he was so weak that it had taken a day to be able to fly home. The risk we were running was that the Slayers now knew we were saving dragons. If they saw one wake up, the only logical action would be to kill it. That's why Ash and I were going to the sleeping dragons. We had saved them once, but now we had to save them again.

Ash had packed a bag with some food in it to give

the freed dragons strength. It was not a lot for a dragon but it was all high-energy food. Fiere had been trapped for approximately a year. Many of the dragons had been trapped much longer than that. Some for centuries. There was no telling what state they would be in when they woke up, and we had no way of knowing how long the two we had freed had been trapped.

Ash flew right over the fiery treetops and landed at the edge of the forest about half a mile from where the fire dragon had landed. I jumped off and threw him some clothes for him to change into.

The forest might have been bright with flames half a mile away, but from here, it looked dark and ominous. It wasn't helping that I could hear screams and the sound of war cries coming from the distant village. I glanced over to see an orange haze filling the sky and wondered just how many of the houses were on fire. Sighing, I rifled through the bag and pulled out a torch. A torch that was now completely useless because Ash had already turned into his human form and there was no way to light it without his dragon breath.

"I don't suppose you can breathe fire in your human form, can you?" I asked as he walked to my side. Okay, it was a long shot, but the couple of times I'd kissed him, I could taste a hint of fire on his breath.

"Nope."

"I guess we are going into the dark then. I'll have to hold your hand because you can see better than me."

"Well, if you insist." He grinned at me which made me feel a little better. It was true that I always felt safe with Ash at my side.

We entered the forest, and it wasn't long before all

the light was blocked out completely. The going was slow as we practically had to feel our way through the trees and undergrowth. The sound of crisp leaves being crushed by our footsteps meant we couldn't go in silently, and I'd bet everything I owned that the place they were keeping the dragons was being guarded now.

A thought occurred to me. "If they know we are saving the dragons, what's stopping them from just killing them now?"

"You know the answer to that."

Did I?

"You said yourself that the dragon's souls make the swords much stronger, much more powerful. If the dragons were truly dead, then surely their souls would go on."

"Go on?" I'd not really ever thought about what would happen to our souls once we died. The Slayers were not a spiritual group of people and death was just something that happened. An ending. No one ever talked about any kind of transition or moving on. Something told me that the dragons thought differently.

"You know, go on. Our bodies decay but our souls go on to a better place."

He didn't elaborate on where this better place might be so I dropped the subject. He was right about one thing. It would be stupid to kill the dragons now. Doing so would only make the Slayers weaker.

It was a strange situation, really. The Slayers needed the dragons to be alive to keep their swords strong, but at the same time, there was always the threat that the dragons would escape. If enough escaped, the Slayers would be overpowered. No wonder they had hidden the truth for so many years. They were scared that this day would eventually come.

After about ten minutes or so of walking, the trees thinned out. I couldn't see them, but Ash wasn't pulling me this way and that to maneuver around them quite so much. Thank goodness for his dragon sense of sight. I'd have crashed into so many trees without him leading me.

Ash held his finger in front of his lips. "Quiet. I see something," he whispered.

I could see it too. In the distance, the trees were lit up which meant we were close. I gripped Ash's hand harder and followed him toward the light. Eventually, I saw stone through the trees. It was a stone wall that disappeared into the trees both ways.

"This has to be it," I said quietly.

"Yep. We just need to find the door. Get your sword out!"

I pulled out my sword with my free hand, glad for the weight of it. For some reason, just holding it calmed me. The wall was very long and as I looked up, I could see it was a taller structure than any other building in the village. It had no windows that I could see, just a flat expanse of grey stone.

Eventually, we got to a corner. I knew there was no roof, but I expected there to be only one door. It was impossible to discern if it was the back or one of the sides, but I knew we'd eventually come to the entrance and that it would be guarded. Just how heavily guarded, I didn't know. If it was by more than one person, which it surely would be, Ash would have to turn back into a dragon to protect us. I could fight one person with my sword, but to say I could fight two or more was pushing it. Ash didn't have a sword of his own, and in hindsight, it would have made sense to bring one. As I'd been carrying the three swords filled with dragon souls, plus my own when we'd set off, it just didn't occur to me to bring another.

"Shhh." Ash interrupted my train of thought.

I couldn't hear anything except the noises from the village in the distance, but I trusted that Ash could.

We crept forward slowly now. And then I saw him. I didn't need Ash to tell me who it was. Even from the distance we were at and in the dim light, I'd know my brother anywhere.

"Jasper!" I hissed under my breath. Next to him were some other men from the village. There looked to be four or five. They still hadn't seen us, so I crept forward to get a closer look. The men with Jasper were all friends of his. Boys I'd know all my life. Young men who would know nothing of the dragons being shifters. They were not poised to fight. Instead, they looked relaxed as they chatted to one another. I heard one of them say something followed by the sound of the others laughing. It was because of this I let go of Ash's hand and marched up to them. As soon as he saw me, Jasper raised his sword.

3

"What are you doing Jasper?" I spit.

"I knew you'd come back. You and your friend." He spat the last word.

"Put down your swords. All of you." I tried to sound authoritative, but in reality, these people were my friends. Jasper knew the secret that the elders of the village had been hiding for so long, but did the others? They looked uncertain. I knew none of them wanted to hurt me, but they were scared to back down because of Ash.

"Ash is unarmed. I have my sword and I'm not raising it to you. Put down your swords and let us talk."

The sounds of battle echoed through the trees. Either the battle had now come as far as the forest or it was just getting louder. The others heard it too.

"You've done this. You brought dragons to the village," shouted one of the men angrily. I recognized him as Joe, Ben's brother. Ben had been injured the previous night. No wonder Joe was angry.

"How is Ben, Joe?" I asked, keeping my fingers crossed that he was okay.

"He'll be fine, no thanks to you and your lot," Joe huffed.

Ash stepped forward and immediately all the men were on their guard again. "Julianna saved Ben's life! If it wasn't for him, he'd have been out right in the middle of the fighting." I knew he was trying to defend me, but he'd made it worse. If I didn't diffuse the situation soon, we were all going to be in trouble.

Joe held the tip of his sword up to Ash's chin. "What's it got to do with you?"

"I don't want anyone to get hurt," said Ash, holding his hands in the air.

"So, you thought bringing an army of fire-breathing dragons into the village would accomplish this 'nobody getting hurt' did you?"

"Joe, stop it!" I demanded, pushing his sword away from Ash and getting in the middle of them. "Do you even know what you are guarding or are you just blindly following orders?"

"We all know what we are guarding," butted in Jasper. "Father told us this morning. He's the one who showed us what and where this place is.

"So, you all understand that we haven't been killing Dragons all this time, but enslaving them?"

"So what?" replied one of the others. His name was Harry. "That's better than killing them anyway."

"But do you understand that they are..." I didn't have a chance to say another word. An arrow zipped past my ear and hit Harry right in the middle of his forehead. Nobody moved as he fell backward, dead.

The Slayers looked in shock over my shoulder. Ash and I turned around to see where the shot had come from. I couldn't see a thing through the dense trees, but somehow, someone was able to fire through them because another arrow flew past. It was so close to my ear that I could hear it. Like a spell that was broken, we scattered into the trees, all in different directions. Ash held my hand as he pulled me away from everyone.

When we thought we were safe, he stopped and pulled me close to a tree, looking around to make sure we were truly alone.

"Who was firing at us?" I asked breathlessly.

"I don't know. They could have been going for you or for the others. Spear promised that they wouldn't attack, only defend, so I think it means it was one of the Slayers."

I hated to think that one of my former friends was shooting at me, but it certainly looked that way. Harry was just in the wrong place at the wrong time. "What now?"

Ash pointed and I looked in that direction.

We were on the edge of the forest now, and through the trees, I could see the battle unfolding in the village. It was far enough away for us not to get caught up in it, but close enough to see the horror of what was unfolding. The sky was lit up by the bright orange flames of the burning buildings, and I could see the silhouettes of some of the dragons in the air. One appeared to be holding something in its claws that looked suspiciously like a human body. As we watched, someone ran down the path near to us. Ash pulled me out of sight, but I could see it was Joe. He was hurrying toward the village at breakneck speed. I couldn't tell if it was to get away from something or if he was running to help the Slayers in the village. We waited for the others, but no one else came.

Jasper was still in the forest somewhere and so were the three others who had been guarding the dragon-keep door. There was also the mysterious archer.

"We need to go into the village," I whispered, feeling utterly useless just hiding in the undergrowth.

"No. We can't help anyone there. We just run the risk of being hurt or killed. I think we need to go back to the keep. The others ran off somewhere and I'm betting that whoever shot at us thinks we are long gone by now."

He had a point, but the thought of going back there scared me. Still, I took his hand and let him lead me back through the forest. It took us much longer to get back than it had taken us to leave. Probably because we were now not running for our lives.

We crept cautiously forward once the fortress was in sight. My eyes kept darting left and right as I anxiously waited for someone to jump out at us. Of course, Ash had been right and no one did. He was also right about the door not being guarded now. There was no one in sight except the body of Harry. I tried not to look at him or the arrow still sticking out of his head.

"There is nothing you can do for him now." Ash pushed on the door, but it wouldn't budge. The huge, wooden doors with ornate inlaid ironwork stood at least three people tall and even with my help, they wouldn't budge.

"Locked," I said. I didn't know why I was surprised. Why wouldn't it be locked?

"Yes, it's locked!"

I swiveled on the spot to find Jasper standing behind us. "Jasper. Why are you doing this? You've seen for yourself that we have both been lied to for all these years. You know that Ash and the other dragons are shifters. Father is a murderer and a liar." I hated saying it, but it was the truth.

"Don't talk about our father like that!" he roared. He enunciated every word, his face as dark as thunder.

"But I don't understand. You know it's the truth. You know Father lied to us. You know he's imprisoned all those innocent dragons."

"That depends on your definition of innocent. He might not have been killing them like he told us, but he was still protecting us. Protecting the village."

"Protecting the village from what? The dragons have never attacked a Slayer, ever."

"Well, I guess he was doing a good job, then. He never gave them chance."

I was fighting a losing battle. The 'truths' he had grown up with were ingrained too deeply for him to change.

"I am not a fighter." Ash stepped forward. "I could change into a dragon and kill you with fire long before you could run away, but I don't want to do that. I don't want anyone to get hurt. I only want to free my family. The dragons in there are my friends, my ancestors. If your family was being kept in an eternal slumber, wouldn't you want to free them? I want to do it without fighting."

Jasper looked like he was beginning to listen, but

when Ash took a step forward, he raised his sword once more. "I can't let you set them free."

"Why not?" I implored.

"Because our swords would be nothing but metal without the dragon souls."

"But if we freed the dragons and lived peacefully, we wouldn't need magic swords. We wouldn't need swords at all."

Just then there was a loud roar from behind the doors.

"What was that?" asked Jasper in a panic, completely forgetting that he wanted to kill Ash just a moment before.

"We freed one of the dragons this morning," replied Ash

"No, you didn't! I've been here all morning. No one has come through these doors and this is the only way in."

"Not if you are a soul and no more. Souls can get through walls. They don't need to wait for the door to open. That's how we found this place. We followed the soul."

Jasper looked confused, and another roar filled the air. He also looked on the verge of running away, but I knew Jasper well enough to know that no matter how scared he was, he wouldn't run.

He fished around in his pocket and brought out a rusty key. "I'm going in there to kill it once and for all."

He inserted the key in the lock but didn't turn it. The dragon was sure to be extremely weak. It wouldn't survive another jab with a sword. It also wouldn't have the strength to escape. I couldn't let Jasper know that though.

"We freed more than one dragon," I lied. "There are four of them. They woke up a couple of hours ago and so will have gotten their strength back by now. You'll never be able to kill them all before they barbecue you."

"Four?"

We'd gotten four swords and Jasper knew that. I could see the cogs whirring in his mind as he decided what to do.

"Why are you opening the door Jasper?" I turned to see another of the men who had been guarding the keep before. I recognized him from the village but didn't know his name. "Don't tell me you are actually on their side now."

"No. Of course not. They freed some dragons. Let them out of the swords they got last night. They are running around in there and unless we do something quickly, they'll fly through the hole in the roof like the first one did. Father would never forgive me if I let them escape."

"So, let's go in there and kill them."

"If we kill them, we lose the magic that their souls provide."

I didn't want to point out that they had already lost the magic. I doubted they would be able to get it back. Being struck by a sword once might imprison a soul, but I doubted the magic in the swords would enable them to do it a second time. I was pretty sure that the dragons were too weak to survive another attack.

"Just open the door, Jasper!" The man barged past

him when he saw that Jasper wasn't moving. He turned the key in the lock.

"Stop!"

We all turned around to see Spear. He was standing there with a sword aloft. I recognized it immediately. It belonged to one of the village elders.

"I'm going to give you two choices. Either open that door and I impale you with this sword, or you can both run back to the village and help them there."

I had to admit, he cut an imposing figure and the sword in his hand made him look almost invincible. Both Jasper and the other man took option two, running through the forest as though their lives depended on it, which I supposed they did.

4

"Spear!" I never thought I'd be so glad to see him. "What's happening in the village? Are my parents okay?"

"I don't know about your parents but there are some injuries."

Ash held my hand tightly at hearing this. "We saw the fighting. It looks pretty brutal."

"It's not as bad as it looks. A lot of the village is in flames, but no one was in any of the buildings we set fire to. I made you a promise, Julianna, and I've stuck to it. We made sure the buildings were empty. Many of the villagers have holed up in about seven houses, and I've given strict instructions for those not to be touched. We have gotten a number of the swords and as far as I'm aware, there have been no fatalities on either side. I can assure you that whoever killed him"—he pointed to Harry—"it was not one of us."

"We think they were aiming for Julianna," said Ash.

The news calmed my nerves a little. No fatalities. It was all I could hope for.

"How did you find us?" asked Ash. I hadn't thought about it, but he didn't have a dragon soul to follow. It was a big fortress, but in a forest this large, it wouldn't be easy to just stumble upon.

"Some kid in the village. Joe something. I caught him running and wondered what exactly he was running from. He blabbed pretty quickly when I held this sword to his stomach. I think it belonged to his father."

I looked at the sword again. I knew I recognized it. It was indeed Joe's father's sword. He was one of the village elders.

Another roar emanated from the keep. The noise spurred Spear into action. He turned the key in the lock and pushed at the gigantic door. In the end, it took all three of us to push the door open fully. Before us was a sight that I would never forget as long as I lived. Hundreds, if not thousands, of dragons were lined up, all appearing asleep. In the back-right corner, the dragons were paler. They got brighter and more colorful the closer to the front. The one that was awake was right at the back and even in the dark, I could see he was pure white.

"Why is he white?" I'd seen a lot of dragons, but none so pale.

"I think they lose their color the longer they are here. He must be one of the first to have his soul taken," said Ash, shuffling around in his bag. He pulled out some of the food we had brought.

As I watched, the huge dragon stumbled and fell

over. We ran towards him, dodging the other unmoving dragons. The white one was still except for his belly, which moved in and out as he breathed deeply. His skin looked mottled and had a tinge of green to it. In places, it was shredding. He looked at us out of colorless eyes but didn't move. Ash bent down and patted his head. He held out a piece of meat, but the dragon didn't take it.

"He's too weak," I said helplessly.

"She," replied Ash. I didn't know how he could tell.

I bent my knees and got to the same level as Ash. "You need to eat," I said to the poorly dragon. "You need your strength. Just a mouthful and you'll feel better."

She stuck her tongue out and Ash placed the meat on it. Immediately it fell off and on to the floor.

"She can't hold her head up!" I moved to the back of the dragon's head and pulled as hard as I could. When Spear saw what I was doing, he came to help. Between us, we managed to get her head upright. Her neck was bent in what looked like an uncomfortable position, but it would have to do.

"Give her a drink." Ash had packed some juice full of medicinal herbs. He pulled out the bottle and carefully began to pour it down her throat. Slowly, she began to swallow. When the bottle was done, Ash threw it to the floor and got out another. This time she gulped it down.

"Try the meat again," said Spear. Ash picked it up and used some water from another bottle to wash the dirt off. She took the meat tentatively and began to chew. It took her more than twenty agonizing minutes to swallow the whole piece of meat, but at least she could hold her head up now. She gave a roar.

"Do you think you'll be able to shift?" asked Spear.

She thought about it for a second and then slowly nodded her head.

"Is that wise?" I asked, but it was too late. The horrible creaking and squelching noise that accompanied a shift was already happening. I jumped back and closed my eyes. I hated watching the dragons shift into their human form. When I opened them again, I saw a wrinkled old woman lying on the floor. She looked so thin and so frail.

Ash pulled out a cloak from his bag and wrapped it around her carefully. "Are you okay?" he asked.

"Yes, I think so." Her voice was croaky as though she hadn't used it for a very long time, which I guessed she hadn't. "Where am I?"

"It's a long story," replied Spear. "We need to get you home and have the village healers look at you. You are not strong enough to fly, but Ash here is. Julianna will ride with you on his back. You will be safe in their hands."

She looked unsure and scared. My heart went out to her. She knew as well as the rest of us did that she was in no position to say no.

"I'll look after you." I put my arms around her and pulled her into a hug.

"We can't go now. What about the fighting in the village?" Ash pulled Spear away from us.

"This is the job you came to do. We cannot leave her. She needs urgent medical attention," Spear answered. I didn't hear the rest as they had walked too far away.

I picked up the half empty bottle of water that Ash had used to clean the meat and passed it to her. She took it from me and sipped at it. I could see the gratefulness in her eyes. She either didn't realize I was a Slayer or didn't care.

It was obvious that neither Spear nor Ash knew her. There was not a spark of recognition from either of them when she changed. Neither of them exclaimed 'grandma' or shouted her name.

"Do you know how long you've been here?" I asked gently.

"Where am I?" she repeated her question from before.

"You are in the forest by the Slayer Village. They imprisoned you along with all these other dragons."

It was only after I mentioned them that she seemed to notice all the other slumbering dragons. Her mouth formed a perfect O shape as she took in the scene before her.

"We are going to rescue them all," I said to try and reassure her.

"But you are a Slayer, too." She said it but she didn't seem scared by it.

"I am... I was. Not anymore. I didn't know what my family was doing. I want to save the dragons."

She nodded her head. I could feel her shivering beneath the cloak. I hugged her more tightly and rubbed her arms. She felt so cold despite the warmth of the weather. I yanked off my tunic and pulled it over her under the cloak. I would be cold up in the air, but she needed it more than I did.

I could still hear a whispered argument going on between Spear and Ash. However much I wanted to be on Ash's side, I had to agree with Spear on this one. The old lady needed to get home. She needed to be somewhere warm and comfortable. Ash must have finally relented because he walked back and told us that we were going home. I thought he meant just the three of us, but Spear followed and explained that he was going to come with us.

"Why?" I asked. It made no sense.

"Ash pointed out that the people in the village will be expecting us to leave. Jasper will have told them that we are taking one of the dragons back with us. He thinks they will try to attack us and with both you ladies on his back, he won't be able to defend you all. I agree with him. You and Ash will go first to distract them, and when I see that the coast is clear, I'll take..."

"Mary," said the old lady.

"I'll take Mary."

"I want to go with Julianna. She has been nice to me."

"I can't allow it, I'm sorry. I need to do what's safest for you."

"What about what's safest for her?" she asked. It was so sweet that she was putting my safety above hers.

"Julianna can fend for herself. She was raised as a warrior." He turned to Ash now. "We need to check that there is no one outside waiting to shoot us. Julianna, can you get Mary to the door?"

I nodded as the boys set off back to the entrance.

"How did you know my name?" I whispered when they were out of earshot. "I never told you."

"Some dragon shifters can read minds. I used to be very good at it, but everything is blurry in my head now. I got your name though and I know I can trust you."

"You can. Can you stand?"

I practically had to pull her to her feet. She was too weak to walk very quickly so I put my arm around her back and held on to her arm to steady her. It was excruciatingly slow and each wobbly step seemed to take a thousand years. She was so light, it would have been easier to just carry her, but I knew she needed to exercise her withered muscles. I wondered why Spear and Ash hadn't come back to help but when we finally got to the entrance, I saw it was because they had both transformed into their dragon form. Spear with his dark green skin and Ash, a flaming red next to him.

It took a long time to get Mary up on Spear's back. She was too weak to climb up herself, so I had to lift her on. It became apparent very quickly that she was not going to be able to hold on herself.

"She can't hold on!" I said to Spear. He was going to have to transform back and come up with a better plan.

Instead, he nodded toward the ground.

I looked over and saw two bags. One was Ash's, the other, Spear's. I picked up both bags, slinging Ash's over my shoulder and opening Spear's. Inside, amongst other things, was a length of rope. As Spear couldn't speak in his dragon form, I had to hope that's what he wanted me to get. I took the rope back to Spear and as gently as I could, secured Mary on. I was confident in my rope tying skills. It was one of the things I studied as a Slayer, but I wasn't as confident that the ropes wouldn't cut into Mary's fragile skin. I only hoped the tunic and cloak would stop some of the chafing.

"Go slowly with her," I said to Spear. "She won't fall, but I'm worried the ropes could rub against her. No sudden moves or diving in the sky!"

Spear nodded his green head.

I hated leaving her, but I knew I had to. I said goodbye and then ran to Ash, jumping onto his back in one swift move. In less than a second, we were off the ground. I held tightly to Ash's neck as we soared above the treetops.

I waited for the barrage of arrows that I expected to shoot at us, but none came. Ash took a route away from the village to keep us safe, and when I looked behind me, I could see Spear and Mary following. It wasn't long before the lit-up village was just a speck in the distance behind us. We had escaped and set Mary free. I should have been elated, but I knew that we had just been lucky. I couldn't say the same about the other dragons. I had no idea how they were faring. Nor did I know if my family were still alive. The little relief I felt at Spear telling me that there were no fatalities had already ebbed away. That was hours ago and anything could have happened since then. I turned back to see where we were going and concentrated on the mountains ahead of us. The Triad Mountains were spectacular. It was such a shame they held centuries of bloodshed in their history.

5

I must have fallen asleep at some point because I opened my eyes to find Ash carrying me through the passage in the mountain. I felt so safe in his presence, warm and comforted, like the last few days had never happened. I breathed him in, a warm scent reminiscent of a campfire. His name suited him so much.

"What are you thinking?" he asked.

"Just how you kinda smell like your name."

He raised his eyebrows and smiled. "How are you? I was worried when I landed and you rolled off me. Luckily, you rolled away from the cliff edge or you'd have been toast. I think you might have landed on your arm."

I felt along my arm and he was right. It did feel a little sore. I was pretty sure I was going to get a bruise on my leg, too, come to think of it.

"I think I'm okay to walk now. I was just tired. I've not slept properly in days."

He let me down gently and held my hand, guiding

me through the dark tunnel. It was still dark when we emerged through to the other side.

"We should have waited for Spear and Mary!" I exclaimed. She was tied to him. He'd struggle to shift into his human form with Mary attached to him.

"They are ahead of us. They landed while you were still asleep. I helped Spear get Mary through the mountain. He's taken her to my house. My mother will look after her. Spear has told me that we are to meet at midday by the campfire tomorrow to evaluate how it went."

"Oh good." I felt so ashamed of being asleep and not helping, but at least Mary was safe and somewhere she would be looked after well. If she was staying with Edeline and Fiere, I would see her tomorrow.

I struggled to keep my eyes open as we made our way down the steps that would take us to the ground. I'd not noticed when we were in the tunnel, but it was the one further along than Ash's house.

"Why didn't we come through the usual way?" I asked.

"Because I didn't want to wake you. I'd have had to when I shifted back into a dragon if we came through the other way. This way I could carry you down the mountain."

He was so sweet. I gripped his hand tighter, thankful to have met him. It was a much further walk to his house coming this way and by the time we reached his door, I was ready to pass out again. I had never felt so weary in my whole life. He led me up the stairs and through a door I'd not gone through before.

"Where are you taking me?" I asked. I desperately

needed to go to bed, but my room was on the floor above.

"This is my room. You are sleeping here tonight. I'll take the sofa in the living room."

"Why?"

"Mary will be in your room. We don't have any more spare rooms."

"I can't let you sleep on the sofa." I yawned.

He pulled back the covers for me on the bed. "Just sleep. I'll be fine."

I was so tired, I couldn't argue with him. I collapsed onto his bed and let him pull the blanket over me. It was pretty dark, but there was just enough light for me to see his room. It was tidier than I'd expected, with a chest of drawers at one side and a writing desk at the other. He rummaged around in his drawers for some pajamas. His bed smelled just like him. Warm and inviting and slightly ashy.

He opened the door to leave and as I saw him silhouetted in the light of the landing beyond, I knew I didn't want him to go.

"Stay."

"What?" He turned his head toward me.

"Please stay with me." I could feel my heart thumping in my chest as I said it, but I knew I couldn't let him go. If he left, I'd follow him to the sofa and sleep with him there. The door closed and I couldn't tell which side of it he was on.

For a half a second, my heart plummeted into my stomach, but then I felt his warm body slip in next to mine. He curled his arm around me and I fell asleep to the sound of him breathing gently beside me.

———

Knock. Knock.

I opened my eyes suddenly after the best night's sleep I'd ever had.

Lucy's voice came through the door. "Mom says that you've missed breakfast but lunch is being cooked down at the campfire if you are hungry."

"What time is it?" shouted Ash back groggily.

"It's half past eleven." Then, "Is Julianna in there with you?"

"Never you mind, brat!" answered Ash. I could hear her giggling as she pitter-pattered down the stairs.

"Morning," he said turning and kissing me.

Food seemed so unimportant to me right now. I wanted to stay here all safe and warm, tucked up in Ash's arms forever, but I knew it was impossible. Sure, we could miss lunch, but we couldn't miss the meeting with Spear and the other dragons.

"I guess we should get up," I said reluctantly.

"I'm sure they won't miss us for ten more minutes." He kissed me deeply and my heart soared again. Being with Ash felt like I was always flying, even when my feet were on the ground.

Fifteen minutes later, we made our way to the campfire. Spear was already there, tucking into a steak between two slices of thick crispy bread. When he saw us, he walked straight over.

"Eat first!" he demanded before we had time to speak. "We will have a discussion later, but now I want everyone to get their strength up. I trust you slept well?"

"Like a log," I said, grinning.

A steak sandwich was handed to each of us and it was only when I smelled the chargrilled meat, that I realized just how hungry I was.

Within twenty minutes, many of the other dragons had joined us at the barbecue. All had been instructed to eat first, just as we had. When everyone had eaten their fill, Spear stood up and began to speak.

"I have talked to many of the dragons that were at Dronias last night. While I cannot call it a complete success, we did acquire a number of swords. There were no fatalities on our side and as far as I am aware, only one on the side of the Slayers. Julianna was there and saw that it was a member of their own kind that killed the Slayer accidentally. Much of the Slayer village has been burned and they will have to share homes until they rebuild. It is not ideal, but it had to happen for us to get the swords. We have added another eight swords to the three we already have."

"Four!" someone interrupted. "We had four yesterday."

"So we did," agreed Spear. "I wasn't counting one of them for good reason, which brings me on to the next bit of good news. Last night, Julianna gave some of her blood to save a dragon. Her name is Mary and she is currently staying with Edeline and Fiere. Edeline tells me that she is very weak but has eaten some food this morning and seems to be gaining strength. No one knows her and she doesn't remember how long she has been trapped. I can only deduce that she is one of the elders of this village, lost for generations. I know you will all be curious to see her and in time you will. Perhaps one of you might recognize her and I am wrong about her age, but I beg all of you to let her recuperate first. Her health is more important right now than finding out her true age. If I am right about her being so old, it proves that Julianna has been telling us the truth the whole time and that we can free all our dragons."

A series of whoops and cheers erupted around me. Spear let the noise abate before he continued.

"There is much work to be done first. I know how eager you all are to set the rest of the dragons free now. We have eleven swords, each with at least one dragon trapped inside, but we all must have patience. Julianna has had a very stressful couple of days. More so than the rest of us, as she has been fighting against her own kind. I'm not going to subject her to more blood loss until she has had time to recuperate herself. I'm also against the plan of going straight back into Dronias. We have been there two nights in a row and we need to rest. We also need to give them time to treat their injured. When we go back for the remaining swords, they will be guarding them much more heavily than before. They will probably have found better hiding places for them and just flying in there as we have for the last two nights isn't going to work. We need to come up with a better plan, which will take time."

"So, you want us to just sit around doing nothing while they hide their swords?" shouted a man at the back.

"No. After speaking with a couple of the dragons that went down there and hearing what Julianna has said on the subject, I think we need to go to the source of the magic."

"What?" asked the man, clearly confused. Judging

by the faces of the others around the campfire, he wasn't the only one.

"The Slayers use the swords, but they do not make them, nor are they the ones that imbue them with magic. The Slayers have no magical abilities themselves. They are warriors, not magicians or wizards. They buy the swords from the Goblins, and it is the Goblins that make the swords magic. The Goblins are not known for being the friendliest species and they only respond to money or gold, but I am hoping if we can get them to talk to us, maybe they will tell us the secret of the swords. If we can somehow free the dragons without Julianna having to sacrifice blood each time, or if we can somehow control the magic remotely, then we will not have to fight anymore.

"The Goblins won't speak to us. Why would they?" the same man shouted.

"That's why I propose we take as much gold as we can find to them. The language of money is universal."

"I've had dealings with the Goblins before," said the man. "They will take your gold and not tell you a word. They are deceitful and secretive and they stick together."

"Coal," Spear said, addressing the man. "If you have dealt with the Goblins before, would you come up the mountain with us to their village? I have only heard rumors about them, but have never actually met one."

"I can if you like," replied the man known as Coal. "But I hate them. They took my life savings to pay for a ring that they never delivered. When I went back to get my money back, they pretended they didn't know me and wouldn't let me into the village.

"But you know the location of the village? You can lead us there?"

"I can."

"I've heard it is high up on the other side of Triad Mountains?"

"It is inside the mountain. There is an entrance to it near the base of the mountain about twenty miles from here. That's how the Slayers get in. They wouldn't be able to get to any of the other entrances as they are high up on the mountain and the terrain is hard going. We could fly to the higher entrances, but I don't think they would like that. We'd be better going in the lower entrance."

"Then it is settled. Tomorrow, we head to the home of the Goblins. Anyone who wants to come, meet me back here as dawn breaks. The rest of you, please consider bringing any gold you can spare to my house. I will add my own personal fortune to the pile, and while it is a considerable amount, I think the more gold we have to offer the better."

"They will steal it from you," warned Coal.

"Yes. It is also a long way to trek whilst carrying gold, so we will not take it with us just yet. I will lock it in my safe until a time that we will need it, but if people bring what they have, I will know how much we have to bargain with."

When it became apparent he had finished, I held my hand up.

"Yes, Julianna. Do you have something to add?"

"I'd like to come with you."

"I don't doubt that for a second. As I said before. Anyone who feels up to making the trek and who wants to, please meet back here at dawn. Make sure you bring some food with you. It will be a long day. As for today, everyone should rest up. Sleep, eat and do whatever it is you feel you need to prepare for the journey ahead.

The crowd began to disperse and Ash took my hand.

"I think we should check on Mary," I said to him.

"Mary is sleeping," said Edeline who had been listening nearby. "I think you two need a bit of time off. It's a beautiful day and you've both been through a lot. Go out and enjoy yourselves."

I kissed her cheek.

"Want to go for a walk?" asked Ash.

"More than anything!" I let him lead me down the dirt track to the meadows on the hillside. We lay on the grass, my head resting on Ash's chest. Edeline was right. The sun was shining and the day was indeed beautiful.

6

The next day arrived with squally conditions. It was not ideal for trekking up a mountain, but Fiere loaned me a thick coat and Edeline let me borrow her boots. They were a size too big, but it was cold enough to wear a thick pair of socks underneath to bulk them out. It was more like an autumn day than a late summer one. Perhaps the weather was beginning to change. Ominous black clouds sheathed the mountain we were heading toward.

"I hope that's not some kind of omen," I said, pointing to the gray and black sky.

Ash hugged me tighter. "It will pass." He didn't sound too sure.

We were standing at the door of Spear's house. It opened and his maid let us in. We were the first to arrive, but within ten minutes, Coal and a number of others had joined us in the drawing room, each kitted out in warm, waterproof clothes and backpacks.

Spear gathered us around him. "The weather is not

on our side. There is a storm heading our way. I propose we fly as high as we can go and then if it becomes too much, we should walk the rest of the way. We need to do this in pairs. One will fly while the other rides holding on to both backpacks. If the need arises, we can swap halfway through."

"You're forgetting something," said Coal, barging to the front. "They won't open their doors to us higher up in the mountains. They are not a trusting people. Our best route would be to go on foot along the base of the mountain until we get to the main entrance there."

"I took into consideration what you told me yesterday Coal. I agree that we must knock on the door where they expect visitors. However, to go along the base of the mountain is madness. The Slayers could see us and attack. Plus, there are countless villages that run along the base of the mountain. I can think of at least four in the first ten miles or so. We don't know if they will show us any hostility. No, I think it would be safer to fly and climb the mountain and then when we are close to the Goblin City, we can head down to the entrance."

"But—"

"Spear is right," I interrupted before Coal could speak. "The next village along has a similar view of dragons as the people of Dronias. The village of Lakate holds a dragon festival every year. I went to it once with my family. They burn effigies of dragons."

"Is there anyone that doesn't hate us?" chuckled Coal wearily.

"It's settled then," said Spear, looking at his watch. "I don't think any more are going to show so if you can get into pairs, decide which one will fly first and we'll be off.

I'll fly up front with Coal, so you can just follow me. Is everyone okay with that?"

Everyone nodded and murmured their assent.

Outside, the riders collected the backpacks and clothes of the flyers.

"How about if I ride this time?" joked Ash as he passed me his bag.

"You wish!" I stuck my tongue out at him. I'd gotten used to seeing the dragon people undress as if getting naked in broad daylight was the most normal thing in the world, but I still blushed as Ash handed me his clothes. I had to close my eyes as they all transformed. I still didn't have the stomach to watch that part, but when I opened them, in front of me were twelve stunning dragons. They ranged in color from fiery red (Ash) to the darkest black (Coal). There were ten of us left in human form. We each hopped onto the back of our respective dragons, leaving Spear and Coal riderless, and one by one, we took off into the sky.

I'd flown on Ash's back a great number of times but the thrill of take-off, as the ground disappeared beneath me, never left me. I'd also never really flown with so many other dragons and it was interesting to see how they flew in formation, a little like flocks of birds flew in a V shape.

I'd also never flown this high in the mountains before. Frokontas was the highest place I'd visited, and it excited me rather than scared me to think that I was going to fly right up to the highest peak of the Triad Mountains, which I'd spent my whole life dreaming about.

The weather was the only concern. It would have

been a glorious flight had the weather stayed sunny, but the rain was already beginning to hit my face and make it difficult to see where we were going. The peak itself was completely shrouded in black clouds and as we flew higher, visibility became worse. As the wind began to batter us, I had to hold tightly onto Ash for fear of falling. In the distance ahead, I could just make out Spear diving downward, quickly followed by Coal and the rest of us. By the time we landed, the weather had really broken and the rain was coming down in droves. I hopped down from Ash's back and took shelter under a sturdy-looking fir tree. The dragons transformed back and dressed quickly, eager to be warm against the lashing rain.

"There is no point anyone else transforming," said Spear. "The weather is making it impossible to fly. From here we walk."

There was no discernible path, although I could see tracks through the undergrowth where animals had worn trails. The paths looked too wide for mere rodents and I wondered exactly what kind of animals lived up here.

Despite the fact that the high peak was hidden by clouds, we all knew where it was and in what direction. Upward! Spear took the lead as he had before and guided us onward, following animal trail after animal trail. Whatever animals did live on the mountain, I didn't see any. I didn't even hear any birdsong. They must all have been sheltering from the storm.

The path wasn't particularly steep, but the air was thinner up here, making the walk tougher. The dragons who had grown up in the mountains were all used to the thinner air, but for me, it meant I was getting out of breath more quickly than they. The terrain underfoot wasn't particularly easy to walk on either, and my feet kept getting caught in brambles and weeds.

"I could do with you doing some fire-breathing on all these plants to clear the path," I joked to Ash. He took hold of my hand and pulled me through the worst of it.

All too soon the terrain changed. The trees thinned and the weeds and plants gave way to the same type of gray rocks near Frokontas. The ground was wet and slippery and became much steeper. A couple of miles in and we were practically climbing over the rocks. I had never been more thankful for Edeline's boots which gripped the wet rocks, helping me to climb. No matter how well the boots gripped, shale kept slipping beneath me causing me to slip back one step with every three or four I took.

"Stop here!" I heard Spear shout ahead of us. He'd found a cave large enough for us all to fit in and it made sense that here is where we would eat.

I rummaged around in my bag and pulled out a couple of sandwiches that Edeline and Lucy had prepared for us. Passing one to Ash, I took a bite out of my own. I'd not realized just how hungry I was, but I finished the first sandwich in a matter of minutes. Thankfully, Edeline had packed quite a few for us. I grabbed another and bit into it. Outside, the rain hammered down so hard it bounced off the ground, leaving puddles everywhere—another thing for us to navigate around. Everyone else looked as exhausted as I felt which made me feel a little better. At least I wouldn't be the one slowing the group down.

"How much farther?" Spear asked Coal who was drinking something from a flask. It smelled like hot soup and as my stomach gave a lurch, I wish I'd have thought of it.

"There are entrances to the Goblin Village all over the mountain. We are actually pretty close. We don't want to be caught up here. They don't like it. They think this part of the mountain is sacred. I say we start our downward course now so we don't accidentally come upon one up here. It will only spell disaster if we do."

"Fine. I understand. Okay, everyone. You heard Coal. We'll take another fifteen minutes to rest and then we shall start our trek down the mountain. I know you are all tired, but it should be much easier from here on out."

I gave a silent thanks and finished off my second sandwich. I didn't think I could have taken another footstep uphill.

The rain hadn't abated as we left our shelter, and if it wasn't for Fiere's coat I would have been soaked to the skin.

Ash took my hand and we both walked beside Coal and Spear who had again taken the lead. As I was now at the front of the group rather than the back where I'd been before, I could at least see where I was going. About two hundred meters below us, the terrain changed from the gray stone and shale back to forest. The going was painfully slow as someone slipped every couple of minutes and we had to wait each time for them to pull themselves up. As the trees got nearer, I spotted something just along the tree line. At first, I thought it was another cave, but this time it had a makeshift door attached to it. The wooden door was open.

"What do you make of that?" I pointed it out to Ash.

"That's one of the entrances to the Goblin City," explained Coal who'd heard me. "We've come too far. We need to walk around it quietly so they don't hear us."

"But the door is open. Surely that's an invitation for anyone to go in?" replied Ash.

"The Goblins don't offer invitations of any kind!"

Ash ignored him and ran over to the entrance. He peeked in and then, before Coal or anyone else could stop him, disappeared into the dark tunnel.

"Foolish boy!" remarked Coal. "We need to get out of here quickly, come on." He upped his pace, giving the entrance a wide berth.

"We can't leave him!" I shouted at the retreating Coal.

"I'm not hanging around here!" was his reply.

I watched helplessly as the others began to take the same path as Coal. Only Spear stayed with me.

"Why is Coal so reluctant to be caught up here? He hasn't mentioned that the Goblins are dangerous to you, has he?" I asked.

"No, but I agree with him. Ash should have left well enough alone. We brought Coal because he knew the Goblins. Now we have two groups which will not help our cause."

"There he is!" I pointed with relief as Ash poked his head out of the tunnel entrance.

"It's empty. There is no one there," he shouted, causing Coal and the others to stop.

"It can't be. There are hundreds of them. You must be mistaken."

"I'm not mistaken. There is a whole city down there. You were right about that, except it is empty. The houses, the shops. There is no one there."

Coal looked dumbfounded.

"Maybe they have left the Triad Mountains," I ventured. The thought of walking all this way for nothing made my stomach fall. It was beginning to get even darker which meant evening was closing in. We had been walking for the better part of a day.

"That's impossible!" argued Coal. "They would never leave these mountains."

He hiked back to where Ash was standing. The others followed and Spear and I joined them. We all peered into the dark tunnel.

"I don't like this," whispered Coal. I had to agree with him. Why would the Goblins leave their own city? Even though nothing had been said about them being a dangerous race, the way Coal spoke about them put me on edge.

I felt nervous following Ash down the dark tunnel, even though I knew everyone else was following.

I had to trust Ash's dragon eyesight as I couldn't see a thing.

All of a sudden there was light. It wasn't bright but it was enough to see the huge cavern that the tunnel opened up into. Holes in the ceiling, protected by glass windows, let in the little light there was outside. To say the cavern was big didn't do it justice. It was massive, with the uneven roof held up by pillars. Thousands of stalactites hung down and here and there, a stalagmite rose up from the ground to join its partner.

It wasn't the cavern that was the most impressive, although it did take my breath away. It was the hundreds of little buildings within it. Set on many levels with roads and pathways connecting each building, they'd managed to build a whole village in here. When Coal had mentioned a Goblin village inside the mountain, I'd expected a series of caves. Nowhere in my deepest imagination could I have conjured this up in my mind.

Ash was right, though. The whole place had an eerie silence. Lights lit up the houses but there was no one walking in the underground streets and the few windows I could see into showed empty rooms. It was as if they had all just decided to move out one day, leaving everything as it was and just disappearing.

The thought of it scared me. What could make a whole village of people just vanish?

Just then a bright flash of light filled my eyes momentarily blinding me.

"Who do you think you are?" roared a voice. It looked like there was someone here after all.

7

As my eyesight returned to me I saw a Goblin standing in front of us. Having not seen one before, I wasn't sure what to expect and his appearance shocked me. He was small and stout with leathery skin and mossy green hair. His hooked nose arched out just above a sneer. I could see why Coal distrusted them.

"We are the dragons from far down the Triad Mountains. We come seeking your help." Spear pushed through to the front to speak to him.

"It is customary to wait to be invited into one's home before just barging in," replied the Goblin.

"Your village is empty," remarked Ash, but as he said it, it became apparent he was wrong. Behind the Goblin, the empty village we'd just seen was now a hub of activity. The shops were full of Goblins. Small vehicles traveled up and down the roads and the streets bustled with activity. "Where did they all come from?" asked Ash in surprise as he noticed them all for the first time. I guessed they used magic for more than just creating swords!

"They have been here all the time. You are just too stupid to have seen them."

Ash looked affronted but did not reply.

"You say you are dragons?" asked the Goblin, addressing Spear.

"That's correct."

"She isn't!" the Goblin replied, jabbing me with a stick he was holding. "She's a Slayer!"

"So, what if she is?" Ash pushed the stick away from me as I rubbed my arm where it had hit.

"Nothing. Just curious, that's all. It is not often we see your kinds mix. In fact, I cannot remember ever having seen it."

"That's why we are here. We need your help with the Slayers."

"The Goblins do not like to get involved with differences of other kinds."

"Who said anything about differences?" inquired Spear.

"You want me to tell you about the swords we provide to the Slayers." It wasn't a question. He already knew.

"We only want information. We've come a very long way. Please."

"Follow me," he said with a wave of his hand.

The Goblin meandered down into the main part of town and we all trooped after him like lost children following their teacher. A few of the Goblins looked at us with curiosity, but most were too busy to give us a second glance.

We walked past row after row of odd looking shops and funny houses, all hewn out of the red rock of the cavern. It made it look both quaint and a bit scary at the same time. I tried to take in all the new sights around me and figure out exactly where we were in the maze of tiny houses. Shops rose up, stacked one on top of the other along the nearest wall of the cavern, stone steps enabling people to reach the higher ones. Below us was a whole town with houses and other buildings. There was a giant town square with decorative rocks placed around the edges in place of flowers. There was nothing growing in this place beyond the Goblins themselves. There were no trees or plants.

Tunnels snaked off in all directions, the largest of which at the very far end of the cavern had a huge sign that read MINE.

All too soon, the Goblin stopped at a building right in the center of town. He knocked at the door and waited for a reply before opening it.

"Krikor," he said to the occupant. "I've brought the intruders. It's only a group of dragons wanting some information. Nothing to worry about!"

"Thank you, Grunch," replied the voice from within. "Let them in."

Grunch held the door open and one by one, we filed in. I was by no means the tallest, but I had to bend almost in half to get through the tiny doorway. We found ourselves in a room that made up for its height by being very large. It looked like a meeting room of some kind with chairs spread out in a circle.

"Please take a seat." He held his hand out to indicate the chairs. They were much too small for us, almost like children's chairs, but we all managed to squeeze ourselves into them.

"Welcome to Kanghar," said the Goblin. "My name is Krikor and I am the king of the Goblins." He was no less mossy than Grunch had been, but he was much older. He walked with a hunch and his green hair was starting to turn white at the temples.

He took the seat in between Spear and Ash.

"I'm sorry we came uninvited," said Spear, "but we stumbled on your village accidentally. We were hoping to come by way of your main entrance at the bottom of the mountain."

Krikor waved his hands, dismissing Spear. "No matter how you got here, we are glad that you have found us. Now, what can we do to assist you?"

"We are having problems with the Slayers," began Spear. He went on to tell Krikor the whole story. When he came to the bit about me turning up in Frokontas, Krikor raised his eyebrow but he kept silent, letting Spear continue with his story.

"I'm sure that Grunch must have told you that we do not take sides. We are impartial to any war going on that does not include us."

"But it does include you," said Ash joining in the conversation. "They are your swords that the Slayers are using."

"I wonder what she has to say about all this." He looked directly at me. I felt uncomfortable, as though he was boring right into my mind and already knew what I was about to say.

"My people...some of my people are murderers. It's

been going on too long and it has to stop. Can you help us?"

"I'm afraid not. Once we sell a product, we do not tell another soul of its magic. That is why people trust us. If we break that trust only once, we will be nothing more than liars."

"And thieves," hissed Coal under his breath beside me.

"Ah, Coal. I wondered when you would return for your ring. I've been keeping it safe for you. The magic you asked will still be strong but you'd be best to take it now. I'll have someone get it for you."

I turned and saw the shocked expression on Coal's face. It made me wonder what kind of magic he'd purchased. Slayers didn't deal in magic. Most actively talked about it as though it was the devil's work and yet their hatred of magic never extended to the Goblin made swords. I wondered why that was.

"They hated the dragons more than they hated the magic," Krikor said, confirming that he could read minds. Ash gave me a funny look and I shrugged my shoulders. "The night is drawing in and you are all wet. I can offer you a bed each to sleep in and a good meal but that is all. I'm afraid your quest for information will not be fulfilled, but I hope you'll honor us and be our guests for the evening."

Spear looked to be considering it but it didn't take a mind reader to know what his decision would be. We were all tired, wet, and hungry. It would be madness to start the trek down the mountain at this late hour.

"Thank you, King Krikor. That is very generous of you."

Krikor stood and beckoned us to follow him. He took us out of the building and across the Goblin city. The sights and smells were all foreign to me and yet the place was so alive that I couldn't help but feel excited to be here.

"That is our best restaurant," pointed out Krikor. I followed his finger to a smart-looking building with a green canopy outside. It had no sign to mark it as a restaurant but the small tables displaying menus meant it didn't need to. "I will meet you back here at seven o'clock and we shall dine together. In the meantime, you all look like you could do with a shower and a warm place to dry if you don't mind me being so bold."

We followed him further into the cavern, past all the shops and houses, and down another tunnel. I would have thought he was taking us back outside if it wasn't for the heat that emanated from it. A blast of hot air breezed past us, making me wonder if we weren't the only dragons here after all.

I heard the roar of it before I saw it, but it was no dragon. It was a huge waterfall, spilling out of a cliff face into an underground lake.

"The water will be much warmer than you are used to, but it's not hot enough to burn. You can bathe here. The little cabin there is full of towels. Take as many as you need. I'll see you all at seven in the restaurant." Krikor shuffled off leaving us all standing looking at each other.

One of the dragons ran past me and with a huge leap, jumping off a rock into the water with a splash.

"Come in!" she shouted. "The water is wonderful."

I still felt cold and damp from the rain and the sight

of the huge lake made me want to join her. I stripped down to my underwear and dove into the warm water. Beside me, I felt a splash and then another as the rest of the dragons joined us. Ash was the last to jump in but when he did, he grabbed hold of me, pulling me down under the water's surface. He kissed me there, out of eyesight and yet within reach of everyone else. When we finally surfaced and sucked in deep breaths, I couldn't keep the smile from my face.

A pleasant couple of hours was spent splashing around in the water, and the aches and pains of the hike vanished, leaving me wondering if the water had some medicinal properties. When we finally got out and dried ourselves using the towels, I noticed that my skin felt softer too. Apart from my rumbling stomach, brought on, no doubt, by only having eaten a couple of sandwiches all day, I had never felt better. I wondered what Goblin food tasted like?

Later, once we had dried and dressed, we made our way back to the restaurant.

Krikor was already waiting for us, along with some of the other Goblins. We managed to squeeze around a large table while a number of Goblin waiters brought us dish after dish of wonderful food. It was like nothing I'd ever tasted before and neither had the dragons judging by the looks on their faces. The food was spicy and hot and utterly delicious. I gobbled it down hungrily, going from dish to dish, savoring the spices and flavors, each different from the last. Despite Spear's best efforts to get information about the swords, Krikor and the other Goblins remained tight-lipped. Once he'd given up trying, they joined in the conversation and were more than happy to share small talk with us.

After the spicy food, the waiters brought out a sweet frozen cream dish which went down wonderfully, quelling the fire in my throat. I'd never had a more delicious meal in my life and I made a mental note to ask for some recipes before leaving.

"I hope we have made you feel welcome. I have had someone make up some beds for you in the room above this restaurant. You will need to go outside and find the stone stairs beside the restaurant and climb them until you come to a building. I trust you'll have a pleasant night.

"I cannot thank you enough for your hospitality, Krikor." Spear held out his hand and the king shook it heartily.

"Coal, you will find your ring there also. Now if you don't mind, I'm an old man and I need my rest. Feel free to stay here as long as you want."

Despite his invitation to stay in the restaurant, we were all tired and so less than half an hour later we wearily trudged up the stairs that had been cut out of stone. The building we came to didn't have beds exactly, but many mattresses and beanbags had been laid out on the floor for us to sleep on. It looked like we were all going to be sleeping in the same room. Ash took my hand and led me to the mattress in the darkest corner. I flopped down next to him and sighed.

He gathered me up in his arms and I laid my head upon his chest. It had certainly been an exhausting day. Even as I thought it, I yawned and closed my eyes.

"You okay?" Ash whispered quietly.

"I guess so. I was just hoping that we'd find out more information. I feel like we've wasted the whole day."

"I know what you mean. This has been a wasted journey and we've still got to hike all day tomorrow to get back. I'm hoping that the weather will have cleared so we can fly down."

"We are no closer to ending this ridiculous war. The only end to it I can see is if we destroy the Slayers and that means destroying my family."

"I won't let that happen!" He held me tighter making me feel safe.

I closed my eyes and began to drift off to sleep. The last words I heard before I descended into a blissful oblivion were, "You are my family now."

8

I woke up wrapped in Ash's arms. The sounds of the others snoring and shuffling in their sleep told me I was the only one awake. The room was still dark although a sliver of light through one of the windows allowed me to see a little. I felt antsy after yesterday's wasted trek, as though I should have done more, but what? I couldn't force the Goblins to tell us anything. I didn't even want to try to force them. They'd treated us well since we turned up unannounced yesterday.

Thoughts rushed through my head, of Ash and his family, of my own family, and most of all, of the mess we were all in.

I couldn't get back to sleep so I decided to get up and do something useful. Stepping around all the sleeping bodies, I headed out into the main chamber of the Goblin village. It was lighter out there but not much. It was also quiet. A couple of Goblins walked past me but didn't speak. Not knowing what to do with myself, I decided to take a walk. I'd not gone far before I had the feeling that the Goblins might think I was snooping or up to no good. In the end, I decided to go back to the tunnel we had first come down and head outside for some fresh air. I saw no more Goblins before I made it outside. It was much lighter outside and colder too. The dawn was just breaking over the horizon, bathing the Triad Mountains in a warm pink glow. I'd not seen it yesterday because of the storm, but now that the clouds had cleared, the view was spectacular. I could see all the way down to the base of the mountains and farther beyond to all the farmers' fields that lay out in tiny squares full of sheep and cows the size of raisins. To my right was the impressive summit of the largest mountain in the Triad Mountains. It was still a long day's trek to reach the top and I could see that snow still lingered, left over from the long winter.

To my right was the rest of the mountain range. Peak after peak of beautiful mountains, the same mountains I'd gazed upon my whole life. On the other side of one of those mountains was Frokontas where Edeline and Fiere and Lucy would be waiting for news, and somewhere along the large expanse of flat farming land, way off in the distance, was my home village, now partly destroyed by fire. It was too far away to see it from here, although I could make out a few small villages which were closer. I felt like a bird, eager to jump from the ledge and stretch my wings and just fly—fly wherever the mood took me, where I wouldn't have to worry about swords and trapped dragons and eons-old grudges.

Thinking of swords made me realize I'd not practiced with mine for a long time. It was something I used to do every day, ironically, before I ever really needed to. The first day I actually had to use my sword, my eighteenth birthday, was the last time I'd really practiced with it. I hadn't realized until now just how much I missed it, the feel of the weight of it in my hand, slicing through the air for the fun of it, not to protect myself or to kill anyone.

I unsheathed the sword and held it up in the air. It felt so good between my fingers. It was so cold up here that I could see my breath which made me all the more eager to warm up my muscles.

I imagined a terrible foe in front of me. Before I'd always pictured an angry dragon, but of course I couldn't use that image anymore. Instead, I conjured up something even more terrible. My idol, Morganna. She was the most famous of all swordsmen and swordswomen. In a world where men excelled at sword fighting, Morganna had turned the notion that women couldn't fight on its head and paved the way for the rest of us. Her sword skills were legendary, having never lost a fight with any man or woman.

She was long dead now though. A dragon finally out-maneuvered her. She was fighting two at a time and didn't notice a third who had sneaked up behind her. She'd put up a brave fight, but she couldn't survive the blast of flame that hit.

I closed my eyes and pictured her. I'd never met her, but I'd seen pictures. An oil painting depicting her slicing the head clean off a dragon hung in one of the community buildings in Dronias.

She was tall and muscular, with long black hair that

she always kept in place with a golden headband. In the picture, she wore a short skirt made out of brown leather and a short top of the same material. Her stomach was uncovered, showing off her tremendous muscles. I doubt she really dressed like that, but the painter obviously wanted to show people her strength.

In front of me now with her sword held high, she took an imaginary stab which I dodged and parried back. One swipe from me and she was down, covered in blood.

"Really?" I opened my eyes, admonishing myself. "You took out the greatest swordsperson of all time with one hit?"

I closed my eyes again and Morganna resurrected in front of me. This time, when I thrust my sword at her, she swiped it away expertly before slicing her own sword back. I dodged and weaved, unable to keep up with her and unable to get another attack in. All my moves were on the defensive.

It was much closer to the truth, although if it was real, I'd have been down for the count within seconds. I knew I was a good swordswoman but I also knew I had a lot to learn. I opened my eyes and took in a deep breath. The sun was higher in the sky now although it hadn't warmed up any. My muscles burned with the exertion and sweat dripped off me despite the cold morning. I guess I'd been practicing longer than I realized. I often zoned out when I concentrated.

"What are you doing? I've been looking everywhere for you. Thought the Goblins had eaten you for breakfast or something."

I turned to find Ash standing behind me.

"You didn't!"

"Ok, no I didn't but I was worried. Why didn't you tell me you were coming out here?"

"You were asleep. I didn't want to wake you."

Ash held out his hand and I took it. He was so warm. "Come on, we are all having breakfast. Spear wants us to head back pretty early. He asked me to check if the weather was good enough to fly home."

"It's beautiful out here. Perfect conditions for flying. You know, I was just thinking how nice it would be to have wings and fly away. I forgot that you can do just that."

"So can you," he replied. "You just have to jump on my back and I'll take you anywhere."

It sounded so nice, the thought of us flying away together, away from all the mess. Of course, it would never happen, but it was nice to dream for a while.

Breakfast was held in the same place we'd eaten the night before and was just as good. Krikor joined us again and as we left he bade us all farewell, telling us that we were welcome to come back anytime. He made it sound friendly, but something in his voice told me he really didn't want to see any of us again.

We were all a little disheartened at our failure as we began our trek down the mountain. Spear had decided that it would be better to get away from the Goblins before members of the group changed into dragons. I didn't know what his reasoning was but I knew better than to question him. Coal was the only one who seemed happy. He kept pulling the ring box out of his pocket and checking that the ring he'd purchased was still there.

My whole body ached as we walked over the difficult terrain. I had pushed myself too far this morning. I was out of practice and it showed.

"Who were you fighting this morning when I found you?" asked Ash.

"I wasn't fighting anyone. I was practicing." I stepped over the rocks, my feet hurting with every footstep.

"You were fighting someone in your mind. Your movements weren't just random. You looked like you were embroiled in battle."

"Okay, if you must know, I was fighting Morganna." I felt silly just saying it.

"Morganna?"

"She was a brilliant swordswoman," I explained.

"She was a dragon Slayer!" added Spear. I hadn't even realized he'd heard us talking. "Killed many of us...or at least took the dragon's souls. She was a barbarian!"

It hadn't occurred to me until now just how different our opinions of one person could be. I'd grown up pretending to be Morganna. She was more than my idol, she was the one woman I'd grown up wanting to be. To hear someone say anything bad about her felt wrong, but knowing what I knew now, I had to see his point.

"She came from your village. Did you know that?" Spear added.

It's funny, in all the stories I'd heard about her, I'd not once considered where she lived or where she was from. Stories of her came from all over the land—the wars she'd fought in, the enemies she had slain.

"We had a festival for her once a long time ago. I was so young I barely remember it. It was then I was told that she had died. At the time I didn't really know who she was, but I remember being in awe of all the fuss that was made. Everyone came out. People were wailing and crying and yet still celebrating her life."

I walked on in silence thinking back to the huge party we'd held for her.

"Oh!" I exclaimed out loud.

"What?"

"Her sword! If she was one of us...one of the Slayers, her sword will have the souls of dragons in it. If the legend of her is correct, there will be hundreds trapped."

Spear stopped and looked at me. "I was just thinking the same thing. Do you know where it is?"

I thought back to the festival. I couldn't remember a sword. Her body wasn't even there. It was not a burial. She had died in a far-off land.

"I've never seen her sword except in a painting. I know exactly what it looks like but I don't know where it is. I didn't even know she came from Dronias until you told me."

"We need to find that sword!"

"I don't know," I repeated. I felt so useless, but I'd never seen the sword in real life. I knew if I closed my eyes I'd be able to picture it as plain as day. I'd stared at the painting of her long enough.

"Can you draw it at least, so we know what we are looking for?"

"Yes!" I replied quickly, feeling relieved that I'd at least be able to do something. "I know exactly what it looks like."

"That's a start," said Spear. "Before you mentioned her, I'd not thought about her for a very long time. She was a legend in our village just as much as she was in yours. I am much older than you and remember stories about her very well. It had not occurred to me that we are not only looking for swords from your villagers but also from the ones that left. You mentioned that the swords of your ancestors were all kept in a vault somewhere. If that is true, could it be possible that Morganna's sword is stored in the same vault?"

I thought for a second before answering. "I don't think so. Morganna was much bigger than anyone in our village. If I didn't know she came from there, I'm guessing it was because she left and never came back. If I was to hazard a guess, I'd say that she would have asked to be buried with her sword."

"And where is she buried?" asked Ash.

"I don't know." I hated how I didn't know anything about the history of my village. How had I grown up knowing so little? It wasn't as though I didn't talk about Morganna much. She was a constant topic of conversation when I was little. It all went back to my father. He'd lied to me about so much, who was to say he hadn't lied to me about Morganna too? He must have known that she came from the village so why had he never mentioned it?

"We change here." Spear stopped the rest of our group. Splitting into pairs again as we had on the journey up, the dragons pulled off their clothes and changed. I hopped up on Ash's back and together we soared through the air.

9

The journey down the mountain was wonderful, the kind of journey I wished would last forever. The skies were clear and the views were beautiful. If it hadn't been for my head filled with thoughts of Morganna and her sword, I'd have asked Ash to stay in the air all day, or at least as long as it took him to tire out.

We landed, once again to a waiting party of dragons eager to know what we had learned. Ash and I left Spear to tell them the bad news and inform them of yet another sword to find. I couldn't face seeing anyone else at the moment and I was sick of talking about Slayers and dragons and the war surrounding us. I was sick of hidden swords and age-old grudges, and most of all I was sick of the lies. I just wanted to be me, if only for one afternoon.

Ash dressed quickly and went to inform his parents and sister that we were back. He returned and quickly turned into his dragon form again. He nudged me to get on his back. When I did, he stretched out his wings and we took off, leaving everything behind us.

It was just the two of us, up in the air without a care in the world.

He landed on the other side of the mountain on a rocky outcrop. The vista below was magnificent, almost as good as it had been higher up in the mountains; I could see for miles. I leaned back and let the sun warm my face as Ash changed back into his human form and put his clothes on. He sat next to me, dangling his feet over the side, and threw me an apple. When I asked him where he'd got it from he told me Edeline had given it to us.

"We are invited to dinner tonight. Mama doesn't want us back late. She insisted that we all eat together."

"Around the campfire you mean?"

"No, just the five of us." It sounded ominous, as if she was going to tell us something. My imagination ran wild as I wondered if she wanted me out of the house. I'd been living there for quite a while now and hadn't paid rent or contributed to the food I ate.

"Don't worry," Ash said, reading me like a book. "She just wants us to be together, that's all."

"Good. Do you think I should bring some food back? I feel bad about living there rent-free."

"Honestly, Mama doesn't care for that. You are the one who brought her husband back to her. You could live there for your entire life and she'll still think she owes you. If you really want to, we could do some hunting. Take something home for dinner?"

"I don't know how," I admitted. We'd started the training with Ally and Stone, but when Stone's soul had been captured, thoughts of training to hunt were put to one side.

"I'll make it easy for you."

"I don't even have a crossbow," I said, pointing out the flaw in his plan.

"You have me!"

"Okay." I smiled. "What can you do that I can't?"

"Look out there." He pointed to the view in front of us. At the base of the mountains, the farmers' fields stretched right to the horizon.

"Fields. Some sheep, some cattle."

"I see dinner."

"Stealing sheep and cows from farmers is not hunting, it's rustling," I pointed out.

"Look again. You see where the fences stop and its just scrubland? It belongs to no one."

I looked to where he was pointing. He was right, there were no markers there, nothing to show that the land belonged to anyone. I also didn't see any animals there. "There's nothing there!"

"We'll see! Just have your sword ready!" Ash gave me that gorgeous grin of his before throwing his clothes at me and changing back into his dragon form. I folded them and placed them back in the bag, hopping onto his back as I did. I held on tightly as he descended at a rapid rate, skirting the tops of the trees, before evening out and flying over acres and acres of farmland.

Small dots appeared on the horizon, which turned out to be a herd of deer. Ash dipped again suddenly, almost causing me to fall off, and sped toward the herd. They were quick, but he was quicker. He scooped one up in his mouth and tossed it into the air. Blowing a plume of fire right after it. The poor thing was barbecued in a second. He caught it again and held it in his mouth.

"Okay, show off. You aren't the only one that can hunt. Fly lower and watch me."

He ducked down lower again and flew right toward the herd for the second time. This time as he flew through the retreating flock, I thrust my sword to the side, right into the heart of one of the deer. It fell immediately to the ground.

"You are going to have to land so I can pick it up!" I instructed. Ash circled back and touched down right by the deer's body. It was much larger than I had expected and so it took me a good ten minutes to load its body onto Ash's back. Now that I'd killed it, I felt dreadful. Even though I told myself that it was for food, it didn't make me feel any better for killing it.

Once we were back in Frokontas, I threw the deer onto the barbecue pit. Ash dropped his, already barbecued deer next to it. There would be enough food to fill the whole village here.

"Can you cook it please?" I asked Ash before he had a chance to turn back. With a fiery blast, the second deer was as cooked as the first. I didn't tell him why I wanted to cook the animal. The truth was that I was scared that its soul would be trapped forever in my sword, or worse, that we'd eat the body and the soul would have nowhere to go. It was just easier to make sure it was dead.

"What's wrong?" asked Ash when he had turned back.

"Do you think the deer's soul is in the sword?"

"I don't know? Does it feel different to you?"

I held up the sword. It still had the deer's blood thickly coating it. Picking up a leaf, I wiped the blade until it shone like new. It felt exactly the same. Other people had told me that when a sword takes a soul, the sword feels stronger, heavier. Mine didn't. "It feels the same," I said.

"Maybe the Goblin magic only works on dragons?" replied Ash. "Come on, let's go tell Mama about the deer."

Inside I could tell we were too late. The most delicious smell permeated the house, telling us that dinner was cooking.

"Mama, we've cooked a couple of deer. They are outside in the fire pit."

"Lovely!" Edeline exclaimed. "I'll get your father to go and cut them up so we can have them another time."

"Julianna killed one," said Ash proudly, making me feel embarrassed.

"Well done. Now, go and sit at the table, the pair of you. Dinner is almost ready."

I followed Ash to a room I'd not been in before. It had a long table which would comfortably fit four, but someone had squeezed an extra chair on one side. Fiere and Lucy were already seated. Seconds later, Edeline came in from the kitchen with a huge steaming pot of stew.

"I wish I'd have known about your venison earlier," remarked Edeline, placing the pot on the table. "It would have been nice in this stew."

"Deer?" inquired Fiere, ladling great spoonful's of stew onto his plate.

"We went hunting today," replied Ash.

"Can you go down after dinner and chop one up for us? The rest of the village can share the other," said Edeline to Fiere.

"Sure. Two deer. Nice job!"

I'd eaten quite a few times with Ash's family, but this was the first time we'd really sat down together without other villagers. It was also the first time I'd had a meal around the dining table. Listening to them chat and tell each other about their day reminded me of my own mealtimes with my family. We always made time to eat together. I missed my mother's cooking, but mostly I missed the time before our lives were ripped apart. It was a bittersweet moment for me. Here I was, having been completely accepted by this new family, and yet I'd somehow managed to lose my own.

They were all completely at ease with me, and although they had taken a while to accept who I was, I was now being treated as any other member of the family. They listened intently to me telling them about the trip up the mountain, and Lucy was fascinated with my description of the Goblins, asking me question after question until Edeline told her to let me eat.

After dinner, Edeline cleared the plates away with help from Lucy and me and then she brought out dessert. Dessert was something I didn't see very often. Slayers traditionally saved sweet food for festivals and special occasions, and this was the first time I'd seen any kind of sweet dish in Frokontas. It was a layered fruit pudding with cake and cream and looked absolutely delicious. Unfortunately, I didn't get the chance to taste it before there was a knock on the door.

"Lucy, will you see who that is, please?" Edeline said while ladling a huge portion of the cream pudding onto a plate.

I heard her running down the stairs and opening the door. Edeline scooped out another portion of the creamy dessert and handed it to me. I was just about to tuck in when Lucy came back in the room followed by Spear.

"Spear! How nice to see you," began Fiere. "Julianna was just telling me about your adventure up the mountain. I'm sorry to hear it was such a bust."

"That's actually why I'm here," replied Spear. "I need to talk to Julianna about something."

"Would you like to join us for pudding?" inquired Edeline, butting in.

"No, thanks, Edie. It's pretty urgent I speak with Julianna. You can all hear it though, it's no secret."

All eyes turned to me. It wasn't the first time. I was almost getting used to it by now. I looked forlornly at the yummy pudding on my plate and wondered if I was going to actually be able to eat it.

"An old friend of mine came to visit me today," said Spear. He turned to the others. "Oak. You know him, Fiere."

"Yes," replied Fiere. I could tell by his face that he was interested to see where this was going as much as I was.

"I told Oak about Morganna. He had some interesting information about her."

"Don't tell me you met Morganna up the mountain?" said Fiere in surprise. "I didn't think she was a big fan of Goblins, nor they of her."

"She's dead," I said. "Has been a long time." I didn't sugar-coat it. It was obvious that Morganna wasn't the dragons' favorite person.

"Actually, that's why I'm here," said Spear. "She's not dead."

"Of course she is!" I replied. "I went to the celebration of her life. She died over ten years ago now."

"I was under the impression she was still alive," said Fiere. "I've never heard anything to the contrary. She's been quiet these past few years, but I just put that down to her finding some other race to torture. Last I heard, she was up north with the Wolf shifters. I'm not sure if she was killing them or living among them. Of course, I've been away for a while, so I could be wrong."

"Oak said the same thing."

"No!" I cried. "She's dead! My father told me." As I said it I realized how stupid it sounded. My father had told me a lot of things, most of which had turned out to be lies. "Why would my father tell me that Morganna was dead?"

"The story Oak told me was that she had a big falling out with the people in your village. She made the decision to leave. The elders put the story out that she had been killed by dragons."

"Why?" asked Ash. He beat me to it. I was wondering the same thing myself.

"Two reasons I suspect. The first being that it added fuel to the fire of hatred the villagers felt about us. If their hero was killed by a dragon, it only served to make the Slayers want to fight more. Secondly, it also meant that Morganna could never come back. The villagers already thought she had been killed."

"Why would she agree to this?" I asked. None of it made any sense.

"I don't know. Maybe she was sick of the fame, maybe she was sick of the fighting? I don't know her motivations, but I do know it's true. Oak has traveled a great deal and has seen Morganna with his own eyes. He has told me exactly where to find her. I was hoping you two would come with me to try and persuade her to part with her sword."

Everyone was silent as we allowed the information to sink in. Another lie told to me by my own father. What else about my childhood was made up? I felt as though nothing I knew was the truth. I looked down at my pudding. What had looked so utterly delicious only ten minutes earlier now looked like something that would make me feel sick.

"I'm coming," I answered. A day ago, I would have done anything to meet my childhood hero but now the only reason I agreed to it was to find out the truth, a truth that had eluded me my entire life.

10

"I want to speak to Oak," I said hours later as we were packing once again for a long trip.

Edeline was upset that we were going out so soon after coming back down from the mountain, but she understood. I was so tired of walking and being away from my own bed that it was only my desire to learn the truth once and for all that kept me going. I think Ash felt the same way and yet he was cheerful as he packed clean clothes into a bag.

"Why do you want to speak to him? Spear will have told you everything."

"Maybe, but how does he know so much about her?"

"He travels a lot. Most of us stay here where it is safe. Many don't even venture down the mountain for fear of being slain."

I felt bad as I always did when he said things like that. It was my people that had caused the dragons to be so isolated. It didn't stop me wanting to see Oak, though.

What did he know and what exactly did he tell Spear? "Do you know where he lives?"

Ash sighed. He knew me well enough by now to know that I wasn't going to give up. The legend of Morganna was a huge part of my childhood and, as I found out earlier, another lie told to me by my father. "Come on. I'll take you there."

I didn't want to drag Ash on yet another journey, albeit a short one. He needed rest as much as I did— probably more as he'd be the one flying tomorrow. "You don't have to come with me. You can just tell me where he lives."

"I'm coming!" He was adamant as I knew he would be. I didn't know why I thought he'd entertain the idea of me going alone.

It was almost dark outside with very little natural light. Low clouds blocked out the moon and the stars, leaving me feeling like I was walking with my eyes closed. There was very little light in the way of street-lamps as the dragons didn't really need them. They had excellent night vision. Thus I found myself relying on Ash's eyes to get us where we needed to go. Now that I was out in the dark, I was glad he'd elected to come. I'd have gotten hopelessly lost otherwise.

I expected Oak to live in one of the bigger houses at the other side of the village and so I was surprised when we turned into the main part of the village. We walked past the place where the town hall used to be before it was burned to the ground by Fiere. Where it once stood was now a wooden framed structure without walls or a roof. Whoever had been rebuilding the new town hall had worked quickly, already having the full frame laid out on brand new foundations.

Ash took me to a small alley I'd not been down before. The houses on either side were higgledy-piggledy, and the alley was so slim that I could touch the houses on both sides if I stretched my arms out. Ash stopped at a door and knocked loudly. The door opened and a man who looked to be in his early fifties answered.

"Ash! What a pleasure. And this must be the lovely Julianna. I've heard so much about you. Won't you come in? I've just warmed some water for tea."

"We were hoping to ask you about Morganna," said Ash as he followed Oak into the house.

"Yes. Spear told me I'd caused a bit of upset when he went to your house to tell you. He expected you might come see me."

"You didn't cause any upset," I said, not wanting to offend him. "It's all the lies I've been told that is upsetting."

"Quite!" he replied. Now that I looked at him, I could see how fit he looked. He had muscular arms and legs and a weathered face. He looked the quintessential traveler. "Sit! I'll bring the tea out."

He disappeared, only to come back moments later with three cups of steaming tea. It was lemon tea by the smell of it, or at least he'd flavored it with lemon.

"So, what is it you want to know?" he asked, passing a cup to me.

I so desperately wanted to ask what she was like, but I knew that sounded childish. Instead, I went with, "When did you meet her?"

"I've met her a few times. The last time I saw her, she was living amongst the Wolvren."

"Wolvren?" It was a term I'd not heard before.

"They are wolf people. There is a tribe of dragons about a hundred kilometers north of here. The Wolvren hate them almost as much as your people do. When Morganna was cast out of your village, she traveled a lot, but it was natural that she would end up with people who had the same mutual enemy."

"The dragons," said Ash.

"Exactly!"

"No one seems to like us really, do they?" mused Ash.

"They fear us. Many a war is started by fear rather than hate. Hate is what fear turns into. It looks less cowardly to hate a person than to fear them. Of course, it isn't. The Wolvren do not like a lot of people. They keep to themselves. Many people fear them, too, for they are shifters just as we are. That's why I was surprised that Morganna ended up with them."

"Her sword must hold more dragon souls than all the others," I said. "Maybe that is why they let her into their village."

"Yes." Oak took a long sip of his tea. "I think you are probably right. She might have been a legend to a lot of people, but she was also an outsider. I think her fame was bigger than she was. The Wolvren allowed her to just be. As far as I'm aware, she hasn't killed a dragon in a long time. Maybe even since she was cast out of your village."

"Why was she cast out?" I asked.

"Ah, I think it comes down to your father," he said, watching me intently for some kind of reaction.

"My father? He always spoke highly of her. His stories of her were what made her my childhood hero."

"He was the best swordsman in town—"

"He is the best swordsman in town!" I butted in.

"Maybe now, but when Morganna turned eighteen, she showed him that he wasn't as good as he thought he was. Even though she was younger and had less experience than him, she killed three times as many dragons as he did on her first attempt. Her legend only grew with each passing year until she became famous outside of Dronias too. Your father had to watch as her fame spread. His jealousy grew in tandem with her celebrity status. When you were little, it became too much for him. He asked her to leave. She refused so he tried blackmailing her. Apparently, he'd seen her with one of the village elders, one of the married village elders. He threatened to tell the village elder's wife. She told me that she loved him and didn't want to hurt him or his family so she decided to leave. When she had gone, she later heard that your father had told everyone that she had been eaten by the dragons. She didn't want to prove him wrong, so she hid away, letting everyone believe she was dead. I think by that time she was tired with all the notoriety anyway. She wanted a simpler life. Your father really had no choice but to say nice things about her. The whole town was in mourning. As I believe, there was even a party for her. A wake, if you will."

"Yeah, I know, I was there," I said, feeling despondent. Why did every story about my father involve him lying to me on a grand scale?

Just then there was a knock at the door.

Spear walked in without waiting for it to be opened. "Ash, Julianna, I thought you might come here. I already told you everything Oak told me."

"Tea, my friend?" asked Oak indicating a chair for him to sit.

"No, thank you. I'm in a rush. It's going to be a long day for us tomorrow." He gave both Ash and me a meaningful look. "I just came for that map."

"Hang on, I'll go get it." Oak stood up and left the room. I heard his feet as he walked up some stairs.

"Did he tell you what you wanted to know?" asked Spear.

"He told me that Morganna left because of my father. He was blackmailing her over some affair. I don't even know if it's true or not."

"If Oak says it's true, then it's true."

"I didn't mean that. I meant if it's true that she was having an affair or if my father interpreted it how he wanted. It could have been innocent. I guess I'll never know. Not without asking him...or her."

"From everything I've heard of your father, lying seems to come second nature to him. Whether he lied to you or lied to Morganna is irrelevant. He's a coward and untrustworthy and needs to be stopped."

I hated to hear it coming from Spear, but he was right. My father was a coward. I thought back to before all this had come out. Morganna might have been my hero as a child, but she was nothing compared to my father. At least that's what I had thought.

"Hang on there, Spear!" said Ash, defensively. "Whatever your feelings about Julianna's father, you

have to remember that he is still her family and upsetting her isn't going to solve any of our problems."

At least Spear had the decency to look apologetic.
"I'm sorry Julianna. Ash, you are right. I should keep my
opinions to myself. This is the problem with age-old
feuds, it's difficult to distance yourself from them."

"Here it is," said Oak, returning to the room with a
rolled-up parchment which he handed to Spear. "I'm
not an artist, but I did my best. I think you should be
able to follow it. If all else fails, keep to the east coast
and keep flying north until you hit the village."

"Thanks, Oak. I think we should all be off now. We
have a very long day ahead. You two make sure you have
a good breakfast tomorrow," he said, turning to us. We
took his lead and left

I was quiet as we walked the short distance back to
Ash's house. Spear's words had stung but it was what
Oak had told me that hurt the most. Once again, I was in
a position where everything my father had told me was
a lie.

I was glad of the cloud cover. It hid my tears well,
although Ash picked up on them anyway. He stopped in
the middle of the town square to hold me. He didn't say
a word, just wrapped his arms around me. It was
enough.

11

By the next morning, the clouds had lifted, leaving a hot sunny day.

"It's going to be hard to fly in this weather. A hundred kilometers is a long way to fly without worrying about the heat. We'd better pack an extra bag of water." Ash ran around the house, sorting the bags out for our journey, occasionally putting his head around the kitchen door to ask Edeline and me to add things to our food bags. By the time we had finished, we had two bags of water, enough food for two days and a bag each with clothes. Ash had packed enough to last us a week which I hoped we wouldn't need.

"Are you going to be able to carry all this?" I asked, feeling how heavy just the water bags were. He also had to have me on his back for the entire duration of the flight.

"I'll be fine. We can land and rest if we need to. Come on, let's go." He kissed Edeline and Lucy on the cheek before heading out into the heat. Spear was outside waiting for us along with a couple of others I recognized from the trip up to the Goblin village.

"Where is everyone?" asked Ash, looking about him as if he was expecting more to arrive.

"This is it," replied Spear.

"Just the five of us?"

"No one else wanted to come. Everyone else is exhausted. We don't need many people. We are only going to talk to Morganna, not wage war on her."

"Didn't Oak say she is staying in a wolf village? Wolves that hate us, no less? We need more people in case they start a fight."

"I'm not about to start fighting with yet another group of people. I am going to ask to speak with them."

I could see Ash getting restless. It sounded in his voice too. "And if they don't want to speak to us?"

"They will," replied Spear.

"How can you be so sure?"

"I don't know Morganna at all, but I'm willing to bet if Julianna comes to the village and asks to speak to her, then she will. I doubt she'd pass up an opportunity to speak to one of her own."

"Are you kidding? We are sending Julianna right into a pack of wolves?"

"It's fine," I said, trying to diffuse the situation. As much as I hated to admit it, Spear had a point. "I want to speak to her. The wolves are not my enemy."

Ash knew when he was beaten. He and his fellow dragons turned into their dragon form and I helped them all secure their own bags on their backs before hopping onto Ash's shoulders.

We soared into the air and out over the mountain

and over the prairies we had seen when we had gone hunting. Spear was in the lead, his long black body cutting through the sky with three dragons and me behind. The sun beat down as we turned towards the east and out to the coast. The ocean was only about twenty kilometers from Dronias, but I had yet to go there. I'd never seen it before and, despite our situation, I felt excited at the prospect of seeing it for the first time.

The sun got hotter as the day wore on, and I found myself pulling a t-shirt from one of the bags to shield my head. Ash, with his leathery dragon hide, didn't need to worry about sun exposure as much as I did, but I emptied one of our many bottles of water over him in an effort to cool him down.

In the distance, the green prairies and pastures turned into the endless blue of the sea. The sun glinted off of it like thousands of tiny diamonds sparkling just beneath the surface. It took my breath away, filling me with awe at its vastness. Hundreds of pretty little boats bobbed on the calm surface, telling me that there was a fishing village nearby. I so desperately wanted to stop to see it up close, to feel the water and sand beneath my feet, but Spear turned a sharp left and headed north just as Oak had told him to.

After a couple of hours, I pulled out one of the sand-wiches that Edeline had made us. After throwing it to Ash, who caught it expertly between his teeth, I rummaged around for one of my own. Just as I took a bite, Spear flew lower in the sky, landing in a field of blazing red poppies.

He turned back into his human form and scrabbled around in his pack for something to wear. "I think this is a good place to stop for lunch. I see that you've already started." He grinned at me as I held onto my half-eaten sandwich. "Don't worry; it was your sandwich that prompted me to stop. I saw you eating when I turned my head and decided it was way past lunchtime."

The five of us went through so many bottles of water that I was glad I'd brought an extra bagful. As the others chomped down on their lunch, I waded through the poppies to see if I could see the sea. I could hear it and I could see the gulls that squawked over it and yet, it was just out of view over a small hill. One day, I would come back and see it properly when I could actually spend some time there.

"You okay?" I heard someone say behind me. I didn't have to turn to know it was Ash.

"I'm just thinking how nice it would be to spend some time by the ocean. I've never seen it before today."

"You haven't?" He sounded surprised.

"You have?" I asked, equally surprised. I'd gotten the impression that he didn't leave the mountain much.

"A few times. I'll bring you back someday."

Lunch was over far too quickly and I found myself packing all the bags as the others turned back into dragons. It had been decided that Ash would take the lead now to give Spear a break. Spear had told him to follow the coast for a few hours until he came to a large forest, and it was there that he should land.

I jumped on his back and he took off with the others behind him in a V-shape. Instead of following Spear's directions, he headed out to the sea—a five-minute detour at most—and flew low over the water. I knew he did it for me. I could smell the salt as the sea sprayed up at us thanks to Ash dangling his feet in the water. He dodged the fishing boats, giving the fishermen quite a fright in the process and then began to rise again, heading slightly inland. It had been a dangerous detour —any of the fishermen could have attacked—but it was one I was grateful for. As long as I lived, I'd never forget feeling the sea spray cooling my face. The rest of the journey was long and uneventful. I occasionally caught glimpses of the sea to my right, although Ash stayed away from it, preferring to stay away from prying eyes, high up over land.

After a good few hours, I finally saw the forest we had been looking out for. What started as a tiny thin strip of green on the horizon soon became an expanse of trees that went right to the horizon line. To the left were high, gray mountains; this was presumably where the other dragons lived. Ash landed at the tree line and turned back into his human form. I threw him his clothes as the others landed.

"Here, check where we need to go," shouted Spear, throwing me a map as he got dressed. I opened it up to find a simple, hand-drawn sketch, no doubt drawn by Oak. A line down the right-hand side of the paper repre-sented the sea, and a huge expanse of scribbles showed the forest. He was never going to make it as an artist that was for sure.

He'd drawn some small buildings to the left and as I looked over, there they were, part of a small village about a kilometer away on the edge of the forest. A dot drawn in red about ten centimeters into the forest was marked with the word "Wolvren." If the scale was correct (which I doubted it was) we were about five kilometers away from the Wolvren village. Flying through the trees would be impossible, so it seemed we would have to walk. I took one of the water bottles from the bag and downed it in one gulp, feeling the still-cold liquid ease my throat. I threw another bottle at Ash and pulled one of the bags onto my back. As we had drunk so much water and eaten our lunch, we were now down to one bag each to carry.

The forest was dark, and with the map being pretty much useless, we took the most worn path, hoping it was created by people—or wolves—and not just some other creature of the forest.

"They are this way," said Spear, taking the lead along the dark path. His voice echoed, sounding eerie. Even though it had been red hot outside the forest, in here it was dark and damp with an unnatural haze.

"How do you know?" I whispered, although I wasn't sure why. The Wolvren were still a long walk away from us.

"I can smell them," he replied. I looked at Ash, and he nodded his head. I'd known that the dragons had unusually good eyesight but I'd not known about their keen sense of smell too. I took a deep sniff, but could only smell the damp moss that clung to the bottom of the trees.

The trail was well-worn and, thanks to the canopy of the leaves, cool enough to be comfortable. Yet there was something wrong that I couldn't quite put my finger on. Yes, the forest seemed to have its own climate entirely, which was odd in itself, but there was something else strange about the place. I kept my eyes open, grateful to be surrounded by dragons. Even so, I kept one hand on my sword, ready in case anything should attack. It was then that I realized what it was that was strange. It was the complete silence of the place. I strained my ears to hear but the only sound was the quiet footsteps we were making through the forest. There was no birdsong or the sound of small creatures scurrying through the undergrowth, both of which I would expect in a forest like this. It was almost as if the whole place was dead and the trees were figments of my imagination. I reached out and ran my hand along the trunk of one as I passed, needing to know that it was real. The bark was cold and damp as if it had been rained on recently. The whole place gave me the creeps.

I'd loved to spend time in the forest near Dronias as a child and could happily spend hours climbing trees. Here, I just wanted to be away, back in the sunshine. We each took it in turns to lead, alternating every fifteen minutes or so. The scenery never changed—just endless damp trees leading off in every direction.

When it was my turn to walk in front, I could feel Ash walking just behind me. The path was too narrow to walk two abreast, so we had to walk in single file. I kept my eyes on the ground, afraid that I'd somehow accidentally lead everyone the wrong way. Not that it mattered with their ability to follow scent, but I didn't want to be the one to mess up. The deeper we got into the forest, the colder it grew. I had to wrap my sweater tighter around myself to keep out the unrelenting damp.

I was just about thinking we should give up completely when I stepped on a branch. I'd stepped on many since entering the forest, but this one was the first to make a sound. The others had been damp and had bent rather than broken under my feet. It gave a loud crack as my weight snapped it in two, making my heart leap. I had just gotten my breathing back under control when there was a large flash of purple light and another crack, this time much louder. My hand pulled out my sword with me barely thinking about it, and Ash ran in front of me to shield me from whatever it was.

"What was that?" he whispered as the light continued to glow. The mist clung to it as though the light was a solid object, pulling it in.

"Magic!" hissed Spear behind me.

I steadied myself, my sword held out in front of me as both the light and the smoke cleared. In its place was a man, but this was no ordinary man. He was at least seven feet tall and had long, gray hair. His face was slightly pointed as were his ears, giving him a lupine appearance. This was most definitely a member of the Wolvren.

I held my sword toward him as Ash readied himself for an attack.

The wolf-man sneered at us. "Your sword cannot handle the soul of a wolf!"

12

I lowered my sword. Not because I thought he was right—although with the magic I'd just witnessed, he probably was—but because I didn't want to appear to be confrontational.

"We came here to see Morganna!" I said, standing my ground. Behind me, I could feel the energy running through the group, each of them ready at a moment's notice to fight if need be. I didn't know how it had happened, but at some point over the past few days, we'd begun to work as a team, and the few of us that were on this journey had become almost one. I knew what they were all thinking and I didn't need to look behind me to know that they still were ready to defend me.

"Dragons aren't welcome here!" he replied menacingly, his features set in a growl, his hackles raised and his jowls set back, baring his teeth. If it was scary on a wolf, it was even more disturbing on this wolf-human person. It was an unnatural expression on someone who stood on two legs. His teeth were pointed, his two incisors slightly longer than the others.

Then, I did something that even I wasn't expecting. I walked toward him. I could feel the fear in Ash even though I didn't feel it myself. This wolf-man was ready to rip my throat out and could in a second, but I hoped that by showing no fear, he would respect me. It was a theory! Only time would tell if it was a good one.

"I'm not a dragon," I said, sounding as brave as I could, "but I think you already know that."

I was standing not five feet away from him now and although the strange purple light had dissipated, I could feel the crackle of magic around us.

"You are either very brave or very foolish," said the wolf-man, but his features were now showing an expression of interest rather than one of anger.

"That's a maybe, but I need to speak to Morganna and I know she is living here in this forest."

"I do not know where you got your information, but I can assure you that only my people live in these trees. I would imagine you have seen for yourselves that no other living creature calls this place home. There is a good reason for that. My kind are carnivores and will eat anything that dares enter this forest. We are a large pack and, as you can imagine, very hungry. There have not been many so foolish to enter here for a long time."

"You aren't going to eat me," I said, hoping it was the truth.

"Hmm," he replied thoughtfully. "You are so sure of yourself. Is it, I wonder, because you believe your dragon friends will save you? That they will turn into fire-breathing killing machines and flame me before I have a chance to kill you?"

For the first time since the wolf-man appeared, I turned to look at my fellow men. Ash was still standing where I'd left him, ready to fight at a moment's notice. The others were not far behind him, their bags on the ground. They were all poised to turn into dragons, just waiting for the wolf-man to make his move. It made me feel ashamed that he was right. I had been brave because of the men behind me. I turned back to him.

"They will not turn into dragons if you give them no reason to."

"They will not turn into dragons at all. Not in this forest, at least. I see that you haven't done your home-work about my pack. Has no one ever told you that you should find out everything about your enemies before heading into their territory?" He was laughing now. I didn't know what was amusing him, but it was wasting both of our time.

"Just let me speak with Morganna and we will be on our way," I said.

He ignored my words and began to tell me about himself instead. "Shifters do not usually carry magic beyond the ability to shift. I assume your dragon friends here can only do that. As you have already seen, my pack has magic that would be considered unusual. I have to admit that as the Alpha wolf, the majority of the magic belongs to me, but there is also a spell on this forest to protect us. It allows only the wolf to shift into their animal forms. We've had enough problems with dragon shifters in the past that I'm afraid it was a necessary precaution. Your friends here will not be able to transform until they are outside of the tree line. I'm afraid you and your sword will be no match for me."

I had no idea if he was telling the truth or not, but I'd seen enough magic from him to believe what he said was true. "You bought your magic from the Goblins on Triad Mountains!" I replied.

For the first time, he looked surprised. "So, you have been doing your homework after all. How did you know? Oh never mind, how you know is irrelevant. As long as you understand that you can't beat me."

"Look, Mr. Tough Wolf," I said, bridging the gap between us. The crackle of magic intensified. "I understand your need to come across as this big bad wolf, but why can't you get it into your stupid head that we are not here to fight you. I have no interest in beating you in a fight, nor do I particularly care about where you procure your magic. I'm only here to speak to Morganna!"

I stood within touching distance of him. I wasn't sure who was more shocked at my outburst, him or me. The already silent forest managed to become quieter still. He stood at least two feet taller than me, so I had to crane my neck to look him in the eye. No one moved for an eternity. I stared at him without blinking, determined not to back down. I didn't need to look behind me to know that Ash had his mouth open in shock. The only sound I could hear was the unnatural boom of my heart pounding. I was under no illusion that the wolf wouldn't hear it too.

After, what felt like a hundred years, but could only have been a few seconds, he began to laugh. Not just a chuckle but a full-on booming laugh that echoed through the forest.

I stood, waiting patiently for him to stop.

"In all my years, I have never known anyone to come into my forest and speak to me this way. It is actually rather refreshing." He clapped his huge, paw-like hand on my shoulder. I heard the others step forward to save me.

"Stop!" he commanded. The magic intensified again, and I knew he'd put some kind of shield between me and the others. "I'm not going to hurt her so there is no need to try and fight me. I've already told you, you cannot win. I like her. She shows spirit. I'll eat anyone, but it would be a shame to eat someone with so much courage, no matter how misguided it may be. I very rarely do this, but I will let you all leave this forest with your lives."

The invisible shield was gone and the crackle of magic disappeared, allowing me to step back and join the others.

"I need to speak to Morganna," I repeated. He seemed to have forgotten the reason we were here in the forest in the first place.

"That is impossible. I know everyone in this forest. All are in my pack. Not one of them is named Morganna. Morganna is not a wolf name." He stepped back then as if he was going to leave us.

"I want to speak to her!" I said again, this time more forcefully.

"It was funny the first time you tried to be sassy, but don't push your luck. I'm letting you all leave unharmed. I suggest you do just that before I change my mind." He turned and began to retreat into the forest. As if a spell was broken, the others came running toward me. Ash enveloped me in his arms.

"It's time to go," he said. "At least we tried."

I looked up at him. I could see the disappointment in his eyes but I could also see the relief. He'd been scared. His one form of defense had been stripped from him, and it had affected him. The others all shared the same look of relief, even Spear. I tried to imagine how I would feel without my sword. Probably as naked as the day I was born. I'd carried it by my side since I'd turned eighteen. It was almost a part of me.

"We didn't try hard enough," I replied. I knew he didn't want me to, but I turned away from him and followed the path that the Alpha wolf had taken into the forest.

13

I ran along the path as quickly as I could. He hadn't just evaporated into a puff of purple smoke, so I knew he wasn't using magic to get away, and yet I couldn't see him in front of me. He was stealthy as was right for a wolf, but it only made me run faster. I could hear the footsteps of the others following me, their heads no doubt coming to the same conclusion I had already arrived at: We were running directly to the Wolvren home.

"Julianna, stop!" I heard Ash shouting behind me but I ignored him. I couldn't stop. I knew the Alpha wolf was not telling me the truth about Morganna and I knew that this would never be over without her, or at least her sword.

"What are you doing?" He was there, the Alpha. I hadn't seen him in the dark and had almost tripped over him. "I told you to leave!"

I knew being "sassy" would not help me now. I needed to come up with a different tactic. "Look, I'm grateful that you've given us the chance to escape and I don't want to disrespect your wishes, but I really need to speak to her. I'm not going anywhere until you tell me where she is."

"You are—"

"I know what you said," I interrupted him, "but you don't understand how important it is that I—we—speak with her. Her sword holds the souls of many dragons, possibly hundreds. They are trapped in there and will be until the end of time unless we let them out."

"This does not concern me. I already told you that I do not like dragons. I only spoke to you before because you are not one, but do not test my patience."

"It's not just the dragons. Morganna herself was done a great injustice. My people treated her badly. More specifically my own father. He lied about her, forcing her to leave the town she knew as home."

"If your people treated her badly, if your own family forced her out, why would she want to speak to you?"

"So you do know her!" I exclaimed. Okay, he'd not said as much, but if he didn't know her, he wouldn't be asking questions.

"I've already told you. I do not know her." He sighed. "This is wearing thin. You need to leave."

"I'm not going until you tell me the truth."

He bared his teeth again, pulling back his lips. His eyes took on a madness I'd not seen in him before and I knew I'd lost the battle. He stepped toward me, growling. Something grabbed me from behind and I realized it was Ash, pulling me away from the beast.

"Come on. We need to go. We can try again later."

"I can't just leave. This is our only chance!" I replied, but I was scared.

The Alpha howled and then gave a warning growl before taking a step toward me.

It was a warning. A warning I wasn't about to ignore. I grabbed Ash's hand and began to run through the forest with Spear and the others in front of me. In the dark, we became disoriented and pretty soon we were running somewhere I didn't recognize. The path beneath us had disappeared, replaced by thick undergrowth which made running difficult. Behind me, I could hear the heavy, guttural breathing of the Alpha chasing us. In front, I saw Spear fall. His foot had caught in a branch that he'd not seen in the dark. It was too late. We couldn't outrun the Alpha, even without one of us falling. We stopped and helped Spear to his feet as the Alpha crashed through the undergrowth toward us. He hadn't turned into his wolf form, but he looked less human and more wolf-like as he came skidding to a stop just feet from us.

"He fell!" Ash said, hoping it would placate the wolf. "He's injured. We're doing what you asked. We were leaving. There is no need to hurt us."

The wolf looked at Spear. There was blood pouring from a cut on Spear's knee. It was a superficial scrape but it proved that Ash was telling the truth.

"I heard what you said to the human."

"What?" asked Ash, genuinely confused.

"You told her that you will come back here later." His face was contorted in anger. Why hadn't we left when he first told us to? Oh, yeah, because I was an idiot who thought I could persuade him to tell me Morganna's whereabouts. This was all my fault. I could draw my sword again but I knew it would be a fruitless exercise. He could overpower me in a second.

"You cannot come back here. I cannot let you. You have shown me that you will not cease hounding me until you are all dead."

"We won't come back. I give you my word. You've made it very plain that we are not welcome."

It was a last-ditch attempt to calm him. It didn't work. "Your word means nothing to me. I have no reason to believe you. The only way that you will stop is your own death and believe me, that can easily be arranged."

He stepped closer and without thinking my hand tightened on my sword. I knew I couldn't win a fight against him, but I'd be damned if I'd go down without trying. Another step closer and I pulled my sword from its sheath.

He grinned, but it was not the friendly grin from earlier. His teeth dripped with spittle and the corners of his eyes narrowed. "As I said before, either brave or foolish." The Alpha stepped closer once again but I held my ground.

Not that I had any choice. The path behind me was blocked by Ash, Spear, and the others. Beyond them, the undergrowth was too thick to run through. I was trapped and he knew it. We all were.

Before he had the chance to leap at me, I dodged to the side. That way, while he was fighting me, the others could run around us and find their way back to the path. At least that was my plan. The Alpha followed me with his eyes. I was right. He was concentrating on only me. It wouldn't give the others much time, but if they found the path pretty quickly and ran as fast as they could, they had a slim chance of escape. The longer I held the Alpha off, the more time it would buy them.

"Run!" I hissed under my breath to the others.

They didn't move. I hadn't counted on them wanting to stay and help me fight even though they must have known it was a fruitless task. None of them had brought weapons with them, thinking that in moments of danger, they were the best weapons. I knew how big and strong they were as dragons, but in their human forms, they were no match for the Alpha.

He growled again and pounced, his clothes ripping in mid-air as he turned into a monstrous wolf. His change surprised me. With the dragons, there was always the crunching of bones and the disgusting way their skin folded and stretched and grew with each shift. The Alpha had shifted effortlessly and had done it within the time it took from his feet leaving the ground to hitting it again. I rolled to the floor, getting out of his way in the nick of time. Getting to my feet quickly, I swung my sword at him, but he was just a hair's breadth away from being struck. He swiped at my sword with his huge paws, almost knocking it out of my hand, but I held tight. Without my sword, I may as well lie down and wait to be eaten. As I thrust, he dodged, and when he lunged, I rolled out of the way, the two of us engaged in a dance that would only end in disaster. Form the corner of my eye, I could see the others scrabbling around in their bags. What were they doing? There were no weapons in there. Nothing that could hurt a giant wolf. They also weren't running away as I had hoped.

I held onto my sword, remembering my training. I thought back to the morning of my eighteenth birthday when I'd practiced with Jasper. I'd beaten him hands down, earning respect from my father. It was a bittersweet memory now. My father's respect meant nothing to me anymore, but at the time it had meant the whole world. I tried to remember how I'd beaten my brother. It had been my stealth. He'd not managed to hit my protective armor because I'd been too quick for him. It wasn't much of a defense against a wolf twice my size, but it was all I had.

He lowered himself, growling, ready to leap. If I was too slow, I'd be pinned to the ground. As soon as I saw the muscles in his shoulders working to push himself up, I jumped onto a nearby fallen log and somersaulted right over him. He wasn't as slow as Jasper had been. He saw what I was doing and tried to turn over in mid-air, hitting the ground on his back. If it winded him, he didn't show it. He was back on his feet and ready to leap again in seconds, giving me no time to attack. I didn't know why I was comparing him to Jasper. He was twice my brother's size and speed. He jumped up, and as I saw his huge claws heading toward my face, I held the sword out in front of me with the hope he'd impale himself upon it. As if in slow motion, he swiped the sword to the side. In that moment, I knew I was a goner.

It was then his head jerked to the side. He landed on me, pushing my body to the ground. I was incapacitated under his enormous weight and yet, he was still. His head rested on my shoulder.

Ash and the others ran over and pushed his bulky

frame away from me. He rolled off as though he were asleep.

"What happened?" I asked, genuinely confused. He was just beginning to come around, but by his groggy expression, he was startled.

"We all threw apples at him as hard as we could. I think Spear threw a canteen of water. One of them hit him in the temple. I think it knocked him out for a second."

"Let's go before he fully wakes," said Spear, grabbing his bag and throwing it over his shoulder.

The others grabbed their bags and followed suit, but it was too late. The Alpha was already back on all fours, blocking our route back to the path.

"I don't suppose you have any more apples?" I joked, more out of fear than trying to be funny. It was pointless anyway. It was a lucky shot that had startled him. Doing it again would be a miracle.

The Alpha growled, saliva dripping from his bared teeth. He got down again, poised to leap at us. This time there was no one left to defend us.

Just before he leaped, there was another huge flash of purple light. It shocked the Alpha, who moved to the side just as a woman appeared from the light. A woman I recognized immediately. I'd stared at her picture enough times.

"Morganna!" I whispered.

"Who dares hurt one of my pack?" she shouted in fury.

I took a step forward. "It was me..."

14

Before Morganna had time to answer, more flashes of light lit up the trees and the surrounding area, like the fireworks we set off at the dragon-slaying parties. Out of the flashes appeared more Wolvren. There were perhaps forty of them, most of which were in their human form, although some were shifted into wolves like the Alpha. We were surrounded in every direction by the snarls and bared teeth of the Wolvren pack, with Morganna in the center.

I did my best to ignore the danger that was all around me—easier said than done. "I'm from Dronias. I came here to see you."

Morganna held her arm out at her side as if to quell the angry mob behind her, or at least to keep them from attacking. Her expression changed from one of pure anger to intrigue, no doubt because of the company I was with. Proving me right, she spoke.

"A Slayer with dragons?"

"Yes, ma'am."

"Hmmm. Interesting."

"We came here to see you," I repeated.

"I have no wish to speak with anyone from my village. Not since...well, not at all, and I especially have no desire to converse with dragons. They, as you are probably aware, are a Slayer's natural enemy."

"Not to mention the wolves' natural enemy," hissed the Alpha, who had changed back into his more human form and who had now taken his place at Morganna's side.

"And yet, I wonder... What has happened that two such enemies would team up just to speak to me? The Slayers hate the dragons more than we do, Alpha. To see them together like this is truly exceptional."

"We can take the dragons and leave the girl if you wish?" Alpha, for it seemed that was his name as well as rank, took a step toward me. Behind me, I could feel the others pull in closer.

"No. Not yet. I need to find out what this has to do with me. If we kill them now, goodness only knows how many others will turn up. I want to speak to them."

"Thank you!" I breathed a sigh of relief. It was obvious she didn't really want us there, but I hoped that once she heard my story, I could persuade her to change her mind.

"Not here, though. You are too close to our village. No matter your reasons, I will never permit dragons into the village. It will violate the trust of every Wolvren here and I refuse to do that to them after they so graciously took me in. There is a clearing about three miles from here due west. If you follow that path and carry on in the same direction, you should get to it. You will know it once you see it. It is a large circle of grass where no trees grow. I do not have the magic to transport you there, so you will have to hike. I'll meet you there and we will talk. You may also set up camp there, although do not misinterpret my generosity. It will be for one night only. After that, I will allow my fellow Wolvren to do what they will with you."

"Thank you!" I said again. I was finally going to be able to find out the truth.

"Do not thank me. I'm doing this because I'm curious. Stick to the path. If you deviate from it I will know. If you come too close to our village to the north, I will know. Do you understand?"

"Yes!"

With that, she and all the Wolvren disappeared in a haze of purple smoke. When the haze cleared, it was just the five of us again, standing in the middle of the silent forest.

"What do you make of all that?" asked one of the dragons.

"If she's a Slayer, she'll have grown up hating us," replied Ash, wrapping his arm around my shoulder.

"And she hates me for what my father did to her."

Spear began the short walk back to the path that Morganna had pointed out. "It is a good job you didn't mention your father's name. She might not have been so accommodating."

"You call that accommodating?" replied the first dragon, following Spear.

"I think we need to be wary," Ash said, following the

others. "She's curious. What is going to happen when we tell her everything?"

"She's not going to be so curious anymore," replied Spear over his shoulder.

"Exactly!"

I kept silent. I was sure they were both right, and yet a huge part of me idolized Morganna. I couldn't believe that she'd do anything to hurt one of her own kind, despite the evidence to the contrary.

The trail was thick with undergrowth and was barely more than a path at all. We'd only walked for ten or so minutes when Spear asked to borrow my sword—not to defend himself, but to cut through the thicker parts of the undergrowth. I hated to part with it. My sword was part of who I was, but unless I wanted to take up the lead, I had no choice. I pulled it from its sheath and passed it over to him. I could hear the *thwack, thwack, thwack* as my sword cut through branches and bushes and had to admit, we sped up considerably from that point.

The journey still took a lot longer than expected and we were all exhausted and sweaty from hiking all day. When we finally got to the clearing, the sun was lower in the sky and thankfully, not so hot. A slight breeze swayed the leaves on the very tops of the trees but did not reach us at the bottom. The clearing itself was exactly as Morganna had told us: a large circle of grass surrounded by dense forest. What she had failed to mention were the beautiful flowers that skirted around it. Bluebells and dainty pink and white flowers that I didn't know the name of. It was beautiful. There was no mistaking we were in the right place but had there been,

Morganna sitting right in the center would leave us in no doubt.

She was alone, sitting on a large red rug which was covered in food.

"I thought you might be hungry," she said as she saw us enter. As I took in the spread before me, my stomach gurgled. When was the last time I'd eaten? After the events of the past few hours, I couldn't even remember.

We took a step forward toward her.

"Halt!"

Spear stopped and I walked right into the back of him.

"You will not bring your weapons in here. I am unarmed as you can see."

I took the sword back from Spear. It felt good to finally get it back again. I placed it back in its sheath. "We were just using it to cut through the forest. The path was overgrown."

"Nevertheless, come toward me slowly with the sword handle pointing in my direction. Just you."

I could feel Ash stiffen beside me, but I knew she wouldn't hurt me. How I knew, I wasn't sure, but if this was what it took to speak to her, then so be it. I held onto the blade's end safely through the sheath and passed it to her. She drew it quickly, leaving me standing there with just the sheath in my hand.

"So you are indeed a Slayer," she said, taking in the detailing on the sword.

"Yes."

"And you come from my village?"

"Yes."

"Hmm." She placed the sword on the ground behind

her. It made me nervous, having it out of reach, but she was not armed as far as I could see. "Come over then. There is enough food for all of us." She beckoned the dragons over, and one by one, we found a place to sit on the rug. Morganna arched her brow as Ash sat right next to me and took my hand, and yet she made no mention of it.

The food was amazing, and yet all of it came from the forest. There were berries of all kinds, big bowls of fruit and nuts, and even a plate of torn up meat. As the whole forest had seemed completely devoid of any wildlife, I couldn't imagine what kind of meat it was, and yet the dragons didn't seem to mind. They took big handfuls and guzzled it down.

I filled my plate with berries and nuts and picked at them as I took a good look at my hero. She was slightly older than the woman I'd looked up to in the painting, but she had aged remarkably well. The painting was at least fifteen years old and yet she looked only five or so years older. She was probably a similar age to my own mother and yet there was not a hint of grey in her long dark hair and her face was remarkably wrinkle-free. She looked closer to my age and yet she had an air about her of having seen everything. A worldliness.

"I've been a fan of yours for a long time," I said, feeling slightly ridiculous.

She laughed. "I didn't realize I had any of those left and certainly not from Dronias. It was made very clear to me that I was not wanted there.

"Not by the people. The people still love your memory."

"My memory?"

"Many of the people in Dronias believe you are dead."

"While it is true that I have been keeping a very low profile these many years, I don't understand why anyone would think I was dead."

"Because my father told them you were. He told us all. He said a dragon killed you."

"A dragon?" she roared. "A mere dragon could not kill the mighty Morganna. Am I not known as the most fearless dragon Slayer of all time?"

"Remember who you are among!" growled Spear.

"Sorry, I forgot," she said, but we all knew she was perfectly aware of her company. She began to study my face, making me nervous. "Your father... Your father couldn't be Rocco, could he? Yes. I see the familiarity." She answered her own question. "If I lived to be a hundred and two, I would never have expected Rocco's daughter to come to speak to me and much less to be in the company of dragons."

"My name is Julianna. The reason I am with the dragons is the same reason I want to speak to you."

"Color me intrigued. A Slayer and a dragon together. What could possibly have happened to have this occur?"

"It probably won't surprise you that it all starts with my father..."

I told her everything, right from the day I woke up on my eighteenth birthday. I told her about how I'd met Ash and the circumstances in which I'd gotten to know the rest of the dragons. I told her about the Goblins and the souls of the dragons being captured thanks to the Goblin magic within all swords. Her eyes became wider as I spoke, leaving no detail out. I ended my story with how we had decided to come find her.

"Well, that's quite a story and not one I was expect-ing. Not that I knew what to expect, but you have floored me. I knew some of what was going on, I'm not going to lie to you. I know what the Goblin swords do. I know they collect souls. I didn't know that it leaves the dragon still alive."

"It's barbaric. My father knew."

"It seems that your father and I are more similar than I thought. While I admit to not knowing about the dragons still being alive, I have killed many, or at least I thought I had."

"Murdering us is no better than capturing our souls," growled Spear.

"Maybe it is, maybe it isn't. I'm not going to ask forgiveness for my actions but I will admit you have given me a lot to think about. In my past, I reveled in the killing of dragons. It was my calling and I was very good at it. In my older years, I realized that it held no fun for me anymore. Your father actually did me a favor. I needed a way out anyway. Him telling people I'd died was probably the main reason that no one came looking for me, and the reason I've been able to live here in peace for so many years. Dragon-slaying is in my past, but it also surrounds my present. The Wolvren have protected me and taken me into their pack. Much like the Slayers, they are enemies of the dragons. I do not kill dragons anymore, but I have given the Wolvren the skills to do it themselves."

"Aren't you tired of all the bloodshed?" asked Ash, who had been silent throughout the meal.

"Yes, I'm weary. Maybe I made mistakes in the past. I didn't always know the dragons were shifters. For many years, at the height of my fame, I thought that killing dragons was no worse than slaughtering any other animal for meat, although you know we never ate the dragons. I suppose I should have questioned where the bodies of the dragons were taken, but I was too happy being idolized that I didn't really care."

"But you know dragons are shifters now?"

"Not all dragons are shifters, but I know it's possible. The ones that live in a colony on the mountain beside this forest are shifters. I found that out myself when I first got taken in by the Wolvren. They had heard of my legend and challenged me to kill one of the dragons. I took off up the mountain alone and found one reasonably quickly. It was a small one, a baby really. I chased it, eager to take it back to the pack to show them. I would have preferred to kill a larger one, but I wouldn't have been able to carry its body. It tried to breathe fire at me, but it was so immature, it could only breath smoke rings. Honestly, it was such a pathetic little thing, and yet I had no guilt about what I was doing. Not until it turned into its human form right in front of my eyes. It was a child. Couldn't have been more than six or seven years old. He was completely naked and shivering. Of course, I couldn't kill him then. I gave him my tunic and told him never to come down the mountain again. I've not killed a dragon since."

"But you're happy for the Wolvren to do it!" Spear said, sounding completely unimpressed by her story.

"I walked back up the mountain the very next day. I spoke to the dragon leader and told him to stay away from the forest. We came to a truce. If the Wolvren stayed in the forest and the dragons on the mountain, neither side would get hurt. I told the Wolvren they could kill any dragon that came into the forest but no further. They accepted it. No dragon or wolf has been killed since I've lived here."

"So, you are lying to your own kind?" asked Spear.

"In a fashion. It keeps them safe."

"Don't you have magic for that?"

"Yes, but may I remind you, my lie also keeps the dragons safe. Now, you've told me a lot of things, some of which has surprised me, and yet you left off the most important part."

"What part?" I asked.

"I'm guessing you didn't just come here to tell me a story. It's a pretty long trek from Dronias. No, you want something from me."

"Yes," I admitted. "The dragons are good people. I wouldn't be here otherwise. They don't deserve the treatment they've had at our hands. I'm here... We are here because we want to save them. All of them. Years and years of dragons are trapped within our swords. I've found a way to defeat the Goblin magic and release their souls." I paused for a second, barely daring to ask what I was about to.

"I'd like for you to give us your sword."

15

"You are asking for my sword?"

"I gave you mine," I pointed out.

"You let me borrow yours to keep us all safe. It's not the same thing. You can see it right here."

"I only want to borrow it. It's not the actual sword I'm after, it's the souls you've trapped."

"Three hundred," she said quietly.

"Excuse me?"

"If what you say is true, there are three hundred dragon souls trapped in that sword."

I let out my breath. Three hundred! It was a massive number. I knew she was the most famous dragon Slayer in our land, but I'd not expected that kind of number. I didn't have to look to know that the dragons were as stunned as I was.

"You have three hundred of my people trapped in your sword?" asked Spear incredulously.

"Not all are your people. There are many dragon colonies, but at least two hundred are from yours."

"We need your sword!" shouted Spear angrily.

"My past has been questionable, and I've spent the last few years living in peace. I feel that by helping the Wolvren, I've atoned somewhat for my mistakes. I barely know you, any of you, so just because you come here with your amazing story does not mean I'm going to give my sword up so easily. No offense, but why should I?"

"Because the Morganna I have grown up idolizing was a fierce but fair warrior. Yes, she killed, but only to keep her people safe," I shouted.

"My people who turned against me."

"My father turned against you. No one else. Don't take it out on the dragons, what my father did to you. He's wronged a lot of people. Now is your chance to make it right. The Morganna I knew would do the right thing."

"You are an idealistic little thing, aren't you? Do you think that if you free the dragons it will somehow make up for everything your father did?"

"Yes, at least partly. I can't change the past, what he did to you or the dragons, or any of the lies he told to the other Slayers, but you can change the future. Let the dragons go so that his years of hurting people can finally be over. You've been in hiding for years. Wouldn't you like the chance to finally finish the man that caused this? Or are you a coward?"

She looked at me, listening carefully to my words. My guess was that she'd never been called a coward in her life. "Why do you hate your father so much?" she finally asked me.

"I loved him. He was an even bigger hero to me than

you were, but he lied. He lied a lot and to a lot of people. He lied to me. My whole life has been a lie and I'm not the only one. The people in the village need to know the truth."

"But why do you hate him?" she repeated.

"Because he's not the man I thought he was.

"No one ever is!" she replied, pulling out something hidden beneath her flowing robe.

I recognized it at once. It was her legendary sword. It made my beautiful sword look dim in comparison. I reached out to take it from her, but she held it back, just out of my reach.

"I can't let you take the sword, but if you tell me the secret to letting the dragons out, I will do it."

There was a flash of light and the purple haze we'd been enveloped in before, now filled the air once again. Had she just left? Used her magic after everything she'd learned and disappeared with the sword? When the smoke cleared, I expected to find the clearing empty except for the dragons and me, but instead, I saw the Wolvren were back, circling us. Morganna still sat in front of me, her sword in her hand.

So it was a trick then. She'd summoned them so they could what? Eat us? Attack us?

"Sit!" she said to them. All at once, they all sat, like sentinels watching over us. She might tell us that she lived in peace with the Wolvren, but I could see she ruled them with an iron fist. Alpha was the only one who disobeyed her command. He walked past us and eyed us warily.

"You drew your sword. We all felt it. Are you in danger?"

"No," she laughed. "I'm sorry Alpha. I had forgotten that particular piece of magic. I draw my sword so rarely now that I should have the summoning charm taken off it. As you are here, you may as well eat with us." She waved her hands and the delicious spread that had laid before us multiplied so that it reached the hungry Wolvren pack surrounding us. It seemed that she had bought quite a lot of magic from the Goblins. No one I knew could perform magic like that.

"Are you okay?" he whispered to her, just loudly enough so I could pick up what he was saying.

"I'm fine. Why don't you sit down and join us? They mean us no harm. In fact, the girl was just about to tell me some of her own magic."

"It's not my magic. It was placed in the sword by the Goblins. I don't know how they did it and they have refused to tell us, but quite by accident, I found out how to reverse it."

"What magic do you speak of?" asked Alpha warily. "Swords hold no magic."

"Mine does, and so does Morganna's. They don't kill. I could stab you right through the heart with my sword right now and it wouldn't kill you. It would cause you immeasurable pain until you fell as if dead, but you would still be alive."

"What good is a sword that does not kill?"

I was aware that to tell him the truth I would be betraying Morganna. Luckily for me, she beat me to it.

"The swords capture the souls of anything they hit."

"But she said she could reverse the magic. After all the dragons you've killed, does that mean we will be surrounded by them?"

"No. The dragon souls are in the swords, but their bodies lie in my village. If we do let them go, there will be a reaction. For some reason, the reversal of this magic causes flames. It would be wise to stand back when we do it."

"Morganna, what is she talking about? Surely you aren't thinking of letting her do this. The dragons are our enemy."

Morganna sighed. "I hoped this day would never come, but I always feared it would. It is time for me to make up for the actions of my past. I am old and weary and have carried this around in my heart for a long time. I have no more fight left in me. The dragons are not bad people. They didn't deserve this."

"You realize if they let the dragons from their colony go, it will also let the dragons from the mountain colony free and we will be overrun by them. Do you understand how foolish this is? How dangerous it is to our community?"

"It is no danger. I've never killed a dragon from that mountain. It is not my legendary sword skills or their fear of me that stops them coming down here. I'm sorry, Alpha, but I have lied to you. When I found out they were shifters, I spoke to their leader. We have a truce to keep out of each other's way. They don't come down the mountain because I asked them to, just as you don't go up the mountain for the same reason. You've kept peace with them for all these years because of that."

"Because you lied to us!"

"Remember how it was before I came to live among you? Dragons were killing your people on a daily basis. There was fighting and pain. I promised you I'd stop it and I have kept my promise, just not in the way you thought."

The atmosphere around the campfire changed at her admission. I could see how uneasy Alpha was and it seemed his fellow Wolvren were equally angry.

"The dragons are not your enemy," I said. "They are peaceful beings who have long since been persecuted by other beings, you included. Don't have your pack end up like my village. For years, we fought the dragons mindlessly, spurred by lies and centuries of hate. The dragons never hurt us, not once, except to defend themselves, and yet we believed that they were the bad guys because people like my own father told lie after lie. I know you dislike the dragons on your mountain but look inside all your hearts. Do you actually know why? Or are you just doing what I did, what Morganna did, and following a tradition of hate rather than thinking for yourselves. Has a dragon ever attacked any of you?"

"Yes. Before Morganna, they would attack all the time," growled Alpha.

"Did they really attack? Or were they defending themselves?"

"The girl is right, Alpha," Morganna admitted. "All this hatred has to stop. I perpetuated it for far too long, and now is the time for me to end it. If you don't want me to be a part of your pack anymore, I understand."

"Of course we want you. Without you, our pack would have disbanded years ago. We would probably have starved to death without you."

"If you only want me to stay because of my magic, you have no need to worry. I can bestow it upon you."

"You know that's not the reason," he said quietly.

For the first time, I wondered if they were involved in some kind of relationship. He certainly seemed protective of her.

"Then let me do what I need to do. I truly believe that now is the time to be strong in our hearts as well as our bodies."

"Very well, but if this hurts us...if it hurts you..." He stopped.

"It will not hurt me, right?" Morganna looked at me.

I hesitated. It would hurt her. I'd been exhausted giving my own blood to save four dragons. I could only imagine how difficult it would be spilling three hundred dragons' worth.

"The magic needs a blood sacrifice. You will need to cut your hand with the sword. The blood of a Slayer is the only thing that works."

"No!" shouted a number of people at the same time as she held the sword's blade to her hand.

"What if they are lying and want to take over our village?" shouted Alpha.

"Everyone needs to get back!" shouted Spear and Ash at the same time.

"We don't want to hurt you!" I said, more for Alpha's benefit than Morganna's. "Everyone needs to get back. The dragons' souls produce a massive amount of heat as they escape. The forest will catch on fire."

"So, she needs to stick her sword in her body and then our forest will burn down?" screeched Alpha.

"No. The neighboring trees might get scorched, that's all. If Morganna stands in the center of the clearing and everyone moves back behind the tree line, it should be fine."

"How much blood will I need to sacrifice?" asked Morganna, getting to her feet.

"I don't know," I replied honestly. It had taken just a few drops for each of the dragons I'd freed, but a few drops times three hundred was a significant amount.

"I guess there is only one way for us to find out." She put the sword to her hand a second time. "You heard her, everyone needs to step back."

The wolves looked unhappy at the turn of events, but they obeyed her orders, retreating back to the tree line.

"Wait. The fire could hurt you too," said Ash. "Let me turn into a dragon so I can protect you. I have fire-proof skin to shield you. I can also fly you up to the sky away from the flames."

"You want to turn into a dragon now? This just gets better and better doesn't it?" Alpha sneered.

Morganna tossed a look at Alpha to shut him up.

"If you harm one hair on her head!" he warned Ash.

"I won't."

Ash ran behind a tree to undress and a minute later, his red wings flapped into the sky through a puff a violet smoke above Morganna. He landed by her side as she held up her sword once again.

From behind a tree, I watched the pair of them. Morganna with her sword held aloft and Ash, magnificent, standing just behind her. For the briefest of seconds, I felt a surge of jealousy. Did Ash and I look that good together? I threw it off. It was a stupid thought, and yet, despite their age gap, they looked good together.

Morganna held her sword up, waiting for the moment to spill her own blood.

16

The famous blade of Morganna glinted in the lowered sun. I cast my gaze around the assembled group of people. What a strange bunch we all were. To either side of me stood my friends, the dragons, all but Ash in their human forms. Surrounding the rest of the clearing were the Wolvren, most in their human form, some as wolves. All looked wary of what was about to happen. And then there was Morganna and me, the only true humans and Slayers to boot. I wondered if these three groups of people, all sworn enemies, had ever stood together in a unified cause before. It seemed doubtful. Every person in that circle would have thought nothing about killing another at some point and yet here we all were, waiting for Morganna to free the dragons.

I could see the doubt on the Wolvren's faces, but it was the face of Alpha that made me the most nervous. He was almost directly opposite where I stood, and both Morganna and Ash shielded my view of him, but every so often, they'd move slightly and I'd see him. He was on edge, it was plain to see, but it was not anger on his face, but fear. Fear for Morganna's life. I didn't know the extent of their relationship, but I was willing to bet that he was in love with her. Whether she felt the same as he did was anyone's guess. I studied her now—my childhood hero. She didn't waver as she brought the sword down to her hand. This was why she was a legend. Her strength was plain to see. She turned and whispered something to Ash, who nodded back at her. She slashed the knife over her palm and red blood spilled out. At exactly the same moment, Ash lifted her fifty feet into the air, out of harm's way. I held on to the tree I was standing behind and waited for the breath of hot air that I knew would follow. I wanted to keep my eyes open, but I wasn't Morganna. I closed them and hid my face behind the tree. I waited. One second, two seconds, three seconds. The heat hadn't come. Was I really so far back as to not feel it? I doubted it. The heat that erupted when I'd freed Ash's father had consumed both my childhood home and the dragon town hall.

"Was that it?" I heard someone shout out. I didn't recognize his voice so it must have been one of the Wolvren. I opened my eyes and peeked around the tree. Looking up, I could see Morganna still in the air suspended by Ash, but the ground and surrounding trees were scorch-free. Had something gone wrong?

Alpha ran into the center of the clearing. I took his lead and met him in the middle just as Ash lowered Morganna carefully to the ground. Alpha didn't ask any questions, he just took her in his arms protectively. It made me feel ridiculous to have been jealous of

Morganna and Ash looking good together, if only for a second.

"Where are the dragons?" Alpha demanded.

"I don't know," I replied truthfully. "Did you watch? Did you see them leave?"

Alpha snarled. "All I saw was Morganna slicing her hand and then being kidnapped by your boyfriend."

Morganna put a firm hand on him. "He hardly kidnapped me. We were just up there the whole time."

"Did you see the dragons?" I asked Morganna.

"I didn't see anything. Nor did I feel any heat. Something went wrong. Did I not cut myself enough?" One look at her hand was enough to tell me she'd cut deeply. Blood still dripped onto the floor.

"Just a minute," growled Alpha. "You've done enough damage to yourself. You'll not be spilling any more blood. It's a trick to weaken you."

There was a movement, so quick it was almost invisible to the naked eye, but Morganna had managed to spear a rabbit on the end of her sword. A rabbit that none of the rest of us had even seen.

"I can assure you, I'm not weakened," she said, passing the rabbit to the startled looking Alpha. "Lunch?"

"You'll need to see to that hand," I said. She was bleeding quite a bit.

"What happened?" asked Ash, reappearing fully clothed. "Why didn't it work?"

"So, it really didn't work? I was hoping we were all too far back to feel anything."

"No dragon souls came from that sword," he replied,

eyeing the rabbit that Alpha was now pulling from the end of it.

"It seems your journey was wasted," said Morganna, taking the sword back from Alpha.

"They are lying!" one of the other Wolvren said. I'd not noticed, but some of the Wolvren that had previously been in their human form had now turned into wolves. We were now outnumbered by our lupine friends.

They were not growling yet, but I could see it wouldn't take much. There was so much anger here. Much like the Slayers, hundreds of years of mistrust couldn't be extinguished in one day. If Morganna couldn't free the dragons, then she was right. Our journey was a waste of time. Or it would be unless we could figure out what the problem was.

Spear stepped up and joined in the conversation. "We are not lying. I've seen it myself."

"Yes, well we have no reason to believe anything you say," countered Alpha. He looked around at the rest of his men. "I don't think we will need the rabbit after all. Lunch will be a feast." He bared his fangs at us and all at once, the rest of the Wolvren began to close the circle around us. One by one, they turned into the wolves they were, each hungrier than the last.

Ash took hold of my arm and pulled me close, but what use was that? He was no match for all the wolves. If he turned back into a dragon, he could pull me up and away, but we would be no closer to freeing the dragons. If we didn't do it now, there would be no second chance. And something told me Morganna wouldn't be lending any more magic Ash's way in order for him to shift again.

"Get ready," he hissed into my ear and I knew he was thinking the same thing. He was going to try to change into a dragon. I had to stop him.

I ran past him and lurched at Morganna. It was a risky move, but it was the only thing I had. I knew I wouldn't be quick enough to grab the sword from her hands. Her reaction earlier with the rabbit had proved how lightning fast she was, but if I could slice my palm down the blade before she moved it, then just maybe my blood would work where hers had failed. It had before, and I could see no reason why it wouldn't work again. Of course, if I was wrong, I'd ruined our only chance at escape.

I held my hand up as I charged and when I got close enough, I brought it down on the sharp blade.

17

"Nooooo!" Ash shouted behind me as chaos erupted. Ash knew exactly what I was about to do and as predicted, he ran forward to stop me. Out of my peripheral vision, I could see the wolves doing the same, although their motive was entirely different. They were out for attack. They'd misunderstood my move as an act of aggression. Morganna stood completely still though, the only one of us that did.

Everything happened as if in slow motion. Morganna held out her sword for me and I slashed my arm across it. As blood welled up from the long cut in my arm, a number of different things happened. The wolves pounced, more than likely to save Morganna, and Ash turned into a dragon. As darkness closed in around me in the resulting melee, it felt as though my mind was playing tricks on me, because Ash seemed to transform much quicker than usual and without the usual sickening sound of crunching bones.

However, it happened, somewhere amongst the shrieks and screams, I found myself under Ash's protective wing. It was quiet under there, although I could hear the muffled noises of both the Wolvren and the dragons as they fought.

I wanted to speak to Ash, to ask him what was going on, but all I could see was the underside of his wing. I could hear his voice calling to me, and yet, like all the other sounds, it was muffled.

Everything was hazy and at first. I thought it was the force of my head hitting the ground—I'd managed to give myself quite a headache—but I soon realized it was more than that. I could smell something burning. Acrid smoke was pouring from somewhere, and the only place I could think that it would originate from was the sword. I looked around, urgently searching for it, but it was nowhere to be seen on the little patch of grass beneath me. I scrambled around on the ground, trying to feel for it in case I'd missed it through the smoke.

I began to cough as the smoke filled my lungs. I couldn't see any fire, but I wasn't worried about burning to death as much as dying from smoke inhalation. I pushed on the underside of Ash's wing, trying to shove it off me so I could get some fresh air. I was nowhere near strong enough to move him, but he must have felt my hands against him because a second later, a gush of air hit me in the face. I took a deep breath, momentarily glad for the coolness, before realizing something wasn't right.

Everything was upside down. At least, that's how my brain interpreted it until I realized it wasn't everything else that was upside down, but me.

Below me (or above me as it felt), the forest grew smaller and smaller. The clearing in which we had been sitting was now in flames, although I was too far above it to feel the heat. Black smoke billowed out, idly drifting off to the west with the wind. We (and I say we because the only reason I could be dangling upside down in the air was if Ash picked me up hurriedly—I was yet to look up and check that this was the case) were traveling in the opposite direction. Just as the clearing itself disappeared from view, I saw the dragons and the Wolvren running away from the flames into the vast undergrowth of the forest. In the distance, I could see the indistinct outline of something I guessed was the souls of dragons, all heading back at blistering speed to their bodies in Dronias.

The people in the village were going to get the shock of their lives when a hundred or more dragons suddenly awakened from their slumber. I could just imagine the look on my father's face. I would have grinned, but a mixture of being upside down with the blood rushing to my head and the blast from earlier was making my head feel woozy.

I closed my eyes, waiting for Ash to put me down, but then I heard a voice. A woman's voice. That couldn't be right, could it? How would a woman be up this high? Unless it was me speaking? I was so out of it that I didn't know anymore. I tried to open my eyes again to make sense of everything, but it was too much effort. Instead, I let myself descend into inky blackness.

"Julianna...Jules..."

"Mmm?" I felt the world around me begin to come back together as the blackness receded

"Julie?" That was new. I knew Ash's voice, but he'd never once called me that before. For some reason, it irked me. My eyes shot open. "Julie?" He looked frantic and yet I could see the relief in his eyes as he looked down at me. "You weren't responding to Jules or Julianna. I thought I'd try something different." He hugged me close to him.

"Just don't call me Julie again!"

I felt him laugh, his body shaking silently.

"Are you okay, Julianna?" It was the woman's voice again, and this time I recognized it. Ash moved back to reveal Morganna and her sword. There was no one else around us, although I could see some basic housing.

I sat up straight "Where are we?"

"When Ash whisked us both up from the fire, I showed him where he could drop us. This is the Wolvren village. Don't worry. We are alone. There is quite a distance between here and the others. I hope they all managed to escape the fire."

"I saw them running into the forest. I think they all got away."

Morganna sighed. "That's good. I will need to go to them shortly. If anyone has burns, I will need to take care of them, just like I did you." She nodded down to my bandaged arm.

"How long have I been unconscious?"

"About fifteen minutes. I used the time to clean and bandage your arm. You've got quite a deep cut there. I made a potion of berries to soothe the pain. You are going to feel it soon, so I suggest you drink it down quickly. It will help." She passed me a goblet filled with a pink liquid that looked like a raspberry smoothie.

I drank it down quickly. It soothed my throat as it went down, taking the taste of the smoke away.

"I had to lend Ash some clothes," Morganna carried on. "It seems he was in such a hurry to protect you, he transformed without taking his off first."

Ash was wearing something that looked like it might have belonged to Alpha. His cheeks were bright red. I felt a hint of jealousy that Morganna had seen him naked but quickly shrugged it off. Morganna had just saved the lives of hundreds of dragons and probably mine and Ash's, too, by bringing us here.

"I saw the dragons," I said.

"Yeah, we did, too." Ash put his arm around me. Even at this distance, I could smell the fire.

"Just how far away is the clearing?" I wondered. I didn't want to be caught in yet another fire if it spread. Maybe the fire had just changed direction and was blowing the smoke toward us rather than away from us now.

"I promise it's far enough away for us to be safe, but if you are worried, there is a small hill not far from here where we will be able to see above the clouds. Do you think you are up to the walk?"

Ash helped me to my feet. I felt unsteady and yet I stood tall, not wanting to show more weakness than I already had. The berry potion had helped clear my head as well as dull the pain, although I could see tinges of red beginning to seep through the bandage on my arm. As usual, I'd plunged in too quickly and done more damage than I should have.

I was unsteady on my feet as I took a few steps, but

with Ash holding on to me, I soon took it in my stride. "We did it!" I smiled. "We freed them all."

"We did what we could," Ash replied. "Spear had some of the others on the lookout for the dragon souls returning. It's going to be chaos there with a few hundred confused, weak dragons. I only hope that there are enough of our people to help them."

I hadn't thought of that. Remembering how weak Mary had been when she woke up, I knew the others in Frokontas would have their work cut out for them, helping so many dragons. Hopefully, the sight of so many dragons waking up would be enough to scare away my brother or whoever else they had put in charge of the dragon keep. If not, there would be another bloody battle. It didn't bear thinking about. Instead, I concentrated on putting one foot in front of the other to get up the steep hill.

"The weather has been wet in recent weeks. I hope that's enough to slow the spread of the flames." Morganna was worried about her forest being destroyed. I only hoped she was right. I'd hate to save the dragons only to destroy the habitat of the Wolvren. "We should be safe here at least," she continued. "We crossed a wide river to get here. I doubt the flames will be able to find a way over."

I knew that flames could always find a way in the right conditions and I was pretty sure she knew the same, and yet I didn't contradict her. She was hoping for the best outcome as we all were.

"How many dragons are left to go?" she asked, not taking her eyes from the fire.

"I don't know," I answered truthfully. "Your sword

held by far the most. Many of the swords owned by villagers have only one dragon, the first one their owners slain once they came of age, but some, like yours, hold many. My father's, for example. He's slain more dragons than I can remember."

It was only when I said it out loud that my jubilance at freeing so many dragons left me. It had seemed like such a big deal ten minutes ago, but now that Ash had mentioned the dragons waking up back home, and thinking about the dragons yet to free, I realized that we still had a very long journey ahead of us. The trail wound up the hill, and soon we emerged at the peak, the whole forest spread out before us like a huge, green blanket. I tried to put my mind to the future and focus on what was left for us to do. It was difficult when all I could see were plumes of black smoke filling the sky and the orange flicker of flames consuming everything in their path.

Morganna stood stock still and stared at the fire. "I need to get back there and see if the Wolvren are alright. My senses tell me they are all alive, but they may need help."

"Do you need me to fly you there?" asked Ash. I know I shouldn't have been thinking that way, but a big part of me didn't want him to leave, not even for a few minutes.

"No. I have enough magic to get me there. I'll speak to Alpha. He probably thinks you kidnapped me."

"He didn't look very happy when I whisked you up away from the fire," agreed Ash.

"He'll be fine once I talk to him and calm him down.

In the meantime, you two are welcome to go back to our home. I'll see you there in an hour or so."

"What about Spear and the rest?" I asked. The other dragons were caught in the same situation as the Wolvren.

"Don't worry, I'll round them up, too. See you soon."

She took something from her pocket and closed her eyes. In a second, she had disappeared.

Ash put his arms around me protectively as we watched the flames lick the sky. In spite of the destruction we had caused, our quest was now in full flight, and I finally felt that we were getting somewhere. It remained to be seen if it was where we needed to be.

18

"How long do you think it will take for them to get back?" It was a completely selfish question. It had been a long time since I'd had Ash to myself and I was enjoying it, just standing there with him cuddling me. I was also exhausted, and the thought of dealing with everyone was something I'd happily put off until a later time.

"Don't worry." His arms closed tighter around me. "I trust that Morganna won't let the Wolvren hurt us."

He'd misunderstood my intention for asking. I wasn't scared. Nothing scared me when I had Ash by my side. "I'm not scared."

"You're shivering. Are you cold?"

I hadn't noticed before now, but I did feel cold. I could feel the tremors racking my body. "Yes, I think so." I was feeling dizzy, too. I slumped against him.

"Come on, we need to get you back to the Wolvren village." He held onto me and began to turn me around.

"I'm fine!" I protested, but I clearly wasn't. The shivering was uncontrollable and getting worse.

"You're in shock. I shouldn't have brought you here. You need to lie down." And with that, he picked me up in his arms and carried me back through the forest to the Wolvren village.

Finding a campfire pit, he set me down, then found some old twigs to burn, two of which he tried rubbing together to get the fire going.

"It's much easier to make a fire when I'm a dragon," he quipped after a few minutes of trying without so much as a spark.

"Please, don't!" I loved him in both his forms, but he was softer in his human form, and he could talk to me. "Stay with me."

He put the sticks down and moved closer, taking my head into his lap. "Morganna did a good job with those bandages. You aren't bleeding through much. Would you like a drink of water?"

"I'm fine. I'm sure I'll be okay in a few minutes. I just went a bit dizzy, that's all. Just hold me and keep me warm." It didn't matter how bad the situation. If I was in Ash's arms, I felt safe. He stroked my hair and I allowed myself to doze.

Sometime later, the noise of the others returning woke me up. I'd not lied to Ash earlier about not being scared, but now the prospect of all the Wolvren coming home to us after they thought we kidnapped Morganna sent chills through me. I sat up quickly, and behind me, I felt Ash go stiff as if he was ready to change into his dragon form at any second and fly us both away.

It was unnecessary though. Morganna appeared

through the trees, hand in hand with Alpha. They were chatting together and there was no look of malice in Alpha's expression. Behind them were the Wolvren, and among them, the dragons. No one was hurt as I had feared. If anything, they almost appeared cheerful.

Upon seeing me, Morganna ran over. "Are you alright? You look awfully pale."

"I'm fine. I went a bit dizzy that's all."

"You need the fire on. Alpha, can you start one, please? I'll make some broth."

Alpha started the fire using a bit of flint pulled from his pocket. The Wolvren gathered around, as did the dragons. Spear clapped me on the back.

"I never had the chance to say it before, but you did a marvelous job back there. I know we've had our differences in the past and I'll admit to not trusting you when I first met you, but I'd doubt there are many dragons that would have done what you did to save their own kind, let alone the lives of their sworn enemy."

"The dragons are not my sworn enemy!" I cried forcefully, but I could see he was teasing me.

"Honestly though. You have proved yourself time and time again. It was a lucky day for us when you decided to come to Frokontas."

"I didn't actually decide to do anything. Ash flew me there, remember?"

"Ah, yes. Either he saw something in you right from the start, or he took a liking to a very attractive young lady." He winked, causing me to blush, the little blood I still had left rushing to my cheeks.

"A bit of both, Spear," laughed Ash.

"What happened out in the forest after we flew

away? We were expecting the worst." I nodded as discretely as I could to the Wolvren.

"We knew what had happened. Of course, we'd seen it before and so we were expecting it. The Wolvren, not so much. As soon as the fire erupted, we ran out into the forest, but it became clear that some of the Wolvren had gotten trapped. We took our clothes off, changed into our dragon form, and saved them. After that, they were willing to listen to us, once we'd changed back of course. We told them that Morganna would be okay. I wasn't a hundred percent sure they believed us, but when Morganna appeared, they relaxed. We've been invited to stay here in their village as long as we need to and our dragon forms are no longer restricted by their magic."

"No."

We both looked at Ash.

"No?"

"Julianna needs to get home. Look at her."

I sat up straight, trying to look stronger than I felt. I didn't want to be the reason we all left.

"She is very pale," agreed Spear.

"I am right here you know!"

"Exactly, and it's because you are so pale that I think we should stay."

"I can see that everyone is the best of friends now, but I don't like it," Ash began. "I like Morganna and I have no issue with the Wolvren, but I still want to get Julianna home."

"Do I have a say in this?"

"Yes."

"No."

Both Spear and Ash spoke at once.

"Fine," Ash conceded. "I don't want to be that guy who causes problems. If you all want to stay, then we'll stay, but remember, Spear, we have a lot of work still to do. It's not all about Julianna. Think of all those dragons freed. We don't know what's happening back in Dronias."

Spear considered this. "You make a good point."

"Morganna and some of the Wolvren are making broth for us," I interjected. "It would be rude to leave before we eat after all they are doing for us. Besides, I have an idea."

"Uh oh!"

"It's not that bad!" I playfully elbowed Ash in the middle. "We need Morganna. I'm going to ask her to come with us."

"Why?" asked both men at once.

I looked over at Morganna. She was stirring a huge pot of liquid over the fire. Some of the Wolvren were throwing leaves and other things in as she stirred. Even doing something as mundane as making soup, she commanded respect. There was a reason she was known as the best Slayer in the kingdom.

"Please don't get me wrong when I say this—"

"Uh oh," repeated Ash, a smile on his face.

"But I'm the only one on our side who knows how to use a sword. Yeah, you guys can breathe fire and bite a man in two, but sometimes, you have to be on the same level as the person you are fighting. Morganna might have been away from Dronias for many years, but she knows everyone there, and more importantly, she'll know how to fight them. She probably knows the elders better than I do. I think we can all agree that I've been kept in the dark about a lot of things. Maybe Morganna didn't know about the dragon souls being trapped in the swords, but she saw a side of my father I hadn't until recently. I think we need her."

Both men were silent for a while, contemplating my words. I could smell the broth now, and it was delicious. I closed my eyes, enjoying the smell, waiting for Ash or Spear to say something.

"You have a point," replied Spear eventually. "Do you think we'll be able to get her to come with us?"

"I don't know, but I'm going to try to persuade her."

One of the Wolvren passed us a bowl each. We watched as everyone began to line up next to the large cauldron. Morganna ladled the broth into each person's bowl.

"I'll get ours." Ash took my bowl from my hands and joined the line with Spear. Five minutes later, he was back with two bowlfuls of hot liquid which smelled like heaven on earth. As we had no spoons, we drank it straight from the bowl. The broth traveled down to my belly, warming me as it went.

When Morganna had finished ladling out the broth, she came to sit beside us. "I'm sorry it isn't much, but as I've told you before, food can be scarce around here. This is made from leaves and roots we find in the forest."

"Please don't be sorry. It's delicious. You are quite a chef!"

Morganna laughed at my words. "Dragon Slayer, master chef. My talents are never-ending." She drank from her bowl before her expression turned serious again. "You are a Slayer, right? I'm correct in thinking you are over eighteen?"

"I turned eighteen a few months ago." My eighteenth birthday. The day I met Ash and this whole thing started. It was the day my life changed in so many ways. It was a day I'd never forget.

"Hmmm."

"What?"

"I was just wondering how many dragons you'd slain?"

I felt embarrassed. I'd not slain a single one. Even though I didn't want to anymore, I still felt stupid and weak admitting to the fact. I was a born Slayer after all. "I met Ash on my eighteenth birthday. I was supposed to kill him."

"And you fell in love with him instead?"

"No, well, not at first. At the last minute, I hesitated and fell off a precipice. I thought that was it, but he swooped down and caught me. At the time, I didn't know that the dragons in the Triad Mountains were shifters. I thought he was a mother dragon. I even wondered if he was taking me home to feed me to his baby dragons."

"You thought I was a girl?" Ash replied.

Spear laughed loudly. "I can kinda see it."

I ignored the pair of them and carried on telling my tale to Morganna. "He took me to a cliffside near his village. I nearly fell off again, this time in shock as he turned into a human in front of my eyes. He was completely naked after changing."

"I'm surprised you didn't jump off the cliff at that point," joked Spear.

"Oh, haha," replied Ash.

"From then on, I met the other dragons and discovered the truth about them. I knew I'd never be able to kill one."

"So you're saying that you've never slain a dragon? Not even one?" Morganna looked at me with amazement.

"Not even one," I repeated her words back to her.

"Interesting."

I'd thought it many things, but interesting wasn't one of them. "Why do you say that?"

"I've been wondering why the sword didn't work for me in the same way it did for you. At first, I'll admit to being slightly jealous; after all, it is my sword and it has served me well for a long time. I couldn't understand why it worked for you in a way it had never worked for me."

"I doubt I'd be able to use it as well as you do. To slay, I mean."

"No, but you had a power over it I could never hope to possess. At first, I wondered if you were somehow special, if you had a magic I didn't know of, but Slayers are not magical beings. Any magic we do possess is bought from the Goblins and can only be used with magical artifacts. The magic you showed back there when you set those dragons free was the magic in the sword and not in you."

"Well, that makes sense," I replied. "I'm not magic. I don't know why it worked for me and not for you. I don't know what I did differently."

"I think it's because you are a Slayer that has never slain. Think about it. How many of those can there be?

Everyone in Dronias over the age of eighteen has slain a dragon. Even those that don't have the stomach for it and don't pursue it. I think the Goblins who made the swords and imbued them with their magic put a get-out clause in there. A way to turn the magic around if the caster of the magic were ever to change his or her mind. I doubt the elders knew about it. It's the only reason I can think of for it working for you. You are the original innocent Slayer."

"Why would they do that, though?" asked Spear. It was a question I wanted to know the answer to, too.

"I don't know, but I'd sure like to find out!"

19

It was sure an interesting idea. Did the Goblins always put get-out clauses in their magical artifacts or was this a special case? Did someone put them up to it? The swords were made so many years ago, some of them going back a century, so if anyone had told them to add that certain piece of magic, they would surely be dead by now anyway.

"We went to the Goblins before coming here," admitted Spear.

Morganna pulled herself forward, interested in what he had to say.

"They were very welcoming despite anything you might have heard, but they were guarded too. They were happy to feed us well, but they'd tell us nothing of the swords or the magic."

"Yeah, I've heard that about them. They like to keep their secrets to themselves. Still, I'm surprised they welcomed you. I've heard they don't like strangers poking their noses in."

"I have the feeling they invited us in as the quickest way to get rid of us. If they'd have shut all the doors and tried to hide, we'd have been curious and kept on looking, probably discovering something about them they wouldn't want us to know. By inviting us in, they could keep a close eye on us."

"I've never trusted the Goblins, even when I was given my very first sword, the one you see over there." Morganna pointed to her sword, which was now blackened by fire. "I was wary. It's funny. After my first kill, I became less nervous around it, and eventually, it became part of me. Before this morning, I couldn't imagine life without it. Now, I'm not so sure.

"It will polish up again," said Ash. "It could look as good as new."

"It's not just what it looks like. Something changed when Julianna set those dragons free. Call me superstitious, but it doesn't feel the same."

"It is the same sword though, and you are still the most famous dragon Slayer in the kingdom. No one can take that away from you," I piped up. I hated to think I'd somehow upset my idol.

"Infamous, more like. After meeting you and hearing all you have to say, being the most famous dragon Slayer in the kingdom doesn't sound particularly great."

"If you are feeling bad, you shouldn't. Just like the rest of us, you were duped. However, if you want to make it up to the dragons, I have an idea."

"She has already made it up to the dragons," said Alpha, overhearing our conversation and joining us by the campfire. "She has given you food and shelter. She has given you her most prized possession—her sword. I'm grateful that you saved many of us out there, but if it weren't for you, the forest would not have burned in the first place. I will call us enemies no more, but we have done enough for your people. Morganna has done enough, and she owes you nothing."

"I didn't mean to offend."

"Let the girl speak," Morganna interjected. "Words cost nothing, after all. What is it you think I can do for you, Julianna?"

"Come home with us."

"She is home," snarled Alpha. "This is her home."

"I know this is her home now. I meant Dronias, her original home. The people there think you are dead. Only my father and possibly a few other elders know the truth about you. The people there are fighting us because they don't know or don't believe the truth. Why would they? They have spent their whole lives listening to stories about how dangerous the dragons used to be. They believe that slaying them is the only way of keeping them at bay. It doesn't matter that there hasn't been a dragon attack in living history; they want to believe what their parents and grandparents have told them. They don't believe me, but they'll believe you."

"Why would they believe me?"

"Because they were all told you were dead at the hand of a dragon. Even if they don't like to think about things, they can't deny that you are still alive if they see you. Your painting still hangs in the village. Everyone there knows what you look like, even the ones like me who were too young to know you the first time around. Once they see you, they'll know that my father has lied in the past. If they know that, they will begin to question all the other things he has told them."

"What you are saying makes a lot of sense, but you are forgetting one thing."

"What?"

"There was a reason I left in the first place."

"I know. You were having an affair with one of the elders. It was a long time ago. Surely the past can stay in the past."

"If I go back, the past won't be in the past though, will it? Rocco will tell Xander's wife the truth."

"It happened years ago. You've all moved on. I think my father has bigger fish to fry than breaking up a marriage over a brief affair that happened so many years ago. If you are worried about seeing Xander again—"

"No, that's not it. I haven't thought about Xander in years. I've been happy here. I just don't want to cause problems."

"There already are problems. There is a war going on over some ridiculous, century-old feud. The dragons are innocent, and the Slayers are blindly following tradition. Neither side needs to die. The Slayers are good people. You must remember that. Surely it's not been so long that you've forgotten what we are all like?"

"I never said I didn't think you were good people. I had many people I loved in that village and I'm not just talking about Xander, but I'm still not convinced it's a good idea to go back there."

"The people love you, Morganna. Just like me, many of them still think of you as their hero. You are practically worshipped there."

Morganna sighed. "It's easier to worship a dead person than like a living one."

"We need you. It's not just the dragons that need you, but the Slayers, too. I can't bear it if anyone else I love gets killed."

"I don't want anyone killed as much as you, but I think you overestimate the reception I'll get."

"I don't think I do. I think that you might be surprised."

Morganna smiled a sad smile. "It's not something I can decide right now on a whim. It's not just me I have to think about, but my people too." She nodded her head to the Wolvren. "I will think about it overnight and let you know in the morning. For now, we all need to sleep. You especially, Julianna. I can see how wiped out you are. You need rest before taking such a long journey. Tonight, you and your fellow dragons can sleep in my hut. It is not much, and there is only one bed, so the rest of you will have to sleep on the floor, I'm afraid. I'll sleep with Alpha."

"Thank you, Morganna, but we couldn't possibly inconvenience you in such a way."

"I'm sure Alpha will not argue with me sleeping with him." She smiled. "My hut is the first one there. I'll see you in the morning." She pointed to a small hut. I doubted it would fit us all, but it was better than nothing. Morganna took Alpha's hand and the pair of them retired to the next hut along. One by one, the Wolvren retreated to their homes, leaving just the dragons and me beside the waning fire.

"Come on, let's go," said Ash, taking my hand. "I'm

sure no one will be upset if you take the bed after everything you've been through."

The others all nodded.

"I want to stay here with you. I'm comfortable. Spear, would you like the bed?"

"I can't take the bed from you. Ash is right. You should have it."

"It's a warm night. I'm comfortable. I'll get a blanket and lay on it. I think I'd feel better out here in the fresh air." The truth of the matter was, I wanted Ash to myself. I didn't want us both squashed up in a small hut with the other dragons. Having a bed wasn't worth it. Besides, I was comfortable. There was something relaxing about watching the stars peeping through the canopy of trees.

Spear and the others trooped off to Morganna's cabin while Ash found us some blankets and something to use as pillows. When he lay next to me, with only the sound of the dying fire crackling to keep us company, I knew I'd made the right decision. He lay next to me so I could lay my head on his shoulder, but I took the opportunity to kiss him. I'd kissed him before, but now we were perfectly alone in the most romantic setting anyone could wish for. Not that I'd have cared about the setting. I'd have kissed Ash anywhere.

He kissed me back gently, almost as if afraid I would break at his touch. Yes, I was exhausted. Freeing the dragons had really taken it out of me, but the touch of his lips on mine rejuvenated me, made me feel alive.

It's strange how the phrase "making out" doesn't sound very exciting at all, but actually doing it with someone you love is a whole different thing. It transports you to places you never knew existed and makes you feel things that you've never felt before. I kissed him hungrily on the lips, then ventured down his neck, planting kisses until he groaned, telling me I was on the right track. As he was wearing a sweater, I couldn't go any further, so I guided my hands up, below the sweater, feeling the hardness of his muscles beneath the warm fabric. I'd never seen him look so beautiful, with his eyes closed in the light of the fire, enjoying my touch on his body. I kissed him again and this time with more force, letting my tongue part his lips. His body reacted to my touch and he pushed himself closer to me. It was new and exciting, and yet I felt so comfortable in his arms, as if we had done this a thousand times. Kissing him felt like home. So raw and so natural at the same time. It was as if my senses were awakened for the first time. I could have spent the whole night kissing him, but as the fire finally went out and we were plunged into darkness, I realized just how exhausted I still was.

He stroked the side of my face and gazed into my eyes. I could barely see him, even with the help of the little starlight that was shining through, and yet it was enough to see that he looked at me with love in his eyes. I rested my head on his shoulder and let him hold me tightly as I fell asleep in his arms.

———

I woke to Ash kissing me. It was the nicest alarm clock I'd ever had. I smiled lazily and opened my eyes. The sky was starting to brighten with the first pink rays hitting the ground. I shivered. It was colder than it had been when we had fallen asleep and somehow, my blanket had fallen off in the night. I pulled it back over the pair of us and covered our heads. Morning could wait a little while longer.

Eventually, the others woke up and came out of their huts, winking at us still under our blankets on the ground.

"I guess it's time to get up." Ash grinned. "Let's go and collect some wood for the fire. I'm starving, and the quicker we get the fire going, the quicker we get to eat."

I pulled the blankets off and stretched. He was right. I was hungry, too. Sticks for firewood were easy to find. There were plenty of them on the ground around the village. I stayed alongside Ash but found it difficult to keep up with him. Not because he was working so fast, but because I was still depleted from losing so much blood. I was confident that the bleeding had stopped, although I didn't want to unwrap the bandages to check. I had thought that a long night's sleep would make me feel better, but I still felt drowsy. Setting the dragons free had taken more out of me that I cared to admit, and yet there were still so many to go.

Ash saw me struggling. "Are you okay?"

"I'm fine. Just a little tired, that's all."

"Come on. Let's get back to the fire pit. You'll feel better after breakfast."

I hoped he was right.

Alpha was there when we got back and he took the sticks from us gratefully. He started the fire and he and a few of the others made some food. I wanted to ask him if Morganna had decided to come with us, but I didn't want to anger him.

Ash didn't have the same worries. "Is Morganna coming back with us?"

Alpha threw some roots into the cauldron. "Yes. You have gotten your way. Morganna is coming with you. We all are. The Wolvren are coming too.

20

"No," said Spear firmly. "The Wolvren can't come. We have enough problems without taking a wolf pack with us. It's Morganna only."

Alpha stood, baring his teeth. "How dare you insult us."

"I didn't insult you," replied Spear. "I merely said that we don't need your help. We have to go in quietly, and I don't think adding any more people will be of use to us."

"You called us a pack of wolves. We are so much more than that and you know it. You are shifters just like us, so please don't think you are superior."

I watched the exchange between the two men. Both had so much anger within them. Sensing a fight and the possible loss of Morganna to our cause, I stood and made my way over to them, positioning myself between the huge men.

"Spear, there is no way we are going to be able to go

in quietly. The Slayers are already waiting for us to attack. The time for stealth is over. However much I don't want to use force against my own people, I think we all have to be realistic, knowing that they will be using force against us. Having the Wolvren as back-up can only help"—I turned to Alpha— "as long as you realize that brute force is our last option. I wanted Morganna to come so she can speak to the Slayers and make them see sense. The Slayers have no real knowledge or fear of the Wolvren, so it shouldn't be a problem for you to come along. I know you want to keep Morganna safe. So, do I. I want to keep everyone safe."

Alpha growled but backed down. Spear gave me a filthy look which I ignored. He liked being in charge and he wasn't taking kindly to being told what to do by me. Still, it made sense for the Wolvren to come. Between the dragons and the wolves, we rivaled the numbers of people in Dronias if you didn't count the small children there. Maybe if they saw all of us, they would think twice before attacking again.

"Actually, I've been thinking about the next part of our plan," said Ash, still sitting by the fire. I resumed my place next to him. "We need to find a time when they are all together. It will be easier to talk to them that way, rather than scaring them by trying to round them up."

"Fantastic idea, Ash," replied Morganna. I noticed she had sat close to Alpha and was holding his hand. I wasn't sure if it was mere affection or if she was doing it to hold him back. He still seemed pretty put out by Spear's words. She turned to me. "Do the Slayers still have town meetings?"

"Yes," I replied, suddenly feeling excited. "Everyone

gathers in the village green in the summer. In the winter or in bad weather, they use the town hall. The next one is..." I calculated the days. "Tomorrow evening at six."

"That doesn't give us much time," concluded Morganna. "We can either set off now and hope to make it in time, or we can put it off a week."

"I don't want to put it off any longer," I said. It's been going on long enough. It has to stop now."

Morganna nodded. "I agree. So we set off today. We need to make a plan and pack supplies. It's a long walk. Alpha, can you get your best men and have them pack supplies for our journey. We'll need provisions for the way back, too, as I'm not planning to stay very long."

Alpha nodded and gathered up the Wolvren.

"We need to let the rest of the dragons know," said Spear. "There are only a few of us here, but there are more that are willing to fight in Frokontas."

I thought about his plan. "I think you are right. Can you and the others fly on ahead to prep the other dragons? Ash and I will follow behind with the Wolvren and Morganna. We can meet at six o'clock outside Dronias' town lines. By the time we go in, the town meeting will be already underway. I know I said that we will need force and that might be the case, but if there is any way Morganna can make the Slayers see sense, I'd like to keep the force down to a minimum. These are still my friends and family."

"We know, sweetheart." Morganna came over and wrapped her arm around me.

"Fine," butted in Spear. "We'll head off now if you are sure you are happy being left with the wolves."

"I'm sure we'll be fine. Thank you for helping me

find Morganna. Having her on our side will make all the difference."

"No problem. We will see you tomorrow night." He gathered up the other dragons. I watched as they took their things behind some bushes to undress and transform. Ash stood.

"I should go help them attach their bags." He followed them behind the bushes just as the sickening sound of their bones crunching let me know they were changing. A few minutes later and they flew up into the air and back to the place they called home.

Ash came back. It felt so serene and quiet without either the dragons or the Wolvren. I'd have been happier if it was just the three of us going back, but we would be overpowered as soon as we set foot in the village. Ash wouldn't have stood a chance, and though I'd like to think that my old friends would let me live, I wasn't so sure anymore. I sighed heavily.

"What's the matter?" asked Morganna warmly.

"I just don't understand how all this has happened. It wasn't long ago I was just a normal girl with my whole life mapped out ahead of me. I knew exactly what I wanted to do with my life and now..." I trailed off.

"You were planning to be a murderer," Ash reminded me. "Things have changed so drastically because, for the first time in hundreds of years, someone has taken the time to get to know the dragons and has stood up for what is right. You should be proud of yourself."

I knew he was right, but deep down I felt like things might have been simpler if I'd just left well enough alone. The dragons could look after themselves without me. "I should have just left things the way they were. You are all big enough to fight without my help."

"There are a hundred dragons without souls locked in a compound in the forest. If what you said was true, that wouldn't be the case. It's because of you that we have saved the ones we have, and it's because of you, we are able to fight for the rest."

"He's right, you know," said Morganna. "I didn't think anyone would be able to talk me into going back to Dronias, but you did. You really are a remarkable girl."

I smiled weakly at the pair of them. It was kind of sweet that they were both trying to make me feel better, but it wasn't getting us any closer to freeing the dragons. "Thanks, guys. Sorry for being so down. We need to come up with a plan because if we let Spear and Alpha charge in, there will be chaos."

Morganna smirked. "Yes, you are probably right. What do you have in mind?"

"Well, we've told the dragons six o'clock. The Wolvren think the same. Why don't we go into the village earlier, just you and me, and talk to the leaders?"

"Not a chance!" said Ash immediately. "I'm not going to let you go in alone."

"I won't be alone. Morganna will be with me. If they won't listen to me, they'll listen to her."

"They know you are with the dragons. They'll attack you on sight."

I sighed. "Some of them, yes, but I was thinking we should go and see Xander."

Morganna's eyes widened like saucers. "Xander? Why?"

"Because he will listen to you. Because he's one of the elders, and if he has any feelings left for you, he'll hear what you have to say."

"I can't go back to him. His wife...his children..."

"I'm not asking you to start up your affair again. I think it's best we keep that to ourselves. But if you can make him see sense before the meeting, maybe we'll have a chance to stop the violence before it starts."

Morganna was silent for a minute. I could see I'd touched a nerve with her. "Xander was my soulmate," she whispered, looking around to make sure Alpha wasn't within hearing range. When she was satisfied he wasn't, she continued. "I knew we shouldn't have been doing what we were doing. I knew he had children and I hated myself the whole time, but it was so difficult to stop."

"It was a long time ago," I said, not wanting to get into a conversation with her about her past infidelity.

"It was, but it's still raw for me. I was going to break it off before your father even found out, but the thought of it nearly killed me. Your father gave me the push I needed to leave."

"This isn't about you," I replied, feeling a little annoyed. While I could sympathize with her about her lost love, the lives of the dragons and the Slayers were more important. "This is about doing what is right and saving lives. You only have to talk to him for a few minutes. I'll be with you the whole time."

She sighed heavily. I could see her struggling with this. Whatever had happened with herself and Xander had clearly made a huge impact. "Of course." She smiled now, but it was a resigned smile. "You are right. It would do me no good to try to talk to your father. Just let me talk to him alone."

"You aren't going to try to start anything up again, are you?" I asked, my voice heavy with suspicion.

She laughed lightly, but with no humor. "No, but there are some things I'd like to say to him while I have the chance. I'd like to tell him the real reason I left and I'd like to wish him well, that's all!" she added when she saw the skepticism on my face.

"Fine, but you can't be long. We have to join the others at the meeting. Maybe you can think about what you want to say on the journey back."

"I already know."

"We're packed," said Alpha, joining us. "We've got supplies to last us for four days. If all goes well, we won't need it all. Here are your bags." He threw Ash's and my bags at our feet.

"Can you use magic to travel with us?" I asked Morganna.

"No. I don't have enough to transport us all. We'll have to go by foot if you can show us the way."

"I guess there is no time like the present," I replied, standing. Ash got to his feet and ran around the same bush the other dragons had transformed behind earlier. He emerged in his dragon form with his clothes between his teeth. I carefully extracted them and placed them in his bag. Then, after slinging it over my shoulder along with mine, I jumped onto his back.

I'd never been more ready to fly away. I missed the sensation of soaring through the sky. Ash took off and hovered, waiting for the Wolvren to collect themselves. We flew slowly over the thick forest, occasionally dipping below the tree line when it became thick, to see if the Wolvren and Morganna were keeping up. We had to fly painstakingly slow, but it wasn't long until we were out of the forest entirely. Ash flew in circles, waiting for them to emerge from the canopy of trees, and when they did, he landed so I could speak with Morganna.

"We will fly on ahead for a while and set up a camp. If you continue due south and look out for our campfire smoke, you'll be able to find us."

Morganna nodded and we took off again. This time at breakneck speed. Ash swooped while I laughed, enjoying every second of our freedom. This was what I loved more than anything in the world. When the sky began to darken, we landed and built a fire. In a couple of hours, the Wolvren would catch us up, but until then I had Ash all to myself.

21

"This is what we are fighting for," I whispered as Ash put another log on the fire.

"For flames?" Ash asked playfully. "Because I've got plenty of those."

"No, for this!" I waved my hand.

"For what?" he asked, confused.

"For freedom, for a chance to be together without it being a problem."

"It doesn't matter how much of a problem being with you is to anyone else. I won't leave you, no matter what other people think."

My heart lifted and I snuggled closer to him. "I know, but there will be others like us. People from the village who fall in love with someone who isn't a Slayer. Look at Morganna. She's with a wolf. We need to change the attitudes of the people there, not just for us, but for future generations. I don't want my children growing up in a town full of prejudice. I want to live in a community of tolerance and acceptance."

"So, we are having children now?" Ash teased, making me grin. "Seriously though, do you really think it's possible?"

"I don't know. People are set in their ways, but that's what we are going to try to do. They can't change if they don't know the truth."

Ash didn't answer. He put his arm around me and we sat like that, keeping warm by the fire until the Wolvren caught up with us. They set up tents and one by one, we all fell asleep.

The next morning it was decided that we all walk to Dronias together. There was no point in Ash flying if we would only have to wait for hours on the outskirts. The journey was long and it made me realize how easy I'd had it flying upon Ash's back.

Eventually, I recognized the pathway on the very edge of the village. We were close enough to see the houses, tiny in the distance, but far enough away that no one spotted us.

"We should set up a camp here. It's not time to go for another couple of hours. We told the dragons six." Morganna began the arduous task of unpacking the tents again.

"I hadn't wanted to camp," replied Alpha, "but my men are exhausted. We'll do what we have to do and set off home tomorrow morning."

He took the tent from her and unfolded it. While he was busy in his task, Morganna and I took it as our cue to leave. We needed to get away from the Wolvren while they were all busy. With any luck, Ash would be able to stall them once they saw that we were gone.

I gave Ash a quick kiss and took off down the dusty road with Morganna by my side.

"Do you know what you are going to say?" I asked her once we were safely out of earshot.

"Not a clue." She kept her eyes on the road ahead, not blinking, but I could sense her nerves underneath her cool exterior. I knew it wasn't the fear of death or fighting that scared her, but the thought of seeing the man who she had once considered her soulmate.

Unlike Morganna, who was silent for much of the walk into town, my head was filled with imagined conversations and plans. I wasn't sure how any of this was going to go, but I was aiming for it to be peaceful. I couldn't stand the thought of any more bloodshed on either side. All the scenarios played over and over again in my head and as the town got nearer, my sense of fear increased.

"Xander lives on the edge of town," I said, pointing to a quaint cottage on the border.

"I remember," was all Morganna said. The house seemed quiet as we walked up the front path. I glanced at the other houses farther down the road and saw no one, although a couple had smoke pouring out of their chimneys, indicating that there was someone in there.

Morganna took a deep breath and knocked solidly on the door. I knew Xander and his family very well. If things went wrong with Morganna, I hoped that my presence would help matters. Then I remembered that my name was mud in town too.

The door opened before I had time to back out. Xander's eyes widened as he took in Morganna in front of him.

"You've got nerve, coming back here," said a voice from just behind Xander. Louisa, Xander's wife, came into view, pushing him to the side. She blocked the doorway, hands firmly planted on her hips.

I guess she found out.

"Louisa, I..."

"Don't 'Louisa' me," Xander's wife shouted, cutting Morganna off. "I thought you were dead. I can't say the thought of it upset me. You should go back from wherever you came from."

"Louisa," I began. She turned and noticed me for the first time. The scowl she gave me was matched in intensity to the one she gave Morganna.

"So, you brought her back, did you? I can't say I'm surprised. First, you bring dragons into the village, and now you are bringing this piece of muck." I had to give her credit. She was a tiny woman, at least two feet shorter than Morganna, and yet she wasn't scared, even though the pair of us had our swords with us and all she was brandishing was a wooden spoon covered with what looked like cake batter.

"We need to speak to you both. It's important. The dragons are coming here tonight and they are bringing wolves with them. I've seen the damage to the village and I don't want it to get worse. I don't want anyone hurt."

"You are the reason there is damage to the village." Louisa's voice rose a few decibels.

"We should let them in," said Xander, speaking for the first time since he opened the door. I could see his expression as he took in Morganna and I didn't like it. It was as if I wasn't even there. Still, if he was going to let us in, I wasn't going to complain. If Louisa got any louder, the neighbors would come out to see what the commotion was about.

Louisa clearly wasn't happy that we were entering her house, and to be honest, I couldn't blame her. She was silent as we trooped past her and followed Xander into the living room, where we both sat on a large, worn-out sofa. Louisa followed us in and made a point of sitting right next to Xander on the other sofa. I hoped that Xander didn't ask her to make us a cup of tea. She looked ready to explode.

"Louisa," Morganna began again, "I came here to apologize and make amends. I know I was in the wrong all those years ago, and since then, it has broken my heart just thinking what I did to you. I'm not asking for your forgiveness. I can't even begin to forgive myself. There has not been a single night since I left that I've not felt shame over my actions. I was young and foolish, but I should have known better. I'm not the same woman I was back then."

I glanced over at Louisa. It looked like her icy glare was thawing a bit.

"Xander is a wonderful man and I know now that part of that is because he has a wonderful woman by his side. I saw what you had—a strong family unit—and I admit I was jealous. Instead of building my own, I tried to break someone else's. It is unforgivable and I'm very, very sorry. I want to make amends for my actions."

"Well, if that's what you came to say, you've said your piece. Now you can go." Louisa's words were harsh, but I could see she wasn't as aggravated as she had originally been.

"That's not the only reason you came though, is it? What do you know about the dragons coming tonight?"

I decided it was my turn to jump in. "You know I've spent time with the dragons. We are not here to warn you; we are here to tell you that they are with us, as are the wolves."

Xander didn't seem perturbed by what I was telling him. Instead, he looked interested. He sat forward in his seat and steepled his fingers. "You were with the dragons when they attacked the village. You should know that the people of the village are extremely scared. Many dragons have been seen flying over our skies recently. Just yesterday, a hundred or more seemed to appear from nowhere. They didn't attack, thankfully, but they caused a stir. I watched as they flew up to the mountains in a group."

Morganna and I looked at each other. They must have been the dragons we released from her sword. "Those were the dragons that the people of this village have slain in the past."

Both Xander and Louisa looked at me with confusion. It was Louisa that spoke. "These dragons weren't ghosts. I saw them with my own eyes. They were real."

"I think we should start at the beginning," said Morganna, and I nodded. I told them everything. How the dragons were shifters, how they only wanted peace but had been portrayed as killers. How my father had lied about everything. When I'd finished the whole story, I waited to see if either of them believed me.

"You are saying that dragon souls are hidden in our swords and that they are human?" asked Louisa incredulously.

"Not human exactly. They are shifters. Part human, part dragon. The wolves are the same. They can shift between their animal form and human form, but even when they are animals, they think as we do. Their thoughts remain the same."

Louisa still looked doubtful.

"I can't prove to you right now that the dragons are shifters, but I can prove part of the story. Can you hand me your sword, please?"

Louisa, like everyone in the village, had slain her only dragon on her eighteenth birthday, and like many others, had given it up after proving she could do it. "Why?" she asked.

"Here, will my sword work?" Xander began to pull it from the sheath at his side. It was a mark of how nervous the village was that he had it strapped to him even in his own home.

"I'm afraid it has to be Louisa's. You've slain many dragons. Every time I release one, it creates a flame. The more dragons in the sword, the bigger the fire."

"You want to release a dragon in my home?" Louisa's voice began to rise again.

"If you don't believe me, you've nothing to worry about. Just in case, I thought we'd go to your back garden."

She didn't say anything but she stood up and left the room. A minute or so later, she brought back a long box that didn't look like it had been opened in many years. From it, she pulled a sword. It gleamed like new. She might not have used it in years, but it was obvious she took great pride in it. It had been polished recently. I could smell the polish on it.

She handed me the sword. I took it and made my way to the garden. It wasn't big, but it had tall trees, hiding it from the neighbors. At the bottom was a fire pit. Perfect.

"You will see a bright flash and the soul of the dragon leaving the sword. The dragons' bodies are in a keep hidden in the forest over that way." I pointed in the general direction of the keep. "You should see the soul head there."

"Are you sure you are strong enough to do this?" asked Morganna, her face full of concern.

I nodded. It was only one. At the fire pit, I raised my arm and with a swift motion, brought the blade down upon it, creating yet another wound on my skin. The flash of fire knocked me to the floor and a dragon emerged like a cloud. I heard a scream as the dragon spirit flew off over the trees.

"Are you okay?" I looked up to see Louisa gazing down at me. She took my hand and helped me up. When she took in the state of my arm with all the old cuts there along with the one I'd just made, she was horrified. "Let me get you in the house and bandage that up."

This was the Louisa I knew. The mother hen who had everyone's best interests at heart. The scorned woman of a few minutes ago had left, replaced by the caring woman I knew she was. I let her guide me inside. As she hunted for bandages, she instructed Xander to make me some tea.

I glanced up at the clock as Louisa came back in. It was twenty minutes to six. The villagers would be assembling for the village meeting. The dragons and wolves would be gathering on the outskirts.

"Do you believe me?" I asked.

"About the dragons being trapped in swords? Of course. I saw it with my own eyes. I can see what you've done to yourself to free them, too." She liberally applied cream to my scarred skin.

"Do you believe the rest? About the dragons being shifters and being peaceful?"

"If you'd told me yesterday that I'd let Xander disappear with Morganna, I'd have never believed it, and yet they are both in the kitchen making tea. I'd say that I'm much more likely to believe your story."

"They will be just making tea, you know," I answered. "Morganna has told me how much it's bothered her, what she did to you."

"I can't tell you I suddenly trust her but I have to trust my husband." She was silent for a second. "They really want peace? It's hard to believe."

"Think about it. Has a dragon ever attacked except in self-defense? I know you've heard all the stories, but have you ever seen it yourself?"

"No," she admitted. "No, I haven't"

"My father has told lie after lie to keep the heritage of this village. We've been known as Slayers for centuries, and he wanted to keep up the tradition. He's known the truth for years. Someone must have passed it down to him when he was young, and I have no doubt that he was training me and Jasper to follow in his footsteps. What he didn't count on was me being saved by a dragon and stumbling on the truth. That's why they are coming tonight. They don't want to hurt anyone. They want to make peace and tell their side of the story. They also want the rest of the dragons back."

"Here is the tea." Morganna brought four mugs of steaming hot tea through on a silver tray. It was almost imperceptible, but I could see a tear in her eye. This was harder for her than she was letting on.

"We need to drink fast," said Xander, looking up at the clock. "The meeting starts in just over ten minutes."

22

The journey to the center of the village was no more than a ten-minute walk, and yet each footstep seemed to take a thousand years. The village I'd grown up in was so familiar to me, though I didn't feel at home here anymore. Some of the buildings had scorch marks marring their once perfect facade from the last battle with the dragons. Some were destroyed completely. It was as if the heart of the village beat no more.

As I rounded the corner to the village square, I stopped short. Holding my arms to my side to stop everyone else, I took in the scene in front of me. My father was on the small makeshift stage, speaking. It looked like the whole village had turned out to hear what he had to say. Once upon a time, I loved sitting in the front row of chairs to listen to my father, but now, listening to him tell lie after lie, the thought of it made me sick. I'd never known the village square to be so full. Usually, only a handful of people turned out to these meetings, typically just the head of each household. It was only on celebration days, in other words, dragon-slaying days, that so many people came out. Today, though, it looked like everyone over the age of eighteen was in attendance. The rows of chairs that had been set out were all full, and people stood along the sides and the back. Everyone, it seemed, wanted to hear what my father had to say.

I listened to him for a moment.

"Last night," he boomed out to the rapt audience, "there was a mass breakout of dragons from the dragon keep. I know most of you saw them. There has been a lot of talk about how this happened."

I bet there had been. The villagers had no idea that the dragons were being kept alive in an endless sleep. They had been told, as I had, that the dragons had been killed. I almost wanted to wait it out and hear what lie my father told to cover it up, but I could see Spear watching the events just out of view of my father. If anyone in the back of the audience turned, they would see him, but they were all fixated on my father. Behind Spear, the other dragons stood. They, too, were still and silent, waiting for a command of action. Every single one of them was in their human form.

Spear looked over and caught my eye. I nodded my head to acknowledge his presence. I also wanted to thank him for showing up in the form he was, without blustering in as a dragon. It would be easier this way. As he was too far ahead to speak to, I hoped that a nod of my head would be enough to convey this. He nodded back. At least I thought he did, but then he kept on nodding and jerking his head to the side.

I wasn't sure what he meant, but when Ash took hold of my arm and pointed to someone behind me, I realized Spear was pointing out the Wolvren who were coming up the narrow road behind us. I prodded Morganna and pointed them out to her.

They had to be silent. None of this could be rushed. There were too many people involved, and I was beginning to think that I'd got myself in way over my head.

I could still hear my father talking to the crowd as I tried to hold in my anxiety. This would only go according to plan if everyone remained calm, but what were the chances? Our plan was a weak one, and beyond "turn up and speak to people," we hadn't really gotten any further.

"They used magic to come back to life," my father shouted. While he wasn't actually wrong about this, I knew he wasn't going to tell the people that it was the Slayers' swords that were magic.

"They have magic, too?" someone from the crowd yelled out in a fearful voice.

"Of course they have magic," my father replied, moving closer to the front of the stage. "They are unnatural creatures."

I saw Spear stiffen, but he didn't move. I needed to do something and quickly. If I didn't, someone was going to snap. Taking a deep breath, I ran past the crowd of people—people I'd grown up around—and jumped up onto the stage.

"It's not true!" I shouted. "My father and some of the other elders have been lying to you your whole lives."

I could see the surprise as people registered my presence. Some looked angry. I knew it was because they'd seen me flying around on Ash's back when we invaded the village. Goodness only knew what lies they'd been told to cover that one up.

"You are in with the dragons. You are under their magic spell," yelled out someone I'd once been friends with. A murmur of agreement passed through the crowd. I was already losing them.

"They don't have magic," said a voice next to me. I turned to see Morganna stepping onto the stage. There was a collective moment of shock as they began to process who it was. No one shouted out, but I could hear the whispers from the people as their shock intensified.

"She's dead!" said someone in the front row.

"I assure you, I'm not dead. I'm very much alive."

"Take her away. She is an abomination," yelled my father, but no one came. Whoever he was shouting orders at was probably wondering how Morganna had suddenly appeared after so many years.

"I was blackmailed into leaving the village many years ago by this man." She pointed at my father who stood there, his mouth open in shock. "I did something very bad in my youth, something I regret to this very day. I've apologized to the people involved and I hope in time, they will be able to forgive me. However, lies were told about me to cover up the simple fact that I was a better Slayer. I killed many more dragons than Rocco ever could hope to. It made him mad, and that's why he sent me away...or so I thought."

The whole crowd was silent now. All eyes were transfixed on Morganna. Behind the people of the village, both the dragons and the Wolvren had come out into the open, but no one was going to take their concentration from Morganna to notice. Only the three of us on stage—my father, Morganna, and I—could see them. My father's mouth opened as if to warn everyone, but as quick as a flash, I pulled out my sword and pointed it right at his gut.

"I'd stay quiet if I were you," I said, standing up to my father. "Morganna has more to say."

He could have reached down and pulled his sword out, spearing me in an instant, but if he did, he knew as I did that the crowd would turn on him. He had no choice but to stay still and keep quiet.

Morganna gave me a small smile before beginning again. "The truth of the matter is, the dragons are not magic. They have no more magic than you or I. They do, however, have one amazing ability."

"Yeah, they eat people," someone shouted out. There was a smattering of nervous laughter.

"They can shift into human form."

The quiet crowd was quiet no more. A ripple of chatter spread through the crowd as people tried to decide if she was telling the truth or not. "Shifters don't exist!" the same man yelled out eventually.

"Really?" growled Alpha. He'd seen the commotion and run up toward the stage, bringing his men with him. The small stage was really beginning to fill up now; if we weren't careful, we were going to fall off.

A couple of the village elders, on seeing that there were more strangers on the stage, came running up and pointed their swords at Alpha. He growled but didn't try to fight them. From the other side, I saw Spear and his men approaching. They, too, tried to squeeze onto the tiny stage. More swords were held up at us by the villagers that still had them. If only I could step down and collect them all.

"To my left, ladies and gentlemen, are the people I've chosen to spend my life with. They are Wolf shifters. To my right are the dragons you are so fearful of."

A look of incredulity spread through the crowd. For all they knew, I'd just brought tens of strangers up here.

"I was on the brink of finding out the truth," Morganna continued, seemingly unaware of the commotion she was now causing. Even though no one was moving, I knew that it wouldn't take much to start a huge battle. Everyone was tensed, ready for attack, just waiting for someone else to make the first move. Morganna had to talk quickly to make sure she said what she needed to say before that happened. "The truth that it is fact the Slayers' swords that are magic." She held up her famous sword. "These swords are given to us on our eighteenth birthday. We all get them. Many choose to keep them hidden away in our houses. Some, like the elders here, choose to use them. Year after year, dozens, if not hundreds, of dragons are killed at our hands. Except they aren't really killed. They can't be killed because then their souls wouldn't strengthen the swords of the Slayers. When a sword is plunged into them, it extracts their soul. Their body is still alive and kept in a hold hidden away in the forest. What you saw last night was them regaining their souls after Julianna freed them."

"They all know she's on their side," spat my father, finally finding his voice again.

"Julianna isn't on anyone's side, but she knows that the dragons are innocent in this. Ask yourselves. Have you ever seen an attack by a dragon that wasn't in self-defense?"

"Yeah, they came and burned down half the village," someone pointed out.

"That's true. They came here to collect our swords. Our swords that have their friends' and families' souls trapped inside. Wouldn't you go to such lengths to get back your brother or mother, cousin, best friend? They tried to come in the dead of night so as not to hurt anyone. It was only because you chose to fight that they had to fight back. Well, they aren't fighting now. They are here to make peace. This fight has gone on long enough and there is no justifiable reason that it shouldn't end tonight."

Some of the crowd were murmuring quietly to each other, but I could tell they remained unconvinced. We were at a stalemate. No one was moving, each waiting to see what would happen. The people in the crowd were beginning to get restless. There was a general feeling of unrest as people decided what to think. I could see we were losing them.

"It's the truth," I said, trying to diffuse the situation. The tension was running high and if something didn't break soon, I could imagine the elders using their swords in a more forceful way. "On my eighteenth birthday, I fell. A dragon rescued me. He took me to his home at the other side of the mountains. There, I saw the people living just as we do. They have shops and houses and a town square just like this one. They are the same as you and I, except that they can turn into dragons. They have spent their lives protecting their village, just as you believe you have, but the truth of the matter is, there is no need. We are not fighting each other, we are fighting a perceived enemy. The dragons want to live in peace, just as we all do."

"Why should we believe you? You've been living among them. You have been caught in their magic." The same man that had spoken up numerous times shouted out again. I wished I could turn into a dragon at that point and bite his head off. I could see Spear getting annoyed at him too. Things had to turn around and quickly.

I saw my father's head nodding out of the corner of my eye.

"They are shifters!" I shouted in desperation.

"Liar!" he shouted back, matching my tone.

Just then, Ash bounded over to the front of the stage. He was on ground level, so a good foot below me. The people didn't know who he was, but they knew a stranger when they saw one. A dozen or so of the men in the crowd moved forward, ready to attack. Before anyone touched him, I heard the familiar creak of his bones. He was going to shift.

The people in the front few rows began to move back as his body contorted in a grotesque fashion. Chairs were knocked over in the panic as people tried to get away from him. His clothes ripped at their seams as a huge pair of red wings emerged from his back. Someone screamed and I saw a woman near the back faint. Not that I could blame her. I still wasn't used to the horrific sight.

Ash, finishing his transformation, spread his magnificent wings and flapped them. More chairs went flying before he took off into the sky.

23

Pandemonium broke out as the villagers scattered. Chairs were knocked over in the panic and screams filled the air. Ash circled around a few times before heading back to the stage. I tried shouting to stop the stampede. Some were running away in fear. Some were running toward the stage with their swords aloft. People were disappearing under the feet of others, running in all directions. Chaos abounded and people were getting hurt. No one would listen to me, no matter how loudly I shouted, my voice couldn't match the panicked noise that Ash's transformation had caused.

I watched helplessly as an old man was knocked over and trampled. Ash opened his wings again and flew to the man, picking him up gently in his talons and flying him to one side, out of the way. Either people didn't notice, or they didn't care, because the rush of people carried on.

"Enough!"

A bright light filled the air and Morganna's voice boomed out. So, she did have a little magic left after all! Her voice rose above the commotion, stopping people in their tracks. "You have walked over your own people to run away from your perceived threat, and yet that threat was the only person helping to save those that you all thoughtlessly trampled on. Look to the side if you don't believe me. Ash was the only one that tried to save one of your own as you trampled over him. If he wanted to hurt you, would he have done that?"

Everyone looked over. The old man had sat himself down in a chair. He was visibly bruised from the trampling, but beyond that, seemed okay. As everyone watched, Ash took to the air again and dove into the crowd. This time, instead of panicking, they moved aside and watched as he plucked a small child from the crowd. The little girl had obviously broken her arm in the fracas. Someone shouted out from the back.

"My baby!"

Ash followed the sound of the mother and delicately flew the girl back to her, letting her go gently in the weeping mother's arms.

Morganna raised an eyebrow. "There, you see? There is the monster that you've feared for centuries. He is a man. A man just like my friends here." She gestured to Spear and the others. "None of these men want to hurt you. They never have. If they wanted to, they could turn into dragons now and burn the village down. Do you see any of them doing that? No! They just want their family and friends back. Family that you have spent centuries taking from them. They don't want justice, they don't want revenge. They just want their loved ones back in their arms."

I looked out over the crowd as Ash flew overhead once again. He circled and landed next to me on the stage. Everyone was silent apart from the young girl, who was still crying. Morganna left the stage and walked right through the crowd that parted to let her through. She took the crying child from the mother and moved her hand up the little girl's arm. Within a minute, the girl had stopped crying and was laughing. Morganna did have more magic than she let on.

"The Goblins!" My father shouted out inexplicably, forcing everyone to turn back to the stage. "The Goblins warned us long ago that the dragons would hurt us."

"You lied to us," a woman shouted.

"I was keeping you all safe!" my father replied, clearly trying to control an uncontrollable situation.

"You knew all this time what the dragons were. What our swords were doing!"

"It wasn't just me," my father protested a little too hard. "The other elders knew too."

"That's not entirely true," Xander stepped forward and addressed the crowd. "I didn't know."

"Okay," my father backtracked. "I left some of you out of the secret. Some of you were just too goody-two-shoes for your own good. I knew if I told you, you'd stop me, but the truth of the matter is, I was protecting my village...your village...all of you. Just like my father and his father before him."

"No!" Xander strode up to my father. "The real truth is, you wanted the power. Your father led this village and you wanted that, too. You knew that the dragons' souls made the swords stronger. That's why you carried on this charade for so long. You know, I often wondered why you accompanied all the eighteen-year-olds up the mountain to their first kill. You always insisted on it. It wasn't because you wanted to help them; it was so that you could make your own kill and therefore make your sword stronger. I've lost count of the number of times you've been up that mountain, all in the name of protecting us. But it wasn't protection of the village you wanted, it was power over the village."

My father looked as though he was about to protest, but Xander stood up to him. There was little difference between them in height, but my father had the edge. In all his years of supremacy and toughness, I've never seen him quell under another man's stare before, but Xander was mad. Mad that he had been duped all his life, mad that the other villagers had, too. My father almost cowered under the stare of the shorter man.

We had the rapt attention of the crowd now. The people who had run were now coming back. The wolves headed into the crowd to help pick up the chairs that were knocked over in the panic. The dragons went down to help. I could see the nervousness of the villagers as they descended into the crowd, but there was no fighting. For the first time in forever, these three tribes were finally working as a team. They were working as one.

It made my heart sing to finally see it.

I watched Alpha put his hand down to help pull up a woman that had fallen in the mêlée. The mother of the child who had been hurt purposefully walked over to Ash and hugged him, even though he was still in his dragon form.

The only people left on the stage were Morganna, my father, and I. Everyone else was helping tidy up the mess. It wasn't just the mess of the panic, but the mess of the last couple of centuries. A lot of the townsfolk kept a wary distance from Ash, but no one tried to hurt him. I had a suspicion he would have turned back into his human form if he'd not ripped his only pair of clothes. Funnily enough, the villagers were less wary of the other dragons. Maybe because they looked human.

I mentioned it to Morganna.

"It will come in time. Look how much you've achieved. Never in my whole life did I ever think I'd see the day when Slayers and dragons stood together."

"Not to mention wolves," I replied.

"It's all because of you." She stood silently for a second, then spoke again. "I came here today because I wanted to help you, but I have to admit, I didn't think it would work. I thought we'd all be driven out of town."

"You really thought we'd fail?"

"I'm sorry to say that I did. I underestimated you. I don't know why. After watching you cut yourself so deeply to free those dragons, I know you are the most fearless warrior I've ever met. You might not have slain as many dragons as I, but you are braver on so many more levels. Slaying was easy. Looking beyond past prejudices and giving a sworn enemy, a chance takes a hell of a lot of courage."

She patted my back. I could scarcely believe what I was hearing. My childhood hero, a woman who was famously fearless, was telling me that I was braver than her. I didn't think I'd ever felt so happy in my life. I turned to my father. He looked like a broken man. My mother and brother had suddenly appeared and were sitting with him on the edge of the stage. My mother's eyes were red-rimmed, as though she'd been crying for a long time. She probably had. She'd aged so much in the past few weeks. The silver in her hair had turned a ghostly white. I wanted to go over and comfort her, but strangely enough, walking over to my family was so much harder than fighting any dragon or talking to a hundred people from a stage. And yet, I couldn't walk away from them. Whatever they had done, they were still my family. My mother was as innocent in this as the rest of the village, and as much as I hated to admit it, so was Jasper.

I took a deep breath and walked over to them. I lowered myself until I was sitting on the edge of the stage. My mother burst into a fresh round of tears and hugged me. Despite her diminutive size, she gave the most powerful hugs known to man. She could barely crack an egg without help, but she held me so tightly that she almost cracked my ribcage. Jasper wasn't going to hug me. He just wasn't made like that, but he gave me a nod of the head, which was enough. There was just my father left. He'd done some terrible, terrible things, but I knew that I wasn't entirely blameless. When my mother finally let go of me, I stood and walked up to my father. Just as my mother had aged, he looked so much older than his years. He seemed to have shrunk too. No longer was he a colossal bear of a man; instead, he was a man who knew he'd lost everything. He'd lost his house, his standing in the community and the respect of the people. He was no longer the big man of the village.

"I'm sorry, Father," I began, but he cut me off.

He didn't speak. Instead, he handed me his sword. The sword I'd admired since I was a tiny scrap of a thing. That in itself spoke volumes. I wanted to say something else, but there was nothing else to say. Fixing my family would be more difficult than fixing the village. Funnily enough, I believed the dragons would be a great help in mending and rebuilding the houses that had been destroyed. They could carry a lot of wood and materials on their backs. I made a mental note to speak to Ash about it as soon as I could.

"I thought I was doing the right thing," my father began in a croaky voice. Even his booming voice had diminished. "The Goblins..."

"You don't have to say anything. Now is the time to build and rebuild, not only the structures around the village but the link between our community and the dragons."

My father nodded solemnly just as Ash appeared at my side. He was still in his dragon form and towered over me.

"See, Father? The dragons don't want to hurt us. This is my friend Ash." I could have told them he was my boyfriend, but I think they had enough to come to terms with in one day. They could probably guess by the way he'd stood by me over these past few weeks. I put my hand up to him, feeling his scaly skin. He looked my father straight in the eye and nodded his head. My father nodded back.

24

The meeting finally ended hours later. One of the Slayers brought out a couple of barrels of ale and another brought out food. It was their way of making amends, although they really had nothing to make amends for. Just like Morganna and me, they had not known the full truth of the situation. As the sky deepened in color and night set in, the chairs were moved from their positions in rows to a circle. In the center, a makeshift fire pit was quickly built up and Ash kindly started the fire for us. Xander went home and came back minutes later with some clean clothing so Ash could turn back into his human form.

It was a weird scene. Dragons sitting with Slayers and wolves, and for the first time in so many centuries, they were all getting along. Even those that had appeared cautious at first were now sitting and chatting with the dragons, probably due to the ale they had been sipping.

At some point, Spear and one of the village elders

had gotten together and rounded up the remaining swords. There was a pile of them next to me. The next job would be to free the dragons within, but Ash forbade me from doing it so soon.

He sat next to me, his arm draped around my shoulder. It was a cold night, but the heat of the fire along with the heat of Ash's body warmed me.

"They have been without souls for a long time. One more day won't make much difference. Besides, if you use all those swords to draw your blood, it will kill you."

He was right. I couldn't possibly free all the dragons at once. It would be too much for my body to take. We would have to come up with a plan to do it without killing me off.

I felt completely at ease with the world with one exception. I thought back to my time in the Goblins' lair. They had welcomed us, although they had wanted us to leave without giving us much information. I'd not really thought about it much before today, but everything boiled down to the Goblins.

I walked over to where Morganna sat. She was sharing a joke with Alpha and one of the Slayers. "I've been thinking about the Goblins..." I began.

"I have, too," she said, standing and pulling me away from the fire. "It's curious that they have been brought up so many times."

"My father told me that they were the ones who told him that the dragons were evil."

"This has been going on for way longer than your father has been around, but if they said that to him, they probably have been saying it for centuries."

"I wonder if it's a way to make more money? Each of our swords costs a small fortune."

"A selling tool?" mused Morganna. "Do you really think that's what this is?"

I thought for a second before shaking my head. "No." I held up my sword. It was a thing of beauty and excellent craftsmanship. "They could charge what they liked for these anyway. Each one is unique and most hold precious stones. They had no reason to tell us to kill the dragons."

Alpha spoke up. I'd not even realized he'd joined us. "I'm sorry for interrupting you ladies, but I heard what you were talking about. I've never told anyone this before, not even you Morganna, but many years ago, when I was still very young, I went to the Goblins with my father. He died long ago, but that is neither here nor there. He wanted magic. We walked for days, taking everything of any value that we had. The Goblins let us in and fed us. I remember as a boy being fascinated by the whole city they'd built indoors."

I remembered it well. It was a feat of amazing engineering or powerful magic.

"I loved it there," Alpha continued. "It was so different from the forest I grew up in..." Spear and Ash headed over to us to hear what was being said. Alpha continued his story. "They fed us the most wonderful food, and for a young boy that had been walking for days and was hungry, it was like heaven. They offered us shelter for a couple of nights, but they would not give us magic. My father was not rich enough. The few trinkets he had brought were of no use to them. I remember them being friendly about it, but I also remember the warning that the head Goblin gave to my father as we were setting off home. He said that a great war was coming between the dragons and the Slayers, and we would be best to get home quickly and stay away from the area. My father believed them. We sped home so fast that I thought my feet would fall off. When we got back, my father realized that his trinkets were gone. At the time, he thought he'd dropped them in his haste to get back, but I always thought that the Goblins had stolen them. I guess I'll never know."

"I've only ever visited the Goblins once," said Spear, joining in the conversation. "But I've heard stories, much the same as you all have. We were also warned about a great war with the Slayers. We have long since been told never to tell the Slayers the truth about the swords for if we did, the Slayers would fight back."

"Well, they weren't wrong," pointed out Ash. "Maybe this was the great war they were talking about."

"They've manipulated us all," remarked Morganna, "but why?"

We stood silently, none of us knowing the answer. The Goblins had a lot more to do with this than any of us previously thought.

I looked over my shoulder at the people. Slayers, dragons, and wolves. The fire was dying out and many had left to go home. A few of the Slayers remained, drinking what was left of the ale. The dragons could fly up to Frokontas, but the wolves had nowhere to go.

"Did you set up a camp outside town?" I asked Alpha.

He seemed to notice for the first time how tired his men looked. It had been a long day. He stood and walked back to the fire pit, addressing all those that were still left. "My fellow Wolvren. We've had a long journey and I think it's time we headed back to camp. I want to invite anyone who would like to join us, be they Slayer or dragon. Tomorrow, we will all talk some more. There is much work to be done."

As if on cue, everyone left around the campfire stood and made to leave. I even saw a few of the Slayers and all of the dragons accept Alpha's invite and follow the wolves to the camp. As the barrels of ale were taken along, I suspected that the party would continue there and no one would get enough sleep.

The only ones left were Morganna, Ash, Alpha, Spear, Xander and my parents. Jasper had left to drink the ale with the wolves and dragons. How times had changed!

"I have something to tell you all," my father said as we sat back down around the dying embers of the campfire. I pulled my cloak around myself more tightly, wishing the fire was still burning. As Ash was now in his human form, I could hardly ask him to turn back and light the fire again. Instead, he caught me shivering and threw a log into it, hoping it would catch the flames.

"The swords..." He gestured to the pile that the villagers had brought to us. My fathers were on top, the most majestic of them all. "This isn't all of them. There are others."

"Where are they?" Spear asked.

"That, I cannot say. For centuries, the eighteen-year-olds of this village have been given swords. Some have been plain, some have been the swords of warriors, but all of them have come from the Goblins. Now, not every eighteen-year-old has become a Slayer. Some chose not to. Many decided to have their sword as a keepsake or memento rather than something they used. However, most used their swords, if only once on their eighteenth birthday. Killing a dragon is a rite of passage in this village, and most like to try, even if they never kill again. Although the families of Dronias can be traced back for generations, there are some, like Morganna here, who chose to leave."

"Where did they go?" interrupted Spear.

My father sighed. "I know the whereabouts of some of those who left since I have been around, but there have been many more."

"Just how many swords are we talking about?" asked Spear, getting agitated. I couldn't blame him. I'd told him how many swords we had to collect without accounting for lost swords from centuries ago. I had a feeling there were a lot more than I originally thought. I held my breath, waiting for my father to answer the question, not wanting to know the answer but needing to know what we had in store for us at the same time.

"There could be as many as a hundred," my father admitted.

I let out a long breath. A hundred swords! I looked over at the pile. There was less than fifty that I could see.

Spear's voice rose, not in anger so much as disbelief. "We have to find a hundred swords to free all of my people?"

"I'm afraid so. Although, that is only my guess. The correct number could be more or less."

"It could be more than a hundred?" asked Ash. He

was having the same difficulty realizing the enormous task ahead as the rest of us were.

"It could be less, too," my mother squeaked. Always the optimist. I squeezed her hand and she gave me a shy smile.

I looked at the assembled people. Just one day ago, I could not imagine we could all sit around the same fire and converse in a civilized manner, and yet here we all were. We'd come so far in so little time.

I stood up tall. "We can find them if we all work together."

"It's an enormous task, Julianna. Impossible even," my mother answered.

"If I'd have asked any of you yesterday if you thought you could sit around a campfire with the people you are with, would you have believed it to be possible? Two dragons, a Wolvren, Slayers. How many hundreds of years has it been since this has been possible? Has it ever happened before, or are we the first? This to me is impossible, and yet we are doing it. No one is fighting and we are all talking to each other. This seems more impossible to me than finding some swords. Between us, we can do it!"

I wasn't sure I really believed it myself, but my speech elicited a round of applause from the group. It spurred them into action if nothing else.

"We keep a registry of all the births and deaths within the village," my mother said. "We can use it to find out who we need to look for. If they were born here and died here, their swords would have been taken to the vault."

"The vault!" my father shouted, suddenly excited.

"I'd forgotten about the vault. There are many swords down there."

"A hundred?" asked Spear hopefully.

"No. Not quite. Thirty or forty maybe, but it's a start. Some people choose to be buried with their swords, too."

"So, we are going to have to dig up graves now?" Ash asked, looking sick at the prospect.

"It's late," said my mother, standing. "We have a lot to discuss, but I fear I'm too tired to get it all through my mind. I would love to invite you all to stay at our home, but unfortunately, we don't have a home at present." She was being nice. She didn't have a home because the dragons had burned it down.

"Those without beds can come back to the camp," invited Alpha. "We can meet up tomorrow and make a plan for the future."

Ash put his arm around me and guided me back to the camp. I was so tired I could barely see, but a bed had been made for us in one of the tents. I rested my head on Ash's chest and fell asleep almost immediately.

25

I woke up to a hive of activity outside. I assumed breakfast was being cooked thanks to all the yummy smells coming through the tent. I guessed that someone had started a fire and was cooking something upon it. I snuggled up to Ash's still sleeping form, reluctant to move from the warmth he provided. I felt happy. It was not an emotion I was used to in recent weeks. Not fully, anyway. Sure, being around Ash always made me feel better, but the war had been plaguing my thoughts and dreams ever since I first met him. There was still so much to do, but for the first time, we were all on the same side.

Ash shifted slightly in his sleep so I kissed him lightly on the lips. His eyes flashed open and he gave me a lazy grin.

"Like a prince, huh?" he mumbled.

"What?" I asked, wondering if he was still caught up in a dream.

"You woke me with a kiss like a fairytale prince would."

"Does that make you a princess?" I teased. He grabbed me and pulled me toward him, enveloping me in a hug that turned into a tickle. I started to laugh until I heard Morganna's voice admonish us from outside the tent.

After a quick but delicious breakfast of roasted bird and bread, Morganna, Alpha, Spear, Ash and I made our way back to the village where we had promised to meet the others. My father had come a long way since yesterday on a personal level and he was the first to greet us as we walked into the village square. The skies had begun to open, drizzling us with drops of rain. He showed us into the townhouse that sat above the vault. The swords we had collected the day before were already piled up, ready for us.

"I've been thinking hard about things," he began as we all took our seats at a large table in one of the town hall's conference rooms. "I've spent my life being a coward and compensated by pretending to be the bravest Slayer. I wanted to be the best, but I ended up being the worst. Julianna, you taught me the real meaning of bravery. I saw those scars on your arms yesterday and I have a hunch I know where you got them. I will not allow you to hurt yourself again. I will free the dragons. After all, I captured many of them."

I saw the pride on my mother's face as my father spoke. It took a great deal for him to speak this way. I guess the years of guilt at what he was doing to innocent people had finally caught up with him.

"You don't have to do it alone," replied Xander. "I

will help, too. My skin is already scarred. I do not mind adding to them."

"We all appreciate your offer," began Spear, "but neither of you can help. It is not enough to spill your own blood. You also have to be innocent of spilling blood before. If you have committed a murder, or in this case, taken a soul, your own blood will be useless."

He waited for this to sink in. Finally, my father spoke. "You mean to tell me that only Julianna can free the dragons?"

"No," butted in Ash. "Julianna has done enough already. She is strong, but I fear that too many more cuts will hurt her beyond repair, kill her even."

My mother made a sound like a cry.

"Anyone who has owned a Goblin-made sword and who has not used it to draw dragon's blood will be able to do the task. Are there any people in your village that can do it?"

"There are some," my father replied. "As I said yesterday, some use their swords purely for decoration. I cannot ask them to injure themselves, though."

"Would you prefer Julianna do it all to wake the dragons up? That is your only other option." Morganna said.

"I'm not letting Julianna do that to herself. She's been through enough!" shouted Ash. I placed my hand on his arm to calm him down.

"No one should have to go through that," my father countered. "I see what Julianna has done. It is my eternal shame that she felt that was the only option. I will never let my daughter go through that again."

I gave him a smile. It was nice to see him sticking up

for me. I remembered how he had always been my hero. How I'd idolized him growing up. I'd lost that in the past few weeks, but with a little time, I hoped we could get back to where were once were.

"What do you suggest?" asked Morganna.

"We need to go back to the Goblins."

"We've already been up to the Goblins," replied Spear. "They won't tell you anything."

"We have two of the most famous Slayers in the kingdom seated around this table. We have dragons and we have wolves. We will make them talk."

Spear nodded his head and with that we were once again at war, only this time not with each other, but with the Goblins. "I agree!" he said, standing up.

"Where are you going?" I asked.

"There is no time like the present. The Wolvren are here now. I have my men ready for action. Let's go today. What say you, Slayer?" He looked over at my father. My father stood and for the first time in centuries, the leader of the dragons and the leader of the Slayers shook hands.

It wasn't as easy as just setting out. We had to gather up the villagers who wanted to go. All the dragons in the village and all the Wolvren agreed to come with us. In the end, there were about thirty of us willing to make the journey back up the Triad Mountains. The dragons could fly, but there weren't enough of them to carry the rest of the men and women who had volunteered so we had to make the journey on foot.

At first, my father said he didn't want me to go, but a swift word from my mother had him quickly changing his mind. She walked with us to the base of the mountains. She wasn't going to come with us, but she wanted to be a part of it if only for a little way. Surprisingly, Jasper appeared and volunteered to come. Even more surprisingly, he didn't try to make fun of me as we set off on the journey.

My mother and some of the other ladies in the village had organized and packed up food for us all. It would be an arduous journey, and we would need all the food and water we could carry. We also had to take extra blankets to keep out the cold now that the weather had turned for the worse.

The dragons led the way, with Spear at the front. It made sense as he had already been to the Goblins' lair and knew the way. My father joined him and from the back, where I walked with Ash, I could see them chatting as if they had been friends for years.

I gave my mother a quick hug as we climbed the wall that separated Dronias from the base of the Triad Mountains. As I put my foot up to climb, she pulled me lightly back down.

"You go ahead," I said to Ash. "I'll catch you up."

He hesitated for a second but headed with the others into the forest which marked the first part of our journey. I waited until he'd been swallowed by the foliage and turned back to my mother.

"I'm so proud of you. I…" A tear followed a trail down her cheek.

"You don't have to say anything," I said, wiping the tear away with my sleeve. "I know."

"No, you don't know. I've watched you grow from this scrappy little thing to being the strongest woman I've ever met. These last few weeks have been tough, tougher than I ever thought possible, but it wasn't losing my home, nor the fight between us and the dragons that scared me. My biggest fear was that I'd lost you." The tears were really coming down now. She made no effort to conceal them or wipe them away.

I hugged her again, my own tears matching hers. "You'll never lose me, Mama. I love you too much."

"I love you, too. More than you could ever imagine." She sniffed and pulled my scarf tighter around me. "Be safe up there. I couldn't bear to lose you again."

"What did I just say?" I smiled. "You'll never lose me. I promise."

"He's a good man you've found for yourself."

I turned to where she was looking behind me. Ash waiting patiently for me between the trees. "He is a good man, Mama, just wait until you get to know him properly. You'll love him."

"I'm looking forward to it!"

I gave her one last hug and vaulted over the low wall. Ash took my hand as we made our way into the forest.

"So many people have told you how proud they are of you, but I don't think I have." Ash's warm fingers intertwined with mine.

"You don't have to."

"I can't believe we started this adventure together. Whatever happens, we'll end it together."

"You mean finding Morganna or looking for the swords?" I asked.

"I'm talking about our lives. Mine began the day you tried to kill me."

"I didn't technically try to kill you. I fell off a ledge if you remember."

He smiled. "You did, and I've never been gladder of anything. If it wasn't for your bad sense of balance, we wouldn't be here now."

"You mean walking up a mountain in the freezing cold on the way to find some Goblins?"

"I mean together. I want us to stay that way. I'll never leave you. Never!"

And as I looked into his eyes, I knew he meant it. Whatever life threw at us, we'd get through it together.

The End

———

Grab the final installment of the Dragon Tamer series here:

https://books2read.com/dragontamerbook3

PROTECTOR

DRAGON TAMER BOOK 3

PROTECTOR

1

I gazed at the people surrounding me, amazed at how far we'd all come. We still had a long way to go to reach the top of the mountain, but I never thought I'd see the day that Slayers, dragons, and wolves would come together for a common cause.

Not that they were all especially happy about the situation. Apart from Alpha, Morganna and, of course, Ash and me, the others had formed very distinctive groups. The dragons took the lead with Spear heading up that group. Rocco followed behind with a group of Slayers. Then, at the very back, were Morganna and Alpha with the wolves. From where I stood, I could see all of them and the long trek ahead of us. I'd made this particular trek before but that seemed so long ago now.

After the fighting and the traveling, all of us were exhausted, including me, and we'd only just set off. It was going to take us a lot longer than it had before to traverse the rocky pathways. We hadn't even gotten through the trees on the lower part of the mountains and I was already flagging with fatigue. The trip to the Wolvrens' home and then back to Dronias, not to mention all the blood I'd lost, had taken its toll on me.

"Are you ok?" Ash asked, noticing my discomfort. I couldn't hide anything from him, he was so perceptive.

"I'm fine," I replied, plastering on a smile. I wasn't fine, but if I said that, he'd either make me turn around and head back to my mother at the bottom of the mountain or insist on turning into his dragon form and carrying me up the mountain himself. I wasn't willing to let either one happen. Truth be told, I was scared that if I left the group, something would come between them. Our solidarity was hanging by a thread as it was and I didn't want to jeopardize that. As much as I hated to admit it, I was the glue that held us all together. Ok, Morganna could technically do the same job. She knew the wolves well and, of course, she was a Slayer, but it still felt like my responsibility to keep everyone together.

"Do you want me to carry you for a while?" asked Ash. "You look really tired."

And there was my second option. The problem was, he looked tired, too, and if he carried me up the hill, the others might expect the same treatment. Besides, I really didn't want to show weakness this early on in the trek. I shook my head and grasped his hand. Just holding onto him gave me strength and if he pulled me up a little and helped me over the rocky terrain, who else was to know?

After centuries of fighting between the Slayers and dragons, it was strange to see us working together. I could still feel the hate and dislike between the two groups. Friendship would take a long time, but with a common enemy in the Goblins, at least we could focus on something other than killing each other. Once we reached the Goblins' cave, bloodshed would be inevitable. I wasn't so naïve as to believe that we could sort out the problems without it. We still had many dragons to save and as I was the only one who could do it, I had to remain fit.

Ash and I had only just left the leafy shade of the wooded area, beginning the long, arduous journey over the rocky, gray terrain that made up the next part of the mountains, when up ahead, Spear came to a stop. I paused under the pretense of seeing what Spear was up to, but as far as I could tell, he was simply gazing out over the view below us. I couldn't see it from where I was near the back of the caravan; I could only see the dark forest behind me, but I knew once I cleared the tree line, I'd see fields of gold and green laid out before me like a patchwork quilt. I'd seen the view enough to remember it well and had even flown over it on Ash's back.

Looking back up at Spear, I could see him speaking animatedly to my father. At the beginning of the hike, before the groups had split, the two had been doing well, chatting about the route, both of them leaving old wounds behind them. But as I watched them now, I could see animosity between them. They were too far ahead to hear what they were saying and the wind that whipped around us swept their voices away, but it was plain to see they were having some kind of disagreement. Nudging Ash, I pointed up at them.

"Do you think we should go see what the matter is?" he asked as he saw what I was pointing at.

I sighed. I'd hoped that we could at least get to the

top of the mountain without problems, but it seemed it was not to be. "I guess so," I said, shrugging my shoulders. I didn't have the energy to run to them, but I knew I'd have to find some from somewhere if I didn't want this journey to turn into an all-out war again. I huffed and puffed as I increased my pace, passing Wolvren and Slayers until Ash and I were at the front of the group.

"What's the matter?" I wheezed at the two men, both of whom looked disgruntled.

"I think we should camp here," my father said to me, "but your friend here thinks we should carry on."

"Look out there," Spear said angrily pointing behind me. The golden fields were covered in a blanket of fog. "If we don't keep going, that is what we will wake up to tomorrow. Do you have any idea how difficult it will be to navigate this terrain with no visibility? We've only just set off anyway. Why are we resting now?"

My legs already felt like jelly with only a couple of hours of walking, but I couldn't be seen taking sides.

My father puffed out his chest. He hated being told what to do. Not being the leader on this particular expedition was obviously not sitting well with him. "We are not like you. We are human. We need a break. You know these mountains. Are you saying you won't be able to find your way in the fog?"

Spear grimaced. "It's not exactly going to make it easy, is it?"

"Look at Julianna." My father pointed to me. Great! Now I was being dragged into this. "The poor girl is exhausted. You can't expect her to carry on walking. We are all tired and hungry. If the fog rolls in, so be it, although I doubt it will get this high."

Spear gritted his teeth as though he was holding back what he really wanted to say. He looked over at me, and despite me trying to appear fine from the journey so far, I was obviously not doing a good job. "You do look tired," he conceded. "Ok, everyone. We are going to set up camp here. We all need to be rested for the next part of our journey tomorrow."

I could hear some of the others, mainly the dragons, mumbling to each other behind me, but none of them would dare to go against Spear's orders. I caught a grin on my father's face, but when I looked at him directly, he let it drop.

All in all, I was glad for the rest. I didn't want to announce it to everyone, but I ached all over, especially where my scars were. My body was a map of scars criss-crossing the skin where I'd cut myself to free the drag-ons. My skin was no longer flawless and never would be again. Some of my scars had faded to thin, silver lines, and others still shone red, but they were all there, plain to see, each one representing the freedom of a dragon.

Two of the younger dragons, Nenno and Fox, changed into their dragon forms to light our campfire. It was getting chilly now the autumn air was coming in and with little to shield us from the wind, we needed all the warmth we could get. Thankfully, my mother and the other villagers had packed us some warm blankets along with enough food for us to feast upon, but as the flames flickered in the wind, I couldn't help thinking I should have been stronger and insisted we carry on further up the mountain where there would be more shelter from the elements.

Fox and Nenno changed back into their human

forms and dressed quickly in the cold air. A couple of the Slayers shifted to one side begrudgingly to let them have space by the fire.

The fire was small as we only had the wood we'd brought with us from the forest, and there were so many of us crowded around it that I could barely feel the heat from it. I had to content myself with snuggling into Ash and wrapping the pair of us in a blanket.

Even around the fire, the group was still separated into three distinct parts. No one was fighting, but no one was making any effort to talk to anyone from one of the other groups either.

"How long do you think it will before someone kills someone else?" joked Ash.

"That's not a bet I'd like to take," I replied quietly. He was trying to be funny, but I knew our expedition was hanging by a thread. Centuries of hatred didn't disappear overnight, and though everyone was doing their best to not get in each other's way, I knew it would take very little for this whole thing to blow up in our faces.

"Your father looks mad."

I glanced over at him. "He always looks like that. I don't think we need to worry about him. He got what he wanted after all. I caught him grinning a while ago. He just likes to be the boss, that's all."

"What about Spear?"

I sighed. Spear was as pigheaded as my father. If any two people were going to come to blows, it was them. Alpha, leader of the Wolvren, seemed happy enough to camp. As I looked over at him, I saw he was chatting to Morganna. Both of them were grinning, caught up in some shared story or joke.

"Maybe we should have brought more women up here," I said, pointing at Alpha.

Ash hugged me closer to him and laughed. "I think it would just give them something else to argue over," he pointed out. Maybe he was right. I couldn't see my mother wanting to make this journey and I wouldn't know who to bring up to keep Spear company. It certainly was a male-heavy expedition, though. Other than Morganna and me, there were a couple of female dragons who were keeping out of everyone's way. All the rest were men.

"If women were in charge, this would be so much easier," I mused.

"The guys think they are in charge, but let's be honest, without you and Morganna, none of us would be here at all. If you ask me, women are in charge here."

I didn't feel in charge of anything, but it was nice to be thought of in that way. I stood and grabbed some food from the pile that had been put out and brought it back to Ash. Between us, we ate bread, cheese, and ham that I made into rough sandwiches, followed by a couple of cupcakes I recognized as my mother's handi-work. Only my mother could think of baking when the whole world was falling down around her ears.

The sky darkened, but I couldn't see any stars. Spear had been right. The fog was already beginning to drift in.

2

I slept better than expected in the cold night. Ash's body heat and the thick blanket helped keep me warm. That was one of the perks of being a dragon's girlfriend: I was never cold. I opened my eyes and blinked. I couldn't see a thing. My first thought was that I'd somehow gone blind, before realizing the damp air around me was actually thick fog. I'd never seen anything like it. I could barely see my hand when I stretched out my arm. I nudged Ash awake.

"Hmmm?"

"Wake up," I whispered. Everything was silent around us as though the fog was hiding the sound as well as taking our vision from us.

"Woah," exclaimed Ash as he opened his eyes.

"Shhh." For some reason, it felt wrong to be speaking aloud.

Through the fog came the sounds of Spear's voice. "I told him this would happen!"

"I can hear you, you know," replied my father

tetchily. I rolled my eyes. The pair of them would be the end of me if they didn't get over their differences.

"Breakfast anyone?" I asked, just to break the tension.

"How are you going to make breakfast?" someone shouted, maybe Nenno. "Are you able to cook in the dark?"

It looked like my father and Spear weren't the only ones in bad moods. The cold, damp air was getting to everyone. I stood, dropping the blanket to the ground. The dampness clung to me. It was going to be a miserable day. I wished I'd not agreed so readily with my father about wanting to stop. Now, if anything, the cold was making my body ache more.

I felt around for my backpack and pulled my warmest sweater from it. The sounds of other people stirring from sleep filled the air. The cloying fog was the main topic of conversation and the main cause of grumbling as we packed up the camp.

Breakfast was impossible. I had to content myself with eating a bar of chocolate that my mother had packed until we got a bit further up the mountain and escaped the fog. I crossed my fingers and hoped that as we climbed, the fog would thin out if only to keep Spear and my father from killing each other.

I whispered this to Ash who smirked. "If they do, at least they won't have to worry about hiding the body."

I rolled my eyes for a second time. It was going to be a long day. The going was extremely tough, not least because we could barely see where we were going. Nenno and Fox turned into dragons and used their fire to light the way. They'd argued that it made more sense for them to fly up the mountain, but both the Slayers and Wolvren argued that it would give them some kind of unfair advantage.

I kept to the back of the group, relying on Ash to keep me going in the right direction with his much better eyesight. It meant I didn't have to listen to the endless complaints as we steadily made our way to the top of the mountain.

By the time we stopped for lunch, even I was getting grumpy. My hair was soaked and my sweater was barely keeping out the cold. The incessant squabbling between all three groups was driving me crazy and to top it all off, I felt sick with the lack of food and exhaustion. A campfire was set and, thanks to Nenno, lit. The fog had thinned out a little—enough to cook a meal—but it was still gray and dreary. I remembered this part of the mountain. We'd gone above the trees and already crossed the scrubland into the rocky parts. Even without the fog, the scenery would be gray and unexciting. I hoped it wasn't a harbinger of things to come.

I helped cook, mainly as an excuse to be close to the fire. As we'd missed breakfast, I elected to cook it for lunch instead. I pulled a pound of bacon and three boxes of eggs from my bag. Someone else brought out a couple of loaves of bread and another person buttered them all. I fried eggs in one pan while Fox fried bacon in another. We had limited supplies, but my mother always liked us to have a cooked breakfast and so she had packed enough for everyone and split it between my father's bag, mine, Ash's and Jasper's. Between us, we cooked up quite a feast.

After we'd eaten and once again set off on our way, I

noticed that people were grumbling less. A bit of food in their stomachs and the atmosphere had changed completely. Well, all except for Spear and my father who seemed to be unable to help themselves.

The actual atmosphere was getting better too. The higher we climbed, the thinner the fog became, until we finally climbed above it. With the gray clouds below us and the peaks of the Triad Mountains rising majestically above us, showing snow caps next to blue skies, it was shaping up to be quite a nice day after all. The sun shone down, drying my hair and lifting the damp from my clothes. Now that I could see, I recognized exactly where I was, and it wasn't far from the entrance to the Goblin city. We'd made it and more than that, we'd made it without anyone killing anyone else.

The last time we'd been here, a small green door had been left open. Ash had walked down the tunnel beyond it to find a very grumpy Goblin. I expected as much today, and so was surprised when I saw the little green door was very much shut. Shut and locked. A huge metal chain with a padlock kept it that way.

"What are we going to do now?" asked my father, glaring at Spear.

Spear shrugged his shoulders. "How should I know? The door was open the last time we were here. Why don't you figure it out?"

What was wrong with these two? They were acting like schoolboys. I marched past everyone else and stood in between them before they began throwing punches. "Father, without you I wouldn't know how to hold a sword, let alone fight with one. Spear, you command a city of dragons. Both of you are fearless and brave. You are both great leaders." They both nodded. "So please act like it," I continued. "You are embarrassing yourselves."

I took a deep breath. I'd been standing up to my father when he was trying to kill the dragons for a while now, but this felt different. I almost expected him to shout at me to go to my room. Instead, he looked dumbfounded.

Spear nodded his head. "I'm sorry, Julianna. You are right. I've not been acting like a man should in my position as leader." He held his hand out for my father to shake it.

I raised my eyebrows at my father and put my hands on my hips, the way a mother would when scolding a child.

"I'm sorry, too, Spear. Please accept my apology." He hardly looked like a man of contrition as he took Spear's hand and shook it, glaring at him the whole time, but it was a start.

"Great!" Someone clapped me on the shoulder and squeezed. I turned, expecting to see Ash, but it was Xander. He gave me a grin and then let go. "Perhaps we should try knocking?" he said heading to the door. "It seems like the polite thing to do."

He had a point. In my head, we would have been knocking it down. Maybe I wasn't so different from my father after all. I tried to suppress a smirk at the thought of it while Xander rapped his knuckles on the peeling green paint of the door. After a minute, he knocked again. I was just about to suggest that we knock it down using brute strength when the door opened a crack.

"What do you want?" asked a high pitched whiny

voice from behind the door. I couldn't see the owner but I could tell it was a Goblin.

Spear stepped forward. "We are here to speak to Krikor."

A mossy hand reached around the door and opened it a fraction more. The goblin—one I'd not seen before—widened his eyes as he took in the sight of our strange crew. "Dragons, Slayers, Wolves. Oh, no. Certainly not, certainly not!" He made to shut the door, but Spear blocked it with his foot.

"I've met with Krikor before. Please tell him that Spear is here. He knows who I am."

The Goblin narrowed his eyes. Goblins were deceitful creatures and like anyone who lies, they never believed anyone else was telling the truth. I could see that the Goblin was either afraid to let us in or had been strictly forbidden to do so.

"Nope. Not going to happen." The Goblin stamped down hard on Spear's foot, causing him to retract it from the door. Half a second later and the door slammed shut.

"Let me put it this way," yelled my father through the door. "Either you open it and let us in, or we'll open it ourselves. The dragons here are desperate to burn something down."

He turned and gave me a wink as though he was doing me a favor. I would have rolled my eyes for a third time that day if it wasn't for the fact his little threat worked. The door opened once again and the small creature stuck his head out.

"Wait here. I'll speak to the king." The door slammed shut once again.

Ten minutes passed before the Goblin reappeared, but this time, he wasn't alone. He had two more Goblins by his side. I recognized the one on the right as Grunch, who had opened the door for us before. I remembered his sneer only too well. He'd been reluctant to let us in last time. This time, he looked absolutely outraged that we were coming back into his home. Nevertheless, he let us all troop past him as we followed the first Goblin. Grunch and the other Goblin I didn't know took up the rear, locking the door behind us. I had a terrible feeling of foreboding about it all. We'd been down here before and gotten out alive. Something told me we would be lucky to do it again.

The Goblin King, Krikor, smiled as we piled into the vast cavern that the Goblins called home. The smile did not extend to his eyes as he shook Spear's hand. "I wasn't expecting to see you again so soon, and yet at the same time, I'm not surprised. What does surprise me is the company you are keeping. First one Slayer and now more." He raised his fuzzy gray eyebrows into an arch. "And who else? Oh my, Wolvren. What a party."

"We aren't here to party, Krikor," replied Spear forcefully.

"What are you here for then? Oh, don't tell me. I don't actually care. I invited you in out of respect, but I think I made my position quite clear last time. I'm afraid you cannot stay. We are busy here and I have to say, the sight of dragons, Slayers, and Wolvren in my home unnerves me."

My father moved forward in an attempt to intimidate the small Goblin. "We'll stay as long as we need to.

You've got some questions and we'll not be leaving until you answer them."

Despite the fact my father was at least three times his height, Krikor stood his ground. "We'll see about that." He smiled coldly. It was a smile that frightened me to my core.

3

He clicked his fingers and a couple of Goblin warriors ran out from nowhere. Dressed in full battle regalia and with anger upon their faces, they looked ridiculous nonetheless as they were both so tiny compared to the rest of us. My father could stamp on the pair of them, crushing them both, armor and all, with no more difficulty than one would crush an ant.

I watched the amusement on my father's face as they ran to him, spears aloft, ready to stab him. "Is this the best you can do Krikor?" he asked, pulling a spear upward and taking the Goblin with it. The angry Goblin kicked his feet in the air. My father threw him to one side where he hit a wall and fell to the ground.

The other spear-holding Goblin looked more apprehensive but held his ground. Krikor clicked his fingers again and hundreds of armored Goblins appeared, all with spears, swords and other assorted weapons raised.

Even my father, as brave as he was, had cause to step back.

I thought about retreating, but something was off. The Goblins looked strange. It took me a few seconds before realizing what it was. "It's a trick!"

My father looked at me. "Bloody good trick," he yelled back. "Come over here, Julianna. Let's go."

"No, Dad. It really is a trick. They are all the same Goblin." I remembered back to the last time I'd been in these caves. Krikor had read my mind. If he could read minds, wouldn't it stand to reason that he could plant images in people's minds, too?

Seconds later all but three of the Goblins disappeared into thin air. "Well done, Julianna," said Krikor, looking impressed. "Usually people run when I do that to them. I see I'm going to have to come up with something better for you."

My father, clearly annoyed at being shown as weak, strode over to the aged Goblin and picked him up by the scruff of his neck. The three remaining Goblins, one of whom was still on the floor after being hurled there, made the decision not to fight him.

He brought Krikor up to eye level.

"Now look here, Goblin. Just because you know magic doesn't mean you can get the better of me. We came here for answers and you are going to give them to us."

Krikor nodded as best he could. My father put him down on the ground where he dusted himself off and gave my father an evil look.

"Please stop this arguing," I said, jumping forward.

Tensions were rising again and I was sick of it. "Your Highness, please tell us what we want to know. We've been to you before and you wouldn't speak, but this has gone on long enough. Too many people are getting hurt."

Krikor nodded his head and beckoned us to a room I recognized. I'd been here before. Krikor pulled a chair out for me at the large, round table and I sat. The rest of my party filed in, taking seats or standing along the walls when each seat filled. Krikor took the largest chair. I'd never seen him look so grumpy before but I couldn't blame him. I guess it wasn't every day he was outsmarted.

"This seat is reserved for the highest member of a party," he said, indicating the only spare seat left. It was almost as large as his chair. Almost, but not quite. I could already see both my father and Spear eyeing it. Alpha didn't seem bothered in the slightest. He'd already found a seat next to Morganna at the opposite end of the table.

As the two men both made a move for the seat, I saw a twinkle in Krikor's eye. He'd purposely done this. He wanted the men to fight. He wanted to exploit their need to dominate. I sighed as they both reached the chair at the same time. As I expected, they began to argue loudly, each of them gripping one of the chair's smooth wooden arms. Instead of trying to stop them arguing, I calmly stood from my own seat and slipped between them, lowering myself into the large chair. Ash, who'd been standing behind me, took the seat I'd just vacated.

"Gentlemen," I said.

Krikor arched a brow in obvious amusement. Both my father and Spear stopped what they were doing and stared, dumbfounded. I was going to pay for this later, but I didn't care. Anything was better than another fight. In the end, both of them had to stand.

"Krikor," I began, "those swords you sold to the Slayers. They trap dragons."

"I know they do. They were made that way. From the dawn of time, the Goblins have made weapons imbued with magic. The Slayer swords are no different. You already know this. Why are you here? We do not offer refunds."

"I don't want a refund." My voice was a little too loud, echoing slightly off of the cavernous walls. "I want to know how to get the dragon souls out of the swords."

Krikor regarded me, his eyes on my scarred arms. "You already know this, too. Those scars. I assume there are more of them?"

I nodded although I didn't need to. I could feel him trying to read my mind.

"Blood is the way. A sacrifice of blood from an innocent. This is the only way to free the souls."

"No!" I yelled, this time not caring that I was being loud. I had to wait a few seconds before my voice stopped echoing. "I've done enough. I've ripped my body to shreds to free the dragons but there are still many more. I don't have the strength to free them all."

"The answer is simple," Krikor responded. "Find another innocent. Take their blood."

I thought about all of the people in my village. I thought about the ones younger than me, the ones not yet old enough to own a sword.

"I can't do that," I replied. "I'm not hurting anyone else. You made these swords, you know the magic. I might not be able to read minds but I can see it in your face. You enjoy being superior to us. This is just a game to you, but it isn't a game to me. I'm not prepared to let the children in my village shed a drop of blood."

"But they already have shed blood," answered Krikor slyly. "I can see it in your head. You and your dragon boyfriend attacked your village. You didn't seem to mind innocent people being hurt then."

"She was trying to stop me," my father said, coming to my defense. "I'm the bad guy here, not her. Give her what she wants."

"And what exactly is it you want, Julianna?"

I shifted under the weight of his glare. What did I want? I wanted all this to be over, for a start. "I want the remaining dragons freed. I want you or your people to use your magic and make them wake up without any more bloodshed."

"The swords need a sacrifice. They were made that way and always have been. Your ancestors asked for it to be so. However, there might be something I can do for you."

"What is it?" asked Ash, jumping into the conversation.

"You can pay me. One thousand gold pieces for every sword left."

I inhaled deeply. That was more than each sword cost to buy in the first place. There was no way we'd ever find that much money. Anger radiated from my father with each passing second.

"That's fine," I heard a voice behind me. I turned to see Spear.

"There are still so many swords left," I reminded him. "How will you be able to afford it?"

"He can't afford it," grinned Krikor. "I can see inside your mind. You don't have that kind of money. None of you do."

Spear walked round to him. "If you can see inside my mind so well, you'll know I was about to make you a deal."

"A deal that doesn't interest me," snapped back Krikor. "Now kindly leave. You've taken up enough of my time as it is."

"Come on, Krikor. Think about it. Isn't it better to get the gold later than not at all?"

"What was the deal, Spear?" asked Morganna from the opposite side of the table.

But it wasn't Spear who answered her. It was Krikor. "He was going to offer me an IOU. He actually thought I'd free all the dragons on a promise of gold.'

"We can pool our money," argued Spear. "The Slayers, the dragons, the Wolvren..."

Alpha, who had been silent up until now, sat up in his chair. "We are not a part of this. We promised to help you because my beloved asked us to, but I'm not giving away the Wolvrens' gold to save some dragons."

An argument erupted around us, with Slayers, dragons and wolves bickering. Krikor grinned. He'd done this on purpose. He never wanted any gold, he wanted to see each group fight.

"Stop!" I yelled. Yet again, my voice reverberated off the walls. "Gold won't save the dragons, will it? You're lying to us."

"No, of course it won't. I already told you that only

the blood of innocents will do it, but none of you seemed to believe me."

I still didn't believe him and now it wasn't just my father that wanted to punch him. However, hurting him wasn't going to help our cause any. There was another way to get the dragons out, I could feel it, but I also knew that Krikor wasn't going to tell us. Maybe the thousand gold coins he asked for would loosen his tongue, but as none of us had that kind of money, it was pointless trying to come up with whatever he was hiding. I stood up from my chair.

"Fine. I'll continue to do it myself."

Ash looked like he was going to argue, but Krikor cut him off. "Good. You do that. It's been working well for you so far. I can't say those scars of yours diminish your beauty at all. Of course, it won't do you much good in the long run."

"What do you mean?" I asked him.

"Haven't any of you noticed that there are more dragons missing than the Slayers have? That's because we found that the swords we made for your ancestors were popular. Other people wanted them too. We could get a lot of money for one sword, but a sword that trapped dragon souls? Oh, they sell for a whole lot more."

My father moved toward him. "What exactly are you saying, Goblin?"

"If I tell you, you must promise never to come here as a group again. I never want to see dragons and Slayers and Wolvren come to my door as a pack. There is too much history between you all and I have no wish to be in the middle of your petty war."

My father looked as though he was going to argue, but Spear jumped in. "Fine. We'll never come to see you together again. I'm actually hoping we'll never have cause to visit you at all. Now, will you tell us what you mean?"

The small Goblin eyed him curiously but didn't answer. This infuriated my father who slammed his fist down on the round table, making us all jump.

"Speak, Goblin, or I'll pull your ears right from your head."

Krikor looked up at him. It was apparent he wasn't used to being spoken to in such a surly manner and it was even more apparent he didn't like it. "There's another Slayer village on the other side of the mountain," he sniffed. "They have Goblin-made swords, too."

4

"Now what?" asked my father as we were shown the exit to the Goblin cave. Krikor had unceremoniously thrown us out after my father decided to make good with his threat and try to pull his ears off. Krikor, being magic, managed to stop him just in time, but refused to talk to us at all after that. Not that I could blame him.

"We go to the other side of the mountain," announced Spear. "What else can we do? We have to collect all the swords."

My father sneered. "Actually, we don't. I promised to help you collect all the swords from our village. I said nothing about scouring other villages. We don't even know where this other village is or if it exists. Why should we believe the slimy toad, anyway?"

I pulled Ash toward my father and Spear. I had a feeling that all-out war was going to break out any minute between the two hot-headed leaders. I gave a silent thank you to Alpha, who, although rather hot-headed himself, chose not to engage with the sparring chiefs.

"We would know exactly where this village is if you hadn't gotten us thrown out," replied Spear angrily.

My father puffed out his chest. "It was a ridiculous idea in the first place, coming here. Everyone knows the Goblins are not to be trusted. It's common knowledge."

"There was nothing wrong with the plan," replied Spear, drawing himself up to his full height. "It would have worked if someone hadn't put his big foot in it."

I could see my father beginning to boil over, his face bright red with anger.

"Dad," I said, taking him by the arm. "I'm sure we can figure this out." I pulled him to one side, getting him away from Spear.

"How about Nenno, Fox and I fly over the mountain, see if we spot the village?" asked Ash, coming to my rescue.

"That's a great idea," I agreed enthusiastically. I didn't like the idea of venturing over the mountain without Ash, but something had to be done to stop the two chiefs warring with each other. My father eyed Ash suspiciously, but after pausing for thought, nodded his head.

Before us, the peak of the largest of the Triad Mountains loomed. The weather had cleared, leaving the snowy peak glistening in the sunshine. As Ash, Nenno, and Fox hid behind a rock to undress and change into their dragon forms, the rest of us plotted a route. Going to the very peak of the mountain would be impossible without proper climbing equipment, but there seemed to be some kind of trail, worn between rocks, around the edge of it.

"I'm not happy about this," my father huffed to me as the rest of the group planned a route up to the trail we could see in the distance. "I agreed to come up here to atone for what the Slayers of our village did. For what I did. I didn't pledge my allegiance to the dragons, nor did I agree to help them with further quests. Their problem with other Slayer villages is not a problem I share, and it shouldn't be a problem you share. This has nothing to do with us."

"Daddy," I cajoled, using a name for him I'd not used since I was about six years old. "This is my problem. You know it is. There's no one else that can free the dragons but me."

"That's another thing," replied my father. "I came up here explicitly to find another way to free the dragons. I did it to save you any more suffering. All we've accomplished is finding more excuses for you to draw blood. I'm your father. My job is to protect you and if that boyfriend of yours had an ounce of decency, he'd not let you hurt yourself in the way you have been. Not that I expect anything else from the dragons."

"Actually, Sir," said Ash, coming up behind us and making us both jump. "I would do anything to stop Julianna from hurting herself. Just because I'm trying to find all the swords to free my ancestors doesn't mean I'm not committed to finding a way to free them without Julianna's help."

Father and I both watched as he picked up the bag he'd left on the ground.

"I forgot it," he said holding it up. "I need it to put

my clothes in." With that, he raced back around the rock.

A minute later, I retrieved the same pack along with two others filled with the dragons' clothes. The three of them—a red dragon, a green dragon, and a sapphire blue dragon—soared majestically into the sky. Spear pointed toward the path we would be taking and Ash nodded before disappearing over the mountain's peak.

My father stomped off ahead, leaving me walking up the mountain with no one to talk to. I noticed that yet again, the group was split into three distinct sets. The Slayers, led by my father, took the front, Spear led the rest of the dragons in the middle, and the Wolvren, along with Morganna, brought up the rear. I decided to wait and walk with them as I'd had enough trying to mediate the bickering between the other two groups.

"Your father is quite a character," Morganna said with a wry smile. "I remember him from years ago. He was always a..."

"Blustering idiot?" I cut in.

Morganna laughed. "I wasn't going to use those words exactly, but yes, it was always important to him that he get his own way."

The path we were taking was extremely steep, and with loose rocks beneath our feet, it made the going rough. However, the crest of the hill wouldn't take long to reach, and then it would be downhill all the way to the other village.

"What did you make of the Goblins?" I asked her, but it was Alpha that answered.

"The Goblins are not to be trusted. I agree with your father. The issue with the dragons is not ours, but we will keep going because it is Morganna's will. As soon as Morganna no longer wishes to continue, she and my fellow Wolvren will head home. I see no need for us to be here." Morganna kissed his cheek.

"You have been more than generous with your time and assistance," I replied. "We would not have been able to do this without you." It was true. The Wolvren were strong creatures and as so, they could carry more than the rest of us. Without them, we wouldn't have been able to bring the supplies we needed.

Morganna squeezed Alpha's hand. "I have to admit, I was not expecting to be away from the Wolvren forest for so long. I have asked so much of you, my love, and yet you've been so supportive." She kissed his cheek again and I could see his chest swelling. It was obvious to me why he was climbing this mountain and it had nothing to do with saving dragons. Alpha would follow Morganna to the moon and back, but would the other Wolvren? So far, they had not complained, but now that our mission had extended, how long could I realistically expect that to last?

I remained silent as we carried on up the hill. I ached right down to my bones; the hike was grueling as the path ahead grew steeper and steeper. The trail that Spear had seen from below was barely a trail at all, but more a patch of small rocks between the giant boulders.

Just before we made it to the crest, a red shape flew over the horizon.

"Ash!" I exclaimed as the flaming red dragon landed beside me.

He nodded his head and then moved it toward his back.

"You want me to get on?" I asked, trying to interpret his motions. He nodded.

I climbed on his back, glad to have an excuse to get away from everyone. I'd listened to enough bickering to last a lifetime. The Slayers, dragons, and Wolvren watched us as we flew overhead and disappeared over the ridge. I was not prepared for the view on the other side of the mountain. A verdant valley stretched on for miles, kept green by the clear river that cut through the mountains, winding as far as the eye could see. Flowers grew abundantly along the banks, creating a tapestry of color below. The source of the river came from the mountain we'd just climbed over in the form of a huge, gushing waterfall which could only be seen from the other side.

A sharp gasp escaped my lips as I took in the spectacular vista beneath us. It was a view so idyllic that it barely seemed real.

Ash fell into a swoop, and I held on tighter lest I fall off. My heart pounded with adrenaline at the speed of our flight. I let out a scream of joy, feeling free for the first time in days. With all the walking we'd been doing, I'd missed this—the freedom of the air. I could tell that Ash was also enjoying himself as he performed rolls in the air, veering right then left.

Up ahead, Nenno and Fox flew steadily, crisscrossing back and forth, looking for the village that Krikor spoke of.

"We should probably help look for the village," I shouted, laughing at the same time. I glanced behind us to see my father and the others finally reaching the ridge. We'd already flown so far, they looked like tiny dots coming over the hill with the very top of the peak to their left.

The sun shone, glaring off the crystalline whiteness of the snow that still hugged the top of the mountain. Snow that covered the peak year-round. With the world below in disarray, I was glad to be up here in the fresh air, tasting freedom. I tore my eyes away from the stunning mountain range behind me to the beautiful valley below. I was up here to do a job, not to have fun. Despite the abundance of water, there was little sign of civilization down there. The grass below was wild, not hemmed in by small wooden fences. The only animals I spotted were a group of wild deer.

Furthermore, I saw no signs of houses nor any type of abode. I even looked at the sides of the hills to see if there were cave-style houses like the people of Frokontas used, but there was nothing. In front of us, Nenno and Fox looked to be faring not much better.

"We are too high up!" I shouted to Ash. "Go lower!"

No sooner had I spoken than he dropped into a swoop again, this time not leveling out until his feet grazed the fast-flowing water of the river.

Ash flapped his giant wings and skimmed the river beneath us as I kept an eye out for houses on the banks at either side. After ten minutes of this, Nenno swooped down to meet us. Ash veered right and landed on the river bank beside him.

He roared something to which Ash nodded in reply. When Nenno took off, Ash followed behind. Fox soon joined us as we headed back to the mountains and our group. Without knowing what Nenno had said, I could only hold on and wait until we were back with the others. Everyone had managed to cross over the top of the ridge and were now making their way back down the other side. When the three dragons landed, I hopped down from Ash's back and joined the group, waiting as they turned back into their human forms.

"Did you see the village?" asked Spear. Behind him, my father arched a brow, silently asking the same question.

"I didn't see anything, but I think Nenno did," I answered truthfully.

Two minutes later, the boys appeared fully dressed.

"What did you see?" my father demanded brusquely.

Nenno ignored his rudeness. "I saw the village in the valley," he said, pointing toward the horizon. "But it's too far to walk in one day, and even if we could walk that fast, the terrain is too difficult to walk over. We are going to have to turn back."

5

I could already feel tempers flaring before anyone spoke. It had been a difficult journey up the mountain. We couldn't turn back now. The three groups were hardly the best of friends, but at least they were talking to each other. Once we were back down the mountain, I had a feeling that our new found truce would crumble after our fruitless adventure.

"So we don't walk!" I said before my father had a chance to speak.

"Are you suggesting we fly?" asked Spear, casting an eye over the large group. "It's going to take a long time to transport everyone down there one by one. It's going to be tiring, too. There's a lot of people and only a third are dragons."

"Not strong enough to carry two people on your back, then?" my father said condescendingly.

Spear bit back. "You wanna try carrying two people on your back and walking down the mountain?" argued Spear.

I got between the pair of them. "Actually, if we go my way, no one will have to carry anyone on their backs. Look down there."

I pointed down to the beginning of the valley. The waterfall had created a large pool filled with clear water which overflowed into the river that wound toward the horizon. At the edge of the pool was an old boat. I'd spotted it earlier when we flew above it, but it was only at this angle I could see exactly what it was. It wasn't the biggest boat, but if we squeezed in, and the dragons flew ahead, we'd probably manage to fit the Slayers and Wolvren on board.

"The river can carry us." I gave the two men a satisfied smile and started down the steep path into the valley. I felt someone take my hand and turned to see Ash walking beside me.

"If it wasn't for you, those two would have killed each other long ago. They are worse than children."

I nodded. "Neither of them is used to letting other people be in charge. Once we sort this out, I'm hoping they become more civil to each other. I can't be there, stopping them fighting forever." I sighed at the thought of it. Maybe I'd been too optimistic when I thought that all the tribes could get on together.

I cleared my mind of the past and looked out over the beautiful valley. Despite the bickering and the pain wracking my body, the view was enough to make me feel happy.

"If I could build a house right up here and live in it for the rest of my life, looking out at that view, I'd die happy," I said, a smile on my face. The sun beat down, warming my face. Even the weather was better at this side of the mountain.

"If I lived in it with you, I'd die happy, too," responded Ash. We needed no other words as we traveled down the dusty path. The pair of us was content to hold hands and enjoy the reprieve from the fighting. Even Spear and my father had quieted down.

It took us over two hours to get down to the lake, but we managed it without incident. The noise of the waterfall thundered in my ears as we hiked around to get to the boat. It was smaller than I imagined, but it was sturdy. The dragons waited as the others got in. When it was full, those left over had to ride on the dragons' backs. I helped push the wooden boat out and watched as it drifted lazily in the current. The dragons changed into their dragon forms while the rest of us waited. I hopped up on Ash's back, and the others—a mixture of Wolvren and Slayers—mounted the others. Nenno took the lead and we followed, flying in formation over the river.

Ash kept low, skimming his feet through the flowing water. My own legs were too short to reach, but the water looked so tempting I made a note to come back here one day and swim. I almost envied those who had gotten a spot in the boat. We swept past them as they lazily drifted downriver, letting the current pull them along.

Up ahead, Nenno flew higher as the river meandered through a canyon. This was the part of the journey he'd mentioned, the part that would have been impossible to climb. It occurred to me then that once we passed through, those on the boat wouldn't be able to get back. Even with the pair of oars I noticed, the river was flowing way too quickly to row against it.

I tried shouting to Ash to turn back to warn them, but it was too late. We were already flying through the canyon. Behind us, the boat followed. We'd either have to somehow attach the boat to the dragons so they could pull it back upstream or we'd have to find another way back.

The canyon's steep walls rose vertically up from the water's edge, towering magnificently on either side. Ash banked quickly to the left as the river curved, and below us, the boat picked up speed through the shallows as the river became much more rapid. Another steep curve and the river straightened out. The banks became lower and lower until they formed beaches which turned into green meadows full of poppies and bluebells and other wildflowers. A group of wild deer, chewing on the grass to our right, ignored us as we passed, and up ahead, I finally saw the village that Nenno had seen. Nenno and Fox were already there, circling the small group of houses. Even from a distance, I could see how pretty the village was. Tiny white houses with red-tiled roofs dotted the riverbank. The main part of the village was to the right, with approximately twenty cute little houses, and to the left four or five more. A small, black metal bridge connected both sides of the picturesque village.

Great fields, separated by small wooden fences, surrounded the village on both sides, sweeping up into the nearby hills. As the village was so small, much smaller even than Dronias, I guessed that farming was the way the people here survived. Ash landed softly in what looked to be the village square, joining Nenno and

Fox and the other dragons. I hopped down to join the Slayers and the Wolvren while the dragons changed back into their human forms.

"Someone should go to the riverbank to let the others know where we are," I said, noticing that the view of the river was blocked by a number of houses.

"I'm not sure that's a good idea," replied Morganna. "Your father isn't going to be happy when he sees this place. It might be better to let them carry on drifting."

I furrowed my brows, not quite understanding. "Why? What does this village have to do with my father?"

"Look around you." Morganna waved her hand toward the surrounding houses.

They were beautiful, so much prettier than anything in my own village. Vibrant flowers grew in boxes at almost every window, although many were overgrown with weeds threatening to take over. Why would they grow flowers and not bother to weed the flower boxes? It was then that I realized what Morganna meant. The village was deserted. Now that I'd realized it, it was hard to believe I'd not noticed straight away. It was eerily quiet and none of the chimneys were smoking. One of the nearby house's front doors was hanging open. Inside, the room was bare.

I closed my eyes, wondering how my father was going to react. I didn't have to wait long. As Spear and the other dragons emerged from one direction, now changed and fully dressed, the people from the boat came from the other.

"Where are the swords, then?" my father asked

jovially, his loud voice cutting through the terrified silence.

Xander was the first to speak. As my father's oldest friend, perhaps he was the only one that dared tell him. "The village is deserted."

My father regarded Xander as though he was joking and when he saw that he wasn't, cast his eyes around the small square.

"What?" asked Spear. "You are kidding, right?"

Xander shook his head. We all watched as my father went to the nearest house and kicked the door in. I wasn't sure whether to be glad there was no one living there or upset by his rudeness. The inevitable roar came soon after.

My father barreled back out of the house, his face set in a menacing stare. "That's it. I've had enough of this. You..." He pointed at Spear. "This is your fault."

"Don't take that tone with me. I didn't make you come up the mountain."

My father stormed across the square to Spear. "I was promised we would find swords. I was also promised we'd find a way to deal with them so my daughter wouldn't have to mutilate herself to save your people."

Spear puffed up his chest and raised his fists. My father took a similar stance. As he pulled back his right arm to take a swing, Alpha jumped between them, teeth bared.

"Why don't we look to see if there were any swords left behind before we start punching the living daylights out of each other?" It was the most vocal he'd been on the whole trip.

When both men agreed and Alpha went back to Morganna's side, I thanked him quietly.

"No problem," Alpha sniffed. "I don't want to be here any more than your father does, but I also don't want to end up carrying bodies out of this place because they've beaten each other to a pulp. No wonder your people and the dragons fought a lot if they were all like those two."

I had to bite my lip from laughing at his words.

"OK, everyone," I shouted, "let's split up. There are approximately twenty houses here. Less than one each. Dragons take the houses on the north side of this square, Wolvren, the houses to the south. The Slayers can check the houses over the river. We'll all meet back here in half an hour."

I hated separating us into groups, but it was the only way I could ensure no one started fighting while I was checking houses. Plus it meant I could keep an eye on my hot-headed father. He stomped across the bridge, sending reverberations back down to me at the back of the group. I hoped it held out long enough for us to check the houses and get back.

My father took the nearest house, and once again, bashed down the door. I hoped the entire village hadn't just decided to go on a group vacation because they'd be coming back to trashed houses if they did. Jasper, Morganna, and Xander each took a house, which left me with the largest house and the one farthest away from the river.

Unlike my father, I knocked on the door and when it didn't open I cautiously opened it. The front room was completely empty. No furniture, no belongings. If they had gone on vacation, they'd packed everything. Going from room to room, I found the same. All were bare. The only thing still there was an old bed frame with a broken leg, and even that didn't have a mattress.

Whoever lived in this village left a long time ago, and it seemed that they took their swords with them. We'd not only wasted our journey, we'd added yet another problem we'd have to figure out. A problem that I'd have to figure out because if I didn't, there was a real possibility the dragons' souls would be trapped forever.

6

I heard him before I saw him.

My father was cursing away, more than likely to himself. He'd found his house just as empty as mine. I couldn't blame him. I was mad, too, and tired. Tired of it all. Tired of going from place to place and not finding what we were looking for. Tired of being lied to and manipulated. This whole quest had been a mission to nothing. All we'd done was waste time while the dragons' bodies withered. I couldn't even claim it a success on the building bridges front. The dragons and the Slayers hated each other more than ever. The Wolvren weren't much better. Okay, they weren't exactly argumentative, but they didn't want to be involved and were only there because Alpha told them to. Alpha was only there because he was in love with Morganna.

Not only was I sick of going from place to place and not actually getting anywhere, I was also physically tired. My bones hurt from all the walking, the sleepless nights, and the weather.

After a final look around the desolate house, I opened the front door and headed out into the sunshine. As I had thought, my father was complaining to Jasper, who, in turn, was nodding his head. They both looked my way as I walked toward them.

"Don't!" I held my hand up as I strode past them. I wasn't in the mood. If they wanted to be angry, so be it. They could keep it to themselves. I was angry enough myself.

Neither my father nor Jasper spoke. Instead, they followed me back across the bridge. I was getting better at this being forceful thing.

As I walked into the town square, the others were already starting to appear from their allotted houses. It was apparent by the looks on their faces that they had been no luckier than us. Spear stood on the other side of the square, his face as dark as thunder, having a shouting match with one of the Wolvren who was waving his hands about. I couldn't hear what they were saying, but I could guess. Everyone was tired. Tempers were flaring.

Sighing, I made my way across to them. So much for the wolves not getting involved. At least it wasn't Alpha, who I could see just emerging from one of the houses empty handed.

"What's going on?" I asked Spear, although it was plain to anyone what the problem was.

"I'll tell you what's going on," shouted my father from behind me, almost knocking me out of the way on his beeline to Spear. "There's nothing here," he shouted at Spear, butting the Wolvren out of the way. "No swords. Nothing. I'm willing to bet that this was all a ploy to get me away from my village. With me all the way out here, your people will be able to sweep in and do what you want. You've wanted to destroy Dronias for a long time but you couldn't, could you? So instead of fighting fairly, you got one of your pretty boys to seduce my daughter so she'd lead us on this wild goose chase halfway around the kingdom."

A familiar figure shot past me before I had a chance to speak, and punched my father square in the face.

"Ash!" I shouted. He'd done no more damage than a split lip, but my father, who was twice his size, looked ready to punch back. I ran toward them but was too late. A couple of the other dragons had gotten there before me and were holding my father back. All around me, I heard shouts and threats as more and more people entered the fight. One of the dragons had accidentally hit one of the Wolvren and so now they had entered the fray, too. The tiny semblance of peace between the three groups had finally dissolved, and now all I could see was chaos.

"Stop!" I shouted, but my voice was lost in the ruckus. No one could hear me above the noise they were all making, and no one was interested in what I had to say, only too happy to finally let out their frustrations. I had half a mind to let them fight it out, but many of them were strong, and who knew what damage they could do to each other. I didn't have it in me to organize getting thirty injured people out of here.

Morganna appeared at my side. Unlike me, she seemed completely composed.

"What should I do?" I asked her, my nerves apparent.

She sighed. "This has been coming for days. I had hoped to get through this without any bloodshed, especially from our own, but years of tension are coming to a head."

"Yeah, but they are going to kill each other." I stepped forward, planning to go into the throng to try to stop it, but Morganna caught me on the shoulder.

"They are bigger than you and they are angry. I hate to say it, but there is nothing you can do without getting hurt yourself. We will have to leave them to it until they realize they are hurting no one but themselves."

I agreed with Morganna in part. I wasn't a match for any of them physically, but I wasn't about to let them kill each other, not when we'd come so far. Scrabbling around in my bag, I found a box of matches for lighting cooking fires when Ash didn't feel like turning into his dragon form. I struck the first and held it to the straw roof of the nearest house. Then I held the second match to another spot on the same roof, not stopping until the entire box of matches was spent and the roof was ablaze. I had no remorse for setting someone's house on fire. No one had lived in this village for a long time and I couldn't see them coming back any time soon.

I hopped up onto the wall of the village well in front of the burning house and shouted again, this time as loudly as I could. Whether it was my voice or the wall of flames behind me, I didn't know, but within seconds, every single one of them had stopped what they were doing and were looking my way.

"Stop fighting, all of you!" I demanded. "I've had enough. We have only one fight, a common cause and that is not with each other. All you are doing is making it harder to solve the problem. You are creating more problems. I've spent days listening to you gripe about each other, but you all know that this is the fault of the Goblins. They lied to us, tricked us again. We know they can't be trusted. This was their plan all along. If we fight each other, we won't have time to go back and fight them, but fight them we must. It is clear to me that all this stems from them and always has, even from the start. I don't like that we have been fooled, but I have to admit that the Goblins have beaten us again.

"However, I'm taking a lesson from this. The next time we go to the Goblins, I will not leave until I get a straight answer. I will not let Krikor or any of them lead me on a merry dance again. I will find out what happened to the swords and I will free the dragons' souls. Either you will come with me, or I will leave you all here to beat each other to a bloody pulp, but I'm telling you now. If you choose the second option, I will go alone. I will not help any of you get out of here when you are too injured to walk. The choice is yours."

I glared down at them, trying to appear more menacing than I actually felt. Inside my heart was hammering beneath my ribs. I'd talked myself into a corner. If they did decide that hurting each other was more important than our mission, I'd be forced to walk out of this valley by myself.

Ash was the first to come forward. He had a bruise on his cheek where someone had punched him. "I'm sorry. It was me that started this," he said, shame filling his face. He walked towards me and held out his hand to me. I took it and jumped down from the well wall. "I really am sorry," he said again, but this time much more quietly so only I could hear. "I know how stupid it was, but I couldn't let your father talk about you like that."

"On behalf of the Wolvren, I apologize, too." Alpha stepped forward and called his men to his side. One by one the others walked toward me and then stood behind me until it was only my father and Spear. My father had a split lip and a dribble of blood was drying on his chin. Spear had a black eye. I couldn't help thinking that they both deserved their injuries.

I raised an eyebrow, waiting for one of them to back down. With a small step, Spear finally moved forward.

Not waiting for my father to move, I turned to walk out of the village. My father was a proud man, but he was also at a disadvantage. He was the only one left. He knew that getting out of the valley was not going to be easy, especially if he tried to do it alone. Besides, he had no one left to fight. His only option was to come with us. As I took a step along the path that would lead us back to the river, with the others behind me. I knew my father would come, too. His pride was wounded, but he wasn't stupid.

Morganna ran up to me at the front. "That was quite something," she beamed. "I was all for letting them fight it out, get it out of their system, let off steam.'

"They would have damaged each other. I'm sure they will find plenty of opportunities to fight, but at the moment we don't have the time. Let them have at it when all this is over. I might even sell tickets and bring popcorn."

Morganna snorted. "You are now my new hero," she said, laughing.

Coming from *my* hero, hearing her say that, filled me with confidence. "Thank you," I replied.

"I mean it. I'm really proud of you. I don't know many people that could stop a whole group of hot-blooded males fighting, but you did. I know I couldn't have done it."

I blushed, not knowing what to say. Instead, I just smiled. With a renewed vigor, I picked up the pace. Those Goblins didn't know what was coming to them. As the river came into view, I couldn't suppress the smile on my face. OK, so we hadn't gotten any further, but Morganna believed in me. Maybe it was about time I began to believe in myself.

"I don't know what came over me," said Ash, taking my hand once again. "I can't begin to tell you how sorry I am. I really shouldn't have punched your father. When he said those things about you, I just saw red."

"Are you sure you weren't just mad because he called you a pretty boy?" I replied good-naturedly.

"That, too," smirked Ash.

Behind us, the flames rose, sending black smoke up into the sky.

7

———

The boat was where we left it, tied to the bridge, bobbing around in the current.

"Now what?" asked Xander. "We can't row upstream. The current is too strong and we only have two oars.

He was right. There was no way we were going to be able to get back to the Goblins the way we came, either by boat or on foot. Farther upriver, the canyon walls were too high and too steep to climb. I didn't fancy asking the dragons to make a few journeys to carry everyone, either. I could only too well imagine the expression on my father's face, not to mention Spear's, if I asked them. No, we'd have to find another way back. We were surrounded by mountain ranges. On the other side of the river, the snowy peaks of the Triad mountains rose above us, sprawling out to the east. Behind us was another mountain range. If we jumped in the boat and let the river carry us out through the valley, we would be heading in entirely the wrong direction. We were going to have to climb.

"If the uppermost peak of the Triads is over there," I said, pointing out the peak to our left, "then Frokontas should be somewhere in front of us." I tried picturing the valley of Frokontas. It did have mountains surrounding it. If I was right, those mountains were just on the other side of the mountain in front of us. "We'll go there and rest up. We are going to need more provisions if we are going back to see the Goblins, and I'm sure you all need rest. Before anyone complains that we are going to the dragon's home, I want to point out that the Slayers and Wolvren have already let us into their villages. Spear, I'm sure you'd like to return the favor and Father, I know you'll be grateful for the invite."

He probably wouldn't be, but tough. He was coming to Frokontas or staying behind.

"So we are climbing mountains again, huh?" grunted Jasper. "Just wonderful!"

"Do you have any better ideas?" I asked, turning to him with my hands on my hips.

"No," he admitted.

"Well then," I said, crossing the bridge quickly. I didn't want to get caught in another argument.

I set a quick pace, more out of eagerness to keep everyone moving so they had better things to think about than fighting rather than enthusiasm at actually reaching our destination.

"You do remember that we can fly up there," said Ash quietly. "It would take a while, but we could possibly make a few trips and—"

"Don't even say it," I interrupted. "Do you really

think Spear will allow it? For that matter, do you want to be the one who asks my father if he wants to ride on a dragon?"

Ash pulled a face. "I see your point."

"I was just telling Julianna how wonderful she was down there," cut in Morganna. "She's turning out to be a true leader and warrior."

"I ALWAYS FOUND something special in her, but she's no warrior," Ash said, but it didn't feel like an insult. His arm wrapped around my shoulder. "A warrior, by definition, is a person of war. I've never met anyone as brave as Julianna, but at the same time, I know she'd never deliberately hurt anyone."

"I stand corrected," said Morganna, smiling while I blushed furiously. The two people I admired the most were talking over my head about me. I was embarrassed sure, but I was also bursting with pride.

"You guys. You do see that I'm right here?"

Ash grinned. "Nowhere else I'd like you to be but right by my side."

Morganna laughed pleasantly. "I'll let you two love-birds go on ahead. It's probably better if one of us lags behind to make sure one of the boys back there doesn't start a fight again.

"That was embarrassing," I said, "but thanks. It means a lot to me that you believe in me.

"I meant it, too, about you being by my side. When we get back to Frokontas, I want you to stay there with me."

"Of course I'll stay with you. Not for long though.

Just until we regroup and rest and then we'll head back up to the Goblins."

"I don't just mean now. I mean forever. I know you've said you'll stay with me, but that was before you rekindled your relationship with your family."

I looked at him. It hadn't occurred to me that he'd be worried that I'd want to go back and live in Dronias. "I'm with you. I'm with you whether you want to live in Frokontas or Dronias or anywhere. It doesn't matter where we are. Wherever I am with you, that is where I call home."

He nodded and smiled, hopefully feeling more at ease. I gripped his hand tightly. I meant every word of it.

The climb up the mountain was grueling. Even though the view made it a much more pleasant walk, the pretty, grassy banks peppered with beautiful flowers were much sheerer than the rocky mountain paths we'd already climbed. By the time we reached the peak, I was having to hold onto clumps of long grass to pull myself up. It took us the best part of the afternoon to get to the very top. Unlike the jagged edges of the mountains to our left, this peak was a plateau. Flat grasslands, too high for farm animals to reach. About a kilometer ahead of us was some kind of precipice. With any luck, it wouldn't be too steep on the other side.

With each step to the edge, all I could think about was the canyon we had come through in the boat. If the sides were as steep, we would be stuck up here and Ash's suggestion of flying would be our only option.

As it was, the edge was only the beginning of a delicate downward slope. Even better, I could see the fenced fields of Frokontas in the distance.

"Home," smiled Ash as he led me down the hill.

It did feel like home. Dronias wasn't my home anymore and hadn't been for some time. I was glad to be back. It had been too long. My only concern was how the people of the town would take my father, or more worryingly, how he would react to them.

He'd been pretty quiet throughout the journey up the hill, but I put that down to wounded pride. Just in case, I held back, waiting while all the others trooped past. My father was at the very back.

"I see Frokontas coming up."

"The dragon village," he replied gruffly. It wasn't a question, more of a statement.

I nodded. "They are good people."

"All evidence to the contrary."

I sighed. "You've met them in the worst of circumstances. Everyone is annoyed and tired. Spear can be a little hot-headed at times, but let's be honest, you've been much worse."

"Hrmph."

"Father!"

"Fine," he conceded. "I could have put in more effort, but..."

"But?" I raised an eyebrow. It was impossible for my father to admit his shortcomings without making them someone else's fault. I waited patiently to find out who he was going to blame.

"This Spear guy. I don't trust him. How do we know he hasn't got half his city waiting to ambush us? This could all be some kind of trick."

"For one thing, look in front of you. Frokontas is hardly a city. It's a smaller village than Dronias.

Secondly, Dronias's bravest and strongest are either out with us or have their souls trapped in our swords. The people left behind are just normal people."

"I'll believe it when I see it," he huffed. I let Ash stay up ahead, deciding to enter the town with my father. I didn't trust him to be civil.

As the ground beneath us flattened out and we began the walk through the village, I linked arms with my father. I'd like to say it was because I was his daughter and loved him, but in truth, it was my way of keeping him close to me. My nerves were running high as we entered the fire pit area, but my stomach rumbled anxiously as I took in the smell of meat roasting over a fire. It had been a long time since I had a decent meal.

The Slayers and Wolvren held back as the dragons were welcomed home. I ran to Lucy, giving her a huge hug. Behind her stood Edeline with Fiere, Ash's recently-reunited parents.

Edeline waited until her daughter had finished with me and then hugged me too.

"Edeline, Fiere, I'd like you to meet someone."

I beckoned my father forward. He looked uncomfortable but did as I asked. By the time he'd walked around the fire pit, he'd gotten over his awkwardness and pulled himself up to his full height. Even at a disadvantage by being in his perceived enemy's village, surrounded by dragons, he was not going to show any sign of weakness.

"This is my father, Rocco."

"How do you do," said my father stiffly, holding out his hand. Edeline ignored it, instead deciding to hug him, too. I had to stifle a giggle at the look of surprise on his face. I don't think I'd ever seen my father blush in his life and yet here he was, his face turning the color of a tomato.

Thankfully, Fiere was much more composed. He shook my father's hand warmly. They were doing a much better job at hiding their dislike for Slayers than my father had at hiding his dislike of dragons. He seemed pretty taken aback by the welcome he'd received and it was with a sigh of relief that I saw him sit by the fire alongside Edeline and eat the food offered to him.

"They say the way to a man's heart is through his stomach," whispered Morganna when she caught what I was looking at. "I think he might have a small crush on Ash's mom."

I laughed. "My father is many things, but he does love my mom. He'd never leave her. I think in this case, he is just really, really hungry.

The dragons served meal after meal until everyone was fed. It was amazing to feel the tension drop after a good meal. I found a place between Ash and Lucy and took an offered plate with freshly baked bread and some of the roasted deer.

Night drew in quickly and with it a cool wind. The fire was kept burning for those of us still outside.

"We should be getting home," my father said, noticing how dark it had gotten. "Can someone tell me the way?"

"It's too far and too dangerous to get to your village at night," said Spear, sidling up to him. At first, I thought he was being nice, until he added, "Not unless you want us to fly you home?"

"No," replied my father hurriedly. "I'm sure we can walk."

"Nonsense." Edeline put her hand on my father's back. "We have room for you in our house. Any family of Julianna's is our family too. I'm afraid you'll have to sleep on the sofa, but I can find you some pillows and a blanket."

I thought my father would say no, but he nodded. "That would be wonderful. Thank you, Edeline."

I opened my mouth in shock. Maybe he did have a teeny, tiny crush on Edeline after all.

"Thank you, Edeline," shouted Spear. "We have a lot of visitors here. Can anyone else offer up a bed for the night? We are going to find the swords, but we cannot do it without the Slayers' help. Please be considerate and let them stay one night."

It was one thing sharing a meal with the Slayers and Wolvren, but I could see a look pass between the dragons at the thought of opening their homes to us.

"I have space," said one woman, putting her hand up. Morganna and Alpha were the closest to her, so they got to go back with her. Once the first few people had spoken up, it didn't take long for the others to volunteer, too, until there were only a few Slayers and Wolvren left. Spear graciously invited them to his own house.

Ash took my hand and led me back to the house he shared with Lucy and their parents. As we crossed the threshold, I could hear my father and Edeline conversing upstairs.

"In all your life, did you ever expect to have the leader of the Slayers staying on your sofa?" I asked in a whisper.

"No," grinned Ash, shutting the door behind him. "No, I did not.

8

I had never slept so soundly in my life. Exhaustion had sent me into a dreamless sleep that lasted way longer than eight hours. In fact, it was mid-morning before the smell of something cooking woke me up. Something that smelled like bacon.

Firecracker, the family dog, greeted me in her usual exuberant manner as I opened the door to the bedroom. Padding from door to door, I saw and heard no one. The house was empty.

"Where is everyone?" I asked Firecracker, giving her a friendly tickle behind the ears. She responded with a woof.

The delicious smell became stronger as I made my way down to the ground floor. Opening the front door, I saw a whole group of people sitting around the fire pit. I picked out my father straight away. He was sitting, chatting amiably with Edeline and Fiere with a plate loaded with food on his lap. It was a nice surprise to see him acting so laid back. The fire pit was always busy, but today, there weren't enough seats for everyone. People were standing around, waiting their turn to take some of the bacon and eggs that were being fried over the fire. Up in the air, the sky was a riot of color, filled as it was with dragons. It reminded me of a kite festival I'd been to once where we'd flown kites of every color.

"So, you're finally awake," Ash said, coming over to me and kissing my cheek. Firecracker wagged her tail at him and then bounded off in the general direction of the food.

"You should have woken me," I replied with a smile. "I've never seen so many dragons up in the air." I looked up and Ash followed suit.

"That's because of you," Ash replied, leading me to the line for breakfast.

I grabbed a plate and joined the line. My stomach rumbled in anticipation. "What do you mean, because of me?"

"A lot of those dragons are the ones you saved. If you hadn't used your blood to save them, they'd still be stuck in the swords."

I looked up again. I'd not noticed before, but now that Ash had mentioned it, they did look like they were happy to be free. One of them did a loop-the-loop before gliding to the ground. It gave me a deep sense of satisfaction, seeing the dragons flying up there, and made me ache to be up there again myself. Having a dragon boyfriend had its perks.

Someone filled my plate with food. I thanked them then found a newly vacated place to sit. I noted that Slayers and Wolvren were also enjoying breakfast among the dragons. Overnight, things had changed. The air of hostility that had been with us throughout the mission had seemingly disappeared. Just like my father, the other Slayers also appeared more relaxed. I saw Xander enjoying breakfast with one of the Wolvren, and even Jasper was chatting with a young dragon girl.

It was amazing what a good night's sleep and a delicious breakfast could do.

I'd almost finished eating when Spear spoke up.

"Good morning all," he began loudly, getting everyone's attention. "I'd like to begin by offering a welcome to our guests and thank you to those of you that gave them a bed for the night. For those of you that weren't here when we got back last night, having Slayers and Wolvren here may seem unusual, but I can see that everyone is making an attempt to get on. For that, I thank you."

I tried not to laugh at him. He'd hardly made much of an attempt to be friendly. I remembered all the arguments I'd been forced to listen to over the past few days. Still, he was being friendly now.

"I'm afraid our mission to find more swords was a failure," he continued. "To say the Goblins were unhelpful is an understatement. The king of the Goblins essentially sent us on a wild goose chase and we didn't retrieve a single sword. Unfortunately, we are no closer than when we set off."

There was a collective round of whispers and mutterings around the fire pit. The disappointment of the dragons that remained was obvious, and I could understand why. It had taken a great deal of faith to take us in, and now to hear that nothing had come of it must have felt like a kick in the face. No one shouted or complained, however. Instead, everyone remained silent to let Spear continue his speech.

"We need to decide the next course of action if we want to free our people. The Slayers of Dronias have agreed to give us their swords, but it isn't enough. There are more out there. All this time, we assumed it was just the one village that was taking us, but we have found out that there was another village on the other side of the mountain. Another village with swords, another group of people slaying dragons."

"Why can't we go to this other village and talk to them, too?" someone shouted from the back.

Spear looked over the crowd. "We did. That's where we came from last night. Unfortunately, the Slayers who lived there have gone. The village is abandoned and the Slayers have taken their swords with them."

The collective mutterings became louder now as everyone processed this new information. For some of them, it meant that seeing their loved ones again was now further away in the future. I could already sense their disappointment.

"The question is, where do we go from here? Does anyone have any suggestions? I welcome ideas from everyone."

"It's obvious, isn't it?" asked Fiere. "We need to find the swords."

"That's not going to be easy," replied Spear. "The Slayer village had been abandoned some time ago. We have no idea where they went, or even why they decided to leave."

"I don't know why they left," I piped up, "but I have an idea where they are headed."

All eyes turned to me.

"How could you know that?" asked Spear. "They left no clues that I could see."

"I'm only guessing, but it seems to me that there was only one possible direction they could go. Behind the village, the mountains were too high to climb. Maybe some people could have scaled them, but I find it hard to believe that an entire village could manage it, especially with all their furniture. The same for the way we took to get back here. The hill was hard enough to climb without bringing all our worldly belongings with us. That leaves either upriver or downriver. If it was you, which direction would you choose to go in? Downriver seems to me to be the only logical direction they'd go. They probably loaded up some boats with their furniture and set off together."

Spear looked thoughtful then nodded. "I agree. However, that doesn't tell us how far they traveled. They could have stopped at the next town or village, or carried on until they reached the ocean. We have no way of knowing."

"I say we go back and pay another visit to that lying toerag, Krikor," chimed in my father. "It doesn't matter about the swords if we can't find a way to get the dragons out of them."

"We do have a way to get the dragons out. Julianna."

I closed my eyes. I could already see that this line of talk was going to descend into another argument.

I was surprised to hear my father keep his voice level. "The Goblin king told us that the swords were in that abandoned village, right?"

Spear nodded his head in acknowledgment.

"But they weren't," he continued. "So, who's to say that he was telling us the truth about them being Slayers too? For all we know, they were living peacefully and the Goblins made them leave."

Spear's eyes narrowed. "What possible reason would the Goblins have for making them leave? According to Krikor, the other Slayer village bought swords from the Goblins. They would be pretty stupid to chase their customers away."

"Chasing people is not the Goblins' way," a man by the fire said. I recognized him as Coal, one of the dragons who had come with us to the Goblins' home the first time we went up. I remembered that he didn't trust the Goblins then, and it seemed that nothing had changed. "They don't chase people, they don't fight people, they manipulate people. They lie and they cheat. No matter what anyone tells you about how Goblins always stick to their word, it is just a myth. The wretched creatures wouldn't know honesty if it hit them in the face."

There was a thud in the distance as though someone had dropped something heavy. I tried to see what it was but there were too many people in the way.

"Be that as it may, Coal, and I see your point, too, Rocco, but he was right when he said there were more dragons than swords. It stands to reason that there are more swords out there."

"No, no, no." My father's voice grew louder. "It doesn't stand to reason at all. You know yourself that each sword can contain more than one dragon soul. Souls are not like people's bodies. They are almost infinitesimal in size. You can't even see them. We only know they are trapped in there because they return to the dragons when they escape. One sword could hold ten dragons' souls, twenty, a hundred, even. In fact, I wouldn't be surprised if a sword could hold a million souls."

Spear considered this.

"You've not speared a million dragons though, have you?" asked Ash in a quiet voice. "You told me that you were the greatest Slayer in the village and you didn't really capture that many. I saw how many dragon bodies were in your dragon keep. How many of those did you pick up on hunting trips and how many did you just happen to find up the mountain, already laid out as if dead?"

"What are you implying? That I'm not brave enough to kill a dragon myself and I only picked them up when they fell out of the sky?"

I closed my eyes and groaned. "Father!" I cautioned.

He looked around him at the glaring dragons. "Sorry, but I did use my sword on your people. You know I did. Why else would I be here?"

"But could it be that sometimes you found the body of a dragon and took it back to Dronias pretending that you had slain it? I would imagine that would bring you a lot of admiration in your village, right?"

My father glared but then nodded slowly. "Ay, there might have been the odd occasion that we brought the fallen body of a dragon down the hill, and I might have said it was me that killed it. It was only to solidify my reputation as the best Slayer. I still killed more than anyone else."

I groaned again. If he kept talking, someone was

going to throw him in the fire pit and I wouldn't blame them. "What do you think we should do?" I asked Alpha in an attempt to take the focus away from my father.

"We do not belong here," Alpha said. "We appreciate the hospitality of both Slayers and dragons, and we also acknowledge the struggle that you are all faced with, but our time is up. We have been away from our home for too long."

I looked at Morganna, hoping she would jump in and change his mind, but she looked resigned. Losing the Wolvren would be a massive blow. They were fearless and I had the feeling we'd need them in the future.

There was another thud as Spear began to speak again. "I'm sorry to hear that Alpha. On behalf of all of us, I want to thank you for..."

An ear piercing scream cut him off. Lucy shoved through the crowd. By the time she got to the middle, she was frantic, tears rolling down her face.

"What is it, Lucy?" Spear asked her.

"Come with me. You have to come with me now!"

9

It was evident from her tone of voice that she was distressed about something. People around the campfire began to get up, ready to follow her. Whatever this was, it wasn't going to be good. I wondered if whatever had distressed Lucy was something to do with the noises I'd heard. Before I'd even had the chance to ponder the question, a large, green object fell out of the sky, landing with a crash in the center of the fire pit and thankfully missing everyone around it.

The ground reverberated beneath my feet like an earthquake as my brain processed what I was seeing in front of me. A huge dragon was now laid out in front of me with flames from the pit lapping around it.

"Someone do something!" Lucy screamed as another thud sounded about a hundred feet away. The dragons were literally falling out of the sky.

I pulled off my sweater and tried dousing the flames lapping at the green dragon in front of me. A number of the others followed suit until the flames were snuffed out completely. Thanks to his thick scaly skin, he'd not suffered much in the way of fire damage, but he looked unwell from whatever it was that made him fall in the first place. His eyes fluttered open and closed, his chest heaving with each labored breath. Now that the fire around him was out, I could see his skin was pale and clammy.

I looked up to the sky. Most of the dragons still left up there had begun to come into land, more than likely fearful of succumbing to the same fate.

Edeline ran up to the fallen dragon and stroked its head. "Can you change back?"

The dragon didn't open its eyes but managed a small shake of its head. It didn't have the energy required to shift forms.

"This is Bolt. He was one of the older dragons," announced Edeline to the shocked group. "His soul was taken so long ago that no one remembered him when he woke up. He's been spending the time since his soul came back catching up on everything in Frokontas."

A number of the group that had followed Lucy came running back.

"How are the other dragons?" I asked. "Are they as ill as this one?"

"Same," shouted one of them. "There are five dragons down and a few more that are still conscious, but barely. None of them have the energy to turn back in their human forms."

I turned back to the green dragon. He was still breathing, but only just.

"Ede..."

My attention was taken from the green dragon to Fiere, who had just cried out for his wife. As I looked over, he fell to the floor clutching his head. Edeline ran from the dragon to her husband. Even from the other side of the pit, I watched him lose consciousness.

Whatever was happening to the dragons was happening to them in both dragon and human form. They were getting sick.

A chatter of fear went around the group as more and more of the human-formed dragons fell. Spear raised his voice once again to get everyone's attention.

"I'm going to need everyone's help. We need to get everyone to my house. It's the only place in the village big enough to accommodate all those who are sick. Lucy, can you head to the village center and ring the village bell? When everyone comes out, tell them to come here to help."

Lucy nodded and ran off as quick as her little feet could carry her.

When the panic had died down, it became apparent just how much of an emergency it was. Dragons were huge creatures and not easy to carry. I joined Ash and about twenty others, and we slung the green dragon between us. Even with so many of us helping, it was still not an easy task to get him all the way across town. If only we had a cart or something, but we didn't. Instead, we each held part of him and moved slowly down the dirt track toward Spear's house.

Bodies littered the landscape. Those dragons that had not been affected helped carry their kin to Spear's mansion, and yet it still took over an hour to collect them all. Those in human form had been taken inside and placed on beds and sofas. The unfortunate ones who had become ill in their dragon form were now laid outside next to each other. It reminded me of the dragon keep in Dronias, where the Slayers kept the dragons without souls.

"Do you think their souls have gone back into the swords?" I asked, seeing them all sleeping soundly. Every so often, one of them would snort in their sleep. I recognized one of the dragons as Mary, the first dragon we'd freed. She looked so peaceful.

"No," replied Edeline, coming outside. "Fiere is unconscious, but some of those inside are still awake. They are sick but they still have their souls. This is something else."

"It's something to do with the swords though, right?" Jasper asked.

Edeline nodded. "I think so. The only dragons that have become ill are the ones whose souls were taken from them. It seems that the longer the dragons' souls were apart from their bodies, the sicker they are. I'm sorry to say, those of you still feeling okay will likely succumb to this sickness, too. It is only a guess, but I think you should go inside and rest. Spear is still trying to organize care for everyone, but the truth is, beyond putting them comfortably down on a bed, there is not much we can do until we figure out what exactly this is."

A number of the dragons took her advice and went inside just as Spear was heading out.

"I was just telling everyone that this is only affecting the dragons who have been separated from their souls," Edeline told him.

Spear nodded and then turned to the assembled

crowd. I'd never seen the whole village out before. There were hundreds of people filling Spear's garden. Spear had to stand at the top of his steps so everyone could see him.

"I know everyone is scared right now" he began. "We thought we had gotten our friends and family back, but as you can see, they are getting ill. Edeline is right. It seems that the ones that have been separated from their souls the longest are the sickest. I have the best care-givers and first aid providers in town looking after every-one. Once they have gotten everyone comfortable inside, they will come out here to take care of the dragons in the garden. At this point, no one knows if this illness is a temporary thing. We can only wait and see."

"What about the other dragons?" one of the villagers asked. "Those that are still without a soul. Won't they get sick too?"

Spear nodded his head. "I assume that will be the case. The longer they have been asleep in the Slayers' keep, the sicker they will get. With some luck, those that have only had their souls taken from them recently will stay well, but I cannot know for sure. I've asked the medics to keep an eye on those that are not sick yet. I promise to keep everyone updated."

"Don't we still have some swords with dragon souls in them?" the same villager asked.

I could already feel people's eyes begin to turn to me.

Spear took a few seconds to answer. He knew the only person that could release them was me and I could tell he was weighing up whether he could burden me with it. "To free the dragon souls, it requires blood and with that blood comes pain." He didn't mention my name which I was grateful for, but I knew I wouldn't be able to hide from my responsibility.

"This is their fault!" shouted a dragon. "Why are they even here?"

"Do you see what you've done to us?" shouted another. "You are nothing but monsters."

It was plain to see that the tide was turning against us. The dragons in the village had been friendly up until now. I couldn't let everything descend into chaos.

"Spear," I interrupted, "please bring me the swords."

"No!" shouted my father. "You don't have to do this. We don't know if freeing them now will save them from whatever this is. We don't even know which dragons are in which swords."

"There is only one way to find out," I replied steadfastly.

Spear headed into his house, I assumed to retrieve the swords.

"What if you free an elder dragon?" Ash asked, gripping my hand tightly. "One that has had its soul in there for a long time. Freeing it will only condemn it to this disease. It might be kinder to keep it where it is."

I thought about it and he was right, but at the same time, if I could save one or more of the dragons whose souls had been taken within the last year, I might be saving their lives. "I have to do this," I insisted.

"No, you don't!" My father glared down at me.

"Yes, I do. It is because of the people in our village that this is happening in the first place. Neither of you can talk me out of it. I'll bleed for a bit and then heal. I'll be fine in a few days, but will the sick dragons be? I need to do this. I need to atone for the Slayers' sins."

My father's glare turned into an expression of remorse. "I hate that it is you that has to do this. If I could take this from you, I would."

I patted him on the shoulder. "I know, Father. Actually, there is something you can do to help."

"Anything!"

Spear brought the swords that still held dragon souls and laid them out in front of us. "Father. You know which sword belonged to which Slayer, right?"

"Of course. I know every sword in Dronias."

"Then tell me, which sword is the newest? Which one has been used the most recently?"

My father studied the line of swords. Each was unique, made especially for the person it was bought for. If my father could tell me which was the newest, I could save the dragons that had been taken the most recently, thereby preventing their illness in the first place.

"This one," my father finally said, picking up a blade with a golden hilt featuring opals. "This belonged to Hecta. She turned eighteen just before you did and made her first kill...er...took her first soul on her birthday."

I nodded. I remembered it well. I'd been so excited watching her go off up into the Triad Mountains and wishing it was me. Taking the sword from my father, I held the blade to my hand. It was already crisscrossed with scars so what was one more?

"Stand back," I warned, knowing that freeing the dragon would make sparks fly from the sword.

I drew it across the meaty flesh of my palm and waited for the burst of fire.

10

Nothing happened. Where I expected flames to shoot out of the end of the sword and the soul of the dragon to whoosh across the sky back to its body, the sword remained exactly as it was.

"Did it work?" asked Spear, staring down at my hand. Blood dripped from the long cut onto the grass below while the people surrounding me looked at me in confusion.

"I don't know," I replied uncertainly. "I don't think so." I gazed up into the sky, searching it for the soul of the dragon, but I already knew it hadn't worked.

Spear took my hand and gazed down at the red line I'd just created. "Why didn't it work?" He searched my eyes for an answer, but I had none to give him. It had always worked before and nothing had changed. I'd not killed anyone, which was the only thing I could think of that could take away my power.

A voice piped up from nearby. "She's a fraud! Why are the Slayers here anyway?"

"We're here to save your asses!" bellowed my father.

"You are the ones that caused all this in the first place!"

So many people were shouting at each other I couldn't tell who was who. A brawl had broken out beside me but all I could look at was the sword. Why hadn't it worked? It always had in the past.

"Maybe you are too tired to release any more," offered Ash, who was also ignoring the chaos. "Come on, we need to get out of here before anyone punches either of us. Let Spear deal with this mess."

I looked up then. Most of the crowd was fighting. Actually fist-fighting. A few people were trying to calm everyone down, but most were too angry to listen.

I saw Morganna trying to pull Alpha from one of the dragons, and Xander was holding Jasper back from one of the Wolvren. All around me, the world had turned to madness again. Spear was now back on the steps, shouting for calm. It was a disaster and I was sick to death of it. Everybody was always fighting, no matter what I did. Ash was right. Spear could deal with it. I'd go back home with Ash and wait it out there. I turned to follow him, but as I did, a thought struck me. I realized what the problem had been with the sword. My father had told us all only a while ago that sometimes he brought back dragons that had already had their souls taken and pretended he'd made the kill. What if he'd done that with Hecta? If Hecta had been too scared to kill, or they simply hadn't found a live dragon, would my father cover for her? I believed he would. Letting go of Ash's hand I dove at the line of swords next to Spear.

Pulling the nearest one to me, I dragged the blade across my calf.

Like an explosion around me, everything turned orange. A loud bang escaped from the sword and someone screamed as I was engulfed in flames. It took a second or two to register that the screams were coming from me. I was on fire. I was burning. The sword in my hand was white hot and vibrating. I dropped it to the ground, hearing it clang as it hit the wooden step.

Searing hot pain flooded through me, filling my senses. I'd gone from a sword not working to this. The sounds of arguing had stopped, replaced by reactions of shock. I could just about hear them over the roar of the flames.

I thought then that I was going to die as fire licked me from all sides. Surely no one could withstand this much pain and survive. Something knocked me to the ground and then everything went black. At first, I thought I really had died, but then whatever had been thrown over me, covering my eyes, was removed.

I blinked. The flames were gone but my whole body was in pain. Looking up I could see the shocked faces of Ash, Spear, and Morganna. Edeline came into view with a bucket which she promptly upended onto me, covering me with icy water. Another woman I'd never met followed suit and threw another bucket of water over me. The coldness soothed my skin.

"She needs to change out of those clothes and get some burn lotion on," Edeline demanded, pushing everyone else out of the way. "Can you stand, Julianna?"

I was in pain but I tried to pick myself up. Ash took

one hand, which was fine, but when Spear went for my other hand, I cried out in pain. It had been holding the sword and was badly burned. I wouldn't let anyone else touch me as Edeline guided me into the house. In the upstairs bathroom was a large claw-footed tub which she began to fill with cool water.

"Everybody out!" she demanded. I looked back to see Ash, my father, Spear, and Morganna behind me. All but Ash back out through the door. Edeline had to push Ash out and lock the door behind him to keep him out.

She peeled my burned clothes away from my body carefully before helping me into the bath.

"You've got some blisters from the flames, but nothing that won't heal given time," she said, carefully wiping blackened ashes from my naked body. "I've got some burn cream which will do wonders, but you are going to be in pain for a few days. You are lucky Ash acted as quickly as he did. He threw his jacket over you and put the flames out."

"What happened?" I croaked. It was the first thing I'd said since going up in flames. Even my throat hurt from the smoke I'd inhaled.

"I don't know. I've never seen anything like it. Once we've cleaned you up I'll go and speak to the others and see if they know."

I wanted to insist she take me but highly doubted that I'd feel able to walk downstairs and have a conversation about swords. Even with the cool bath water, I was still in agony. My skin was an angry red color, and most of it was marked with small blisters. Edeline let me drip dry rather than use a towel, which I was grateful for. It meant I took longer to dry, but the thought of moving a towel over my skin was enough to bring tears to my eyes. I had no idea how I was going to put clothes on without screaming.

"This is a miracle cure," Edeline assured me as she took off the lid of the burn cream. "As you can imagine, in a colony of dragons, we had to come up with something amazing to treat burns. We can withstand high temperatures in our dragon forms, but we can burn in our human form."

I nodded, not expecting much, but as she applied the cream, the pain began to dissolve. It was as if the cream leeched the pain right from my skin. By the time she'd slathered it all over me, I was able to put on a light cotton dress she'd found for me.

"You'll have to wear that for a couple of days, but you'll find that the cream will get rid of those blisters pretty quickly. I'll let you have the tube." She handed it to me. It smelled like nothing I knew, floral with a hint of something else, coconut, maybe.

"Thank you," I said, placing the tube in one of the dress's pockets.

She bustled about in a cupboard and came back with a roll of bandage. "You are going to need this on both hands and your calf. You've certainly done a good job of hurting yourself!"

She cut the bandage into three strips of equal length. The first she wrapped around my leg where I'd sliced it with the sword, then she wrapped both of my hands—my right because of the cut on it from Hecta's sword and my left from the burn from the other sword. I was such a mess.

"I guess I won't be entering any beauty contests anytime soon?" I joked.

Edeline laughed. "You look beautiful to me, and I'm betting there is a young man down there that only wants to know you are alright. Do you feel well enough to go downstairs and talk to the others?"

I nodded. We found them in Spear's study. The last time I'd been in here, we'd been planning to raid Dronias. Now my father sat in there, munching on a cookie. How times had changed. When I walked through the door, everyone stood. Ash came running up to me.

"How could you have done something so stupid?" I could see the tears in his eyes as he approached.

"Stop!" Edeline demanded when he was still a foot away. "She's burned her skin. You can't touch her for a few days. She'll not thank you for it. Her skin is very delicate at the moment."

"I wasn't going to," objected Ash. "Is she going to be OK?"

"I'm right here!" I said. "And I'm fine. Your mom's burn cream has taken most of the pain away. She thinks I'll heal within a few days."

Ash nodded and gave his mom a small smile. "You shouldn't have done it though," he insisted.

"No, she shouldn't have," agreed my father. "I told her not to. I've been telling everyone, including her, that this is too much for her, and now look what's happened."

"I'm agreeing with you," said Ash forcefully. "I didn't want this any more than you did. I hate that she got hurt."

"You were close enough to stop her," replied my father angrily. "If you didn't want her to do this, why did you let her pick up the sword?"

"I'm right here!" I repeated, this time loudly. "Stop talking over me as though I'm not here. I am here and I can hear you. Does anyone know what happened? Why did the sword do that?"

Nobody said anything. I looked at the sword I'd picked up. Spear had it propped up next to him on the sofa. It was blackened by the flame, but I knew which sword it was. When I'd first picked it up, I'd just grabbed for the nearest sword, not thinking of who it belonged to, but now I could see it was my father's sword. Even though it was covered in soot, I recognized the shape of it. That's why it, and me along with it, had gone up in flames. I'd not released just one soul, I'd freed many. All the dragon souls my father had caught were now free.

"How many were there?"

"A lot," said Spear "You did it, Julianna. You saved many dragons."

"How many, Father? Ten? Twenty? A hundred?"

My father bowed his head. "At least."

I smiled. Soon, over a hundred dragons would be flying across the sky and coming home. It was worth the pain. It was worth everything.

"You're not doing this again," my father demanded. "I won't let you." He turned to Spear. "You hear that? She's my daughter. She's been hurt enough. I'm sorry about the rest of your dragons, but there is no way I'm going to let you subject her to that again."

Spear nodded. "You are right. Julianna has done so much for us already. I won't ask her to do it again."

They were talking over me again, but I didn't have the energy to argue. In fact, I didn't have the energy for anything. The room began to spin and I felt myself falling to the ground. Everything around me went black.

11

I awoke in a room I'd never seen before. Light shone through a window, illuminating the white walls. It was sparse but large, with a large, ornate wardrobe at one side and a soft chair next to the bed I was lying on. Slumped in the chair, Ash was fast asleep, his mouth slightly open, one arm hanging over the side. I watched him for a while. The rhythmic rise and fall of his chest, the way his eyes moved under his eyelids. I wondered what it was that he was dreaming about.

The rest of the room gave me no clues as to where I was. There were no pictures on the walls and no personal items. I only knew I wasn't in Ash's house, with its walls carved out of the cliff rock, nor were we in any house in Dronias. The houses there were beautiful and quaint, but they didn't have the perfectly straight lines of this room.

Someone knocked on the door lightly, waking Ash from his slumber.

"Come in." I tried sitting up to welcome whoever it

was, but pain shot through me. I cried out as Edeline ran through the door.

"Don't move!" she commanded. "I'm here to put more of the lotion on you." I did as she asked and stayed still. To move was agony, anyway. "I was hoping this would have worked faster," she said, pulling the light cotton cover gently away from my skin. Underneath, I still wore the white cotton dress.

"Where am I?" I asked as Edeline got to work, smothering my dry, cracked skin with the cream. As soon as she started to apply it, the pain began to subside.

"This is Spear's room," Ash said, taking my hand. "He said you could stay here as long as you need to. He's been sleeping on a couch downstairs."

Sleeping on a couch? "How long have I been up here?"

Ash gave his mother a look.

"Tell me," I demanded.

"You've been out of it for a week," Edeline began. "I'd hoped that the lotion would work a lot faster, but you've been through so much that your body is taking its time to heal. The blisters are gone now and your skin is looking a lot better than it was." She gave a slight, comforting smile.

It certainly didn't feel any better. Nor did I feel better knowing I'd been asleep for so long. "A week? What's been happening?" I tried to sit up again. This time, it was slightly easier thanks to the soothing properties of the lotion.

"Please don't panic. You've not missed anything."

I saw another look pass between her and Ash. There

was something they weren't telling me. "What is it? You are hiding something."

I saw Ash fire a warning look at Edeline, but she ignored him. "The dragons you saved haven't returned."

If I'd been asleep for a week, it meant the dragons' souls returned to them at the same time. They should have been back with us by now. "What happened?"

"We don't know. Spear is forbidding anyone to turn into their dragon form at the moment. The disease seems to be contagious. Some of the other dragons have caught it, but no one has contracted it in their human form. Because of that, we are all trapped here. No one can fly. We've been spending the week looking after the sick dragons. Your father has outdone himself. He got together a crew and between them, they've made a shelter outside. It's almost like a hospital for dragons."

"My father is still here?"

"Of course," replied Ash, taking over for his mother and applying the lotion to my arms. "He can't go because no one can get out, but I doubt he'd leave anyway. Not with you still here like this. He's been checking up on you every couple of hours."

"But what about the steps up the cliff face? Has no one gone up there?" I remembered the time I tried going home. There was a steep set of stairs carved into the cliff with a set of tunnels through the mountain to the other side. It was a grueling journey, but it was certainly doable.

Edeline shook her head. "The stairs are impassable. Heavy rain caused parts of them to wash away."

So, we were well and truly trapped here. The only way out of Dronias was from the south, the way we'd come in a week ago. I sighed and closed my eyes. Nothing was going to plan. The Goblins had lied to us, we'd failed to collect any more swords, and I'd almost burned all my skin off freeing the dragons. Worse still, the ones I did free hadn't returned, and there was no possible way to find out why.

I thought back to Dronias, to my mother. We should have been back by now. She would be beside herself with worry. I wondered how the Slayers were dealing with the dragons. If they were ill like the ones over here, they would need caring for. Would they do that? I didn't know. It was one thing to open the doors to let them go free, but it was quite another to actively care for them, and that's if they knew they were ill in the first place. If the souls had returned to them and then they'd promptly fallen ill to the ground after waking up, there was every chance that the villagers wouldn't have even spotted the souls returning.

"Can I speak to Spear, please?" I asked Edeline. She looked unsure of what to say but nodded her head.

"I'll go get him. He wanted to be the first to know when you woke up anyway."

She left me alone with Ash. He didn't speak as he carried on applying the lotion. My skin, no longer hurting, tingled under his touch.

"Kiss me."

He looked surprised by request. "Are you sure? I don't want to hurt you."

I gave him a smile. It had been so long since he'd last kissed me, I could barely remember. Our lives were a maelstrom of chaos and adventure, and because of that, we'd not had time alone for a long while. I almost wished I'd sent Edeline away instead of to fetch Spear.

"My face wasn't burned, and even if it was, I'd still want to kiss you."

He leaned forward and kissed me lightly on the lips. I leaned into him, but at that moment, Spear opened the door and we shot apart.

"You look to be doing better," smirked Spear. I felt the blush rise to my cheeks. Typical. My face was the only part of me that wasn't already bright pink.

"Edeline tells me you want to see me."

"Yes," I nodded. "I want to know what our next move is."

"To be honest with you, Julianna, we've been too preoccupied to come up with a plan. Everyone has been busy looking after the sick." He sat on the only place he could, the end of the bed, careful to stay away from my feet and legs.

"How is everyone?"

Spear sighed. "The dragons that were ill that managed to change into their human form have recovered, but those that were too weak to transform back are still sick. I don't know what to do for them. Thanks to your father, they're sheltered from the weather and being kept warm, but unfortunately, there seems to be no improvement."

"What about the swords?"

Ash jumped up. "What about the swords? You aren't suggesting cutting yourself again, are you?" He turned to Spear. "I won't allow it. Look at her. The blast nearly killed her."

"Calm down, Ash," replied Spear gently. "We have

all agreed —the dragons, the Slayers, and the Wolvren —that Julianna cannot possibly offer herself up again. I think the blast gave everyone a wake-up call, even the doubting dragons. No one wants, nor expects, Julianna to hurt herself further." He looked right at me. "I hope you agree to that."

I nodded gratefully. The truth was, my whole body had been put through enough. I knew, as Spear did, that we'd have to do something, but for now, all I wanted to do was rest. "Thank you, Spear."

Over the course of the next few days, I had many visitors. My father came to see me at the end of every day. Morganna kept popping in to update me on everything, although there was very little news to tell me. Lucy often came to read me stories. Throughout it all, Ash never left my side. He brought food up to eat with me and moved from sleeping on the chair to sleeping with me on the bed once I'd healed enough to be touched.

After a few days, thanks to Edeline and Ash looking after me, I was finally allowed downstairs. The lotion had worked enough that I could move quite freely and without pain. My skin was covered in scars that would never fully heal, but it was a small price to pay for the return of the dragons.

The day I was able to get up, a meeting was called in the parlor. Spear had deliberately only invited a few people. Beside myself and Ash, there was also my father, Morganna, Alpha, Edeline, Fiere, Xander, Jasper and, of course, Spear. A plate of cookies and a pot of tea were brought in by a maid and set on a small side table. I grabbed a cookie before sitting on the sofa next to Morganna. Ash took the place beside me.

"I've already told Julianna that we've all agreed that she cannot hurt herself any further to free the dragons. I think we can all agree that she has gone above and beyond what any of us could expect of her. I, on behalf of the dragons, want to thank you, Julianna, for everything you have done for us. Your bravery is unsurpassed and my gratitude knows no bounds."

I cast my eyes down at his words. It was so embarrassing being praised so publicly, and yet my heart jumped with pride.

"However," Spear continued. "We now have a problem. Julianna is the only person that can free our ancestors and family members. Because of this, we have to find another solution and we have to do it quickly. The dragons outside do not appear to be getting worse, but at the same time, they are not getting better either."

"I say we head back up to pay those Goblins another visit," My father broke in.

Surprisingly, Spear agreed. "Yes, I have to admit, it's looking like a trip back up the mountain is our only way to solve this. The Goblins have gotten away with this for far too long, and I, for one, am sick of them tricking us."

Everyone nodded. I nibbled on the cookie, not too sure. We'd all gone up there before, twice in fact, and nothing good had come of it. I didn't see how dragging everyone back up the mountain would help.

I quickly finished the cookie. "We promised Krikor that the dragons, Slayers, and Wolvren would never return to the Goblin city together."

"And he promised us that there were more Slayer

swords in that village," my father reminded me. "They can't be trusted, so I see no reason why we shouldn't just go up there anyway."

"Actually I agree with Julianna," cut in Morganna. "They might be more willing to cooperate if only a few of us go."

"Are you volunteering?" Spear asked her.

Morganna nodded. "I'll do whatever I can to help. Of course, we are going to have to figure a way up the mountain first. With the dragons being ill, we cannot do anything." She looked right at me as she said this, something that Ash picked up on right away.

"You surely aren't going to ask Julianna to go with you?"

"Why not? She's better now. I can't go with you or with Alpha or with most of the rest of you. We have to show that we can be trusted, even if they can't. I need to go up the mountain with another Slayer. It's the only way."

"What about me?" my father asked. "Or Jasper, or both of us? Why does it have to be Julianna?"

"Because I trust her with my life, that's why, and you should know you can trust me with hers."

I filled with pride at hearing my hero talk about me in such a way. Of all the people in this room, many of whom were bigger and stronger than me, it was me that she picked. I couldn't help the grin that appeared on my lips.

Unfortunately, not everyone agreed. "I won't be separated from her," argued Ash. "I love her too much to let her go."

"I'm not letting my daughter go up the mountain in

the state she's in," roared my father. Pretty soon everyone was squabbling again.

I was just about to chime in, to tell them what I thought of the plan, when the room went dark. Something was blocking the sunlight. I turned to see a dragon landing, then another.

"It's the dragons!" I shouted. "They are back!"

12

I don't know who got out of the house first, but we were all in the garden within a minute of spotting the first dragon. Three or four of the dragons had already landed, but the sky was filled with many more, too many to count.

"Someone go inside and grab some clothes for them," directed Spear, running toward the first dragon. Jasper, Xander, and Alpha ran inside, following Spear's orders.

The first few dragons changed into their human forms. I recognized one of them immediately. It was Stone. The last time I'd seen him was when he and his brother Ally were training me to hunt. It felt like so long ago.

"Where's Ally?" I asked Ash, trying not to look at Stone's naked body.

"I think he's in the dragon hospital your father helped build. The last time I saw him, he was helping out in there."

I looked to where Ash was pointing. A huge shed now took up most of Spear's garden. My father had done an amazing job.

"I'll get him," Ash ran off toward the shed.

Ally was going to be so happy. He'd been so utterly depressed that his brother had been killed. Even when we found out that he'd not been killed, but his soul reaped, he was still upset. I don't think I'd seen him smile since the last day we were all together.

"What happened?" asked Spear, pulling his jacket off and handing it to Stone. "Why has it taken so long for you to get back? Your souls were released a week and a half ago."

"We were confused. There were so many of us waking up at the same time. Some had been trapped recently like me, but some of the dragons had been trapped for decades. There were also many that didn't wake up. We tried everything we could, but nothing would wake them."

"That's because Julianna only released the souls from one sword. There are still so many swords to find."

Stone looked confused. "That's what happened? Our souls were harvested?"

"I guess you could put it like that," replied Spear. "What happened next?"

"I thought we'd all come back from the dead. I wasn't the only one. I wanted to come home, but some of the others wanted to find out what had happened to them. When we left the building our bodies had been kept in, we found ourselves in the woods at the base of the Triad Mountains. A quick flyover showed us to be near the Slayer village. The village where Julianna comes from."

Stone glanced over at me. "I wanted to get revenge. Most of the others did, too, so we flew down to the village."

I closed my eyes, not wanting to hear the rest. The biggest and bravest of all the Slayers were here in Frokontas. There was no one left to defend the village against all these angry dragons.

"What did you do?" roared my father, rushing up to Stone.

At that moment, Xander, Jasper, and Alpha came running up, their arms full of clothes. One by one, the dragons began to shift into their human forms behind Stone. Stone raised his hands.

"It's not what you think," replied Stone quickly. "No one was hurt."

"They'd better not be!" yelled my father, poking his finger against Stone's chest.

Spear pulled it away. "Enough. You heard him. No one was hurt." He turned back to Stone. "So what did happen?"

"We went in to attack but Julianna's mother came running toward us with a white flag. Actually, it was a white dress on a stick, but we got the message. We thought we'd won without having to fight, but when we shifted, she told us about everything that had been happening. About how Julianna had done what she set out to do and turned the Slayers and the dragons into friends. Of course, I didn't believe it at first, but the rest of the village came out and corroborated her story. They were so nice to us."

"That doesn't explain why it took you so long to get back," argued Spear.

Xander threw a pair of pants at him, which he slipped into. Stone looked embarrassed now. "We didn't know we were friends before seeing Julianna's mother, so we might have...kind of...well, we might possibly have burned down a few buildings."

I sighed. So many of the buildings in Dronias had already succumbed to the fire of the dragons.

"No one was in them, but we felt bad so we all agreed to stay and rebuild them. I know we could have sent someone home to tell you that we were okay, but we didn't know you were waiting for us. We decided as a group to help out there and then all come back at once. We wanted to make a splash, so to speak."

I looked up. The skies were still filled with the returning dragons. "Well, you've certainly done that," I commented.

"You burned down part of the village?" My father was close to having another temper tantrum. I ran up to him and whispered into his ear.

"Daddy. You were the one who took these dragons' souls, forcing them to be trapped. Some of them have been in there for over twenty years. Don't you think you might want to cut them some slack? After all, they are the ones who should be mad at you." I raised my eyebrows at him. He nodded, slowly accepting my words.

"I'm going to need you to go to the fire pit," announced Spear loudly so all the newly returned dragons could hear him. "We have much to tell you and my house will not accommodate so many people.

Julianna, do you think you are well enough to round up everyone and ask them to meet us there?"

I was just about to answer when I heard a yell coming from behind me. I turned to see Ash coming toward us with Ally.

"Brother!" Ally yelled, rushing toward Stone. Stone grinned as Ally crashed into him, knocking him to the ground. The pair of them play-wrestled for a few seconds before Ally pulled Stone to his feet and gave him a huge hug.

"I'll do what I can," I said to Spear over the commotion.

It took over two hours to get everyone around the campfire. The dragons kept on coming, so I had to wait until the last one had arrived. Someone lit a fire and a wild deer was roasting above it. Flagons of beer were passed around, and the noise of conversation was almost deafening. The whole thing had turned into a party of sorts, so when it was time for Spear to speak, he had to shout loudly to be heard.

"Welcome back to those of you who came home to us today. I'm sure many of you will want to catch up with old friends and family members. I'm going to ask you all to stay in your human forms. You've probably heard the rumors over the course of the past couple of hours, but for those of you that haven't, a lot of the other dragons that came back to us got ill not long after coming back. It's already been well over a week since you got your souls back so I'm assuming you will come down with whatever it is. If you stay in your human form, you will recover. At the present time, we cannot find a cure for those that fell ill in their dragon form. I do not want the same fate to happen to anyone here so it is imperative that you do as I say for your own health. At the first sign of any illness, you may come to my house to be looked after or you may stay at home to be looked after by your families."

"What about the rest of the trapped dragons?" asked someone I didn't recognize.

"As you all know, the Slayers and the dragons have called a truce of sorts over the past few weeks. That is largely thanks to Julianna. Julianna, where are you?"

I raised my hand. Hundreds of pairs of eyes fixed on me. I gave everyone a shy smile.

"Julianna not only brought our tribes together, but she is also the one who is responsible for freeing you. To free you she has had to draw her own blood time and time again. I will not ask her to do it another time and I don't want anyone else asking her to either. We are going to have to come up with another plan to free our people."

"We already have a plan, Spear," said Morganna, standing up. "Julianna and I are going back up into the mountains. We are going to speak to the Goblins."

"No!"

I had thought it would be my father or Ash that spoke up first, but it was Alpha. He'd not left Morganna's side this whole journey. I could understand why he wouldn't want her to go back to the Goblins alone. He'd wanted to take his men back to their village, but because of the dragons' illness, had been unable to. I felt sorry for him because I could see the determination on Morganna's face. He wouldn't be able to stop her any more than Ash would be able to stop me. He gripped my hand tighter as though he knew what I was thinking.

"I'm going to go," I whispered so that only he could hear.

"I know you are. I know that there is nothing I can say or do to stop you, and yet I don't want you to go."

I turned to look at him. "Morganna is the strongest person I know. Not one of the men here would beat her in a fight. I'm safer with her than with anyone else. Besides, I can take care of myself."

Ash sighed in resignation. "I won't stop you, but do me a favor. Wait a few days until you are fully healed. Your body has barely recovered."

I nodded. It was only fair to honor this one request.

"You're not going to let her go, surely?" my father asked Spear.

I stood up, letting go of Ash's hand. "It's not up to him, Father. I am my own person and I make the decisions for me. Morganna, I will go with you. I just need a couple more days to recuperate and then I should be strong enough to climb the mountain."

Alpha and my father stood up. They both looked ready to fight

"Gentlemen," Spear began, talking to the pair of them. "I am not their keeper any more than you are. They have both decided to go to the Goblins. It makes sense that it should be them. They are both Slayers and they are both fearless. The Goblins will either talk to them or no doubt they will be forced to talk to them."

"You can't get up the mountain," my father said, suddenly thinking of it. "The only dragons that are in that form are too ill to fly, and the rest of them can't turn into their dragon form because they'll get ill." He crossed his arms and raised his eyebrows, smirking now that he had found a way to thwart me.

He had a point. The only way out would be to scale the sheer cliff, and I had neither the equipment nor the talent for such a thing.

"I'll fly you up," said Fiere, standing up. "I've already had the illness and recovered. I'll shift, fly you up the mountain and then come home and quickly shift back."

My father looked at him with daggers in his eyes, but there was nothing he could do.

Morganna and I were going back up the mountain.

13

Fiere flew us almost to the entrance, leaving us about a twenty-minute walk away. I expected him to drop us off then fly back. The longer he was in his dragon form, the more dangerous it was for him. None of us knew what would happen to him if he stayed too long in this form. He'd had the illness once and gotten over it, but there was nothing to stop him getting it again.

He didn't fly off though. He rounded behind a tree and shifted into his human form. I threw him a shawl I'd packed, which he wrapped around his middle.

"Shouldn't you be going home?" I shouted across to him.

He came over from the tree. "I just wanted to talk with you before I left you here."

"Okay."

He placed his hand on my shoulder. "I haven't known you for a long time, but I've seen the way my son looks at you. I almost decided not to bring you this morning. I was worried you'd get hurt or worse, and it would break Ash's heart."

"What made you change your mind?" I asked.

He gave a small laugh. "It was Ash. He came to me early this morning. I told him that I was going to tell Spear that I wasn't going to take you, but he told me that I should. He said that you were so stubborn that you'd only find another way if I didn't. He asked me to look after you."

"You can't," interjected Morganna. "The Goblins want us to come alone. I don't know why they only want one tribe at a time—maybe they are afraid we'll break into war right in the middle of their underground town —but we promised that we wouldn't come with another group."

"I understand that," he replied, "but I owe it to Ash."

"You've got no armor. You don't even have any clothes," reasoned Morganna. "How will you be able to protect us?"

It was true that Morganna and I had dressed for this. We were both kitted out in the best protective clothing that the dragons had to offer and most importantly, I still had my sword. Fiere only had the shawl I'd given him.

"I'm a dragon, remember? I don't need clothes. I'll follow you up the rest of the way and keep out of sight."

"No," I shook my head. "You've been ill once. The longer you are in your dragon form, the more likely you are to become ill again. I couldn't bear it if you became ill because of me. Once we are done with the Goblins, we'll head back down the mountain. I have a flare in my backpack. I'll set it off once we get close to home so someone can fly up the cliff to get us."

His face looked pale, his forehead clammy. "But..."

"But nothing, You're already getting sick. I can see it. Now get back down the mountain before you become too ill to shift back."

He nodded. Just before he hid behind the tree again, he called out to me. "Shoot that flare if you're in trouble. I'll make sure someone comes and rescues you."

"I will," I promised, however I had no intention of needing to be rescued. I'd spent enough time having people look out for me. It was about time I did something by myself. Okay, not exactly by myself. I had Morganna, but I knew her well enough to know she wouldn't overprotect me like the others would.

Fiere disappeared behind the tree. I heard the disgusting yet distinctive sound of his bones grinding and cracking as he changed back into a dragon. It was a sound I'd never get used to as long as I lived. His wings unfolded and he took off, leaving only my shawl behind. Morganna and I watched him fly away until he was only a speck.

"Do you think he'll be okay?" I asked Morganna, turning around and looking back up the trail. Flying the pair of us up here had obviously taken it out of him.

"Hopefully he'll be able to glide back down to the village and shift there. I think he'll be alright. Come on, let's get a move on. I don't want to be out here all day."

It was a calm day, but cold so high up in the mountains. I wrapped the shawl over my shoulders and began the hike to the Goblin city. It took us longer than the twenty minutes we had planned to walk. The combination of the cold weather and rocky ground beneath our feet slowed us down. It didn't help that we'd landed lower than we planned to in the first place.

An hour and a half later I could finally see the door ahead of us. Once again, it looked abandoned, a trick of the Goblins to make people think that there wasn't anyone there.

I sat on a boulder and pulled a bottle of water from my pack. We'd both traveled light, expecting to only be out for the day, and had only brought a couple of bottles of water each. I unscrewed the top and handed it to Morganna. She took a swig and handed it back.

"Are you alright?" she asked as I gulped down the rest of the bottle.

The truth was, I'd felt better. I ached much more than I should for such a short walk, and even though I'd mostly healed from the burns, my skin was still delicate in some areas and was not being helped by the thick, protective leather clothing we were wearing.

Instead of admitting that, though, I took a deep breath and nodded my head. I didn't want her to think I was weak.

"Come on." I stood and packed the empty bottle back in my bag. Just then, a flash of red caught in the corner of my eye. I whipped my head around to see a red dragon circling above us.

"Ash!" I hissed. He couldn't hear me as he was too high above us, but I couldn't shout lest the Goblins hear me.

When he landed, he dropped something from his mouth which I recognized as his clothes, then quickly turned into his human form and pulling on his clothes. "What are you doing here?" I asked. "I've just sent your father home and now you're here. Don't you trust me?" I felt angry with him. When I'd left, he'd been totally fine with me coming up the mountain. Well not fine exactly, but I didn't expect him to follow me.

"As soon as you were out of sight, I panicked. I'm sorry. I do trust you and I know you can look after yourself, but I thought I'd come for back up."

"What if you become sick, too?" I huffed. "Your father was looking ill."

"I'm fine."

"Ok, just stay here, then. Morganna and I will go up to the Goblin city. We'll shout to you if we get in trouble. For goodness' sake, stay out of sight."

He nodded and sat down behind a boulder.

"He just cares about you, you know," Morganna said to me once we were out of Ash's earshot. "Don't blame him. He loves you, that's all."

"Hmm," I grumbled. "How would you feel if Alpha popped out from behind a bush right about now?"

"Oh, I'd kill him," she replied with a sly grin. I snorted with laughter.

The door was still hanging from its hinges, so we stepped into the tunnel that would take us into the Goblin Kingdom.

It was quiet. Too quiet. It reeked of Goblin trickery.

"Krikor!" I shouted out down the tunnel. My voice echoed back to me.

The tunnel ended, opening into the large cavern I'd seen before. It was empty. There was not a Goblin in sight.

"Where are they?" I asked. The usually busy city was now silent except for our own footsteps. "Hello!" I called out. Again my voice echoed, but this time it was much louder, reverberating off the cavern walls.

"Check the buildings," said Morganna, pointing at the holes in the wall of the cavern which I remembered to be rooms cut out from the rock.

I went one way as she went another. She took the small restaurant I'd eaten in the first time I'd been here. I climbed a long set of stairs that led me almost all the way to the roof of the cavern before coming to a balcony. I turned and looked out into the cavern. I could see the whole place from up here. The buildings cut from the rock and the exit to the left, the tunnel to the mines in front and below me, and the rest of the cavern disappearing into the darkness to the right. Behind me was an open doorway. I stepped through it into the darkness. Once my eyes adjusted to the lack of light, I saw a number of closed doors leading from the tunnel. I opened the first one to find a small room with a tiny bed. This was where the Goblins slept. I checked the next room. It was exactly the same.

I didn't need to continue down the corridor to know that this was their sleeping quarters. I also didn't need to search further to know it was deserted. The beds hadn't been slept in for days and there were no personal effects. I opened a wardrobe door to confirm what I already knew. The wardrobe was empty. The Goblins were gone.

"Julianna!" I heard Morganna shouting. I dashed back to the balcony to see her standing below, just outside the restaurant. "The place is deserted," she confirmed when I got back down to her. "We should have let Ash come with us after all. Do you think we should search the place?"

"What for? If they've gone, they've gone. They seem to have taken everything with them. Even the bedrooms are empty."

"Hmm." Morganna walked away from me slowly. She looked around her as if searching for something, but I couldn't say what. I followed her to the entrance to the mines. I'd never been down there before; the thought of it unnerved me. The small bit of light that flooded into the cavern through holes in the ceiling didn't quite reach down here, and once again I found myself walking in the dark. I followed the sound of Morganna's footsteps in front of me, wishing I'd brought a torch with me.

As if reading my thoughts, Morganna clicked her fingers and the tunnel lit up.

"What just happened?" I asked, finally seeing down the tunnel.

"I got sick of walking in the dark and decided to use some of my magic. I have so little of it left and hate to waste it, but at the same time, I don't want to break a leg by tripping over anything."

The light flickered and went out. Morganna clicked her fingers again, illuminating the tunnel. Just as quickly, the light was extinguished again.

"That's strange," Morganna remarked.

"You're out of magic?"

"No. I've got enough to last me a bit longer. This is something else. It's as if magic isn't working here."

"Well, you'd better hurry up and get it working," I said, gripping hold of the hilt of my sword, "because I can hear something and I think it's coming this way."

14

Gripping the hilt of my sword, I readied myself for a fight. I could hear Morganna's steady breathing in front of me and beyond that, the noise of footsteps. They came closer. I listened as whoever it was ran up the tunnel toward us. The sound was faint but unmistakable. My breathing increased along with my heart rate as the footsteps were almost upon us.

Closer, closer, closer...

Morganna clicked her fingers and the tunnel lit up. There was no one there. I whipped my head around, looking up and down the tunnel, but apart from the two of us, it was empty.

"What happened? Where did they go?"

The footsteps had gone past us and were now getting fainter again. Morganna's light went out.

"Follow me," she said brusquely. "I think I know what's going on and I think I know how to stop it."

"Stop it?" Stop what?

I held onto her arm as she guided me slowly down the pitch-black tunnel. I heard another sound. Water. The tunnel finally ended and for the first time in over ten minutes, I could finally see. Small shafts of light illuminated another cavern. This one was almost as big as the first, but much colder and damper. The water I'd heard was a huge underground river roaring through the cavern. This had to be the beginning of the river we had floated down to get to the deserted village. I remembered the water as being warm, but here, further down the mountain, the cavern was cold. Stalactites dripped water into the already ferocious river and a seam of a silver-colored metal ran diagonally through the rock, sparkling in the pale light. A small bridge crossed the river from where we were to what looked like a mine at the other side. A small track ran the length of it with an abandoned mine cart flipped on its side. Pickaxes littered the floor, dropped, no doubt, when the Goblins left. There was no one there and yet I could hear the very faint *tap, tap, tap* of tools on rock over the sound of the river.

"There's no one here," Morganna announced loudly, "Let's steal the tools."

Why would she want to steal the pickaxes? We had no need for them. She began to cross the bridge, but some unseen force knocked her back. She fell on her butt just in front of me. A smile played on her lips.

"What's happening?" I asked, taking her hand to help her up.

"None of this is real. The Goblins are playing a trick on us."

"A trick?"

"Yes. This place isn't abandoned. I knew they'd try something like this. They are all here, we just can't see them. Isn't that right, Krikor?"

The sound of the tapping got louder. Images began to appear, at first indistinct before coming fully into focus. I opened my mouth as I took in the scene now. Whereas it had been desolate just moments before, now it was a busy working mine. Hundreds of Goblins were working, the abandoned pickaxes I'd seen now in their hands, being used to mine the metals they needed to make their magical weapons. The mining cart on its side disappeared and a fully working one zoomed down the track, filled with stones.

"I could have wasted more magic to erase the glamour they'd put on themselves, but I figured threatening to steal their stuff would do the trick." Morganna grinned, sweeping the dirt from her clothes.

"Come this way!" An angry goblin appeared in front of us, a sword in his hand. It looked like one of the Slayer swords. "The king wants to see you."

"Put it down, Shorty," snapped Morganna. "We are here to see Krikor, anyway."

He marched us back up the tunnel. It was now lit with what looked like fairylights, although they had to be run on magic. Krikor was back in the conference room where we had seen him the last time we were here, but unlike then, he was alone. The Goblin who had escorted us here bowed and left, closing the door behind him.

"Back so soon?" he asked, sounding resigned. "I can't seem to keep you away, can I? Tell me, what is it that draws you to me like a moth to a flame? My good looks, perhaps?"

I stifled a snort. Never in a million years could anyone say that Krikor was good-looking. Even for a Goblin, who were an ugly bunch to begin with, he was unattractive.

"Don't kid yourself, Krikor," snapped Morganna. "You know exactly why we're here. You sent us on a merry dance down to that village, knowing full well that there would be no one there."

Krikor arched a brow. "What makes you think that? I have no interest in where Slayers go once they've taken their swords."

"You might not care about the Slayers, but you do care where they go because you care where your precious swords end up. Isn't that right?"

"I might like to keep an eye on them, yes," replied Krikor smoothly. "But that doesn't mean I know where they are."

He was lying and we all knew it. "Tell us where they are," I said, holding my sword to his neck. I'd had just about enough of the garbage he was spouting.

His eyes widened as he took in the sharp blade at his throat, but then he looked me in the eyes and grinned. "You won't hurt me. I can read you like a book, remember? There's a reason the swords empty their souls for you. You are an innocent. You'll never purposefully hurt anyone, not even me."

I pushed the blade further, leaving a small cut on his neck. A small drop of blood worked its way down his leathery green skin. "Want to try me?" He was right. I would find it difficult to kill, but when I thought of all the dragon souls he'd helped capture, the dragons that were now sick and might die because of the swords he made, I actually thought I might be able to do it.

He held his hands up but didn't drop eye contact. He was goading me into doing it. I felt the anger rise within me. Could I do it? Could I really kill him to get what I wanted?

And then it hit me. Killing him wouldn't get me what I wanted. Killing him would get me nowhere.

I lowered my sword.

"I knew it." Krikor sneered.

"Yes, you did. You knew I wouldn't kill you, but you also know that I could. You saw into my mind. You saw how angry I am. Why have you been lying to us for so long?"

"Why should I tell you the truth? You come to me, time after time, even though I've told you that you are not welcome. You already know how to free the souls of the dragons and yet you wouldn't accept it when I told you. You know that there are other Slayers who come to us for swords, and yet you are here again. I don't know where they are. Is that what you want to know? I was keeping an eye on them, but they left their village a few months ago. I don't know where they went to. Are you happy now?"

"Not particularly. Yet again, you've told us nothing. We are no closer to helping the dragons now than when we walked through your door the first time."

"That is no concern of mine. Why should I care if you free the dragons or not? Selling swords was my job. If you misuse them, then that is on you."

It was clear that I wasn't about to get any information out of him. He had a way of not really answering any questions meaningfully. Getting a straight answer out of him would be unlikely.

"Talking of selling swords," interrupted Morganna. "I need a new one. My last one is ruined thanks to Julianna letting the dragons out of it."

"You have no money," Krikor stated.

"That is true, but I do have some Goblin magic left. Sell me a sword and you can have that."

Krikor raised an eyebrow intrigued. "You have our magic and yet you chose not to use it to see us."

"I didn't need to. It was pretty obvious you were all still here. We could still hear them working down in the mines."

"Hmm. I guess I'll have to do better," replied Krikor thoughtfully. "However, I cannot sell you a sword."

"And why not?"

"We do not make swords anymore." I looked at his odious face, split by a wide grin

Another lie. I'd seen a pile of them in the mine. I thought about all the lives that had been ruined by this Goblin. The dragons, suffering the loss of their loved ones. The Slayers, giving their innocence to fight an unnecessary war against a friendly species Something in me snapped. I picked my sword up, raising it upward, ready to swing. With months and months of pent-up rage coming to a climax, I swung at the small Goblin's neck with a scream.

I braced myself for the impact, the feeling of resistance before the blade sliced the Goblin's head off, but it never came. I blinked, trying to register what had happened. The scenery had changed. We were no longer in the conference room. We were outside. I looked around, trying to get a sense of what had happened. Morganna stood beside me, but Krikor was nowhere to be seen.

"What happened? Where are we?"

"I used what was left of my Goblin magic to transport us outside. Now that the glimmer has been erased, I could build up enough energy to use the magic. We are just above the entrance to the Goblin city. Look."

I looked down the mountain a little way. The small green door was still hanging off its hinges. "Why did you do that?" I asked, still feeling angry.

"I didn't want you to kill him," she replied simply.

I thought about her response for a few seconds before realizing why. "You knew if I killed him, I'd no longer be innocent. If I'm not innocent, I won't be able to set the dragons free."

"Actually, I'd not thought of that. I stopped you killing him because I like you and I know that you'd never be able to live with yourself."

Her answer brought peace to me, and the anger I'd felt just moments before now dissipated. She was right. Murdering someone, even someone as repellent as Krikor, would only cause me more pain. Yet I couldn't help but think that we'd made yet another wasted journey up this mountain. I looked around for Ash, feeling dejected. It was only then that I realized that he wasn't there. Ash was missing

15

"Ash?" I shouted, stumbling down the mountain to where we'd left him. Beneath my feet, the shale-like rocks made every step a potential hazard.

"Don't panic. He's probably behind the boulder," called Morganna behind me.

It was possible but unlikely. Why would he be hiding behind a boulder? When I got to the boulder, I didn't find Ash behind it, but I saw something much worse. Shreds of fabric lined the ground. Shreds that I recognized immediately as the clothes Ash had been wearing. I picked up the biggest bit—a part of his shirt. There was no mistaking it. It was Ash's, alright.

I held it out for Morganna to see as she rounded the boulder. "He shifted so quickly, he tore his clothes in the process."

"Is that usual?" asked Morganna raising her eyebrows.

"No. He always takes his clothes off before he shifts.

He's meticulous about it. I've never seen him leave his clothes in this state before."

Panic filled me as I wondered why he had felt the need to go so against character. Peering around, I realized there must be some kind of threat or he wouldn't have done it. I saw nothing but the valley and the tops of the trees that marked the border of the Triad Mountains so far below us. I looked around and up, but there was only the gray shale that covered the desolate landscape right up to the snowline of the mountain's peak.

"Something happened. He wouldn't just leave us," I panted, running back up to the entrance of the Goblin city.

"Stop!" yelled Morganna, following me. "I agree, it does seem odd that he would just vanish, but I don't think it has anything to do with the Goblins."

I hesitated. "What makes you think that?" Who else could it have been?

"Goblins do not fight. Not the way Slayers do. They use cunning over brawn. It's unlikely that they would have come out here to get involved in a fist fight. Even if they had weapons, they would have been no match for a dragon and they know that. They would have had to use magic."

"They probably did use magic," I argued.

"No. Magic leaves traces. Just like inside earlier when I could sense that magic was being used, I can tell you with absolute certainty that no magic has been used out here recently."

I wavered, halfway between going through the doorway and outside. "Are you sure?" I trusted her, but I couldn't see where else he could be."

"I'm positive."

My mind whirred, trying to come up with a possible scenario in which he would have disappeared. "What if he just decided to walk down the tunnel to find us?"

"What? As a dragon? That tunnel was built for Goblins. There is no way that a full-grown dragon would be able to squeeze through it. No. Something else happened, but I don't know what. Perhaps we should head back and see if he went home."

I shook my head. "He wouldn't have gone home. Not without me." He'd flown up all this way to protect me. What would be the point of leaving the second I went inside? But what other option did I have?

Morganna began the slow descent down the mountain back to Frokontas. I hesitated, taking one last look around, and followed her. Something was wrong, but I could hardly stay up the mountain on my own.

"The flare!" I said, remembering I had it in my backpack. "We can set it off."

"What good would that do?"

"Maybe Ash will see it and come to us. Maybe the people down in Frokontas will see it and fly up here."

"I thought you didn't want the dragons flying? Surely it's safer that they stay in their human forms as long as possible?"

I sighed. If Ash was in his dragon form, then he was more likely to develop the illness. Why, oh why, did he shift?

"What's that?" asked Morganna, peering down the hill.

Far below us, something was moving. I pulled out a pair of binoculars I'd packed and focused on whatever it was. When I saw what it was, I couldn't believe it. I passed the binoculars over to Morganna. When she saw who was coming up the hill, she gasped.

"What the...? What are they doing here?"

Alpha and the rest of the Wolvren were charging up the hill. Even though they were so far below us, they were clearly rushing.

"Something's happened in Frokontas," theorized Morganna. "Maybe that's why Ash left so suddenly?"

I took the binoculars back and trained them toward Frokontas, but I couldn't see it from here. Ash wouldn't have been able to either, not even with his amazing sight. The only way to find out the problem was to run down the hill to meet the Wolvren.

I thought it would be easier to go downhill than up, but with the small rocks, we had to take it slowly for fear of slipping. The Wolvren got bigger as we ran toward each other. When we were close enough to see their features, I wasn't comforted by the look of alarm on their faces.

"What is it? What's happened?" I huffed, trying to get my breath back as they approached.

"Didn't you see it?" responded Alpha. "There was smoke on the mountaintop. We thought the Goblins had set fire to their home with you in it."

"Why would they do that?" asked Morganna.

Alpha, in a rare show of affection, hugged her close. "I don't know. I just saw the smoke and I panicked. I asked the dragons to carry us up the cliff face so we could come and check on you. They refused to carry us all the way in case they fell ill, so we ran from the cliff top."

I looked behind me and up to the entrance of the goblin village. "There's no smoke," I said, pointing upward.

"You can't see it from here, but around the side, you could see it from Frokontas. Not that it matters. Now that we know you are both safe, we can take you home."

"No. Ash is up there." Just because I couldn't see any smoke didn't mean there wasn't any. If Ash was in trouble, I needed to get to him. I turned around and began to run back up the mountain, not even hesitating to see if the others were following me.

I heard it before I saw it. About a hundred feet above the entrance to the Goblin village, there came the sound of growling. There was an unmistakable smell of burning in the air, and as I rounded the mountain, I finally saw the smoke that the Wolvren had described.

This side of the mountain was much steeper than the side I was used to. I had to be much more careful as I hedged my way around the side of the peak. Snow crunched under my feet, snow that never melted no matter the time of year thanks to the cold temperatures this high on the mountain.

"Ash!" I called out his name, hoping the growling would stop, but it wasn't just him making the noise. There were two distinctive growls and it sounded as though they were snapping at each other. "Ash!" I screamed again, sending a small avalanche of snow down the mountain just ahead of me. Once the snow had settled, I carefully walked further around the mountain until I saw him.

To my surprise, the other set of growls was not a mountain lion or bear as I'd thought, but another dragon. A yellow-scaled dragon, slightly smaller than Ash, but with dagger-like teeth and bright green eyes. They were on a ledge high above and hadn't noticed me yet.

I was just about to call out for the third time when the earth began to shudder. The Wolvren and Morganna had followed, thundering around the mountain, and had set the snow off again. My feet slipped out from under me, sending me sliding down the mountainside alongside the snow.

Everything in my vision turned white as I began to topple, over and over in the snow. The snow covered me as I tumbled, my hands scrambling and finding nothing but cold wetness, and I fell to my certain death. Either I was going to go over a precipice and die of the fall, or I would be buried in the snow. I wanted to scream, but the snow muffled any sound I made.

A sharp pain seared my side and I found myself falling upward. In my disorientation, I didn't even question my change of direction, just put it down to dizziness, but as my vision cleared and the snow fell away beneath me, I saw that I wasn't falling at all, but being lifted.

The pain I'd felt was, in fact, Ash's talons in my side as he pulled me from the snow. Fire escaped his lips, directed toward the yellow dragon, which had decided to give chase. The yellow dragon breathed fire right back at Ash, narrowly missing me hanging below him. Ash didn't flinch. He wouldn't have felt it thanks to his thick dragon hide, but he turned and headed back toward the mountain, dipping in low and dropping me in a pile of snow near Morganna and the Wolvren.

"Are you ok?" Morganna asked, rushing towards me. Her and Alpha pulled me out of the snow and stood me back upright on the path.

"I'm fine, I think. Just a couple of bruises." I brushed myself off as I watched Ash continue his flight with the yellow dragon hot on his tail. They both headed back around the mountain to the entrance of the Goblin village.

"Who was that chasing Ash?" Alpha asked.

"That is the big question," I replied. "I honestly have no idea."

I took the path back to the safer side of the mountain extremely slowly, cautioning the others to do the same. I whispered to them to keep their voices down as we didn't want to start another avalanche. If we made it to below the snow line, we'd be much safer.

I could hear the snarling again. It seemed the yellow dragon had caught up with Ash. I'd seen plenty of yellow dragons in Frokontas, but I'd never seen one so bright as this one. I tried to picture who it was but came up with nothing. It had to be one of the newly-escaped dragons from my father's sword, but why would he have come up the mountain and what reason did he have for attacking Ash?

I finally made it back to the relative safety of the side of the mountain I was used to and saw Ash again. His giant claw was on the back of the yellow dragon, holding it flat on the ground. It seemed that Ash had won this particular fight, although he wasn't unscathed. Both dragons were covered in scratches and bite marks from the fight.

16

The yellow dragon tried breathing fire at Ash by twisting its neck and aiming for him, but this time, only a puff of smoke emerged. It was apparent that this dragon was weak. As I got closer, I could see the tiredness in its eyes. Chasing Ash through the sky had zapped it of its strength. Still, I didn't want to go too close just in case he found a new burst of energy to barbecue me. I stayed a good distance away, watching to see what would happen next. At first, I thought it was shrinking, but quickly realized it was shifting. As the body turned from a dragon form to that of a human, Ash took a step back. Once it wasn't a dragon anymore, the rest of us could watch it, allowing Ash to shift back, too.

"I need some clothes," I said, turning to the Wolvren pack. "Extra coats, tunics, anything you have on."

It was cold up on the mountain and most of the Wolvren had a lot of layers on. Alpha took off his own coat and handed it to me, followed by a few of the others, removing just one item of clothing each. Between them, we managed to get two full outfits together, one for Ash and one for the yellow dragon. I dropped the clothes for Ash by his feet. He chose to go back behind the boulder we'd left him at originally. The other dragon changed where he was, too weak to do otherwise or unconcerned about being seen in the nude.

As soon as he turned back, it became apparent he wasn't a he at all, but a young woman. Her yellow scales translated into a mane of long, luscious blonde hair, and her sparkling green eyes followed her from one form to the other. I threw the Wolvren clothes at her and waited until she dressed before attempting to speak to her.

She dressed slowly, keeping an eye on all of us. Now that she was in her human form, she looked nothing like the terrifying beast she had been as a dragon. She looked like a young woman, younger than me even, and the fear in her eyes was unmistakable. This was no monster. She was a young girl who was afraid. As I moved toward her, she stepped back.

"I'm not going to hurt you," I said, pulling a first aid kit from my bag and holding it out to show her. "I just want to help you."

She turned and ran, but unfortunately for her, she ran right into Ash, who had just appeared from behind the boulder. She tried to escape, but it was no use; she was too weak. He carried her over and set her down on the ground. I opened the first aid kit and began to work on her cuts and scrapes.

"You'll feel better once I've bandaged you up," I assured her, taking in her wide eyes and look of terror. She didn't say a word as I cleaned her up and bandaged the worst of her scratches.

I'd almost finished when she finally spoke. "Where am I?" she asked in a small voice.

"This is the Triad Mountains," I answered. "Don't you know? How did you get here?"

She gazed around her as if trying to remember something. "I was here," she began. "It was a long time ago, I think. I don't remember exactly when. I was hunting for food when...when someone attacked me with a sword. He was a huge man with a shaggy beard. Then, a few days ago, I came back. I feel like I've been gone a long time, but I don't remember anything since then."

No prizes for guessing who the man with the shaggy beard was. My father. That's why she'd appeared up here and didn't know why. My father must have attacked her at some time in the past and taken her soul. When I let the dragons go, her soul would have come back to her body. I just couldn't understand why her body hadn't been taken down to the Slayer village like all the others. I also didn't understand how he'd managed to climb all the way up here. It was incredibly difficult to get so high up the mountain without the help of a dragon.

"Did my father...Did this man attack you up here?"

She shook her head. "He attacked me farther down the mountain, but after he stabbed me, I managed to escape. I flew up here and then everything went black. I felt a whooshing sensation as though I was being pulled from my body."

"That would have been your soul," I replied, moving from her to Ash, who had also suffered from scratches and bites in the fight.

"What?" she asked, confused.

"My father's sword didn't kill; it trapped dragon souls. He tried to get you, but he didn't push the sword in far enough. It meant that it was only later when your soul escaped and, as you say, 'whooshed' down the mountain to his sword. I let all the dragons free from his sword a week ago. That's when you came back up the mountain to your body."

She gazed at me uncomprehending as I turned to Ash, to bandage up his scratches.

"Why did you attack me?" he asked her.

"Is that what happened?" asked Morganna. "She attacked you?"

"Yeah. I was just sitting here waiting for you to come back when she flew out of the sky and attacked."

"I'm sorry," she said, bursting into tears. "I was scared. I didn't know what had happened to me and then I saw you and thought you might hurt me."

"Well, you did a good job of hurting *me!*" He held out his arm so I could clean the dried blood from it.

"Do you know each other?" I asked.

"No," they chorused.

"She's not from Frokontas."

"I'm not from around here at all," she admitted. "I ran away from home. I can't even remember how far I traveled looking for food before flying up this mountain. I thought I might find a mountain goat to eat, but instead, I found the man that hurt me. He was your father, you say?"

"It's a long story, one for another day," I said, finishing up with Ash. "Do you know how to get home?"

She shook her head sadly. "My brain feels fuzzy, like I've been asleep for a very long time. I can't even remember which direction my home is. I wish I'd never left."

I turned to Ash. "Do you know of any other dragon colonies near here?"

"No," he answered, standing up and checking the bandages I'd put on him.

"I've heard of other colonies in this mountain range," remembered Morganna. "I wanted to go and find them in my youth. I wanted to be the one who slayed all the dragons."

The girl flinched at this admission.

"Don't worry, I don't do that anymore," she assured the girl. "But I do know of other colonies to the south. It's possible she came from there."

"Do you remember your name?" I asked her. I couldn't keep thinking of her as 'the girl.'

"Avery."

"Well, Avery, we can't leave you here. You can come down the mountain with us. You'll be looked after in Frokontas. It's a dragon village."

Ash pulled my arm and took me to one side. "Do you think that's wise? She might get sick like the others."

I looked back at her. Her face was pale, her lips chapped and she looked so tired with black circles under her eyes. "She was trapped in my father's sword like the others. There's a good chance she's already sick."

He nodded. "I guess you're right. If she is sick already, we'll need to keep her in her human form so she doesn't get worse."

The journey down the mountain was arduous. The muscles at the back of my legs burned with the exertion. Ash offered to fly me down the mountain, but I refused, knowing it wouldn't be fair to everyone else, not least to Avery who looked as worn out as I felt. The original plan had been to walk down to the cliff top and set off the flare so that someone could come and fly us down the cliff into the village. However, because of our slow going, it was already dark by the time we reached the cliff edge.

The lights of Frokontas twinkled down below, but the huge fire in the fire pit was extinguished for the day. Nevertheless, I pulled out the flare and set it off. It lit up the whole sky, then fizzled out. I found a rock to sit on and waited. After five minutes it became apparent that no one was going to come for us.

"Ash, you're going to have to fly down there and let them know we need help."

He nodded, pulling his clothes off quickly, disappearing behind a bush. "You can come down with me and find Spear," he commanded. "I'll fly back up and bring some more down. Between the two of us, we can get everyone down to the ground in only a few journeys."

"I can fly some people down," said Avery, gazing down into the valley.

"No!" we all shouted making her jump.

"Stay in your human form," I said. I didn't want to tell her that the dragons who were trapped in my father's sword were getting sick. She was afraid enough as it was.

"You look tired," I improvised. "And you don't know exactly where to drop us."

She nodded, accepting my reasons.

Ash's voice came from behind the bush. "Julianna, can you come back here, please?"

I looked at Morganna who shrugged. The scene that greeted me when I walked around the bush made me open my mouth in shock. He stood there with his trousers on, but no top, exposing his bare chest. Across the chest and over the shoulder was a deep scratch that was still gushing blood.

"Why didn't you tell me about this earlier?" I asked, scrabbling for the first aid kit once again. I thought about our long walk down the mountain. The t-shirt he'd been wearing was drenched in blood. He'd tossed it to the floor along with a coat he'd been wearing over it. That's why I hadn't noticed.

"I didn't know it was so bad. I thought it would stop bleeding."

I looked down at the cut. A first aid kit wasn't going to help much, but at least I could clean the wound. "You are going to need stitches." I pulled out some cleaning ointment and poured it on a cotton swab. He winced as the fluid dripped into the deep cut. "Lift your arm," I ordered, pulling out the last of the bandages.

"There's no point putting that on. It will only tear off when I shift into a dragon."

I looked him square in the eye. "That's not going to

happen. Turning into a dragon will rip your skin to shreds in this condition."

"So, how will we get down?"

"It looks like Avery will have to go down for help after all."

17

I quietly explained to Morganna the problem with Ash. She agreed that we'd have to ask Avery to go for help.

Avery was sitting waiting on a rock, looking down at the ground. She appeared upset and unsure. I could hardly blame her. She was stuck on a cliffside with a group of people she didn't know, including two self-confessed Slayers, one of whom was the daughter of the man who trapped her in his sword for so long.

"Avery." She looked up and gave me a shy smile. I just wanted to pick her up and put her in my pocket. "Ash is injured. He can't shift without hurting himself. Would you mind going down the cliff after all?"

Her hand went to her mouth. "Oh, I'm sorry." She looked behind me as Ash emerged from behind the boulder, now with his shirt and coat back on.

He smiled warmly back at her. "It's no problem. You were scared. I hurt you, too. We'll have to chalk it up to experience, but I can't shift. My skin is torn across my shoulder."

"I said I'd go down and I will," she said, standing up. She looked even smaller now. I'd put her at seventeen or eighteen years old, but now that I'd looked at her properly, I saw I was wrong. I'd be surprised if she was a day over fifteen.

"Can you see that house over there?" I asked, pointing to Spear's house in the distance. She nodded. "Fly down there and find a man called Spear. He'll send someone up to carry us all down. Tell him that Ash is okay but unable to shift. You don't have to tell him that it's because the pair of you were fighting. Don't turn back into your dragon form."

She nodded again, this time disappearing behind the bush that Ash had just emerged from.

"Wouldn't it be better if one of us goes down with her?" asked Ash. It hadn't occurred to me, but he was right.

Less than a minute later the bright yellow dragon came out and readied herself for flight. I ran up to her, hoping she'd hear me before flying away. She hesitated and looked at me.

"I'm coming with you. Is that alright?"

She nodded, so I jumped on her back.

It felt weird being airborne with someone other than Ash. The thrill of flying was still there, but I found I had to hold on tighter to Avery. We weren't as in sync as Ash and I were when we flew together. I'd been flying with him for so long now that I knew instinctively which way he was going to turn, whether he was going to do a dive, or when he was just gliding through the air. I could fly on his back and almost never have to hold on, just adjust my body to match the way he was flying. With Avery, I had to hold on to her neck. She glided all the way over Frokontas, coming to a stop in Spear's garden. I hopped down and told her to wait where she was. Running inside, I bumped into Edeline.

"Julianna!" she exclaimed. "You're back. How did it go?"

I shook my head. "Not great. The Goblins wouldn't tell us anything. I doubt they ever will. Is Spear around?"

"He's outside with the sick dragons. Are you ok?"

"I'm fine, but Ash got hurt and couldn't bring us down the mountain. He's okay," I reassured her. "Nothing that a few days of healing won't cure, but everyone is trapped up there."

"I'll go get them. Are they on the ledge?"

"Yes, but I'd prefer Spear to go. I've got another job for you if you don't mind."

"What is it?"

I guided her to the window. Avery was still in her dragon form, curled up on the grass.

"Who is that?" Edeline asked.

"She's a runaway from another colony. She's been in my father's sword so long, she can't remember her way home. I was hoping you could find some clothes for her, then bring her inside. She's very thin. I think she's in sore need of a good meal."

Edeline nodded and followed me outside. I ran to the makeshift hospital while Edeline went to help Avery. I found Spear talking to my father at the far end of the hospital. So many dragons were laid out on the floor unconscious that it looked just like the prison in the woods near Dronias, except these dragons did have their souls.

"Julianna," he greeted me. "Success?"

"Not really. I'll tell you about it later. The others are up on the ledge. Can you go and get them?"

"Can't Ash bring Morganna down?"

"No, he's hurt. It's not bad, but he can't shift right now."

Spear furrowed his brow. "So how did you get down?"

"It's a long story. It's not just Morganna up there. Ash is still up there, and the Wolvren too."

Spear sighed. "I really don't want anyone turning into their dragon form at the moment. Too many dragons are getting sick."

"You can't leave them up there, Spear," responded my father.

To my amazement, Spear clapped him on the shoulder as one would an old friend. "You're right. I'll do it myself and bring them down a couple at a time. It shouldn't take more than half an hour to get them all."

"What was all that about?" I asked once Spear had left.

"I've been on my best behavior. We've come to a truce of sorts."

"I'm glad to hear it," I replied. "Dare I ask what brought about this turn of events?"

He looked around him at all the dragons with a look of regret on his face. "I've seen dragons looking like this many times. I'd often go to the building where we held the bodies to rejoice over my power. I know it sounds pathetic now, but back then I thought I was all powerful. Seeing just how many bodies I'd slain made me feel like a big man. Spear and I have our differences, but seeing how much he wants these dragons to get well has made me realize just how much damage I've caused. Slaying dragons didn't make me a big man. Quite the opposite. It made me very small indeed. Trying to save the people in the village, doing everything in his power to help them, including giving up his time and garden. That makes Spear a bigger man than me. I never cared about the people in Dronias as much as Spear cares about the people here. I pretended I did, but the truth was, I wanted everyone to look up to me." He grabbed a cloth and began to mop the brow of one of the slumbering dragons. "I feel such guilt at my actions."

I smiled at him. "It sounds like you are willing to put things right."

"I am. I said that when we first started this journey, but again, I think I was trying to exert my power. Now, I really do want to help. I don't know what is wrong with these people but I'm going to do everything I can to fix it. I know you said that the Goblins wouldn't help you, but I'll bet everything I own that they know what's wrong."

I sighed. He was probably right, but after three attempts at climbing up there, I'd finally given up hope of them ever helping us.

"How did you get down here if Ash didn't bring you? Don't tell me you climbed down."

"I'd break my neck attempting to do that. Come with me and I'll show you."

I took my father into the house. Avery and Edeline

were both in the dining room. Avery was devouring a salad that Edeline had made for her. A plate of mini muffins was next to it on the table.

"Father, this is Avery. She's a dragon from another colony. Avery, this is my father, Rocco."

At me mentioning who he was, her eyes went wide. The fear in them was obvious.

"Are you..." My father turned to me. "Was she in..."

"Yes, Father. Avery was one of the dragons you slayed. When she was released, her soul went to the mountain peak where her body remained. We found her when we were visiting the Goblins."

"My child," he said, moving toward her. She flinched. "Please don't be afraid of me. I'm not going to hurt you. Not anymore."

"I remember you now," she said.

"I'm sorry. Truly sorry for what I did to you. All I can do is promise that it will never happen again. Please forgive me."

I watched with bated breath. She had no reason to forgive him. It was because of him that she was lost and alone.

She gave a timid smile and picked up the plate of muffins, offering one to my father. He took the whole plate, set it down on the table, and gave her a hug. I couldn't see his face from where I was standing, but his body moved as though he was sobbing silently. I decided to leave them there. My father had a lot of making up to do and it was up to him to decide how he was going to do that. An evening speaking with Avery might be good for both of them. If my father meant what he said, and I believed he did, then maybe when this was all over, he'd help Avery find her way home.

Outside, I only had the starlight to help me see Spear, but as I watched, a dark silhouette of a dragon carrying three people came in to land. Morganna, Alpha and another of the Wolvren hopped down and headed over to me.

"It's been a long night," Morganna said to me as Spear took off again. "We are going to head to bed." She took Alpha's hand and the two of them headed to the houses in the cliff face. The other Wolvren walked past me into the house. Spear must have let him sleep there.

Ash was the last to be brought down. Once Spear was back in his human form, we took Ash to the outside hospital where Spear patched him up a lot better than I had. Stitches pinched together the long hole in his shoulder and chest that Avery had made in the fight.

"That's going to scar," said Spear, finishing up his work.

"It's okay, we'll match," I said meaning the scars on my own body. I took Ash's hand and bade farewell to Spear.

Together, we walked the same path Alpha and Morganna had taken fifteen minutes earlier. The night was quiet, with a slight hint of a chill. Ash took off his coat and gave it to me, exposing the bloody mess of his shirt.

"Do you think this will ever be over?" I asked him. "It seems that no matter what we do, nothing gets any better."

He put his arm around me. "I want to be positive and say yes, but I honestly don't know. I don't see how we can fix everything without the Goblins, and they are refusing to help. Maybe it's time that we admitted defeat and treat those soulless dragons back in Dronias as dead. That's what we thought they were for the longest time. We've already done our mourning for them."

I sighed. I hated that he was talking this way. I had been hoping that he would cheer me up like he always did. "It's not just the dragons back in Dronias though, is it? The dragons here are sick, too."

"Maybe we should mourn them, too," Ash replied.

With that sobering thought in mind, we let ourselves into his house and fell asleep in his bed.

18

Ash slept fitfully, moaning in his sleep due to the pain in his shoulder. My own body was still sore, and even though I'd been liberally applying Edeline's burn cream, it still appeared red and flaky in patches. Because of his moaning and my own pain, I couldn't sleep. I got out of bed and made my way to the balcony in the hopes that some fresh air would make me feel sleepier. In the dim moonlight, I saw someone heading up the path to the fire pit and cliffside houses.

I waited until I could see definitely who it was before heading downstairs to open the door and welcome her home.

"You're out late," I pointed out as Edeline walked through the door.

Firecracker ran up to her, wagging her tail, to which Edeline gave her a stroke behind the ears. "Yeah," she replied wearily. "It's been a long night. So much went on since you left."

She looked so tired. I'd been so caught up in my own stuff, I'd not really put a thought to the people of Frokontas who were working through the night in shifts to look after the ailing dragons.

"Would you like me to make you a pot of fruit tea?" I offered as she took off her coat and hung it up.

She gave me a grateful smile. "I'd love it. Thank you."

I was eager to find out what had gone on over at Spear's house. It had been pretty quiet when we left and I couldn't imagine what could have gone wrong now. And something had gone wrong. Edeline looked not just tired but resigned, too.

I ran up to the kitchen and poured a couple of cups of fruit tea. Edeline appeared a few minutes later with a bottle full of clear liquid which she added to her cup.

"Sleeping draught," she answered my unasked question. "I'm so utterly exhausted, but I know I won't sleep. There's just too much going on. Would you like some? You look pretty sleepy yourself."

I shook my head. "I'm not going to be able to sleep even with that. Ash is tossing and turning and moaning in his sleep. Spear stitched his shoulder, but it still hurts him."

"I'll sort him out," she said, picking the sleeping draught bottle up and leaving the kitchen. Five minutes later she was back. She poured what was left of the clear liquid in my cup.

"It's herbal and won't hurt you," she said with a wink. "I've given some to Ash, too. That will knock him out for the night. You'll both wake tomorrow morning feeling like you've had the best sleep of your life. You'll probably need it after hearing what I'm about to tell you."

I grabbed a couple of cookies that Edeline had baked earlier and handed one to her. I had a feeling I was going to need some sugar.

"So, what happened? Was it my father?"

If there was trouble, I could count on the fact my father was involved. Despite what he said to me earlier about turning over a new leaf, I wouldn't be surprised if he was already getting under people's noses. It was in his nature.

"Actually, no. It was that girl you brought home, Avery."

I arched a brow. "Avery was causing trouble? She did attack Ash, but she said she felt threatened. I believed her."

"Oh, I'm sure she did. I don't mean she was trying to hurt anyone. Quite the opposite. The poor thing is terrified. She's just a kid. Rocco has taken her under his wing and given her a bed to sleep in at Spear's house. He's decided to stay there, too, to protect her. I told them both I'd head back tomorrow."

"Protect her? Why?"

"It all started when Spear had some people over for dinner. The Wolvren who were staying with him, the dragons that had developed the sickness in human form, and all the volunteers helping with the sick dragons. He's got quite a house full at the moment."

She paused to take a sip of her tea, leaving me hanging.

"Then what happened?"

"The Wolvren mentioned to everyone where they

found her, up on the top of the Triad Mountains. One of the Slayers, I think it was Jasper, asked her how long she'd been there. It turns out that in the couple of days she was lost up the mountain, she heard a bit about what was going on with the Goblins. Apparently, they didn't realize she was there as she spent the last week curled up and hiding behind some rocks. She overheard quite a bit about us and the Slayers when they came and went from the entrance."

My heart jumped. All those times we'd gone up the mountain and learned nothing and Avery had heard something by accident. Maybe we should have spent time hiding behind rocks by the entrance rather than blustering in every time. "What did she hear?"

Edeline put her head in her hands. "She seems to think the Goblins are out to get us. That they wanted to be rid of the dragons a long time ago and that selling swords to the Slayers was their way of doing it."

"I don't understand. What would selling the swords to the Slayers do for the Goblins?"

"The dragon souls are what power Goblin magic. Avery says that a long, long time ago, they killed the dragons themselves, but they are small creatures and do not have the skill for fighting. So, they invited warriors and village leaders in from the nearby villages to offer to make them magic swords. That's how the Slayers became Slayers. Before that point, the people in the villages and the dragons had lived peacefully."

I could quite well believe that the Goblins had somehow started this, but it made no sense. "If the dragon souls create the Goblin magic, how does it help them if the Slayers have the souls?"

"That is the question," she replied, standing up and rinsing her cup out. "Avery doesn't know. She didn't hear any more."

I felt the sleeping draught begin to take effect. My eyelids became heavy and when Edeline yawned, I caught it. I headed to bed, my mind racing, but almost as soon as my head hit the pillow, I was out.

Edeline was right. The sleeping draught helped me sleep like a baby, but nothing could stop me waking up to the noise outside the next day.

"What's that?" Ash mumbled from under the covers.

I snuggled up to him, enjoying the warmth of his body, wishing that just for once, there wasn't a problem to deal with. It had been a long time since we'd slept in a bed, and getting out of it hadn't been on my to-do list for today.

"I don't know. It's probably got something to do with what Avery told your mother last night." I sighed, pulling the covers further over my head to block out the noise. I could already tell that there was an argument brewing outside and no doubt I'd have to deal with it.

"What did she tell her?" he asked, jumping out of bed and inadvertently pulling the covers off me. He found a clean shirt from his wardrobe. I watched as he pulled it over his scarred torso. We really were a pair, covered in scars. It suited him, made him look dangerous.

I reluctantly dragged myself out of bed and tripped on the bloody shirt from yesterday that was still in a heap on the floor. I picked it up, along with the other dirty clothes, and made a mental note to wash them if I ever found the time. I dressed quickly and followed Ash out of the house.

It seemed like half the town was already at the fire pit, including all the Wolvren and Slayers. Unfortunately, no one had thought to light the fire and start breakfast. My stomach rumbled as I remembered I'd not eaten dinner yesterday. There was a lot of noise, with everyone shouting to be heard. I scanned the group to find my father. He was uncharacteristically quiet, sitting between Edeline and Avery, but then he did have a sandwich in his mouth. Once again, I wished I'd thought to get something to eat before coming out.

"What's going on?" I asked Edeline, finding a place to sit beside her. Ash took my other side.

"The Wolvren told everyone about the Goblins. The dragons are really mad."

"I bet they are. What do you think, Father?" I asked, peering around Edeline to speak to him.

"I'm keeping out of it," he replied, taking a bite of his sandwich. "I told you last night that I wasn't going to argue with people anymore, that I was going to try to keep the peace. Well, now, I'm going to go with the majority. I'll let someone else decide for a change. Besides, the Slayers are getting their say." He nodded towards the other side of the fire pit.

I looked over to see Jasper screaming at one of the Wolvren, while Xander was in a heated discussion with one of the dragons. "Why does it always descend into chaos when the three groups get together?" I sighed.

Ash chuckled. "I'm just surprised your father isn't in the middle of all this," he whispered in my ear.

"He's a new man!" I informed him.

I listened to the arguments going on around me. It sounded like everyone had a different opinion. The dragons wanted to go back up to the Goblin village and burn it down. The Slayers weren't so sure, as they feared the magical repercussions if they tried. Morganna reasoned that if they did manage to kill all the Goblins, no one would be able to find the rest of the swords, and even if we did, we wouldn't be able to free the dragon souls from them. Finally, the Wolvren just wanted to go home.

I was just about to try and do something to stop the shouting when Spear arrived, looking distraught. He seemed as annoyed at the ruckus as I was. He stood on the side of the fire pit and tried shouting to get everyone's attention. Unfortunately for him, I was the only one who noticed him. His shouts were ineffective over all the noise.

I stood up and Ash grabbed my hand.

"Where are you going?"

I pulled my hand back. "You'll see."

Heading back into the house, I ran up the stairs, Firecracker hot on my heels, and emerged onto the balcony. Below, I could see everyone arguing. Some had already come to blows.

"You might want to go inside for this," I warned Firecracker. She just looked up at me and wagged her tail. Putting two fingers in my mouth, I whistled as loudly as I could. Everyone—every dragon, every Slayer, and every Wolvren—looked my way. I was going to verbally kick some ass and they all knew it!

19

It was strange having everyone look at me, but I didn't feel daunted. The ridiculous fighting had gone on long enough.

"We are all on the same side!" I shouted down to them. "We all want to live in peace, side by side, but we can't do that with the incessant, petty squabbles that occur daily."

As I spoke, a few of the people in the crowd nodded their heads.

"Our three tribes have a long history of hatred between each other. You all know that, but you should also know how that hate started. The Slayers weren't always in the business of killing dragons, and the dragons didn't always hate the Wolvren. One time in history, we all lived together peacefully. However, a great many years ago, the Goblins realized they could harvest magic in the form of dragon souls. It's no secret that dragons are magical beings."

"We can't do magic," shouted Ally.

"Of course you can. You might not be able to wave a wand, but you can shift your entire bodies. That is magic. You defy physics every time you change from a dragon to a human and become a quarter of the size. Dragons are born with a magic that is pure. The Goblins saw that and wanted it for themselves.

"For those of you who have met the Goblins, you'll know they aren't built to fight, but they are cunning. They spread the rumor that the dragons were killers. Just a hint here and there, but before long, those hints became full-blown rumors. When it was common knowledge that the dragons were dangerous, they offered to make special swords for the people in the surrounding villages. Over time those people became Slayers. The Slayers hunted the dragons because they thought they were dangerous, and the dragons fought back, thus proving the Goblins were telling the truth."

I paused for a breath and to let everyone take in this new information. I was embellishing on what Avery had said, filling in the gaps.

"Once the Slayers were slaying, the stockpile of dragon souls grew. The more swords the Goblins made, the more souls were collected."

"None of this makes sense," replied Ally. "The souls have been in the swords for a long time. Some of them over a hundred years. If the Slayers still have the swords, or had them up until recently, then the Goblins didn't even have the souls."

He had a point. We still had the swords and therefore, we still had the souls, too. I'd been so caught up in what Avery had heard and spun my own theory around it without thinking it through.

Below me, everyone began to argue again. I'd messed up. What did I know about being a leader? I couldn't even get everyone to stop bickering for more than two minutes. Kick ass. Ha!

"There has to be meaning behind this," I shouted down, "Maybe the Goblins have been trying to get the swords back, or to figure a way to release the souls themselves."

"You'd think they already know how to do that," another dragon replied, not bothering to hide the contempt in his voice. "They were the ones who made the swords. They'd be a bit stupid if they made them to collect souls without making a way to get the souls out."

"Fine," I agreed. "Maybe they just haven't found a way to get the swords back yet." I said it, but I didn't believe it. They'd not even attempted to get the swords back. In all the times we went up to the Goblin village, no one tried to take our swords from us. I was missing something, but I didn't know what. There had to be meaning to it, but I couldn't quite see it.

"Can I come up and see you?" someone asked. I looked for the voice and saw it was Morganna. After I nodded yes, she cut through the crowd and made her way through the house up to the balcony.

"Well, I really messed that up, didn't I?" I asked, feeling dejected. Sure, the squabbling had temporarily abated, but my theory had hit a blank wall. Maybe Avery had misheard the Goblins, or I'd interpreted what she'd heard wrongly.

"Actually, I've been thinking about something ever since we were up at the Goblin village. I think you're right and I think I know why."

"Why?"

"When I was there the first time with you, I felt the magic all around us. I felt it when I first went to the Goblins many years ago to purchase some of it, and I felt it again this last time. Each time I visited, the magical energy was more diminished, as if it was getting smaller. Magic is just a form of energy like any other. It might be slightly more mystical than, say, the electricity in a lightning spark or the flow of a river, but it is energy, nonetheless. The first time I ventured up there all those years ago, the air crackled with it. You could feel it on your skin. It was almost too much to be in the village for too long. The energy I felt the last time we were up there was almost non-existent."

"You mean they're running out?"

"I believe so, yes. Because magic is energy, it lasts eternally unless it's used. The Goblins could have had enough of this magic energy to last a great number of years. Hundreds even. If they took back the swords from the Slayers after a year or so, the Slayers would stop coming to have them made, and so the Goblins would have very few souls to work with. Why not make swords for as long as they could get away with it, or as long as their magic held out, until they decided to take them back? Goblins live for much longer than either humans or dragons. A hundred years or so is nothing to them."

I mulled over what she was saying. "So you think the Goblins are close to the last of their magic?"

Morganna nodded her head sagely. "I'm sure of it. I think they'll be coming for the swords soon."

"Well, they've got no chance of getting them," I huffed. "The ones that still hold dragons are at Spear's house. If they even tried getting down the mountain into the valley, they'd have to fight dragons, Slayers, *and* Wolvren.

"You forget who we are talking about. The Goblins will not fight. They are too clever for that. I think they'll try and take the swords some other way."

"What other way?" I asked, not liking the sound of what she was telling me.

"I don't know, but Goblins are extremely dangerous. They hide it well, but they don't hurry things. Whatever they are thinking of doing will have been their game plan for a long time. They'll stop at nothing to get what they want, and they'll think nothing of killing anyone who tries to get in their way."

"We need to tell Spear!"

I ran downstairs and asked Edeline and Fiere if we could invite some people inside. It wasn't just Spear we had to tell. We brought in Spear, my father, and Alpha as the three leaders, along with Fiere and Edeline themselves. Edeline brewed a pot of tea while Morganna shared her thoughts with everyone.

Spear furrowed his brow. "Are you sure about this?"

"No, I'm not sure," replied Morganna. "Most of what I've told you is conjecture, but I think it would be reckless to ignore the signs. The Goblins will have held just enough magic power back to annihilate all of us if they need to. I believe we are headed for a war, ladies and gentlemen, and it isn't going to be pretty."

No one spoke for a good minute until my father broke the silence. "I bet you wish you could go back to just worrying about the Slayers now, eh?" He clapped Spear on the back.

"We need to come up with a plan," I jumped in. "If Morganna is right and the Goblins are about to attack using the last of their magic, we need to make sure everyone is safe. Spear, can you organize the dragons? Tell them that they have to stay indoors until we can determine the threat. I think they'd be better bringing everyone to the houses in the cliff face. They are safer than the houses in the village. You'll have to ask the inhabitants to let more people in."

"The people in these houses are already allowing Wolvren, Slayers and those returned dragons with no homes to stay with them. There's no space."

"They'll have to make space," I insisted. "People can sleep on couches or the floor. It's only until we figure out what the Goblins are up to."

"We can fit more in," offered Edeline as she poured the tea for us. "Lucy can sleep in with us for a few nights, can't she, Fiere?"

"Of course," he replied. "We need to keep the people in the village safe."

"Father, can you take the Slayers home?" I asked as I looked to Spear. "Spear, he'll need someone to shift into their dragon form to get them up the cliff so they can go through the tunnels to the other side."

"Okay, but we'll take them right back to Dronias. It's not much difference. I doubt anyone will get sick in the time it takes to get there and back."

"Hang on a minute," my father interjected. "Why are the Slayers going back to Dronias?"

"Because Dronias is the first place they'll look for the swords. Everyone there needs to be kept out of harm's way, too."

"So, you want me to just go home and hide, do you?" he blustered.

"Not at all. I want you to organize the village, get everyone safe, and then come back so we can plan how to deal with the Goblins."

He nodded. "I understand what you are saying, but I'm needed here. I'll send the others back, putting Xander in charge. Jasper can go and take your mother to safety."

I turned to Alpha. "I know you want to go home. I'm not going to stop you. I'm sure the dragons will fly you back up the—"

"Stop right there," he said, cutting me off. "It's true that this fight does not involve us. We have no swords or souls, but I would not think of abandoning you at this time. I would not abandon Morganna, and I know she will want to stay to fight."

"Too bloody right I will!" she responded, giving him a kiss.

"That's settled then. We'll make sure everyone in Frokontas and Dronias are safe and then we'll meet back here and decide what we are going to do."

I picked up my tea and drank it down in one gulp. I had a feeling that I was going to be too busy over the next few days to be drinking tea again. I stood up as if to leave, but before I could, Ash came rushing through the door. His face was red and he was breathing heavily as if he'd just been running. Fear was etched onto his face.

"What is it?" Edeline asked in alarm, taking in the expression on her son's face.

"Good, you're all together," he wheezed. "You need to come with me. Something weird is happening.

20

Ash didn't give us time to question him; he was already out the door. Chairs squeaked on the floor as everyone else stood up in a panic. All I could think as we followed Ash out of the house was that the Goblins were attacking. Would we even be safe out there? Would everyone else be safe? We'd not had the chance to tell everyone to stay indoors yet. Had we run out of time?

Part of me remembered Morganna saying that they didn't attack individually. They didn't fight in the way we did with swords, but then I remembered her telling us that a war was coming. If they were going to attack, they would do it with what was left of their magic. As we ran outside, I looked for signs of what this magic might be, but apart from a few startled people still around the fire pit, nothing had changed. I looked upward toward the Goblin village. It was impossible to see from here, but I figured if anything was going to come for us, that was the direction it would come from.

Everything appeared normal there, too. The sky was a lovely shade of pale blue with a few clouds lazily scudding across it. There was nothing to suggest that we were close to an attack. The only sounds I could hear were the usual sounds of birdsong. If it wasn't for the panicked look on Ash's face, I wouldn't have thought this day was different from any other. He was already a long way ahead, sprinting, it seemed, to Spear's house. I felt a knot in my stomach at the thought that it might be something to do with the sick dragons. Maybe something weird was happening to them and it had nothing to do with the Goblins after all.

I watched Ash run up the stairs to Spear's front door ahead of me. A minute later and I followed, with the others behind me. Ash stood in the entrance hall, bent doubled over as if completely winded by the run.

"What is it?" asked Spear, crashing in behind me.

"Come with me." Ash beckoned us into a room I'd not been in before. It was sparsely decorated with only a couple of chairs. In the very center were two piles of swords. I knew them immediately. On the left were the swords that I'd freed the dragon souls from and on the right were the swords I had yet to do. Seeing them side by side, it was obvious which were which. The ones with the souls still in them looked brand new. They sparkled, whereas the others were dull with burn marks on them from when the dragons had escaped.

Behind me, the others filed in as Ash pointed to the pile of sparkling swords. I tried to figure out what was wrong, but they looked the same as they always did. There was something wrong with the air though. I couldn't put my finger on it. It was a feeling that something was wrong. The hair on my arms stood on end.

"Goblin magic," Morganna said. "It's strong here. They must be using a lot of it."

So that's what I could feel. The room felt charged somehow, but apart from the feeling, I couldn't see exactly what the Goblins had done.

"What did you see, Ash?" asked Fiere.

"When you all went into our house, I decided to check on the sick dragons. I'd just got to the house when I heard a loud bang. When I came inside, there was another bang. Actually, it was more like a popping sound. It took me a few seconds to figure out what was making it. The swords. They are disappearing."

Almost as soon as he'd said it there was a loud popping sound followed by a whoosh of wind. One of the swords disappeared into thin air in a flash of light.

"Since I last looked, about ten have disappeared just like that."

"Ten in the last fifteen minutes. At this rate, they'll all be gone by the end of the day," I said.

As I spoke there was another pop. This time, I dove on the top sword that was glowing slightly. The whoosh of wind flew past my ears and the sword lit up brightly before disappearing from my hands, scalding them as it went.

"I think I'm going to need more of your cream Edeline," I said, looking down at my red palms. They weren't burned badly, but enough to know that it was impossible to stop the swords from disappearing.

"Are you ok?" asked Ash, running over to me.

I nodded. "It's nothing major."

Ash rolled his eyes. "Why is it that whenever something explodes, you are in the center of it?"

"It hardly exploded," I countered. "That's not really the problem right now. Our main concern is knowing if this is all the Goblins are going to do or should we expect worse to come?"

All eyes pointed at Morganna who shrugged her shoulders. "I don't know. I already told you that I was theorizing."

"Well, it certainly seems that you were right about the Goblins wanting the swords. If they are taking them that way, by magic, then I assume that they won't need to come into Frokontas. However, I don't want to leave it to chance. We'll follow the original plan and get everyone safely in the cliff-side houses before planning what to do next. Edeline, Fiere, can you go and round up as many people in the village as you can and get them to the cliffs? Alpha and Morganna, can you go and knock on the doors of people in the houses there and ask them to let the others in? Tell them I said they have to if they refuse."

The four nodded their heads and made to leave, but my father stopped them.

"Wait. What about the swords?"

"What about them?" replied Spear. "They've gone and we can't stop the goblins from taking more." Just as he said it there was another pop and whoosh of wind and another went. "See?" pointed Spear. "We'll deal with it later, but now I have to get my people and your people to safety."

"What I mean is," began my father patiently, or as patiently as my father ever was, "if Morganna is right and they are taking the swords to use the dragon souls to turn into magic, wouldn't it be better to let the villagers fend for themselves and get the rest of us up the mountain before they essentially kill those dragons?"

We all looked at him as his words sank in. We had to make a decision and fast.

"What do you think?" asked Spear, surprising me. Everyone looked at me.

They wanted me to make the decision. The weight of everything felt heavy upon my shoulders. If I chose wrongly it could cost a great many lives. I weighed up what we should do before speaking.

"I didn't see any signs of magic outside, but we are vulnerable here. This valley is enclosed which makes us sitting ducks. I say we go with the original plan and get everyone to the cliffs as quickly as possible." I looked down at the pile of swords. There were still a lot there. It would be a few hours before they all vanished. We had a bit of time. Not much, but enough.

"We'll all go. It will be quicker with the eight of us doing it. Then we can work out what we are going to do from there."

"Who's going to guard the swords?" asked Edeline as another one vanished into thin air.

"There's no point keeping guard over them. We can't stop them disappearing, whether we watch them or not. We need someone to stay here to watch over the sick, though. There are still a few people inside the house and the dragons in the building in the garden."

"I'll stay," Ash said. "Just make sure you come back

for me when you go up the mountain. I don't want to miss out on some prime Goblin kicking."

"Thank you," I said, kissing his cheek.

The eight of us dashed out of the house, with my father turning one way to the makeshift hospital and everyone else racing into the village. Spear and Edeline took the farmhouses while the rest of us knocked on doors in the village center.

It took nearly two hours to get everyone into the cliff houses. Many of the dragons were scared and more than a few had to be persuaded to leave their own houses. With each second that passed, the fear in me grew. Fear that we were about to be attacked down here, fear that we were leaving it too late to save the dragons in the swords, and the nagging thought that I could have solved the problem by using the swords to cut myself, thus releasing them all. I tried to put the thought to one side. I would be dead long before I got through all of them, and yet I still felt guilty, as though I should have done more.

"I think that's everyone," puffed Spear as we met around the fire pit. A few others had joined us after finding out why we were moving everyone. All the Wolvren were there, as were all the Slayers, save my father who was still back at Spear's house. Ally and Stone were there, as were a number of other dragons.

"We have quite an army," I pointed out as we all formed a circle around the fire pit. I looked up to see Lucy looking down at us from a window. Firecracker was beside her, but the rest of her family were with me by the fire. A lump formed in my throat as I realized, there was a chance she'd never see any of them again if we did head up the mountain.

There was still no sign of magic. The beautiful weather belied the situation we were in, but I knew then that we were at war. Whether the goblins came down to us, or we went up to them, it didn't matter. Fighting them was inevitable.

"Right, everybody!" I shouted. "You are here because we are going to fight the Goblins. This is not going to be a war without casualties. I'm not going to ask any of you to come with me up the mountain. The choice belongs to each and every one of you, but I want it to be clear that we are going up there to fight."

I looked at the people at the fireside, waiting for some of them to turn away, to go to the relative safety of the houses, but no one moved. All I saw was the resolute expressions on their faces. Every single one of them had been affected by the Goblins somehow. Every one of them had a reason to fight.

"As you have all made your choice, follow me." I turned toward the path that led away from the cliff face.

"Follow you where?" one of the dragons asked. "I thought we were going up the mountain?"

"Oh, we are, but there is someone we have to pick up first."

There was no way I was leaving my father behind. He might have been a lot of things, but he was a Slayer first and foremost. There was no one I wanted on my side more than him. We were going to kick some goblin butt!

21

The bit of lawn in front of Spear's house that wasn't taken up by the dragon hospital was covered with armor, the metal and leather pieces laid out neatly.

"What's this?" I asked as my father came out of the house, his hands full of swords.

"War!" replied my father with glee. He placed the swords on the ground, one next to each outfit. "I hope you don't mind, Spear. I found all this stuff in your basement."

Spear shook his head. "It's fine. As dragons, we have no need for armor. Our skin protects us, but as the town leader, I had some made just in case. It's been sitting in my basement unused for years."

My father nodded, a wide grin on his face. I'm not sure I'd ever seen him so happy. The promise of war thrilled him. "The swords are our old swords, the ones without the dragon souls in them. I figure it's about time we fill them with Goblin souls, don't you?"

"What about the other swords?" Morganna asked, referring to the ones with the souls still inside.

"Oh, they are still vanishing." He dismissed it with a wave of his hand as though he didn't care about the swords anymore. He was too focused on the upcoming battle.

Seeing my father's fervor and the weapons really brought home how dangerous this was going to be. I'd been on quite a number of adventures since my eighteenth birthday, but this time, there was a great possibility that someone was going to get killed.

I'd spent my childhood imagining the Goblins as these sweet, peaceful characters who happily made swords. I'd spent my whole life dreaming of the day I'd get my own. Little did I know that would be the day my life would change. And oh, how it had changed. As I strapped into the armor my father had set out for me, I looked back over the past few months. It felt that everything I'd gone through had come to this point, this moment in time. I fingered the hilt of my sword, the same sword that had started all this. I'd worn it almost constantly since then. It had almost become a companion to me. It was the only one of the swords that still retained its shine. It was the only one we had that hadn't had a dragon released from it. The Goblins wouldn't try taking this one back since it didn't hold a dragon soul, but even so, I held onto it as though a Goblin might sneak up and snatch it from me at any second.

"We don't have enough swords to go around," pointed out my father as he pulled his own armor on.

"Jules only freed a few dragons. We need to decide who gets one."

"I'll take mine," said Morganna, coming forward and picking it up, placing it in her scabbard.

"And I've got mine. Jasper, here's yours." He threw the sword, still in its scabbard, to Jasper, who belted it around his waist. "Who else wants one?"

"We don't need them," said Ash, referring to the dragons. They didn't need armor either. Their skin was armor enough.

There were still so many people without swords. None of the Wolvren had one and most of the Slayers didn't. The armor we were wearing was not really fit for purpose. It was nothing like the armor that everyone owned in Dronias. Back there, every villager had theirs fitted to them. Everything was made to measure by a tailor in the village. Here, we were wearing a cobbled together mishmash of items, none of which really fit, and most which offered very little protection.

The Goblins were no more warriors than the dragons were, but they had swords. They had our Slayer swords, not to mention all the other weapons they had made over the years. Who was to say if they had stockpiled some or not? They most definitely had armor, I'd seen them wearing it. And let's not forget magic. It might have been running low, but the disappearing swords told us they weren't completely out of it yet.

Another problem we had was clothing. The only way we could get up the mountain was if the dragons carried us and to do that, they had to be naked. That meant they wouldn't be able to change back once we were up there, not unless we took clothes with us.

Unfortunately, taking bags full of clothes would slow us down in a fight. In the end, I came up with a solution.

"Dragons. Drop your clothes in this sack. I'll take it up the mountain and drop it once we get to the top."

The dragons nodded and one by one, they went behind the hospital to change.

There were more Slayers and Wolvren combined than there were dragons, so we had to sit two people on each. Morganna hopped on Ash's back just behind me, my father and Jasper jumped up on Spear, Xander and Alpha sat upon Fiere's back, and the rest found others to fly on.

"In my entire life, never did I dream that one day I'd be flying on a dragon," shouted my father as Spear ran into a take-off. I heard my father give a whoop of joy as they leaped into the sky.

In any other circumstance, his delight in flying on the back of a dragon would have me grinning from ear to ear, but I was a bag of nerves as we set off, taking up the second position behind Spear. Morganna held tightly to me as we soared through the air. Below me, the other dragons were ascending in formation as Frokontas grew smaller and smaller.

Knowing the Goblins would have come to this point with or without me didn't lessen my anxiety. Their magic running out now would have happened anyway, but I couldn't help feeling guilty, as if this was somehow my fault. I tried shaking the thought away. If I'd not come up the mountain on my eighteenth birthday, the Slayers would have continued slaying and there would have been more dragon souls trapped in the swords ready to be turned into magic by the Goblins. The ones that had been freed would still be in there. Still, the thought of all the people I loved flying up to fight an army of Goblins who had magic to command made me feel sick to my stomach. If anyone was injured or worse, I wasn't sure I'd forgive myself.

The sun shone down on the peak of the mountain, glistening off the snowy cap. It was so bright, I had to close my eyes as we landed so I wasn't blinded by the glare. As planned, we didn't stop right at the entrance to the Goblin village but flew right over it and landed in the snow farther up the mountain. Ash fell into a dive before leveling out and landing right next to Spear, Jasper, and my father.

My father jumped down, landing squarely in the snow, a broad smile splitting his face. "What a rush!" he yelled, holding his dull sword skyward.

"Shh. Avalanches!" I reminded him, pointing at the snow. I'd told them all about the possibility of avalanches down in Frokontas. Either he'd not been listening or was too excited to care. I suspected the latter. I'd never seen anyone so ready for battle.

One by one the others arrived. Thankfully, they'd listened to me and spoke using hushed tones. As they were all assembling, I gazed down the mountain. The entrance to the Goblin village was about two hundred feet below us. I saw no sign of movement, but that didn't mean they weren't ready.

"This is going to be too easy!" whispered Jasper in my ear.

"Don't underestimate them," replied Morganna who was standing right next to us and overheard him.

"There's no one there. Look!" insisted Jasper, who

seemed to have inherited his lack of fear and brazen attitude from our father. I wished I had half their confidence.

"They are there," Morganna said, shielding her eyes from the sun. "Just because you can't see them doesn't mean they aren't there. I can feel the Goblin magic. It's pretty strong. Can't you feel it?"

I'd felt it in Spears house when the swords were disappearing, but up here all I could feel was the icy breeze, which had the same effect, standing the hair on the back of my neck on end.

"We go down in waves," said my father quietly. "I'll go first with Alpha, Jasper, and Xander, then the Wolvren can follow. The dragons can take to the air and defend us as they see fit."

A couple of the dragons nodded their heads and prepared to take off once again.

"Wait!" shouted Morganna. The snow behind us shifted slightly, making me nervous. "What about me? What about Julianna?"

My father looked over at me. "You two can follow the Wolvren. We need someone to hold back."

"And you picked the two girls?" Morganna put her hands on her hips. "Not happening. You know I'm a better Slayer than you, and you've seen how brave Julianna is. I'm going down with you."

My father looked like he was going to protest but thought better of it. "Fine. You can head up the front. Julianna, you stay to the rear."

Now I was mad. Hadn't I proved I was good enough to lead the group? But there was no time to protest. Everyone was already setting off. My father held his sword aloft again, and with a war cry, began to run down the mountain. Behind me, the earth shuddered. The snow was beginning to crack. In a spur of the moment decision, I ran toward the dragons that were beginning to take off and launched myself onto Ash's back just as his feet left the ground. If my father didn't want me on the front line, fine, but I wasn't going to sit back and wait in the snow.

I'd flown with Ash enough times to anticipate his every move and so when he rolled right, I leaned left. We were a team and with us working together, we were stronger than if we were apart. Below us, my father charged to the entrance. I expected him to run straight but something was stopping him. I just couldn't see what it was.

"Lower," I shouted to Ash, who immediately went into a dive. As we neared the entrance, I saw a dome-shaped barrier covering the doorway. It was almost invisible, but I could just about see its outline. I watched as my father began hacking away at it with his sword, but it wasn't having any effect.

"Get back!" I shouted down at him. "Ash, blow fire at it, see if that helps."

Ash waited until everyone was a good ten feet clear of the entrance, then, stretching out his neck and opening his jaws wide, he let out a blast of flame. The magic dome was much easier to spot now as the fire burned around it, but it didn't penetrate it. I couldn't believe it. We'd come all this way to fight them and they'd made themselves safe using a magic forcefield. If we couldn't find a way past it, they'd be free to do what they wanted with the swords and there would be nothing we could do to stop them.

Ash flew back up into the sky so high that the people below us looked like ants.

"What are you doing?" I screamed, holding onto him tightly. I loved flying with him usually, but at this height it was terrifying. Below me, I could see the whole mountain. The peak was below us and to the left. If I looked right, I could see Frokontas on one side of the range and Dronias on the other side. In the distance, I saw other small towns and villages with a patchwork quilt of farmlands separating them. Below us, the rest of the dragons circled, waiting for something to happen.

Ash circled around the peak. He couldn't speak to me in his dragon form, but he was trying to tell me something.

"What is it?" I asked pointlessly. Then I realized what he wanted to say. The entrance we knew of to the Goblin village was one of three entrances. The second entrance, the one that the Slayers used to buy swords, was down at the base of the mountain somewhere, but there was another higher one on the mountain, too. If we could find it, there was a chance we'd be able to get in there.

We were too late. I didn't need to look for the entrance. I could already see it and there were hundreds of Goblins swarming out of it and running down the mountain to where the Slayers and Wolvren were standing.

The Goblins had known we were coming and they'd been ready to ambush us. We were sitting ducks!

22

Ash saw them at the same time I did. He fell into a dive so quickly I almost didn't have time to hold on. Fire burst from his mouth in an attempt to fry the invading goblins, but they were ready for him. They were using the same magical force field they'd used at the entrance to shield themselves. The fire bounced off of the invisible umbrella over them and spat out in all directions.

"Warn the others!" I screamed.

Ash turned slightly and glided down to the main Goblin entrance.

"They are here!" I yelled to the Slayers and Wolvren. "They are coming around the peak of the mountain at any second and they have a forcefield around them."

The people below me readied themselves for the attack, but I already knew it wasn't going to be enough. The Goblins may have been small, but the Slayers and Wolvren were hopelessly outnumbered. The dragons, after hearing what I'd said, followed Ash back up the mountain. The Goblins were still running down. In less than five minutes, they would be at the lower entrance and our people couldn't hope to fight them.

"Maybe we should call it off," I whispered. If we could get everyone on the backs of the dragons, we could get them all down to safety.

Ash shook his head. He was right, we couldn't call it off. If we did, the Goblins would only come right down the mountain to Frokontas or Dronias and kill everyone in the villages. We had to fight them, to stop them, but how?

On either side of me, the dragons flew past, circling the angry Goblins from above. Every so often, they'd let out a burst of fire, but just as it had with Ash, their fire didn't penetrate their protective field. I panicked, not knowing what to do. I could jump down from Ash and try to kill them with my sword, but there were too many. I'd be dead in less than a minute. I was just about to ask Ash to turn back to the others when inspiration hit.

"Fly higher!" I shouted at Ash, pointing to the mountain peak.

As we neared the top of the mountain. I began to scream. I shouted at the top of my voice. At first, Ash turned his head to see if I was alright, but when he understood what I was doing, he joined in, letting a loud roar escape his lips. The other dragons came to investigate and when they saw our plan, one by one, they added their voices to the mix. Our combined efforts rattled down the valley. Anyone below us would wonder what was going on.

"Blow fire down there," I instructed, pointing at a particularly precarious patch of snow. He did as I asked and it was all it needed to give way. Thousands of tons of snow began to crash down the mountain. We'd caused a massive avalanche.

In my head, I'd only thought to cover the goblins. I thought that we'd dislodge only enough snow to reach them, leaving our people free, but now I saw what we'd done. What I'd done. Snow, too much snow, was hurtling down the mountain at an impressive rate. It wasn't only going to envelop the goblins, it was going to smother those on our side too.

"Quick! Go down and pick up the others," I instructed, urging him to speed up.

Ash turned and flew as fast as he could down the mountain, letting gravity help. We flew over the Goblins who had now noticed the snow tumbling towards them and had picked up their pace. But it wasn't enough. The snow rumbled down, knocking the Goblins over and smothering them. Their forcefield was not a match for the sheer weight of the snow. Ash flew over them and swooped down so we could pick up some of the Slayers and Wolvren by the lower entrance, but it was too late. The snow was almost upon us.

"Ash!" I screamed as we were engulfed in white powder. I tumbled from Ash's back and rolled, unable to stop the motion. What had I done? I thought I' be saving us, but I'd only succeeded in getting everyone caught in the avalanche.

Everything went from white to black as the snow above me got deeper and still I was tumbling, spinning over and over with only the roar of the snow in my ears.

Then everything stopped. The tumbling ceased and I found myself encased in snow. Snow that would become my grave if I didn't find a way out soon. I cried out for Ash but my voice disappeared into the snow. I was completely alone.

I was disoriented and didn't know which way to dig. I tried listening, hoping that someone would be shouting for me, but everything was silent, the snow drowning out all sounds from above. I took in a couple of breaths, knowing that I didn't have much oxygen left, and tried to clear my head. Trying to figure out which way was up was impossible, but to stay still and do nothing was a death sentence.

I chose a direction, not knowing if it was the right one, and began to dig, pushing freezing snow away from my face. I knew I only had minutes left, so I worked hard and fast, trying to get as much snow away from me as possible. I was just about to give up when a strange vibration passed through me and the snow. It was enough to loosen the snow and for me to punch my way out. From there, someone grabbed hold of my hand and yanked me free. I took a great lungful of air to shake the dizzy feeling, then looked about me.

The whole mountainside was covered in snow, but at least it had stopped moving. All around me I could see people clamoring out of the snow. Many people. The avalanche had not been as deadly as I thought it might be, but it had done damage. I could see that. The entrance to the Goblin village was now buried.

"Morganna used the last of her goblin magic to loosen the snow," my father said, pulling me to my feet. "I think you are the last to be pulled free."

"Everyone survived?" I asked incredulously.

My father nodded. "Thanks to Morganna and the dragons, yes, I believe they did."

"The dragons?"

"They used fire to melt the top layer of snow."

"What about the..." I hadn't finished my question before I got my answer. A mob of angry Goblins was heading our way.

Weapons raised and angry looks on their faces, they charged at us. As the farthest down the hill, I watched as they began their attack. There were about a third of them than there had been before. The snow had taken them by surprise, crushing their forcefield and burying many of them.

The thought of it was enough to spur me on. We were now on an even footing. Pulling my sword out from its sheath, I raced uphill, ready for battle, my father following closely behind.

Ahead of me, Morganna and Xander were locked in a battle of swords with a couple of the Goblins. Jasper had forgotten his sword completely and was using his fists to clobber one of the taller Goblins. Above, the dragons spat fire and snapped at the Goblins at the back, picking them up with their teeth and flinging them over the precipice. I watched as Ash swooped down and grabbed one of the Goblins. He flew over me and hurled the screaming creature down the mountain.

A pack of wolves ran past me, their teeth bared, ready for a fight. I jumped, wondering for a second where they had come from, before realizing they were just the Wolvren who had shifted into their wolf form. It had been such a long time since I'd seen them as anything but human that I'd forgotten they were shifters. Snarling and snapping, the wolves attacked the Goblins, biting down on any limb they could sink their teeth in to.

Everywhere I looked, people and Goblins were fighting. Some with weapons, some with fire, and some with magic. I scanned the chaos, looking for Krikor, but before I found him, I saw Alpha being held upside down in the air by some invisible force. Below him, a Goblin held up his hands, using what was left of his magic.

I ran toward him, and before he had time to react, I barged into him, knocking us both to the ground. Without the magic holding him up, Alpha fell on top of the pair of us, knocking the air out of all of us.

"Thanks," Alpha said getting to his feet. He held his hand out to pull me up, but another Goblin was already upon him. Without any weapon, Alpha was at a disadvantage, but the small goblin underestimated his strength. As I pulled myself up, Alpha turned into a wolf, surprising both me and the Goblin on his back. He turned and with his huge jaw, he grabbed the Goblin, pulling its arm clean away from its body. I closed my eyes and tried not to throw up at the sight of blood spurting from the Goblin's arm socket as the piercing scream hit my ears.

"No time for dawdling." Someone pulled me up. I opened my eyes to find my father once again. He was locked in a sword fight with one of the Goblins but had still managed to take my arm and pull me out of harm's way. Behind him, another sword-wielding goblin attacked. I jumped between them and pointed my sword at the attacker. Behind me, I heard the sound of metal clanging together, of sword upon sword as my father fought. In front of me, I knew I'd have to do the same. It had been a long time since I'd had to battle anyone with a sword but it came naturally. The Goblin came right at me, his sword outstretched, but I managed to knock it to one side. I quickly recovered from the attack to get in my own blow, but the Goblin was good. He parried my blow and lunged forward, but I was too quick for him. I jumped to my left and attacked again, this time ripping a hole in his sleeve and tearing the skin of his arm slightly. He kept up with me, defending my attacks expertly and getting in some jabs of his own. Behind me, I still heard my father fighting with the other Goblin, his back against mine.

I tried another move, this time shocking the Goblin into taking a step back. I was winning! As I was about to deliver a final blow, another Goblin jumped in. Now I was fighting two of them. I was good, but not that good. Keeping two swords at bay was taking up all of my concentration and skill.

"Daddy!" I shouted as the first one leaped forward.

A flash of silver from my father's sword and the Goblin's head came clean off his shoulders, flying down the mountain. The shock of it was enough to make the second Goblin pause. I took my opportunity and lunged at him, but he was quick and managed to dodge out of the way. He turned and fled, leaving me with just my father.

"Thank you, you saved my life," I said, turning to my

father, but he wasn't standing behind me as I'd expected. He was on the ground, a sword protruding from his eye socket. I knelt, feeling numb, and pressed a finger to his throat. There was no life in him.

He was dead because of me.

23

At that moment, the world ceased to exist. Everything went quiet, the fighting stopped. Nothing mattered. My father was dead. I tried to shake him awake even though I knew it was pointless. The Goblin sword had pierced his brain.

All around me, the battle raged on. We'd started off strong thanks to the avalanche, but the Goblins were using both magic and weapons stronger than ours. I recognized the sword that killed my father as one that had disappeared from Spear's house.

Tears fell down my cheek, dropping onto my father's face, mixing with the blood. I pulled the sword from his eye and threw it as far as I could away from him.

My father had given his life to save me. If I'd not called out his name, called to him for help, he wouldn't have lost concentration. There was no way a lowly Goblin would have been able to kill my father, not even with my father's sword empty of dragon souls as it was. My father was a slayer, a warrior, a protector. It was all he ever had been. He'd died on the battlefield as he always wanted to.

Movement to my right jolted me out of my reverie. It was the Goblin that had killed him, and he no longer had a sword. Jumping to my feet and with an anger I would never have thought I could possess, I charged at him, screaming. My sword pierced his heart.

He dropped to the ground, blood pouring out of him as he took his last breath. He died, his eyes still open, now unseeing. He was my first kill, but he wouldn't be my last. Anger and frustration surged through me. I screamed so loudly that I was sure they heard me at the bottom of the mountain. I lifted my sword skyward and vowed to kill the Goblins. I'd kill all of them for what they had done, not just to my father, but to all the Slayers and dragons.

My sword felt different, heavier somehow, and yet more powerful. It took me a few seconds to realize what had happened. I'd not killed the goblin at all, despite driving the sword right through his chest. I'd stolen his soul just as the goblins had taken the dragons' souls.

I could feel the magic around me, and for the first time, understood what it felt like to own a soul-filled sword. I felt invincible. Invincible and extremely angry.

People were fighting all around me. It was chaos. Fire rained down, melting the blood covered snow, revealing the dead bodies of those Goblins who had fallen in the avalanche. The smell of burning meat, which could only be coming from the charred bodies of the Goblins that the dragons had attacked, permeated the air. To my side, a couple of the Wolvren still in their human form were fending off a particularly nasty group.

I ran past them, slaying each Goblin in turn before they even saw I was there. With each kill, my sword grew stronger and my anger deepened. Adrenaline fueled my rage as I killed Goblin after Goblin, not pausing between each kill, and not caring for the souls I was taking.

It was just desserts for all the years we'd suffered, for the dragons who'd lost family members. To have the soul sucked out of them by their own magic served them right.

I swung left and right, sucking away soul after soul, and with each one, I felt stronger. Not just because I now held a soul-filled sword, but because I felt sure of myself. For the first time in my life, I knew what it was to be a Slayer. I wasn't doing it for glory or for tradition, as the others in my village had. I was doing it for survival, but I had to admit to myself, it felt good. I now knew why my father had fought the dragons for so long. This was what I was born to do.

I looked around. Morganna was the closest ally to me. She was expertly fighting two Goblins at once, but she was sure of herself. She didn't need my help. The Wolvren were also fine without me. In battle, they'd shown themselves to be aggressive. They didn't need weapons; they had their teeth and they were using them brutally. The strewn-about limbs of fallen Goblins were testament to that.

That's not to say we hadn't suffered casualties of our own. A couple of Wolvren were down, as was one of the dragons. It's blue-green scales told me it wasn't Ash. I wanted to go to them, to see if they were still alive, but there were more pressing needs I had to attend to.

Slightly farther up the mountain, I could see Jasper. He was hopelessly outnumbered, and yet he was doing a magnificent job of keeping them at bay. I ran, jumping over the scattered bodies, pushing my muscles to the extreme, to get to him. I wasn't about to lose another family member.

There were six or seven of them surrounding him and he was struggling. I jumped in the circle of Goblins and brother and sister fought together for the first time, engaged in a battle for our lives.

These particular Goblins were good. Not because they had superior skill at fighting, but because they were using magic to fool us. One minute they were there, then they were gone, only to reappear moments later a few inches to the right or left. I could tell that their magic was waning by the way they were jittering in and out of vision. Their glimmer wasn't working as well as it should, thankfully for us, because if it did, I was positive Jasper and I would both be dead. As it was, we were able to anticipate their movements and attack as soon as they appeared. I speared the first and he went down quickly, giving a slow death rattle before succumbing to his wound. I felt a slight jolt as this soul left his body and entered my sword, strengthening it further. Behind me, Jasper fought as we circled around back-to-back, trying to keep one step ahead of our opponents. I heard a scream, too high-pitched to be Jasper. He must have killed one, too.

I was currently battling three of them, one of which kept disappearing on me. He was the one I needed to get first. The other two would then be a piece of cake. He was sneaky, though. As I did everything I could to defend myself from the other two, he'd appear and try to get an attack in. As soon as I lunged for him, he was already gone.

I knew he was still there, just invisible, but he was quick, and every time I delved my sword into what should have been his body, he had already jumped to the side.

Suddenly, a sharp pain in my side made me jump. I looked down to see a bloom of blood appear on my tunic. The pain seared through me, clearing my head. I didn't need to fight these guys. I didn't even need to see them. I could kill them all with one swoop. The two Goblins I could see had hesitated, taking in my injury. They were probably waiting to see if it would kill me. I raised my sword to my side and with a cry of "Not today!" I swiped it at their neck level. One, two, and finally three heads flew clean off, the invisible one suddenly appearing long enough for me to see his head roll down the mountainside.

Feeling triumphant and stronger than ever thanks to the souls of the three I'd just killed, I turned to help Jasper. He was down to two Goblins himself, neither of whom were using magic. I crashed my sword down to the first, who jumped to the side and launched an attack of his own. I was ready, though, and as he ran forward, I held out my sword at arm's length. The stupid fool was running too quickly to stop and impaled himself on my sword way before his reached my body. His eyes went wide with shock before he slumped, his lifeforce leaving him. I lowered my sword to let his body fall off and once again, I felt the now familiar jolt of his soul entering my sword. At that moment, another Goblin fell. I turned to see Jasper with a huge grin on his face. At some point, he would find out about our father, but now was not the time to tell him. I let him indulge in his victory for a few moments before pointing down the hill at a group of Goblins who were attacking Alpha.

He ran down the mountain with a war cry, leaving me alone. I looked down once again at my tunic. The Goblin had managed to spear me at the very edge of my body in the one place the protective leather didn't cover. It was a flesh wound and hadn't hit any major organs, but if I didn't get it bandaged soon, I was at risk of bleeding to death. Ripping a bit of clothing from one of the dead Goblins, I did the best I could to make a bandage. I wrapped it around my waist and at the point of the wound, I stuffed in more fabric to stem the bleeding. It was gross but better than dying.

I scanned the scene below me. As I was the highest person on the mountain, I was able to see the whole battle. It was still going strong, although with far fewer people and Goblins. Bodies littered the ground and the stench of blood was unmistakable. It filled my nose, making me want to vomit. I had to keep breathing, though. I was feeling dizzy with grief and with loss of blood, but I couldn't fall now. Fainting would probably kill me. I didn't want to have to go through all this to die because of exposure to the cold. I felt weak now, but my sword and my heart felt strong. If I could keep myself standing, I could see this through to the end.

To my right, a flash of red stole my concentration as it always did. It was Ash. It was like my eyes were trained to seek him out. A group of Goblins was firing arrows at him and as I looked more closely, I could see that some had already hit their mark, their shafts sticking out from between his scales. He was in pain. He wasn't making any noise, but I could see it in his face. He blew a gust of fire at his attackers but was way off the mark. He needed my help. I raced around the mountain to where the Goblins stood. They were right on the very edge of the precipice where I'd been at the first avalanche, when I'd gone over only to be rescued by Ash. It was fitting I'd be able to return the favor.

Standing on the edge of a cliff with their backs to me, they were easy targets, or they would be if I was quick. I didn't need my sword for this, I just needed speed. I sheathed my sword and pelted at them with full force. All it took was a quick shove and the first was screaming down the cliff face. Without pausing, I moved on to the second and then the third, pushing each one to their deaths. The last one saw me, but it was too late; before he'd even had the chance to aim his bow at me, he was already hurtling to his death.

"Ash!" I called out loudly. He followed the sound of my voice and came in to land beside me. As gently as I could, I removed the arrows that pierced his body. When he turned back into his human form, he'd be covered in the scars of war, just as I was. We'd both been through so much in such a short time and now it was nearly over. As I turned to look behind me, I felt Ash's long tail curl around my body and his head rest on my shoulder.

The Goblins were dead. All of them. We'd won the war. There were so many injured and dead from our side, too, but many were still standing. Morganna, Jasper, and Xander were checking the mountainside for our wounded. Up in the air, Spear and the other dragons flew around in circles, checking that everything was clear before they landed. The silence was deafening. After a couple of hours of listening to the sounds of war, all that was left for us was the clean-up. I stroked Ash's head, glad to have him by my side. Our scars would fade in time, but the psychological scars would remain forever. I knew we had a long road of healing ahead of us, but I knew with him at my side, I'd get through it.

I took a step forward, planning to help the others tend to the injured, when something passed quickly in front of me. Whatever it was, it was almost invisible, but the way the light bent told me that magic was in play. Without thinking, I ran toward it and leaped into the air. As I suspected, I connected with something before knocking us both to the ground. I heard an "umph" below me as I landed on it.

"Show yourself!" I demanded, holding my sword to where I suspected his neck to be.

In front of my eyes, a Goblin appeared. It was Krikor.

24

"Krikor! I should have known you'd be cowardly enough to leave." I dragged him to his feet, my sword still at his neck. "I have the souls of many Goblins in this sword," I said to him as menacingly as I could. "We need to talk, and I don't want any more tricks, not unless you want there to be another Goblin soul in here. I have to say it would be quite fitting."

He looked scared. With his people dead and his magic almost completely gone, there was nothing left for him to do and he knew it. He gazed at me with sorrow in his eyes, which unnerved me. I was expecting anger or defiance. "What do you want?"

"You know what I want."

"The souls of the dragons."

"Yes. I want them back and I don't want to spill any more blood."

"Your blood would be useless now, anyway. You are

no longer innocent. You are a murderer just like the rest of the people in your village."

"I killed to save my people," I spat at him. "Something I wouldn't have had to do if you hadn't trapped them."

He raised an eyebrow. "Your people? How interesting that you call the dragons your people, when in fact your people are the ones that slayed them."

"The dragons are my people Krikor, but I don't expect you to understand that. You've manipulated us all for too long and today, it's going to stop. I know you can free the dragon souls without my blood. You would need to be able to in order to turn their souls into magic."

"So, you know?"

"No, it was only a theory, but I know now. How much magic do you have left? I know it can't be a lot."

"It isn't. Why do you think we were taking the swords back? We needed the dragon souls to generate more."

"Do you have enough to bring my father back to life?" It was a long shot, but I had to ask.

He regarded me curiously. "You father died at the hands of a Goblin?"

"Yes."

"If he died on a sword, the sword would trap his soul, just as your sword has trapped my fellow goblins. You only need to free him."

Hope rose within me. I could save him. "He was speared through the brain."

"Ah, well, in that case, there is no hope. The brain is the one part of a person that can't be fixed by returning a soul. There is only one way to fix this, and that is to use magic. A lot of magic."

"So, do it!" I insisted.

Krikor looked at me, a sly smile on his face as though he knew something I didn't.

"What?" I asked, holding the sword right up against his neck.

"There is only one way to get all the magic we need and you know what that is." His grin widened as I realized what he meant. To get enough magic to bring my father back to life, I'd have to sacrifice the souls of the dragons still trapped in the swords. I heard footsteps to my right and left. A war was raging in my head. I couldn't let my father stay dead and yet, could I really give all those dragons to save him?

Tears sprang to my eyes. Tears of frustration. A loud, guttural scream escaped my lips at the injustice of it all.

"The dragon souls left in the swords might have been there so long that no one remembers them," said a voice. It was Ash. He'd turned back into a human. "You can save him."

He was right. Dragons like Mary had been captured so long ago that they no longer had living family. No one would care if they just disappeared. No one really knew them. That is, of course, if they were all captured a long, long time ago.

I turned to Ash. He was wearing one of the spare sets of clothes we'd brought up and already there were patches of blood from the arrow wounds. I loved him so much right then. "My father died to save them," I murmured. "He wouldn't want me to choose him over them. Saving the dragons was what all this was about, what it's always been about."

I turned back to Krikor. His grin was gone. "My father died the way he would have wanted to. Making amends. Saving the dragons."

Krikor grimaced, but he knew he had no choice. My sword was at his throat. "So be it," he said. "Follow me."

With one of my hands holding onto the scruff of his neck and the other with my sword to his throat, I had to walk slowly while Krikor led us to the entrance of his village. It was still partly submerged, but Ash and Morganna managed to dig enough of a hole for us all to fit through.

"Over here!" I yelled to everyone else. It took a while, but eventually, they all converged around the entrance. "Is that everyone?" I asked, not wanting to leave anyone behind. They'd fought for this, and they needed to see it. The dragons and the wolves had all changed back into their human forms and gotten dressed.

"It's everyone that's still alive," Spear grunted.

My heart fell as I took in how few there was left of us. A couple of the Wolvren were injured with various wounds. Xander had a nasty cut on his head and blood dripping from his arm. Most of the dragons looked uninjured, thankfully. Ash seemed to have come off the worst.

The tunnel was darker than I remembered it, but before now, it had been lit by magic. Now, we only had the faint light from the entrance to guide us. In the main chamber, holes in the ceiling let in enough light for us to see.

"This way," Krikor said, leading us to the far end of

the cavern and into a tunnel I'd not seen before. It was almost pitch black, but Krikor knew his way without the light. I held on to him tightly, knowing if I let go, he'd be gone in a flash.

The tunnel seemed to go on for miles downhill. I was beginning to think it was some kind of trick to escape when we came into another cavern. This one was a lot smaller than the one I'd seen so many times up near the top of the mountain, but the beauty of it took my breath away. Intricate patterns carved into the walls surrounded us, and each one was decorated with precious jewels just like the ones the Goblins used in our swords. The artistry was magnificent and awe-inspiring, but it was not this that took my attention.

There, in the middle of the floor were swords. Not just our swords, but the swords of others too. Other Slayers' swords, just like the ones from the abandoned village downriver. They were not piled up as they had been at Spear's house. Instead, each one was mounted in a placeholder that held them so the sword blade pointed upward and inward. They were in layers of circles, rising higher and higher around a central spire. My eyes followed the line of the swords to the very top, where there was a crystal, larger than any precious stone I'd ever seen before. Light emerged from it and it was this that enabled us to see.

"What's that?" asked Ash, taking a step towards it.

"Don't!" Morganna held him back. "There's very powerful magic in this room."

"Not enough of it," remarked Krikor dryly.

I pulled the sword away from his neck but kept a firm hold of him. "What now?" I asked wearily, desperate for all this to be over. I was exhausted and losing blood at such a rate, I didn't dare look.

"I have to climb up and touch the crystal," Krikor replied.

I didn't want to let him go, but at the same time, I wanted to finish this. "Circle the room," I said to the others. "Morganna, can you stand by the exit in case he tries to escape?" Morganna nodded and moved into position. The others circled the wall and joined hands. If I let go of him now, there was no place for him to escape to. "No tricks," I hissed in his ear.

I let him go, but held my sword up to his back should he try and run. He didn't, though. He walked forward and began to climb. Each foothold and hand-hold was between the blades of two swords. He was risking hurting himself with each step, and if he fell, he'd be extremely lucky not to skewer himself. Still, I held the sword to his back, lifting it higher and higher until he was beyond my reach. The crystal was about twenty feet up and so it took him a while to climb, picking out his route between the swords. I wouldn't have been able to find my way up there. He hesitated for a fraction of a second before reaching out to touch the crystal. I wondered why he didn't try to escape. As soon as he freed the dragon souls, everything was over for him. Not that I'd left him much choice in the matter.

"Wait!" yelled Spear. "The dragons we already freed are dying. If we release the rest, won't they fall prey to the same illness?"

Krikor looked down at him. "Your dragons are not dying. They are being reborn."

"Reborn?" asked Ash. "What do you mean?"

"The illness is not an illness at all. It is part of the magic. When someone stabs you, even with a magic sword, damage is done to your body. When the dragons' souls went back to their bodies, the internal damage was still there. Healing requires a lot of energy. Right now your sick dragons are literally rebuilding themselves. Within a month, they will begin to wake, newer and fresher and younger than they were even before their souls were taken. Their outer skin will shed, leaving them with a beautiful new complexion. They will be reborn."

"But some of the dragons whose souls were not taken have fallen ill, too," I remembered.

"The magic works in the same way as a disease. It is contagious. They will be reborn, too. You'll have a village of young, vibrant dragons. You should be pleased. It won't work if you stay as humans though, so I suggest you all go home and stay in your dragon forms until the day you can rise again, free of illness, free of old age and free of any injuries you have sustained." He eyed Ash as he said this. Blood was still dripping from him and he looked so pale. Was this another trick? I had no idea, but if we didn't let him free the trapped dragons, they may as well be dead anyway.

"Do it!" I shouted up at him.

He held his hand out once again and this time touched the crystal.

A bright flash of light caused me to close my eyes. With everything else going on, I'd completely forgotten about the intense heat that blasted out of the swords when the dragons were freed, and this time there were so many of them. I braced myself for the fire and flames, but they didn't come. Instead, a powerful wind wailed around the room, knocking us all over. I curled into a ball as the wind roared. The noise was intense, like being in the center of a hurricane.

When it was all over, I opened my eyes. The others were laid on the ground as I had been, and the light from the crystal was out.

I blinked a few times, wondering how I could see everyone, even dimly, when I saw there was a small shaft of light coming from behind a part of the carved wall. I'd not seen it before because the light from the crystal had been so bright.

"Daylight!" I shouted, running toward the crack. My voice echoed through the cavern.

"I think this was the way the dragon souls went," said Spear who'd been right next to it. Between us, we pulled on the wall making the crack wide enough to get through.

I turned back to get Krikor but he wasn't there.

"Where's Krikor?" I asked, desperately searching the room. "He couldn't have come this way. The crack was too small until we pulled it open."

"I'm sorry," said Morganna, "I think he escaped back up the tunnel. The wind knocked me over. I felt something jump over me, but I thought it was the dragon souls."

He'd escaped, but as I looked down the tunnel through the wall and saw bright daylight flooding in, I knew that so had the dragon souls, and so would we.

25

The exit led to a dirt road at the base of the mountain. I knew this road. If we followed it, we'd end up in Dronias. It was a road I knew I'd have to take, even if Ash and the others decided to fly back over the mountain to Frokontas.

On the way out of the tunnel, I'd told Jasper what had happened to our father. He'd nodded, resigned, and told me he'd seen his body as we were fighting.

Ash dawdled behind our group as we walked the path home.

"I'm going home," I said and he nodded.

"I was hoping you'd want to come back to Frokontas and stay...permanently."

I gave him a small smile. He looked so sad at the thought of me leaving. "I meant I have to go home and tell my mother about father. Then I'm going to bring her home. To our home, in Frokontas."

He smiled widely then and kissed me on the cheek. He looked so pale. We all did. Just getting everyone up the mountain was going to be an effort, but before that, I had to go back to Dronias and tell them what had happened. My father wasn't the only Slayer killed up there. Jasper, Xander, Morganna and I survived, as did one or two more, but we would be going home in smaller numbers. I also had to make sure the last of the dragons escaped the dragon keep in the forest. I'd hate to think of leaving any behind.

When we were far enough down the road, Spear announced that the dragons were taking anyone who wanted to go back to Frokontas.

Morganna came to me and kissed me on the cheek. "I know you are going back to Dronias. Alpha and I have decided to go back with Spear, just until we are all healed. Many of the Wolvren were injured and Spear has promised us all medical aid. Once we are better, we will return to our own home. I hope you'll come and see us before we go."

I hugged her hard. My idol had become my friend. "Ash is going to bring me back tomorrow," I explained. "I'm just going to do what I have to do in Dronias first."

"What about Jasper?" she asked, seeing him walking slightly further ahead, deep in his own thoughts.

"Jasper's a grown man. He's been living in my father's shadow for too long. Maybe now he'll be able to live life the way he wants to."

"Do you think he'll come to Frokontas?"

I shook my head. "No. Dronias is his home, and now that my father is dead, he will be the leader. I have a feeling that will please him. He always did like to be the best."

Hours later, when everyone else had flown back to Frokontas, we arrived in Dronias.

My mother took the news of my father's passing better than I thought she would. She insisted on coming to the dragon keep with us to help any left behind dragons, but there were none there. They'd all been matched to their souls.

"We've done it," I said wearily to Ash. He held my hand tightly. They were free, but this was just the beginning. If what Krikor had said was true, they had a month or two of illness to look forward to.

That night, after doing her best to patch us all up with her limited first aid knowledge, Xander's wife, Louisa, made us all dinner. My mother had been staying there since my father had come to Dronias with me, but she wasn't happy. Her home had long since burned down and now that Xander was back, she was eager to move out. Jasper offered to build her a home, but she chose instead to live in Dronias with Ash and me.

"Rocco did a great many things in his lifetime," she began over dinner. "Not least of which was to impose a lot of pain on the people of Frokontas. Now here I am, being invited to live among those very people. It is humbling to be asked. As for Rocco, he was a good man deep down. He only ever wanted the best for Jasper and Julianna. He was, above all, a family man. It seems like he did everything he could to make up for his mistakes in the last weeks of his life, and it is that for which I will remember him."

"Hear, hear," cried Xander, raising a glass. "To Rocco!"

The next day we were surprised by Spear knocking at the door. Behind him were two dragons.

"To what do we owe the pleasure?" asked my mother, recognizing Spear.

He bowed, actually bowed to her. "I come with my deepest condolences on the passing of your husband. He and I were natural enemies, but in the end, we became the best of friends."

She thanked him and invited him in.

"I'm afraid I cannot come in. The dragons have no spare clothes to change into and the doorway is too small for them to fit through. I came knowing that Ash was injured and thought that he and Julianna might like a lift back home."

"It's going to be my mother's home, too," I said, coming up behind her. She rested her arm on my shoulder and grinned.

"Of course. We will be honored to have her. I was going to invite her to the party anyway."

I raised an eyebrow. "Party?"

"Yes. Krikor was telling the truth. The dragons that got sick first have already begun to wake up. It's pretty disgusting to watch them shed their skins like snakes, but when they do, well, you should see them."

"I can't wait," I grinned.

"You don't have to wait. We decided last night to invite all the inhabitants of Dronias to the party." He beckoned us outside and pointed skyward.

I looked up to see a sky full of the most vibrant dragons I'd ever seen. A rainbow of color filled my vision, reminding me of a kite festival. One by one, they landed. Xander, Jasper, my mother and I ran through the town, knocking on doors and inviting people to join us.

Of course, not everyone wanted to come. Decades of hatred were a hard thing to forget, and many of my fellow Slayers decided to stay at home. Many did come out though, and each one who did was transported on the back of a dragon. The whoops and excited yells of the people flying for the first time reminded me of how happy my father had been when he'd flown on Spear's back. The grief over losing my father would never leave me, but having been able to spend so much time with him in the last few weeks, and fighting next to him, was a small consolation.

Once my mother had hopped up on Stone's back behind Jasper, there was only Ash and I left to go. Spear shifted into his dragon form. His skin was dull and patchy and I recognized it immediately as the first stage of rebirth. Soon, he would fall asleep and wake up brand new. I had a feeling he was looking forward to it.

Ash helped me up and then jumped up behind me. As Spear took off, he grabbed hold of my waist tightly.

"Ouch!" I shouted. He was clamping down on the gash in my side. He shifted his grip a bit lower down.

"What's the matter with you?" I asked as the Triad Mountains passed beneath us.

"I've never flown on a dragon's back before. It's kinda scary!"

I had to laugh

Frokontas was a hive of activity when we landed. The flames in the fire pit were roaring and the delicious smell of cooking meat emanated from it. Tables had been set out at the outer edges and filled with all manner of food and drink, and all the people of Frokontas had brought chairs out to accommodate the arriving Slayers.

Dragons mixed with Wolvren and Slayers around the fire, while Edeline and some of her friends served food. Some of the dragons stayed in their dragon forms to give pleasure rides to the children of Drorias and to Lucy, who seemed to be enjoying it more than anyone else.

My mother jumped in and insisted that she help, too, and when she introduced herself, Edeline gave her a bone-crushing hug.

Fiere thrust a glass of beer in my hand, then passed one to Ash before heading into the crowd. A band of musicians started to play in the background and I watched with surprise as Alpha pulled Morganna from her seat and began to dance with her. Alpha had never struck me as the dancing type.

Ash took my hand and led me to the edge of the party, away from everyone else. Firecracker saw us leaving and decided to follow, gamboling around our feet as we walked slowly up the track that would take us to town and beyond that, to Spear's house.

"Are we going to visit the sick dragons?" I wondered aloud.

Ash stopped and put his full beer glass on a nearby fence post. "I wasn't planning to, but we can after, if you like."

"After what?" I asked.

He responded by kissing me. My heart thumped wildly as it always did when Ash kissed me. My own beer sloshed down my side but I didn't care. I was home. It was the only place I ever wanted to be.

Later, we did walk to the sick dragons. A couple that had emerged that day after shedding their outer skin walked past us. They gleamed in the sunshine.

"Maybe I should try this illness thing," mused Ash, taking in one particularly vivid green dragon.

"You probably already have," I said. You were injured by a sword, and you've been looking ill for days, even before we went to battle. I bet if you turn into your dragon form now, you'll be asleep by the end of the day. I think Spear will too. He looked pretty ghastly earlier."

"Don't tell him that," chuckled Ash. He looked into my eyes. "Will you wait for me while I sleep?"

I kissed him lightly on the lips. "I'll wait for you forever."

As we got close to Spear's house, it occurred to me that the beer was soaking through my trousers. I would need to change. I pulled off my sheath with the sword still in it and examined my pants. They were soaked through and I smelled like a brewery.

"I'm going to head into the house and see if he has a spare pair of pants laying around," I said to Ash who nodded.

When I picked my sword up I noticed something unusual about it. It was dull and no longer looked shiny and new.

"What the..."

And then reality hit. When Krikor freed the dragons from all the swords, he'd freed the Goblins from mine, too. No wonder he hadn't tried escaping before touching the crystal.

I looked upward to the peak of the largest mountain in the Triad Mountain range.

The Goblins were still up there, only now they were going to be mad!

For more books by Armitage & Culican, check out the Realm of Light and Fire series: https://www.jaculican.com/realm-of-light-and-fire/

SAVIOR

A DRAGON TAMER NOVELLA

1

As I took one last look around my cottage, I could scarcely believe that I was never to see it again. The house I'd grown up in, the village that had been my home since the day I was born, the people I'd counted as friends and family. I had to leave them all.

I purposely left my sword until last. None of this was real while my sword still stood against my bed where I always kept it, ready for the next fight. I picked it up and held it, feeling the weight of it. It was so familiar to me and I was glad that I would be allowed to take it with me. It was the smallest of mercies on a day like today.

My eyes were dry as I left the house, stepping out into the darkness. I was a famous warrior and even though there was no one around to see me leave, I wouldn't allow myself a moment of weakness. Morganna never showed weakness! That's how I got to where I was, by never showing fear to an enemy. Not that the people living in the cluster of small houses that made up the village of Drionas were my enemies–well, not all of them. I was one of them, almost a leader. I was respected and looked up to. At least I had been. Not anymore. Now I was a coward, leaving in the dark of night because I'd been told to by one of the village elders. I never thought my life would come to this.

It didn't take long to find the path leading away from the village. Even in the dark, I knew I'd find my way. My eyesight was perfect, even in the inky blackness. It was one of the reasons I was so good at what I did—slaying dragons!

I had no clue where I was going. It was unlike me to not have a plan, but then I hadn't been expecting the visit from Rocco two hours earlier. Rocco was a village elder, a fierce dragon slayer in his own right. One of the best. Except, as I found out tonight, 'one of the best' wasn't good enough. He wanted to be *the* best dragon slayer in the village but that wasn't possible while I was still around.

I'd never taken him for the jealous type. What did he have to be jealous of? He had a wonderful family, he was well respected, and he could kill a dragon in his sleep. I guess you can never really tell with some people.

When he'd knocked on my door, I'd invited him in for a cup of tea, assuming that he wanted to talk about next week's dragon hunt.

He didn't stay long. Just long enough to tell me that he'd seen me with Xander and that in exchange for him keeping quiet, I should leave the village and never return.

What choice did I really have? Xander was the love of my life and another village elder. He was also married with three children. Sure, I could have stayed and let the pieces fall where they may, but I couldn't do that to him. I loved him too much. I loved him enough not to break up his family. He'd be thrown out of the village for having an affair. I afforded myself a little daydream of us both taking this journey together. His wife would eventually pick up the pieces and his kids would forget him in time, but I'd never be able to forgive myself. What had started as a little bit of fun had gotten out of hand and Rocco seeing us had given me the push I needed to end it. End it and escape any backlash. Xander would now be able to concentrate on his family.

The path curved as it reached the village marker. I turned and took one last look at my home, but it was in complete darkness and there wasn't anything to see. Clouds filled the sky, blocking out the moon and stars, leaving my parting view of my home as dark as the feeling in my heart.

Rocco was going to tell the village that I had befriended a dragon. Of all the things he could come up with, that was the most ridiculous. Morganna, the best dragon slayer in living history, befriending a dragon? It was absurd. And yet, in the end it didn't matter what he told the other villagers. I wouldn't be there to defend myself. I should have killed him right then and there. I certainly could have. He was a magnificent warrior, but I had the edge and he knew it. But, just like with Xander, Rocco had children. A young boy and girl, neither older than five or six. However much I hated Rocco right now, I couldn't leave their children without a father, no matter how much of a low-life he was. Why did it always come down to the children? I laughed out loud. Hearing my voice breaking the silence made me feel lonelier than ever. I'd never cared for children and yet here I was, running away to protect the kids of two different men. I knew the names and ages of all of Xander's children, but Rocco's were just a couple of nameless kids running around with toy swords and dirty knees. Why was I giving up my whole world just to protect them?

"Maybe I've got more maternal feelings than I thought!" I whispered to myself, shaking my head. Maybe I was just going insane?

The woodland that skirted the Triad Mountains thinned out the further I walked away from Drionas. I'd been walking over an hour and still didn't know where I was headed. To the right were the Triad Mountains. I knew them well after years of hunting dragons in their peaks, but there was no place for me to live up there. Not unless I really did want to befriend a dragon. That would certainly be a turn up for the books, if I showed up in Drionas in a few days riding on the back of a dragon.

I was feeling too sad to chuckle at the thought of it. Morganna, the greatest dragon slayer, riding a dragon. Like everything else that had happened that night, dragon riding was a ridiculous thought.

Sick of wandering aimlessly, I found a rock to sit on to give me time to clear my head. I was usually so focused, so sure of what I was doing and where I was going. This aimlessness was alien to me.

Taking a deep breath, I assessed my situation. Whichever way I looked at it, I was in a mess. Drionas was a tight knit community and as such, we didn't travel much beyond its borders. In some ways it was nice, but in others, such as this situation, it meant that I knew no one and was woefully lacking in geographical knowledge.

I knew, for example, that if I carried on walking in the same general direction I was already heading, I would hit the coast way past daybreak. I didn't, however, know the names of any of the small towns and villages that populated that little bit of coastline. Living by the sea had its own appeal, but it wasn't the type of environment I was familiar with. I needed trees and mountains and valleys. Climbing over the Triads would be difficult, so I made the decision to head north. I picked up my bag and sword and took the first fork in the road that would take me in that direction.

The first fingers of sunshine were creeping into the sky as a man with a horse and cart drew up beside me. A cursory glance at his cart told me he was a merchant, more than likely on his way to market somewhere. In the back were rolled up rugs and carpets. Maybe it was lack of sleep or just so many years living in danger from the dragons, but my imagination took over. What if those carpets held bodies? They were certainly long enough. I gripped the handle of my sword tightly, ready to draw it in a split second if needed.

"Good morning, miss. You look lost. Can I offer you a lift anywhere?"

I exhaled, unaware that I'd been holding my breath. He was just stopping to help me. It wasn't something I was used to. In my village I held a certain role: that of a woman who gave help instead of received it. "Thank you." I climbed up and took the seat beside him. At closer quarters, he looked harmless enough and I felt foolish for thinking otherwise. I still kept my hand on my sword though. Those that lost focus were the ones that usually ended up killed first.

"Where to?" He clicked and the horses resumed their steady trot along the cobbled road.

"I don't know. North."

"I'm going as far as the market in Fossville. That's about an hour north of here. Will that do you?"

I guess it would have to. "Thank you."

I'd never heard of Fossville, but if it had a market, it meant I could get breakfast there.

The man talked the whole way there and I listened, not giving up any information about myself. The less people knew, the better. I didn't want it getting back to Drionas where I was. I needed a clean break.

When he asked me questions, I nodded my head or murmured uncommittedly, giving him only my name.

He seemed content to talk about his work and family which suited me fine. When we arrived at Fossville, I gave him a couple of coins. He tried to argue but I insisted, though when I checked my coin purse later, I wished I had let him win. I'd left all my money in Drionas's vault. In my haste to leave, I'd brought only my coin purse, which didn't hold a lot. The money I had would pay for breakfast with maybe enough left to feed me for a week. After that, I would have to find a job pretty quickly.

I bought the cheapest breakfast I could find—two eggs and a chunk of bread—and sat in the cheap-looking cafe to eat.

Finding a job? It wasn't going to be easy. In Drionas, I was a celebrated warrior. I'd saved the village so many times from dragons that the other villagers brought me gifts such as food and gold. I'd earned enough to live for multiple lifetimes and had put it in the central vault. It was as good as useless to me now. I had no other skills beyond slaying dragons. I couldn't make clothes or fish. I took the last bite of my bread feeling more despondent than ever.

I'd never not known what to do. I'd always been so sure of myself and here I was, moping around like a five-year-old that had lost his mommy. I took a deep breath and stood up. I wasn't completely useless. I had my sword and the skill to use it. I would continue north and learn to feed myself. If I knew one thing, it was how to kill. Killing a rabbit or deer was bound to be easier than killing a dragon. At least neither of them breathed fire. I'd teach myself to hunt! As I walked through the market, I saw the merchant. I gave a wave, feeling much more cheerful, and he waved back. I was just about to walk past when I saw something that caught my eye on the next stall over. It was a crossbow. If I was going to hunt, I needed the right equipment. The stall sold all manner of weapons, including swords. None of them came close to my own sword but at least the prices were right. The crossbow would set me back nearly all of my money, but if I were to feed myself with it, it was a bargain. I even managed to get the weapon's merchant to throw in a quiver of arrows for free.

I felt stronger as I left the village, taking the north road. I didn't know what lay ahead of me, but at least I was prepared.

I walked for hours in the baking sun, determined not to stop until I found somewhere to hunt. I passed many creatures that would be delicious cooked over an open fire, but all of them were in farmers' fields and I was many things but I wasn't a thief. I could have tried out my new crossbow on the birds that flew over head, but they were so quick, I was afraid I'd lose too many arrows before hitting one. I needed to find somewhere where bigger animals roamed free.

By the time evening rolled around, I was exhausted. My stomach was complaining of the lack of food and my muscles burned with the effort of walking all day. And yet, in the distance, there was a sight that warmed my heart—a line of dark trees which could only mean the edge of a forest and, even better, the snowy peaks of a mountain range beyond.

I'd find both food and a place to shelter in the forest, and if I was lucky, maybe a village that I would be able to call home.

I dragged my protesting legs along for another hour until I reached the edge of the forest. It looked just like the forest near Drionas with tall pine trees, and just for a second I felt a pang as I thought of home. There was something different about this patch of trees, though. It was deadly silent. Nothing moved through the undergrowth and I couldn't hear the sound of birds overhead. It was so quiet that the sound of my own breathing seemed magnified. Breaking the silence, I pulled my sword from its scabbard with a clatter and held it in front of me, ready to attack. There was a reason that this forest was so quiet and the only explanation I could come up with was that some big creature was eating all the smaller ones. It could even be dragons, which would suit me just fine.

Slowly, I walked through the forest. It was much

bigger and darker than I imagined and after walking for a couple of hours, I realized that my biggest problem was that I still hadn't found food, not that I'd end up as food. I pulled a handful of leaves from a tree but they tasted bitter, so I spit them out. I knew nothing of edible plants. My stomach had long since given up growling at me and now was tightening with spasms of hunger. I was so exhausted I could barely see through the thick branches and my muscles ached so badly, I had trouble holding myself up. When I tripped over a branch and hit the ground, the resulting blackness was more than welcome.

2

I heard it before I saw it, and yet I didn't open my eyes. So much for being a warrior. Before yesterday, I'd have been up and ready for the kill at a moment's notice, but today, I'd happily let whatever it was that was shuffling around near my face eat me for breakfast. I was so tired that just the thought of opening my eyes felt like a feat of endurance. But when the noise turned into someone or something licking my nose, I thought I should probably see what it was.

My eyes peeled open to see a hairy snout in my face. I pulled back and saw that the snout was attached to a wolf of some kind, except it was like no wolf I had ever seen before. It was much larger than a common wolf with longer limbs. This one didn't act like a wolf either. Its teeth were not bared as I expected any wolf to do when facing an enemy. I pulled myself up into a sitting position and stared at the strange creature. He stared back at me as though sizing me up.

"Are you a shifter?" I asked, feeling foolish. I'd heard

stories of animals that could turn their whole being into a human form, but it was nothing more than a myth, a story handed down from generation to generation to scare the young ones.

He cocked his head and growled. Funnily enough, his growl sounded almost human. He wasn't scared of me, that's for sure, and I could tell he meant me no harm. Didn't normal wolves attack no matter what?

Another noise startled me although the wolf seemed at ease. Behind him in the undergrowth, other wolves were heading this way. For the first time since waking up, I felt nervous. I searched the ground near me for my sword but it had fallen out of my reach. My breathing became more rapid as I realized that there was no way out of this situation alive. If I couldn't reach my sword, I may as well lay back down and let them eat me. Then it came to me.

My crossbow!

I could feel it still strapped to my back.

I waited until the first wolf looked back over his shoulder toward the others and carefully pulled the crossbow out. I'd never used it before, but the wolves were close enough and still enough for me to get a good shot. OK, so I'd probably not be able to kill them all before they attacked, but at least I'd go down with a fight.

I'd just gotten the crossbow into my hands when the first wolf barked something that sounded like an order to the other wolves. I was startled when they all retreated and left just the two of us alone that I forgot what I was doing and dropped the crossbow to the ground in front of me.

"They listened to you?"

I felt stupid talking to an animal that was really no more than a wild dog, but he seemed to understand my every word. There was intelligence in his eyes and the way he looked at me. He was like no wild animal I'd ever seen before. He just sat and stared at me. I longed to reach out to him, but something told me that this wouldn't be the right thing to do, and yet I had to do something. We couldn't just sit and stare at each other all day.

I was turning away to retrieve my sword when the wolf moved out of the corner of my eye. Something about the way he moved was odd, but it was only when I looked back at him directly that I saw what it was. I had been right. He was a shifter. His body was folding in on itself in the most grotesque manner. His snout became shorter as his already long limbs lengthened even more. He stood on his back legs and grew until he was over six feet in height. I should have been scared but I was mesmerized by his transformation. When it was complete, he stood before me, a young man with the same greyish-brown hair that fell down his back and the same cool grey eyes that had been staring at me for the last ten minutes. He held out his hand to help me up out of the dirt.

I took it, figuring that if he wasn't going to kill me as a wolf, he wouldn't do it as a man.

"What are you doing in our forest?" His voice was strong and commanding, exactly how I expected him to sound. He was a man in charge.

"I'm lost."

He laughed then although I wasn't sure why.

"No one gets lost in these woods. No one would dare to enter, and yet here you are with your sword and crossbow. You are armed and yet you chose to lie on the ground for us to find you and kill you."

I didn't like his tone, although he had a point. In all my time of being a dragon slayer, I'd never felt or acted so helplessly. It was embarrassing. It was also making me angry. How dare he talk to me in such a manner?

I pulled myself up to my full height. I was a tall woman and yet I still fell a few inches shorter than him.

"I'm a dragon slayer. If you let me get my sword, I'll prove it to you."

"Here," he said, picking up the sword and throwing it to me. "No need to prove anything." He was laughing again.

Now with my sword in my hand, I knew I was invincible. He didn't have his legion of buddies behind him now. It was just me and him, and I was the one with a weapon.

I held the point of the sword to his throat and adopted my most menacing expression. "Don't laugh at me or I'll kill you where you stand."

He held his hands up but there was no fear in his eyes, just the same amusement he'd shown before. "Is that any way to treat a man who helped you up?"

I lowered my sword slowly, although I kept a tight grip on the handle. One foul move from him and I'd chop him in two.

"You should leave this forest. There is no space for you here."

"Maybe I will, maybe I won't."

I'd already planned to leave. I'd found no food and if

I didn't eat soon, I was going to be completely useless. I just didn't want him to think he could tell me what to do.

"You are a feisty young thing, aren't you? Are you having fun in my forest? Find enough food?"

I hesitated. He could tell I'd not eaten.

"There is no food here. Not for you. Not unless you know where to look and I suspect you don't. Your cheeks are hollow and you have circles under your eyes. I'd wager that you haven't eaten in at least twenty-four hours. Well, you've come to the wrong place."

I calculated how deep in the forest I was. I'd walked for hours before I fell. I didn't have the strength to walk back without sustenance. I needed water at the very least.

"You know where I could get food."

He'd said there was food here if you knew where to look for it. My guess was that he knew exactly where to find food and water, and I wasn't leaving until he showed me.

He laughed again.

"I'm so glad I'm a source of amusement to you."

"Turn around."

"Why?" I didn't want to take my eyes off him. Despite the fact he hadn't threatened me, I was wary.

"Just turn around and look up. Just above your head."

I turned and looked. There was a bunch of funny-looking green fruit hanging just above me. I'd not seen them before. I plucked one from the tree and took a bite. The sweetest juice I'd ever tasted dribbled down my chin. I ate the whole fruit quickly and turned to pluck more. As I gazed upwards, I saw the fruit higher in the tree was bigger and more abundant. There was one particular piece that was huge compared to the others and I had to have it. I pulled my hunting knife from my belt and threw it at the stalk. It sliced the fruit clean off the tree, dropping it cleanly in my hand. The knife continued spinning until the handle hit the truck and it too fell. I caught it and placed it back in my belt before taking a bite out of the juicy fruit.

"That was impressive," said the wolf man. I'd almost forgotten he was still there since I was so absorbed in getting nutrients into my starving body.

"I told you, I'm a dragon slayer. Killing a dragon is much harder than bringing a bit of fruit down. You should see what I can do with my sword!"

"I thought you were joking. You don't look like a dragon slayer."

"Because I'm a woman?"

"Partly, yes." He didn't even seem bothered by his sexist attitude although I couldn't blame him. Female dragon slayers were in short supply. "Partly because I can't understand why someone with the skills you possess would end up starving and asleep in the undergrowth."

"It's a long story."

"You aren't lost, are you? Are you here looking for us?"

"No. I didn't even know that wolf shifters existed. I mean, I'd heard stories but I didn't believe them. I came in here looking for food, but as you pointed out, I didn't do a good job finding it."

"So, you are lost?"

"Does it mean I'm lost if I don't know where I'm going?"

"It does sound like a long story! Maybe you should come with me and tell me about it."

"Why would I want to do that?"

"Because there is a stream that runs through my village with the clearest water you've ever seen. Plus, your knife throwing skills are exceptional. Maybe I could help you."

I didn't think I wanted his help and yet the thought of drinking from that stream was tempting.

"The other wolfren will not harm you. I am their leader. My name is Alpha."

"Wolfren?" I'd never heard the term before.

"It is the term we use for werewolves, or wolf shifters if you will. My people listen to me. You will not be harmed."

I had no reason to trust him and yet, I'd no reason not to trust him either. I followed him through the dark undergrowth for about half an hour until we came upon a clearing dotted with small huts. Some of the other wolfren looked astonished to see me but they said nothing as I walked through the village.

Alpha led me to a stream and he wasn't lying when he said it was crystal clear. I could see the fish swimming through the water and the pebbles that lined the bottom.

I took great gulps of the water, feeling more refreshed with every gulp.

"You were thirsty!" Alpha said behind me.

"Why are you called Alpha?" I was being rude but I

didn't care. Alpha was a weird name. "I thought the alpha was just a generic term for a leader.

"For a wolf leader, yes. We take on the name as if it is our own once we become the alpha."

"So, what was your name before?"

"You ask many questions and yet you have not told me how you came to be here."

"It's none of your business," I answered sharply, feeling a pang of pain in my heart. Xander would know I've left Drionas by now.

Alpha's eyes crinkled up at the edges as he began to laugh again. It seemed I was an endless source of amusement to him.

I was just about to say something else when the sky darkened. I looked up to see the underside of a dragon fly overhead. The villagers all ran for cover as the dragon rained fire down on the clearing. One of the small houses began to burn.

Without thinking, I leapt up and chased the dragon. It was something I'd done a thousand times. I knew how they thought and how they worked. Running through the trees was hard, but with the water and fruit, I had renewed energy. The dragon circled back and I knew he was going to make another pass at the village.

I turned back to follow him, keeping his pace.

Once we were out in the open, I'd be able to get a clear shot at him.

As we both came into the clearing, I pulled out my sword, waiting for the dragon to fly lower. He was not here to play games; he was here for food, and to get food, he would have to fly lower. In the center of the clearing, I stood and waved my hands. Let him think I was on the dinner menu. If he came to me, it would make it easier.

He swooped, his jaws open to carry me off, and just as he was about to take me into his mouth, I jumped and plunged my sword into his eye. The dragon let out an almighty screech and flew onward, leaving a trail of blood and taking my sword with him, still in his eye socket.

Alpha ran toward me.

"You are amazing. You stopped the dragon from taking any more of our people."

I was not amazing. I let him get away with my sword.

"I need to go find him. He has my sword."

"You need to rest. You've only had a little fruit and you look exhausted."

"I need my sword!" I replied forcefully.

"I'll do you a deal. Rest here for the night, and tomorrow I'll show you where the dragons live."

It was a good offer.

A campfire was set up and the other wolfren gathered around. Someone had skinned an animal and was now roasting it on the fire. I couldn't identify it although it looked like a small deer of some kind.

"I thought there were no animals in this forest?" I said, breathing in the delicious aroma of the barbecued meat.

"There are not a lot left. The dragons have eaten almost everything. My people will have to move on unless we can eradicate them. We have been at war with them for decades and it looks like they will win. Although with no food, they will probably have to move on, too."

"It sounds familiar. My own people are slayers. We have also spent many years at war with the dragons. That is how I know how to fight them. That one you saw was the first I failed to kill."

"You are very tired, do not berate yourself. Without you, we would surely have lost another of our pack. We have lost many already."

"You need to learn how to use a sword," I replied. Someone passed me a chunk of the cooked meat and I tore a piece off with my teeth. It tasted as delicious as it smelled.

"Perhaps we do. We rely on our strength and brutality but in truth, that does not get us far.

"I can teach you how to kill dragons. I've been doing it all my life. You saw what I can do. If I'd eaten this meal first and been rested enough, that dragon would be dead at our feet right now."

I don't know what made me say it. Here I was, asking a perfect stranger to give me a place to stay, and yet I felt safe with him. He was in the same position as I. The dragons had tormented his village as much as they had done in Drionas, except here, they were wolves and not slayers. As much as I hated to admit it, even to myself, I needed to be here. It was already beginning to feel like somewhere I could call home.

"I don't doubt it."

I could see he was mulling my proposition over. I could tell that they didn't let strangers into their pack lightly. Alpha had been kind and patient with me, as had the other wolfren, and yet I could see mistrust in their eyes. Every single one of them was a wolf shifter. Not quite human and yet not fully lupine, either. I waited for Alpha to answer. He stood and conferred with a couple of other wolves. It didn't take long for him to come back with an answer.

"You can stay in exchange for helping rid us of the scourge of dragons. As long as you are teaching us, you will be allowed free reign in our village."

"Done," I replied, holding my hand out for him to shake. "I'll go and retrieve my sword tomorrow, then we shall begin."

He shook my hand and nodded his head slowly. I had a feeling that this was going to be a decision that would affect my whole future.

3

Early the next morning, I left the den before the others awoke. Alpha already knew I was planning to retrieve my sword; I'd told him the night before so there was no need to wake him. He knew I'd be back. He'd told me that he wanted to come with me in some misguided thought that I couldn't look after myself when it came to dragons. Ha!

I wanted to be alone. Even without my sword, I still had my knife and the new crossbow. It would be enough.

I knew the dragons lived in the mountains. I'd spent enough time around them to know the types of places they liked to live. Finding them wouldn't be a problem. I could see the peaks of the mountains above the tree line and I estimated that it would take me a couple of hours trekking through the forest to get to their base. How long it took me to find them after that would depend on how high up they made their nests.

The path to the mountains was relatively clear and

the journey took less time than I had anticipated. Luckily, there was also a pretty clear and easy route up the mountain, so I wouldn't have to climb the whole way. The path was rocky but the incline wasn't so severe that it strained me. With the early morning sun, it would be a pleasant walk.

It wasn't long before I was above the tree line and could fully appreciate just how huge the forest was. It stretched for miles and, even though I couldn't see the Wolfren camp, I could gauge where it was from the distance and direction I'd walked. I'd thought it was somewhere near the center, but seeing the vastness of the forest, I could tell it was really only on the edge. The forest would take days to walk through from one side to the other. I wondered what other creatures lived among its leaves and branches.

Even though I'd never been here before, I recognized the terrain. The grey rocks were identical to those in the Triad Mountains and if that wasn't enough to convince me of dragons living nearby, the unmistakable smell of sulfur would do it. It permeated the air. Not too strongly, but enough to convince me I was on the right path. It would only get stronger the higher I climbed. The path became much rougher and after an hour or so of hiking, I found that I had to climb more and more. I was almost grateful I didn't have my sword with me as its weight would only be a burden.

The heat of the sun began to burn and sweat dripped from me. In my haste, I'd forgotten to bring water with me.

"Idiot!" I said to myself. Of all the things that could kill me in a place like this, dehydration was number one.

Dragons I could cope with, but lack of water was not something I could fight with a knife. I needed to find water and soon. One thing I knew about mountains was that there was always water there if you knew where to look for it. Hidden lakes, streams, waterfalls. The Triads had them all. Even a puddle would be enough to sustain me for a little while. I'd never really mastered the art of water divination. I knew others could find water just using a couple of sticks, but I'd never taken the time to figure out how. I'd have to rely on my other senses. I stopped still and listened for the sound of running water. It was eerily quiet, just like the forest. What was with this place? Surely a forest this size and mountains as large as they were couldn't only have two species inhabiting them. Even if there were only dragons up here, they would still need to drink. Nothing could survive without water.

I climbed more, listening for the sound of a brook babbling or even better, a river raging, but I wasn't in luck. Wherever the source of the water the dragons drank from was, it was much higher than here.

I carried on regardless, despite my mouth getting dryer, my tongue beginning to feel rough, and the headache that was creeping around the edges of my brain. I knew I should turn back, but that would have meant defeat and defeat was not something I would ever admit to. After another hour of climbing, when the forest was way below me, I finally heard the sound I'd been listening out for. The faint strains of a stream winding its way down the mountain reached my ears. I ran toward it as fast as I could, keeping my senses open for the dragons. I was yet to see one, but the smell of sulphur had intensified and the scorch marks on some of the rocks told me that I needed to keep my wits about me.

As I rounded a corner, I saw it. A stream full of clear water. It was probably the very same stream that ran through the wolfren village. I fell to my knees as I put my whole face in, drinking up the cool, lifesaving liquid. I gulped it down, desperate to hydrate myself, and when I'd had my fill, I splashed it all over my face and arms to wash of the salty sweat. When I was sure I'd cooled down enough and taken enough of the water to keep me going for a while, I stood, wishing I had some kind of container so I could carry it with me. It was then that I recognized I was not alone. I became aware of a presence watching me from further up the stream. Normally I would have noticed straight away but the dehydration had made my brain foggy.

I looked up to find a small dragon, much smaller than any I'd seen before. It must have been a baby or at least a young one. Even from the distance between us, I could see that it would only come up to my waist, even if it stood up to its full height. I walked toward it cautiously. It may have been young, but it could still breathe fire. If anything, it could be more dangerous than an adult. Adult dragons could control their fire. Younger ones couldn't. I took a cautious path toward it. I didn't want to scare it but at the same time I didn't want to be barbecued. If I scared it off, I'd only have to chase it to kill it, which would take up way more energy that I wanted to waste. If I could move slowly enough that it didn't move, I could get it in one swipe of my blade. It would be a good souvenir for Alpha. It might even have enough meat on its bones to provide a pre-dinner snack for the wolfren.

"There now," I said as sweetly as I could. I didn't have a maternal bone in my body and was useless with kids, but I thought if I kept my voice gentle, it might be enough to keep the dragon calm. It worked until I got about twenty feet away from him. My closeness had gotten to be a little too much and he scrambled on the rocks behind him to escape. Why didn't he just fly? He was young, but he was certainly old enough to use his wings. As I caught up with him, I could see why. His wing was bent at a funny angle. He was frantically trying to get away from me, but his wing dragged behind him, slowing his progress. I caught up to him quickly and reached out to grab him. Killing him would be a walk in the park. I raised my knife, but before I brought it down into his flesh, something came over me and I paused. It didn't feel right, killing this tiny creature. The dragons I'd killed were huge and ferocious. This one was helpless. I could feel him trembling beneath my fingers. He wasn't even trying to escape my clutches now. He must have known it was useless. I was much too strong for him.

He looked at me, fear evident in his eyes, and as I held onto his front arm, I knew I'd never be able to kill him.

"You are probably going to die anyway," I said, dropping my hold on him. "No dragon can survive with only one working wing."

I expected him to carry on scrambling up the rocks but he just sat there, trembling. What was I going to do now?

The best option would be to leave him where he was. He didn't have my sword. One of the larger dragons would have that somewhere, probably in a nest. I searched the sky, wondering when the dragon's mother would show up. The mother dragons were the worst. They'd do anything to protect their young and would think nothing of frying a slayer on the spot if it meant safety for their babies.

I sat down and stroked the small green dragon absent-mindedly whilst I tried to come up with a new plan.

My touch seemed to calm him a little. Maybe I did have some maternal bones in me after all.

He began to twitch, which I put down to fear and maybe pain from the broken wing, but as the tremors became more violent, I realized something else was at play here. I stepped back in shock as his whole body went into spasms. Then the familiar but still sickening sound of bones crunching and skin stretching filled the air. What was happening to him? His whole body seemed to be folding in on itself.

I could hardly bear to watch as his skin shuffled itself around and his body rearranged itself into—

He was a shifter!

The small green dragon had gone and a young boy sat quivering and naked in his place. For a moment, I was too shocked to move, but I recovered quickly and pulled my tunic over my head, giving it to the boy. When he slipped into it, I could see that his shoulder was sore on the same side where his wing had been damaged. It looked like he'd dislocated it.

The shock at finding out he was a shifter was so overwhelming that I didn't know what to say to him.

He looked to be about seven years old, although he was small for his age.

"Thank you," he said in a small voice.

"Who are you?"

"My name is Drake. Who are you?"

I could hardly tell him I was a dragon slayer. "I'm Morganna. Does your shoulder hurt?"

"A little," he replied, and then winced as he tried to move his arm. "I think I can help you. I'll need to push the top of your arm near the shoulder. It's going to hurt but only for a second and then the pain will almost be completely gone. Would you like me to do that for you?"

The poor kid looked terrified, but he nodded his head all the same.

I walked slowly over to him so as not to scare him.

As I got closer, I could see that I had been right. A swift push would get his arm back into the right place. I was just worried that he would scream. If he did, that would alert all the other dragons to my presence. The other dragons must be shifters too. What about the ones on the Triad Mountains? Were they shifters too?

I couldn't even begin to get the idea through my mind, so I concentrated on the boy instead.

"Look at me and not your arm, OK? I'm going to talk to you while this is happening. It will hurt for a second and then the pain will disappear, like magic. Can you tell me how old you are, Drake?"

I popped the shoulder back into place as hard as I could, not giving him time to answer. I was hoping that if

I took him by surprise, it would be over before he knew it. He didn't scream as I'd expected him to, but his mouth formed a perfect O shape. Tears began to form at the corners of his eyes, but to his credit, he kept it together.

"There, is that better?"

"You didn't warn me!" he said, although I could tell by the way he was able to move his arm now that I'd done a good job.

"I'm sorry. How does it feel?"

"It feels OK. I can move my arm again. How did you do that? Are you magic?"

"No," I smiled. He was a cute kid with a crop of unruly black hair. He looked nothing like his dragon self, apart from the cuteness. "Your bone just needed to pop back into place. How did you hurt yourself?"

"I fell and when I stood up, I couldn't move my wing. Are you one of the wolves because you don't look or smell like them."

"I'm not a wolf, no. I'm a human."

"What's a human?"

How could he not know? He looked just like one.

"I guess I'm just like you but I can't turn into a dragon."

"Or a wolf?"

"Or a wolf."

"So, what do you change into?"

"I don't. Humans stay exactly like this."

He considered this for a minute before replying. "That's boring!"

I had to laugh. "It sure is kiddo!"

When I was sure he was OK, I asked him where his family was. For the longest time, I'd thought nothing of killing dragons. It was no worse than swatting a fly, albeit a large, fire-breathing fly, but now I knew they were people, too. I was going to have to be more careful about how I approached them. I couldn't kill them, that was for sure. Not now, knowing what I did. My mind fleetingly went to all the dragons I'd already killed, but I pushed it away sharply. I didn't have the time for regrets. I was sure it would haunt me in the coming months.

"I'll show you. We live not far from here."

I began to follow Drake and as I did, I wondered how the older dragons were going to react to me when I finally got to them.

4

As we climbed higher, the stench of sulphur intensified, making breathing difficult. The air was thinner up here, too, which didn't help, and yet Drake seemed unaware of it. I guess he was used to the altitude and had adapted to it. I had to ask him to slow down once or twice, because now he had the use of his arm back, he was practically skipping up the rocks in the way that only kids can do.

The sky went dark. As it was a cloudless sky and I wasn't aware of any eclipses due, it could only mean one thing. I looked up to see the underbelly of a huge dragon. I didn't want to kill it anymore, but at the same time, if it was a choice between its life and mine, I'd go for mine every time. My hand gripped the handle of my knife, but at this distance it would do no good. The crossbow would be my best shot but getting it out would show that I intended to kill them. Either way could spell disaster. The dragon circled closer, flying lower and lower in the sky. It was almost upon us and I still hadn't figured out what to do when the dragon attacked.

It opened its jaws and flew straight at me. My hand tightened on the knife and I could feel my pulse racing. My first instinct was to slice its throat as it flew over as I had done hundreds of times, but how could I do that knowing that it could be Drake's mother or father? I was going to have to kill it. I had no choice. I was just about to bring my knife out when Drake pushed me out of the dragon's path.

It flew past as I dusted myself off. The large dragon came to a standstill and perched itself on a nearby rock, staring at me. It looked confused, unsure of itself. I wasn't surprised. It would have seen Drake saving me. Drake had also tumbled and was wiping the dust from the tunic I'd given to him.

The sound of bones crunching alerted me to the fact that the large dragon was shifting. I'd already seen it once with Drake, but it didn't stop the horror I felt at witnessing it all over again.

I closed my eyes. When the horrible sound stopped, I peeked. A naked man stood before me. He was older than me, maybe in his early fifties, but I could tell by the muscles on his chest that he liked to keep in shape. He picked something up from behind a rock and threw it over himself. It was some kind of cloak. They must have them dotted around the place for times like this. Having to shift without clothes on could lead to some embarrassing episodes, I mused.

"Who are you?" shouted the man, climbing down the rocks towards us. He sounded menacing.

"She's with me," cried Drake. I was thankful he was

with me. I was afraid this man would kill me in a heartbeat otherwise.

"Drake, get away from her."

"She helped me, Papa."

Papa? So this was Drake's father.

"I fell and hurt my arm and she mended it."

The man was almost upon us. I straightened up and looked him in the eye, determined not to show how scared I felt.

"He'd dislocated his shoulder. I just popped the bone back in. He needs to rest it for a few days and be more careful in the future."

"Indeed," replied the man. His tone had softened although there was still an edge to it. At least he didn't sound like he wanted to push me off the mountain anymore.

"Drake, go see your mother. She will need to look at that shoulder of yours."

"Yes, Papa!" Drake scurried away, leaving only me and his father on the mountain.

"You can come with me."

His words didn't make it sound like an order, but his tone did. I followed him a little way up the mountain until we got to a small cabin. He opened the door and gestured that I should go inside.

I was surprised at how nice the house was. It was obviously lived in, with three comfy chairs and a fireplace. Doors led off the main room to other rooms. If I didn't know otherwise, it could have been any one of the homes in Drionas.

"I always thought dragons lived in nests," I remarked. I turned to look at the man and he just scowled. I'd put my foot in it as usual. Still, I didn't think he was going to kill me. Doing so would mess up his lovely home.

"Would you like something to drink?"

OK, so I didn't think he was planning to kill me but him offering me a drink was not what I expected. It seemed so civilized for a dragon. Had I gotten them wrong this whole time?

"Yes, please."

"We have tea, juice or water."

"Water will be fine thank you." Dragons drank tea?

"Take a seat and I'll be right back." He nodded toward one of the seats.

I sat in one of the comfy chairs and watched as he disappeared through one of the doors. He came back about ten minutes later with a glass of water for me and some juice for himself. I also noticed that he'd gotten dressed. Instead of the cloak, he now wore trousers and a short-sleeved top, both in cream.

"It's not often we get visitors up on the mountain. May I ask what you are doing here?"

I tried to think of some reason for being here that didn't sound bad. Nothing came to mind so I went with the truth. "I came to kill dragons."

He raised his eyebrows.

"I'm a dragon slayer. That is all I've ever done."

"So, how is it that you saved my son? He is a dragon, or did you not know that?"

"I know he's a dragon. I saw him in his dragon form. His wing was injured. When he turned back into his human form, it translated into a dislocated shoulder. I couldn't kill him. He was just a little boy."

"I'm a man and a fully-grown dragon, and yet you are here in my house taking drinks with me. Why are you not killing me?"

He sounded genuinely curious and not the slightest bit mad that I'd just told him I wanted to kill all his people.

"I didn't know you were shifters. I've been hunting dragons in the Triad Mountains all my life and I never suspected they could turn into humans."

"That's rather arrogant, don't you think?"

"I didn't know. I could hardly call it arrogance."

"I wasn't referring to your knowledge of what we are; I was referring to you saying that we turn into humans. Only a human would say that. I do not consider myself human in any form. I am still a dragon."

"But you look and sound and act like a human."

"Maybe humans just look and act and sound like dragons when we are in this form? Have you ever thought about it like that?"

"That's a bit pedantic, don't you think?"

"Not if you are a dragon. It's just how we think. I take it you've changed your mind about killing us all now that you know the truth."

"Of course. I never would have if I'd have known the truth."

"You are the exception to the rule then. Many humans still try to kill us even when they know the truth."

"I'm not one of them."

"So, I take it you'll go home to wherever it is you came from, then, and not disturb us again?"

I took a sip of the water. It was deliciously cold. I needed to get my sword but how could I tell him that? In doing so, he'd know it was me that blinded one of the dragons. And yet I couldn't go without it. It was part of me.

"I came from the wolfren village."

He sat forward in his chair.

"You are with them? You are not one of them!"

"No. You already know I'm human."

"I'm surprised. They like intruders even less than we do."

"They asked me to come and kill you in exchange for a place to stay. I have nowhere else to go."

"I can think of a million places I'd rather be than with that pack of dogs," he spat.

"They have been nice to me."

"Hmmm." He didn't sound as though he believed me.

"Why do you fight them?"

"Why does anybody fight anybody? This war has been going on since way before my time. It was to do with food originally. The wolves and the dragons both eat meat. With two groups of hunters, the forest soon became empty of other animals. If you've lived among the wolfren, you'd have seen it yourself."

"I have noticed. It's very eerie."

"Not really. Just the other animals have been hunted to extinction in this particular place. It left us with only the wolfren to eat and they were left with only us to eat. It was a case of eat or be eaten."

"That sounds bad!"

"Not so much anymore. We now fly to the other side

of the mountains where there are wild deer and farm animals."

"The wolfren were eating something that wasn't dragon."

"Yes, there are wild deer in the forest now, too. The wolves only need to travel a short distance deeper into the forest to find food nowadays. There is enough to go around."

"So, why are you still fighting?"

"Much the same reason you still fight dragons. It is all we have ever known. Our feud is so old that I'm sure no one really remembers."

"So why don't you stop?"

"If it were only that easy. If we stop fighting, the wolfren will take it as a sign of weakness. They will come up here and kill us in our beds."

"Not if I told them not to."

"I'm surprised you have much sway with them. How long have you known them?"

"A day."

"A day? A whole day." He started to laugh. "You are either more stupid than you look or have a very strange idea of who the wolfren are."

"I'm not stupid. It doesn't matter how long I've known them. They are fighting you for the same reason you are fighting them. That reason is nothing. You both have enough food. There is no reason to fight. It's this whole war that is stupid, not me."

"Aye, perhaps you are right."

"I am right. They don't want any of their people hurt or killed any more than you do."

"Maybe that's so, but if you tell them to stop fighting

just because we've decided to stop fighting, they will come up here and kill us all the same."

He had a point. I sipped my water and tried to come up with a plan that would work. Then it came to me.

"What if I tell them that I've put a spell on you. Something that will stop you from being able to come into the forest. Some kind of force field. That would stop them."

"You can do magic?"

"No, but they don't know that."

He laughed again. My plan meant that I would have to lie to Alpha and the other wolfren, but if it meant saving their lives, I would do it.

"It's certainly an interesting concept. It would mean getting my people to agree."

"It would also mean that the wolfren would never come up here again and your people and Drake would finally be free as long as you keep to the other side of the mountain."

He mulled it over and then slowly nodded his head. He invited me to meet all the other dragons. His prospect made me nervous after everything I'd told him about being a slayer, but he was nice enough not to mention it.

The afternoon went by in a whirl, but I knew I had to get back to Alpha and the others. They would be wondering where I was. The last thing I needed was a pack of wolves coming up the mountain to find me.

I bade farewell and as I was leaving, Drake passed me my sword. I'd not even mentioned it. It was like he just knew it belonged to me. I ruffled his hair and made my way back down the mountain.

5

The journey down the mountain was much easier than my journey up. It helped that the dragons had given me a bottle filled with water to quench my thirst and keep me going. I'd have to throw it away before I got to the wolfren village because I'd never be able to adequately explain it to Alpha, but that was fine. I only wanted the water anyway.

With the weight of my sword firmly attached to my belt, I felt much better about everything. The last two days of my life had been quite the adventure and even though I couldn't help but think of Xander and those I'd left behind, I knew that I needed to get away. Rocco had given me just the push I needed to break away from the village. Security was one thing, but I'd never grow as a person there. It was just too small.

My thoughts crept to the dragons on the Triad Mountains. They were probably shifters too, locked in the same stupid, pointless war with the slayers, as the dragons and wolfren here. Fighting for the sake of fighting. I knew I'd have to go back and tell the people the truth one day, but with Xander's young children at risk of being hurt by our indiscretions, that day would be a long way off. I only hoped they would find out themselves and then the ceaseless killing could finally stop. It wasn't my war anymore. I was too busy ending this one. The shade of the trees was cooling and I was glad to be back amongst them. I drank the last of my water and hid the bottle behind a stone. I could have thrown it away, but a part of me knew it wouldn't be the last time I'd visit the dragons, and maybe I'd need that bottle again someday. The trail back to the wolfren village was a clear path, probably used by the wolfren to hunt the dragons. I'd only been walking a few minutes before I heard his voice. Alpha was calling my name.

"Alpha! I'm here," I called back.

He came crashing through the trees and when he saw me, he grabbed me roughly by my arms.

"You've been gone so long. I thought the dragons had surely killed you!"

I was just about to answer when he pressed his lips to mine, taking me by surprise.

His kiss was forceful and almost violent and yet at that moment, it was just what I needed. I kissed him back, matching his passion and surprising myself at the same time. Two days ago, I wouldn't have believed anyone who told me I'd be kissing someone other than Xander, much less enjoying it, and yet kissing Xander had never felt this right. Maybe because Xander was never really mine in the first place.

The kissing was fierce and yet when he finally

pulled away, he had nothing but tenderness in his eyes. He truly cared about me.

"That was unexpected," I finally managed to say once I'd gotten my breath back. We both broke out laughing.

Of course, I'd seen him before and yet after our kiss, I really saw him. His eyes were beautiful. The light grey sparkled when the sun hit them. They were like mirrors and looking at him was almost like looking at myself. His hair was the same grey but with streaks of light brown and his body was to die for. How had I not noticed those muscles before?

"You have the sword."

I held it up for him to see.

"And you are not hurt?"

"I'm fine. Not a scratch on me. The worst part was that I forgot to take water."

"You shouldn't have gone without me. You could have been hurt."

"I could yes, but I told you I was a slayer. Slayers know how to defend themselves against dragons."

"So, I see." He was impressed. I felt like a fraud.

"You are truly a wonder. How many did you kill?"

I swallowed. I didn't like lying to him before that kiss, but now it felt even worse. The kiss had meant something and I knew I wanted more. And yet, not lying to him meant death, to the dragons, to the wolfren, maybe even to him. It was the only way.

I took his hand and began to walk with him back to the wolfren village. Even though he must have known this forest like the back of his hand, it was me that led him along the path.

"You told me that the dragons ate all the food," I started, deliberately ignoring his last question. "Is that the full truth?"

"We can find food. We don't have to eat dragons. It's just I'd rather eat them than they eat us. The animals that live deeper in the forest are harmless. There are deer, squirrels, rabbits. None of those fight back."

"So, if the dragons were gone, no one would starve?"

"That's right. Now don't tell me you killed them all."

"Not exactly, but I have stopped them from being able to come into the forest."

He stopped in his tracks. "How could you do that? Are they all injured?"

Now was the time. I was going to lie to him. I hated myself, but I uttered the words nonetheless.

"No. I used up some magic I was carrying with me. I'm not a sorcerer, but magic is something you can buy if you know where to get it and have enough gold to pay for it. It just so happens that I had a little left. I used it to create an invisible barrier between the forest and the mountains. The dragons will not be able to come down here and hunt for you and you will not be able to hunt them."

"An invisible barrier?" He sounded unconvinced. I never was a good liar, which was probably why my relationship with Xander didn't work out. I wasn't sneaky enough and Rocco caught us.

"The forest is yours again and as long as I am alive, the dragons will not be able to hurt any of us."

"So, you retrieved your sword before setting up the barrier?"

Crap! I'd forgotten about the sword. I wracked my brains to come up with something quickly.

"I found the sword lying on the ground. The dragon must have dropped it." My lie made me realize that I'd not seen the dragon I hit in the eye. I had never felt more terrible in my life. I was a liar and a murderer. From now on, I vowed to be a better person. No more cheating, no more lying and one day, when the time was right, I'd avenge the dragons on the Triad Mountains. Today was not that day though. Today was a day for getting to know Alpha. Deep in my heart I knew he was connected to my future. I gripped his hand harder and pulled him round to face me. I kissed him again. This time it was a kiss of promise. Even though he didn't know it, that kiss meant I'd never lie to him again. I hoped somehow, he understood what I was trying to say to him in that tender embrace.

It accomplished something. When we finally broke apart, he didn't ask me another question about the dragons or the magic barrier.

"I barely know you and yet I feel as though I've been searching for you my whole life."

"I feel the same way, too."

He held me close, pulling me into his arms. I'd never felt so safe in my whole life.

"You have saved my people, and more than that, you have saved me."

"I only did what I promised to do."

"You are the bravest warrior I have ever known. I want you to stay."

"In the village?"

"With me."

As we walked back to the village, I knew I'd found my new home. I was one of the pack!

The End

———

Continue the Dragon Tamer Series with book 1, Slayer.

https://www.jaculican.com/dragon-tamer/

J.A. ARMITAGE

J.A lives in a total fantasy world (because reality is boring right?) When she's not writing all the crazy fun in her head, she can be found eating cake, designing pretty pictures and hanging upside down from the tallest climbing frame in the local playground while her children look on in embarrassment. She's travelled the world working as everything from a banana picker in Australia to a Pantomime clown, has climbed to the top of Mount Kilimanjaro and the bottom of the Grand Canyon and once gave birth to a surrogate baby for a friend of hers.

She spends way too much time gossiping on facebook and if you want to be part of her Reading Army, where you'll get lots of freebies, exclusive sneak peeks and super secret sales, join up here

https://www.subscribepage.com/v7o8k4

J.A. CULICAN

J.A. Culican is a USA Today Bestselling author of the middle grade fantasy series Keeper of Dragons. Her first novel in the fictional series catapulted a trajectory of titles and awards, including top selling author on the USA Today bestsellers list and Amazon, and a rightfully earned spot as an international best seller. Additional accolades include Best Fantasy Book of 2016, Runner-up in Reality Bites Book Awards, and 1st place for Best Coming of Age Book from the Indie book Awards.

J.A. Culican holds a Master's degree in Special Education from Niagara University, in which she has been teaching special education for over 16 years. She is also the president of the autism awareness non-profit Puzzle Peace United. J.A. Culican resides in Southern New Jersey with her husband and four young children.

THE
DRAGON
TAMER
SERIES

ACKNOWLEDGMENTS

Cover Designer: Christian Bentulan
Edits & Formatting: Dragon Realm Press